THE VISIONARY AND THE JUMPER

THE VISIONARY AND JUMPER

SONJA SKIPPERS

CASCADIAN COTTAGE

PUBLISHING LLC

First Edition: August 2023

Cover Design by jesh_art_studio on fiverr

Cascadian Cottage Publishing, LLC

PART ONE

BABYLON

Chapter 1: Daniel

 Deep in a hollow asteroid in the Goethe solar system, Daniel's sisters and mother rustled through the Christmas storage box for their favorite nativity sets and strings of lights in order to decorate their living quarters. Daniel, sitting nearby, placed a holly ornament on the Christmas tree, and then the creator God pulled Daniel into a vision.

Constellations shook free, rose from their orbits in the Milky Way and positioned themselves above the galaxy, at the Eye. The space between the stars filled and became four beasts. These creatures paced on top of the Milky Way, as if it were merely a disc of dirt or a shallow pool.

The first was like a lion, and it had the wings of an eagle. Daniel watched until its wings were torn off and it was lifted from the ground so that it stood on two feet like a human being, and the mind of a human was given to it. The lion's wings were torn off.

The second beast looked like a bear. It was raised up on one of its sides, and it had three ribs in its mouth between its teeth. It was told, 'Get up and eat your fill of flesh!'

The third beast looked like a leopard. And on its back it had four wings like those of a bird. This beast had four heads, and it was given authority to rule.

The first three beasts disappeared into constellations. Their stars were ripped apart by the fourth and final beast—terrifying and frightening and very powerful. The beast had large iron teeth; it crushed and devoured its victims and trampled underfoot whatever was left. It differed from all the former beasts, and it had ten horns. This last beast, with the fewest sentient features, spoke to Daniel. He didn't understand the words, but the tone was boastful.

When Daniel came out of his vision, he was weak for two days. His oldest sister, Magdalene, and his mother, Sherah, took care of him. The soft lights on the Christmas tree were like faint copies of the stars he'd seen, and he gazed at them as he rested on the couch while he thought about the galaxy and the animals in his vision.

At the next dinner he ate with his family, Daniel first concentrated on the little things. The rice was sweet and puffy. The pearl beans were creamy. Artificial gravity was working, so he poured water from a jug into an open cup with a scoop of powdered milk. Christmas rugs hung on the walls, covering the dark rock of the asteroid. The low ceiling made the room feel cozy today. Sometimes it felt claustrophobic.

"Did anything happen while I was in my vision?" Daniel asked his family. "Is there any news from Gospel of John?"

Sherah said, "No."

At the same time Daniel's youngest sister, Salamasina, yelled, "Yes," and punched a fist in the air. Hippolyte, the middle sister, pushed her fist down, but Salamasina shook herself free and dove for Daniel's lap.

"I missed you too." He smiled and held her on his lap, pushing her curls away from his face.

"I have news, but we can talk about it in private later," Sherah said.

"Why do you have to talk later when we already know about it," Salamasina complained.

"Is it about Gospel?" Daniel asked. "Have there been any more bombings?"

"No." Sherah shook her head. "We have heard nothing from Gospel."

"How is the enclave?" Daniel asked, trying to think of all the important things, which included the million exiles who lived in the asteroids.

"All my little sheep are flocking together still," Sherah answered. "Worried about you, but listening to me like they should—"

"The king sent you and Maggie and Hippo a letter!" Salamasina yelled, unable to contain the news.

"What's this? King Nebuchadnezzar? Why would he do that?" Daniel looked around the table, but his other sisters stayed silent.

"Now is not the time," Sherah scolded. "After dinner, naughty girl."

"I'll find out soon enough," Daniel said, squeezing his sister and giving her a bowl of rice. "Hippo and Sally, how are classes going? Who's been teaching since I haven't been there? I imagine Magdalene isn't helping." He winked at her.

Magdalene gave her usual answer. "You pick up my slack, not the other way around."

"What about the contract for the Axima moon?" Daniel asked.

"My dear son, we can get along without you for a few days. We always do."

"But no one else is a lawyer. Have you found contact information for Te'oma yet?"

"Well, no, but now—he's doing business on Babylon, isn't he? I'm thinking—"

"No," Magdalene interrupted.

"Mom, that's right, no thinking," Hippolyte said.

After some awkward silence Daniel said, "Someone else try picking a subject."

His sisters talked in fits and starts. Salamasina usually talked at length about a classmate or new game, but today she just cuddled on her brother's lap and ate her rice one grain at a time.

"Why everyone in a mood?" Daniel asked. "I think it's time to share."

Sherah reached behind her to a small table, grabbed something, and placed it on the table in front of Daniel. It was an expensive envelope addressed to the Rosefinch-Ravauviro family with a letter inside saying:

To all noble families exiled from their home Paradisian solar system with the worlds Gospel of John and Revelation of John: King Nebuchadnezzar of the Chaldean empire requires the attendance of Paradisians from the royal family and the nobility—young women and men without any physical defect, handsome, showing aptitude for every kind of learning, well informed, quick to understand, and qualified to serve in the king's Etemenanki palace on Babylon. We will teach them the language and literature of the Chaldean empire. Their presence is requested by the month of Sunumunna. The young women and men will be trained for three years, and after that they will enter the king's service.

Daniel contemplated it for a few minutes, pushing his beans and rice aside and petting Salamasina on the head. "It looks like we need to leave within a couple of days because of how far we are from the Goethe Gate." The Gate, which was a few connections away from the empire capital, was in orbit around the inhabited inner world, which would take a few weeks to reach from the asteroid field.

"No, we aren't going," Magdalene said. "I'm not going, and I don't see why you have to."

"Birbirru said I'm too young to go," Hippolyte said.

"Yes," Sherah said, "a representative of the king needs to perform a set of exams, including medical. They are on Cottiae waiting for you, Daniel." Cottiae was a close-by asteroid. Daniel sent a message to the contact on the invitation.

"It would be for the best if you failed the exams," Magdalene said.

Sherah didn't reprimand her eldest. But Sherah had just stuttered over whether she could contact Te'oma. If Daniel went to Babylon, he might. So his mom wanted him to go but didn't want to overtly influence him.

"Maggie, did you purposely fail?" Daniel asked.

"No, she didn't," Hippolyte said when Magdalene just glared. "There isn't a way, so she just left before it started. She's been ornery."

"I don't want you to go!" Salamasina said.

"Of course not," Daniel agreed, "but, you know, when I was your age, I had to leave Gospel. I didn't have a choice then, and I don't now. Wow, it's hard to realize we've been here for ten years." He hugged his sister tighter.

"So you want to go?" Salamasina whimpered.

"I want to keep you and our sisters and mom and our enclave safe, and this might be the best way."

"No, it's not!" Magdalene said with excitement, reaching a hand across the table. "Come with me to Revelation of John. If we don't do as the king commands, we'll have to leave this solar system, and I'm sure there's a place for us in the militia."

Daniel squeezed her hand. "I'm going to follow the rules a little bit and get the exam done. Maybe I will be disqualified, and I can stay here."

"No, now's the time to leave," Magdalene insisted. "You can't possibly want to stay here. On *asteroids*."

"We've been relatively safe and comfortable," Daniel insisted in his own way.

"Safe and comfortable? Do you hear yourself?" Magdalene asked. "This is how we lose our culture. The empire takes the best of us. If you go, you're placing basic survival before any other value."

"You are the best of us," Daniel said. "Not me."

Magdalene rolled her eyes.

"My dear daughter," Sherah said, "what I hear you say is that we have only two options; resistance until physical death, which is all the militia promises, or conformation until spiritual death. Do you truly see no other option?"

"There is no third option. And I choose the first; I'd rather be on the Zharqua estate or in a Revelation militia than here." She shook off Daniel's hand and left the room.

Salamasina started crying. "I don't want anyone to die."

Daniel rubbed her back, and she buried her face in his Scythian sweater.

"Well, what about you? What choice do you make?" asked Hippolyte, gesturing to Daniel.

"I think there's a third option," Daniel answered. "God would not give me visions for nothing. I can't see an easy way forward, but I have faith that this will work out."

"Is that what faith is? And we just let you go?" Hippolyte asked.

Instead of answering with words, Daniel reached a hand out to Hippolyte, which she held tight. Sherah put an arm around her. Hippolyte had spent her youngest formative years in abundance but didn't have any solid memories to grieve for what the others had lost. Magdalene and Daniel remembered their Valla Varra vineyard estate. Hippolyte didn't suffer the way the older siblings did, but she had a certain cynicism.

Daniel received a message from someone named Birbirru on Cottiae. "I need to leave now for my exams."

Sherah sighed. "This is why I wanted to wait until after dinner."

A long row of asteroids was connected like pearls on a necklace by tram from Martigny, their home asteroid, to Cottiae. If Daniel didn't want to travel by tram, there was also a reliable shuttle service.

Neither of these options was acceptable today. Daniel was too much on edge to use public transportation.

He traveled by star surfing.

His day time clothing and shoes had the shielding he needed for space travel. The Rosefinch-Ravauviro family stored helmets and gloves with their surfboards near the airlock. Daniel clicked on a helmet and a pair of gloves, and slid a board from its spot, the surface smooth and shiny in the light.

Once Daniel was outside the airlock with the surfboard attached to both feet, the gravity field of the tram line gently pulled him over. He used that force to push down the line, away from Martigny.

When he lived on Gospel, ocean wave surfing was his favorite vacation activity. The feeling of home was echoed in the gliding and pressing against gravity while star surfing.

Being outside was not like his vision. Yes, he was tiny among the stars, but he missed the living, seeing beyond sight, the perspective of seeing the entire galaxy, but still small and fearful. Despite enjoying time with his family, reality was always translucent for a few days after a vision. Despite everything else, he held onto a core of peace and confidence.

He continued moving away from his home asteroid. He surfed from one tram track to another, making a 180 degrees upwards spin in reference to the first track, pushing against that gravity for momentum so that the gravity of the second track would catch him. This second track had stronger gravity, which gave him room to do some rolling tricks on his way. At one point, a tram sped by as he safely glided out to the edge of the gravity well. He depended on his disc to alert him of dangers. He had stuck it on his skin below his collarbone so it wouldn't get lost. It projected information through his clothes and shielding.

After a half hour, he changed from the fast track to a local track. It went parallel to the living areas of a set of asteroids connected with glass tunnels. He watched for gardens and trees. The translucent walls of one asteroid showed a mossy, humid area with a grove of miniature redwoods that he especially liked. The well-developed asteroids were like witch balls his sisters liked or tidy terrarium globes.

By the time he landed at Cottiae, he felt much more soothed.

The empire specialist had set up in a doctor's office. Daniel had to wait a half hour. Waiting at all was new to him, as he usually received rushed service since he was a member of the exiled nobility. But he was beginning a new life. Soon enough, he was brought back to a room set up with strange equipment.

"Hello, my name is Birbirru Kanasu, which is Akkadian for sparkling flower. I hope you speak Akkadian," this specialist spoke in Akkadian with a smirk. They were dressed in Scythian pants and sweaters and had purple hair in long braids.

"Yes, I do. Thank you," Daniel said awkwardly. His home language was Kahi, the common tongue in the Paradisian solar system, but he was forced to learn Akkadian in order to deal with the Chaldean empire on educational and business issues. He was conscious of his heavy accent, rolling his r's and not pronouncing consonants harshly enough.

"I hope you'll be a better patient than either of your sisters."

"I'm sure it would be hard to be worse," Daniel smiled.

Birbirru laughed and their sly tension broke. The examinations were invasive, but they were as polite as possible. Daniel kept his dignity intact by never asserting it. They catalogued his tattoos and piercings, which included an estate tattoo of grapes on the back of a shoulder, a Martigny identification tattoo around his forearm, bands around his biceps in honor of his deceased father, and ear piercings that were traditional to men from his father's home island estate.

Their casual chatting was enjoyable, but Birbirru had an eye only for the very organic, physical, material health of his body. They wanted to wave Daniel's visions away as mere dreams. He had no traces of compounds from mushrooms or other plants to trigger a different mental state; no signs of epilepsy or other conditions associated with altered mental states; the idea of God choosing to communicate via visions was absurd to them. Birbirru was not from the Gospel of John, so Daniel didn't push them.

The visions became a sore point. They were the one issue that might keep Daniel from Babylon.

"How is the rest of your family, or enclave? Do they report similar symptoms?" Birbirru asked. "Maybe there was carbon dioxide build up that cleared out of your system." They were watching Daniel. An uncooperative noble would be information to pass on.

"No one else," Daniel answered with a gentle smile.

"I have the technology to perform a biochemical and protein survey. It would create a three-dimensional model of your brain. Do I have your permission to move forward?" Birbirru asked, still watching like a hawk.

Daniel thought about it. The empire would have some very in-depth information about him on file forever. Magdalene's frustrations and Hippolyte's warning came to mind. But if everyone in the Rosefinch-Ravauviro family failed nobility tests, what would happen?

"You may move forward with whatever you think is best."

The specialist did so. Soon, they both sat at a redwood table to review the results. "Your brain is in healthy order. There are no imbalances, or oddities, or noticeable deviations from what I consider appropriate for a Paradisian noble. There's no organic explanation for your visions."

"I am quite happy to see how healthy I am. It has quite taken a load off my mind."

Birbirru stared at him, wondering if he was being sarcastic. He smiled, and they relaxed.

"So you are a specialist who works for the empire?" Daniel asked. "Are you testing just my family or are there others?" He wanted more information about what was going on, but his Akkadian and formal manners were too unpracticed for him to know how to phrase things politely.

Birbirru swept their purple braids off their shoulder. "Just your family in this solar system. Other specialists are assigned to other solar systems. You are so far from the center of the empire compared to other Paradisian nobility. This was the least desirable posting. But I'm only a minor patrician. I suppose I'm lucky to work directly for the palace." They wrinkled their nose.

"Yes, all the news we get is weeks and months old. You'll get to leave soon."

"And it looks like you'll be coming with me. I'll give you a couple more days to wrap things up." Birbirru poked at their information disc.

Daniel's nerves lighted with thrills and fear hearing the inevitable conclusion. "The Gate is quite a distance. Has Jumping improved at all? Have you been on a Jumping ship?" Daniel asked.

"No. Jumping is still unsafe for everyone. Empire citizens from the high courts and universities don't have access to safe Jumping. We will stick to the Gates. Only the recently recovered ships can Jump. I had an opportunity to travel in one, but I'm glad it didn't because we haven't heard from it, so it's marked as lost as the others." They pulled on their braids and twiddled a stylus as they continued working on Daniel's file.

The unsuccessful Jumping news disappointed Daniel. If Paradisians had a working Jumping ship, they could visit each other without the Chaldean empire monitoring them through Gate travel. More selfishly, if Birbirru had a ship right now, he could stay with his family longer.

"Let's finish talking about your visions and then we'll be done for the day," Birbirru said with a smile. "Whatever passes for a day here. According to what I'm reading, your creator God supposedly gives interpretations. Have you had one for your recent vision?"

"No. In the past, a messenger from God gave me the interpretation."

"Why not skip right to the interpretation? Why a bunch of imagery if you get the literal meaning? I thought visions were supposed to be vague, anyway."

"I think you're going to remember a lion with eagle wings, right? It's a little impressive I think. Or I'm not explaining it right."

"Honestly, I've never heard of this," Birbirru said, taking notes.

"I am a prophet." Daniel unexpectedly felt his face get warm from blushing. He hadn't ever said that so directly to someone outside his enclave before. "When I say that we are given visions and interpretations, I am talking about prophets. God has a specific plan for my people, Paradisians; God rescued us from Aegyptus, gave us a solar system, and has given us information that She is sending her Daughter, just as God's Son has already been sent. But now we have to leave our Paradisian solar system for decades."

"You haven't left Paradise," Birbirru snapped. "King Nebuchadnezzar has seen fit to remove the leadership so that the planets can be ruled properly. Breadbasket worlds like Gospel of John are rare and must be treasured. I thank Marduk that so many of you have voluntarily chosen exile. Fewer to kill."

Daniel nodded. He tamped down his anger and grief. Other Paradisian prophets said that Paradise deserved the treatment, that it was punishment from the creator God, but that didn't change that a specific empire with a specific king was choosing violence. Being angry at the king was like being angry at God or tornados and hurricanes.

Birbirru let him go and he took a tram back to Martigny. On the way home, he stopped for a visit to the asteroid with the redwood forest. He didn't know what was waiting for him and this might be the last chance to be alone with his grief.

Chapter 2: Daniel

Daniel's goal in life, whether as teacher, lawyer, or whatever God decided, was to serve his people. Magdalene agreed with him, but they disagreed on how that service should look. Now that Daniel was leaving, the siblings had one last argument, the last time they were alone together, when they returned the Christmas storage boxes to their storage area.

One reason Daniel had come to the storage room was to comb through their belongings for items to bring to Babylon. Sherah had already set some things aside during his vision, but she had encouraged him to look with Magdalene for company.

At first the siblings were business-like, moving boxes from the cart into the storage room and moving other belongings around. Magdalene's pale skin glowed ghostly in the dim light before the lights switched on. They both had features from each parent, but a unique mix and match for each. Magdalene had straight, dark hair like their dad and pale skin with sharp features like their mom. Daniel had curly hair like his mom and other sisters, but kept in a tight bun, and had tan skin like his dad; everyone else's tan had faded once they moved to the asteroid.

As Magdalene organized the Christmas boxes, Daniel went deeper into the storage room and found the boxes from his favorite holiday, Easter, and sat down to examine the contents of one box. He opened it and unwrapped the decorations, painted crystalized eggs and golden cups the size of Salamasina's head.

"Maggie, do you remember this cup? It was on the mantel in the solarium at home." Daniel rubbed the grape vine sculpted around the base.

Magdalene came over and rummaged a bit in the box but took

nothing out, then paused and crouched by Daniel.

"Danny, if you want to go to Babylon because you're tired of poverty, Revelation of John can find a cushy administrative position for you."

Daniel looked at his sister, aghast. "This isn't about poverty! I want to stay here more than you do. I wish we could both stay here. You still need training to inherit from mom and I always meant to back you up."

"Are you leaving just to protect us? Danny, we can find a way without you sacrificing yourself. No one wants that."

"God, speaking through the prophets, has been very clear about what he expects from us. I have to go."

"If the prophets are real—"

"*If?* Maggie, you take care of me and you don't believe?"

"If your visions are true, God is bringing violence on us. Do you want me to believe in a violent God? I'd rather believe in no God." Magdalene was also aghast now, the same expression on their faces, the boxes ignored.

"The violence is a consequence of our own choices," Daniel said. "Plenty of Paradisians have created idols of gods from other solar systems, and corrupted the meaning of their temples—"

"There are innocent Paradisians who are suffering. Even our own sisters don't have the life they should. Maybe the Revelation leaders are corrupt, but Gospel has nothing to ask forgiveness for." Maggie put a hand on his shoulder and leaned to him.

"Have we done nothing wrong?" Daniel tapped the cup against the floor for emphasis. "The life you want for our sisters is dead. Our family may have not committed the abuses of the former kings and queens, but we are not innocent. God wishes us to care for refugees, but we profited from their labor or turned a blind eye, even on our own estate. Where would our sisters learn to do otherwise? We need repentance and humility."

"We can't take care of every refugee in the galaxy. Serving a violent, cruel king is not repentance."

"Serving God is the most important, and we each have our own ideas. Maybe I'm thinking too highly of myself, but I can help our people better from Babylon. While I want to keep our family safe, I also want to know more about my visions. I'm not going to find those answers here, or by joining a militia."

"I can't stand this." Magdalene got up and left.

Daniel rubbed the cup again. He had forgotten—the beauty and happiness this represented would never, should never, come again; his grief was arrogance. He felt a sudden upwelling of anger that his family ever put this cup in his hand. He put it away.

Daniel had similar conversations during his last day. All the enclave citizens in the Goethe solar system wanted to talk to him. He met with cousins, mothers, miners, the original people who settled Goethe, among others. The enclave citizens repeated with anger and hope the story of Abram, ordered by God to sacrifice Isaac.

Once Daniel was ready to leave, a somber crowd followed him from the living quarters to where the Chaldean shuttle with Birbirru waited for him. People lined up against the walls when the halls were narrow. Perhaps he could do something besides be born to wealth and have visions to earn their reverence. When people asked him for last words —as if he were going to die—he would say to remember that healing would come, and to bring that knowledge forward. As he got closer to the shuttle, he heard "please pray for us" "please pray for me" "please pray."

Sherah grabbed his arm and raised an eyebrow. She thought Daniel should pray aloud, and she knew what his prayers were like. Daniel looked around for the man who led prayers. He raised his eyebrows, too.

A few paces from the shuttle entrance, Daniel stood on a piece of his luggage, with his hand on top of his mom's head for balance. He closed his eyes and bowed his head. "Let us pray:
"In God we make our boast all day long,
    and we will praise your name forever.
But now you have rejected and humbled us;
    you no longer go out with our armies.
You made us retreat before the enemy,
    and our adversaries have plundered us.
You gave us up to be devoured like sheep
    and have scattered us among the solar systems.
"How long, Lord? Will you forget us forever?
    How long will you hide your face from us?
How long must I wrestle with my thoughts
    and day after day have sorrow in my heart?
    How long will our enemy triumph over us?
"For I know my transgressions,

and my sin is always before me.
Against you, you only, have I sinned
    and done what is evil in your sight;
so you are right in your verdict
    and justified when you judge.
"Where can I go from your Spirit?
    Where can I flee from your presence?
If I go up to the heavens, you are there;
    if I make my bed in the depths, you are there.
If I rise on the wings of the dawn,
    if I settle on the far side of the sea,
even there your hand will guide me,
    your right hand will hold me fast.
"For I am convinced that neither death nor life,
neither angels nor demons, neither the present nor the future,
nor any powers, neither height nor depth, nor anything else
in all creation, will be able to separate us from
the love of God that is in Christ Jesus our Lord."

Press Release from King Nebuchadnezzar

It is I, your king, dear people. Thank you for the kind words and celebrations. This day five years ago, we finished our conquest of the Gospel of John and the Revelation of John. Paradisians from that solar system live among us now.

It is in times like these that I see the true nature of the Galaxy; mine to take and subdue and rule over.

I am developing one of my incredible plans, the kind that can't fail, and I must share it with you.

My plan: invite all the noble Paradisian exile young women and men to Babylon, my own residence and glorious capital of the Chaldean Empire.

Point One: We must turn the weirdness and strength of the Paradisians into Chaldean assets. The last serious bombing occurred years ago. It is time for all of us to put that old history behind us. It is time for the Paradisians to be fully integrated into the Chaldean Empire. I have invited their best and will train them properly. They will become Chaldeans, and then I will give them a home here on Babylon. Some people say they adhere to their culture too strongly to be assimilated, but I've seen how their kings and queens act and don't believe it.

Point Two: They are hostages. I've heard that despite my kind and generous lack of violence for years, there's some dissent on their two home worlds, so now I will have their elite exiles under my thumb. Their special sons and daughters will be in an even deeper exile.

Why am I doing this? I have a vast army, the greatest in the galaxy. I have the ambition to gather one solar system after another into my benevolence. They must come for themselves to see how things really are. Please give them a warm welcome when they arrive.

Chapter 3: Daniel

The trip from Goethe to Babylon was uneventful. Daniel acclimatized himself to Babylon's daily rotation, which the ship's cycle was based on, including the time zone of the Etemenanki palace, which was in the city of Babylon on the planet of Babylon in the solar system of Babylonia, in the Chaldean empire. He forgot the length of a Gospel hour. Once his ship attached to the Babylon space station, Birbirru pointed him in the direction he should go and then Birbirru disappeared.

The palace coordinated special space elevators to meet his ship and the other ships delivering young men to the North Pole palace so that they would all arrive at the same time. Other young nobles were being delivered to the South Pole, where they would receive an education.

Daniel's space elevator opened into decontamination procedures, which were the most uncomfortable he had experienced, and seemed to be like that by design, not from incompetence or being cheap. Some strobe lights and puffs of powder puffed onto the entirety of his naked body. After this weird series of tests, he asked the technician what would happen if this triggered a seizure or some kind of sensory sensitivity.

"If arrivals can't get past this point without medical help, then we don't allow them on the planet," the technician said, not even looking at him.

This would cut out quite a few people, and might have gotten Daniel, if his visions had leaned into the epileptic direction.

He took his time putting his clothes back on, using a conscious slowness to bring his body back to normal and to remind himself why he was here.

Feeling calm, he stepped out of the processing center and found the other three, dressed in the Paradisian flying style, coveralls with collars that folded crisscross, and printed with patterns from home, each from distinctively different parts of Gospel of John. Daniel's heart ached with happiness and homesickness. This felt almost like a global gathering, like the time of year when Paradisians celebrated Arrival Day.

Hananiah, the tallest person around and who could see Daniel the easiest, waved and gave him a smile and handshake when he reached them. "I saw you last at my sister's wedding a few years ago."

Daniel nodded, "The cake was snowballs?" It was over ten years ago.

Hananiah laughed. "By the way, I liked the prayer you gave to your enclave. It's been filtering through to other enclaves."

"Thank you." Daniel turned to the other young men, Mishael and Azariah. Mishael had arrived from a Chaldean moon; he hadn't undergone the decontamination procedure and his black, braided hair was still sleek and clean. Azariah might have also had black hair, but it was messy with the orange decontamination powder. Daniel wondered how orange his own hair was.

Mishael shook Daniel's hand with ease and self-assuredness. "I've been here before. I was here last ten years ago, I mean back on Babylon, and no idea I might be back under such circumstances." Mishael held his hand tighter. "I am with you in any decision. Your reputation and visions precede you, I'm sure."

The swing in attitude threw him off for a minute. Daniel wondered if Mishael's estate was preparing for violence.

After thinking about that for a moment, he turned to the third, Azariah, who kept his arms crossed and didn't smile. "I understand nothing and I'm not a noble and wouldn't mind getting kicked out." The non-smile deepened into a scowl for a moment before returning to neutral.

"Of course you're not noble. Zharqua has no aristocracy. What are you doing here?" Mishael said, haughty.

"Patroness Shelomith is still in charge of the Zharqua estate," Azariah flicked the rose on the shoulder of his coveralls. "She adopted me the day before we left the planet. No one asked what I wanted. I have no idea."

"Did you truly come straight from Gospel?" Hananiah asked. "How's Saint Domminick really doing? North or south pole." The entire Paradise solar system had been under a communications shadow; only specific kinds of messages got out, and no personal communications.

"And Darh Dothoma," Mishael added.

"Stop it," Azariah said, holding up a hand, irritated. "Just stop it. I don't ever want to talk about Gospel. Unlike you, I don't know when or if I'll ever hear from my family again. I'm done talking. All I want to know is how they are keeping track of us and where the food is."

"I had instructions to meet a special advisor named Oshpenaz Baghdasaryan at the east gate of the Etemenanki palace. I've got about a half hour to get there," Daniel said. Everyone agreed. Once Azariah had settled in, he might talk about Gospel.

Mishael, with bravado covering a bit of uncertainty, led them to a particular exit expanse. The gravity and humidity of the tropical jungle surrounding the city pressed down hard on Daniel. There was a thickness to the air that reminded him a bit of Gospel, but it was too, too different.

Before leaving the archway, Mishael showed them a map engraved on the wall. He traced the route they would walk.

"Where are quicker thoroughfares with some kind of transportation? Does the palace expect all of us to walk?" Daniel asked. He didn't want to step out. He was light-headed already.

"Walking is self-sufficient, which is an important quality," Mishael answered.

"Is there a map we can take with us?" Hananiah asked. "My disc won't interface."

"Just take a manual picture," Azariah answered, helping Hananiah with his disc.

"Mishael, were you really self-sufficient when you visited?" Daniel asked. "Weren't you seven years old?"

"I remember getting lost a lot. But I had my mom."

They started up the sandy path as indicated. Daniel kept his head down, watching where his feet were going. There were steps, sharp turns. After a particular set of steep stairs, Hananiah said, "Good thing we packed light like they said."

"Good thing we have strong bodies."

"And tall."

Daniel pursed his lips. If this path was like the other paths, there was no room for baby prams or rolling chairs or any type of movement weakness. Rich people could afford anti-gravity technology.

A steep climb and a sharp turn, the view in front of them changed from layers of trees with big, thick, green leaves, to opening up to a beautiful view.

"Hey, let's stop for a minute," Hananiah said. "I haven't ever been to a planet that looks like this."

In the ten minutes of walking, and given the natural elevation of the station, they had climbed high enough that the city spread out below them on either side of a turquoise-colored river; probably called the Babylon River. Daniel backed up until his back was against a tree with its big leaves shading him. Beyond the river canyon, the jungle-like growth faded into sand off in the distance. No red sand like home, but something that burned white in the strong sunlight, so bright it seemed purple. The temperature in the sun was almost halfway to boiling. The shade under the tree was only a little cooler. They needed water.

"That's beautiful," Hananiah sighed, and stepped forward. The path was quite narrow; people elbowed the three young men, obviously foreigners, in their backs, pushing them closer to the edge.

"Hananiah! Step back. There's no guard rail," Daniel said.

"Oh I'm fine," Hananiah said.

Azariah looked over his shoulder when Daniel called out to Hananiah. He sauntered across the path and stared at the bag Daniel carried. It was a challenge. Azariah didn't have a bag like the other, and Daniel was more tired than anyone else. Daniel held onto the strap and looked right back at him, saying nothing. He shrugged and went back to the guys at the edge of the cliff. Daniel stayed under the tree. The two other guys were letting him rest in a more discreet way than Azariah's blunt offer.

"This path isn't good for blind people either," Daniel said once they started walking again. "What else is left?" He disliked this planet. The gravity was wrong, the air was wrong. He was tired already. But more than that, his parents had taught him to use his elite status and abilities to ease the way for others. But here, these paths to the palace would leave as many people behind as possible. If off-worlders wanted to get to the palace, they had to use all their strength for their own selves.

The young men made it to the Etemenanki palace without further incident. An assistant to Oshpenaz was waiting for them and led them to the chamber they would share for three years. Their living quarters were a glorified dormitory without separate rooms, only personal alcoves surrounding a sunny common area, with drapes they could close for privacy. There was a shrine to Marduk in one corner facing north and another shrine to King Nebuchadnezzar in another corner.

They had one bathroom. It had water plumbing. Daniel took a five-minute shower, hurrying in case someone was coming to meet them. His hair was too curly to easily take down from its roll to clean, so he wiped it with a damp cloth to get the orange powder off.

The bathroom ablutions gave him a minute to absorb everything about the last hour—the environment, the culture, the next three years. Hananiah was a known quantity. Mishael was probably a known quantity, and Azariah was bent on being unknown and angry.

Three years and then…. No going back to Gospel. Hopefully not going back to the claustrophobic goethite asteroids. Find a post here? Maybe a different planet would have a culture that would feel more natural. Nothing felt natural here. Daniel dressed in a clean moss-green robe he found in a closet.

Oshpenaz entered with bustle and noise and assistants, filling the common area with their presence. Daniel got up and shook their hand and introduced himself. He was glad he could shake their hand clean with Babylonian soap, with all the weird powder from the decontamination and the dirt and sweat from the hike washed off. Oshpenaz noticed, as seen by just the slightest raise of their eyebrow and a lack of judgment rather than any actual praise. They spoke Akkadian, and Daniel answered in the same language, which he picked his way through slowly. Daniel could understand more than what he could speak.

Mishael interrupted Daniel using fluent Akkadian. "Excuse me sir, but it is inexcusable that I don't have my own quarters or bathroom, and that there are shrines; these are all things I required specifically, that I would be coming only on the understanding that the palace would respect my requests."

"The palace decided your quarters based on the consensus that I received ahead of time, which was explained to you. If all four of you agree on changes, that would provide enough demand." Oshpenaz waved their hand to show courtesy.

"I'd like the shrines gone," Daniel volunteered.

"My apologies to Mishael. My parents told me to accept whatever was given, though I wouldn't mind having the shrines gone. If I'm the only hold out for personal rooms, then I'll switch sides." Hananiah gave Mishael a little bow, who kicked him lightly in the shins.

"Azariah?"

"Shrines gone for sure," he replied. "This is the most personal space I've ever had. I don't see how this isn't a room. Look, you can't even see me." He stepped inside the alcove he had chosen, across from Daniel's, and closed the drapes and didn't even open them again.

Mishael gave a growl of frustration and stomped off to the bathroom. They could hear him knocking things around.

Hananiah had found a moment to wash his hands and face and change into clean clothes and greeted Oshpenaz politely. He and Daniel followed them around as they pointed to things and introduced them to the chief servant, Samwel Chande.

"I would like to officially meet Azariah," Oshpenaz said with another funny gesture, flipping their hand. It didn't mean anything to Daniel.

Azariah was dozing on his bed, not having washed or changed. His bag plopped on the floor in front of the table that it was supposed to be set on.

"This is Azariah Ramzi," Daniel whispered. "He is the adopted son of the Zharqua estate's nobility, or what passes for nobility."

Oshpenaz nodded solemnly. "That matches the information I have. We do, in fact, accept adopted nobility; we have decided to trust the nobility that we have so indulgently accepted into our empire's embrace."

Daniel nodded, "Thank you, Oshpenaz."

"What do you think of him?"

"Oh, you can't hardly depend on my opinion, but given all that, from what I've seen so far, he'll be a credit to the empire in three years, I'm sure."

"Three years, of course. That is why the king set three years. Who knows what will happen before then?"

"Is this project fully funded?"

"It currently is, yes, and there is more than one reason to keep it funded, but the king must be indulged at every turn."

"I will oblige."

"I wondered what type of noble we would receive. We prepared ourselves for ignorance, narrow opinions, and distressing manners, but these are not incurable faults." The way their eyes rested on Azariah made it clear what type they thought Azariah was. Oshpenaz gave Daniel a sincere smile. "You will dine soon. The aptitude testing will start tomorrow."

Once Oshpenaz was gone, Mishael came out of the bathroom with a frown. He was clean, his hair wrapped up, and changed into a deep carmine colored robe, muttering about how stupid things were.

"For our families," Daniel whispered.

Mishael's frown softened. "I have a sister."

"Only one?" Hananiah and Daniel said together.

"And what if we have no family? What if I don't care about the Gospel's nobility? Is that all that's worth saving? I don't like that greasy man." Azariah had pushed his drape open at some point. His new scowl was even worse for all the dirt and the new setting, with bright light through the skylights. He had mentioned having a big family, so his obstinance was deliberate.

"That's why you're here," Daniel answered. "You are worth saving. How many people have to tell you that, including that person who you should know better than to ever insult again? Sorry, that came out rude. I need to eat. Clean up and get dressed. Or not."

"Samwel, I put on just the first thing that looked interesting. Could you help me choose something appropriate for my first dinner?" Daniel asked.

"It's your first day, just go eat, you've had a big day," he was about ten years older than Daniel with a world-weary look, wearing a schenti the color of a hopbush flower with bronze embroidery. He spoke Kahi, the common language of the Paradisian solar system, which was a relief.

"Please? Am I expected to wear coveralls? Or a jumpsuit? That's very different from what I'm wearing."

Samwel bowed politely and gave Daniel a tour of the closet, which was bigger than the private alcoves and had windows. The general style of clothing was like what Daniel wore on his Gospel estate, just adjusted for a warmer climate. He had worn coveralls on the asteroid. Robes, dresses, schentis, and so on were for planets with consistent gravity. Mobility and practicality weren't the primary concerns of Babylon. Samwel pointed out fifteen different styles of loincloths. Daniel picked up one that was about knee length. Very different from his daily outfit that could protect him in a vacuum. Samwel said that Daniel's robe was a little informal and gave Daniel something he called a *hullanu*, which looked identical until he pointed out nuances in the length and type of fabric.

Daniel double checked that athletic gear made from high-tech fabrics was available. He would rather swim naked than in a cotton swimsuit. When he pointed this out to the others, they were interested. Samwel told them about a bathhouse on the canyon floor on the Turquoise River, available for use. Azariah wanted to check it out immediately, but they convinced him skipping the first meal was unacceptable, so his bad mood continued.

Finally, they were at dinner, which was served on low tables and cushions. Dishes spread out before them, with a servant saying they would be served from the king's table. One dish had stuffed frogs. Another dish had geoducks on the shell. An odd soup was made from birds' nests. More seafood, more meat. Daniel's heart sank. He looked around. Everyone showed the same uneasiness, even Azariah, though he was putting food on his plate.

"I don't have any fight left in me," Mishael groaned and flopped down onto a cushion, leaning his head against the edge of the table.

So Daniel got up, talked to the server, and got Oshpenaz involved. He spoke about strict religious dietary needs, etc. They were concerned, annoyed, etc. Daniel asked for something very simple, beans and rice, or quinoa, or dishes with vegetables only. It was all worked out. He went back to the table, and the servers started picking up the dishes. Azariah helped, though not with a pleasant attitude. Daniel thought about telling him to stop, but Azariah knew what he was doing; he did not want anyone under any circumstance to mistake him for nobility.

Oshpenaz asked Daniel if there was anything else, if perhaps the wine was to his liking. There was a funny inflection—daring him to object and curious as to his opinion. He took a sip and almost spat it out. It tasted like vinegar with rancid notes.

"I've read about the vineyards in this world," Daniel said, as an indirect answer. "I've been curious to taste some from the Charax Spasinou region. But maybe there's none available. I know Babylonian wines are the rarest in the galaxy."

"Perhaps rare to you, but it is so common in the palace. We wished to present you with one of the most expensive wines we currently have."

Daniel tried to think of a way to politely ask what could possibly make that expensive.

They saw his face and talked about how far the vinegary wine had come from the other side of the galaxy.

Daniel was less annoyed. They saw value in the wine because it was from far away. Good to note. The palace was possibly not actively trying to poison them or, worse, make fun of them.

"I must insist on trying your Charax Spasinou," Daniel said. "Please consider it a favor for a brand new off-worlder."

"I will have the New Helio wine replaced immediately," Oshpenaz said.

Daniel went back. Azariah was pouring himself a glass.

"Please don't," Daniel said.

"Is it poisoned?!" Azariah asked, looking at the wine.

"It would be better if it had been," Daniel said. "No, sorry, perhaps I'm being a wine snob. I don't know what you might enjoy."

Azariah tried a sip and the ghastly look on his face made Daniel laugh.

"You have Oshpenaz's favor," Azariah said accusingly.

"Yes," Hananiah apologetically agreed. "I was trying to join the conversation and Oshpenaz enjoyed brushing me off."

Daniel ignored that. As the last dish settled onto the table with Azariah's help, Daniel said, "Mishael, you come from a line of priests? Why don't you say the blessing?"

Chapter 4: Azariah

Azariah didn't float through life talking one on one with God like some people (like Daniel, this is a reference to Daniel), and didn't know what he was doing on Babylon. He was not noble but only a lowly son of a teacher and a field worker, and not some slave like the rest of the young men had, or whatever special word they use. Azariah's home estate was on the opposite side of Gospel from Daniel, where they fought to the death over a lot of things. That's a bit too dramatic. But Azariah had become newly exasperated with how the nobility managed every estate on Gospel.

Yes, Gospel of John is a world perfect for vineyards. Talking with Daniel, one would think that was the only thing Gospel was good for. Overall, Gospel was the breadbasket of four sectors of the Sagittarius Arm of the Milky Way. They grow lots of things and they're good at it.

Azariah had worked on a wheat plantation. He loved how the blue skies and yellow wheat were hardly ever gray. It took two days to travel by ground truck from one end to the next. He would ride big machinery around all day, eyes to the horizon when he wasn't tucked under the big machinery trying to fix it.

Who was riding his favorite truck right now? Will the Chaldean Empire destroy and replace it? Or will whatever slave labor the Chaldean empire provide use his truck? Now that he was on Babylon, it was a little embarrassing to remember, but he had left some notes. *The lights don't work, so don't get caught in a strange field when the sun goes down; the radiator doesn't work, so don't let the truck idle and get hot and you'll want to be careful with the gasoline allotment.* But what would even happen? 1. No one else would ever read the notes. 2. Someone—friend or foe—would read the notes and laugh at how pathetic Azariah was. 3. Someone—friend or foe—would appreciate the notes, whatever.

So Azariah has his farmer's tan on top of his natural tan, his calluses, and never planned to see space, never liked those space adventure stories, nor did he have some secret dream of being a prince or owning a rocket ship. He wouldn't mind reading a rocket ship manual, but growing up, the truck and farm equipment manuals kept him busy and happy enough. Yet for some reason the lady of the estate, Patroness Shelomith, Dictator Shelomith to some, put his name on the list of her dependents, and he was forced into exile on Babylon instead of being left behind and forced into a militia. She was being mysterious, so Azariah got a blood test done, and no, he wasn't some long-lost nobility. He was regular third generation salt of the earth, planned to be a farmer since he knew what one was, before he learned he didn't have any other choice, anyway.

On his second day, Azariah took aptitude tests. It was hot. He went native and wore a schenti thing, Aegyptian style, a color similar to Samwel's, and no shirt. (Has he beat you over the head enough with the class warfare? Maybe not.) Didn't sweat as much as the first day. His new comrades-in-arms were sleek, well-groomed, not very traumatized, all the qualities requested. While Azariah wanted to make a point, he didn't want to appear at a disadvantage.

A few hours later, Oshpenaz sent an assistant to bring Azariah to him; the Etemenanki palace was much beyond the efficiencies of any feed message. Azariah walked from the sun spilled portico with blue cushions where he'd been writing letters on his own, down the walkway shaded by orange trees—but he recognized them as mock oranges, only the smell, no fruit, useless, disgusting, and into another pavilion, with gold cushions. Every detail of the palace was exceedingly ostentatious. Azariah wanted to kick everything. He could complain about all of this to the others, but Daniel had been a good example of appearances going a long way. If not for him, Azariah would have been eating food he was uncomfortable with; hiding his anger and saying 'please' and 'thank you' were minor sacrifices he could make, especially if he could still be true to what he believed in. Azariah tucked his anger away.

Once Azariah was settled, Oshpenaz activated some heat shields, blocking the blistering sun from coming in and blocking sound from getting out, but otherwise invisible. He'd run into plenty on Gospel. New to being on the secretive side. Azariah looked out at the view, the best he'd seen so far. White sand, the ziggurat buildings carved into the sides and bottom of the canyon, and the jungle trees with monkeys nearby were much too foreign.

Azariah dropped the natural sullenness of his first day and used proper manners. He'd watched the real nobles and had refined the skills his patroness had given him. Oshpenaz relaxed.

"My dear young man, you have the most striking results of the group."

"Mr. Oshpenaz, I am incredibly flattered by any attention. As you can imagine, having the attention of King Nebuchadnezzar's advisor is beyond anything I could expect." Azariah's tone was sincere and also conveyed a *we know this is ridiculous* aspect. His patroness was a wonderful teacher, but she might have been out-of-date or, like, barbaric without knowing.

"By striking, I mean that you obviously manipulated the results. You do not want the Chaldean empire to know you. What is it you want?"

I want to go back home. This place is ridiculous. I want to sleep under the stars in a wheat field. I want to eat rice and beans in a crowded apartment.

"I would be happy to take advantage of what you are offering, but I want it to be on my terms." Azariah didn't want the Chaldean empire to contaminate him. There, that was the right way to put it, and not something he could say out loud. He clenched his jaw and then relaxed and gave the king's representative a gracious smile. Azariah didn't have that certainty of purpose that the other three had. He could fall deep and happily on Babylon. Oshpenaz and King Nebuchadnezzar would enjoy having a Gospel native as a warlord at the front of the Chaldean empire expansion, or the type of administrator who's happy to make things worse for people as the king sees fit. And Azariah could feel it. But he could still heavily feel the pull of Gospel, his fields, his truck.

"Perhaps you prefer to live in the rural country, but yet you must do your service like any young noble. I could see you establishing the empire on a new planet, or planets, and then retiring, setting an example of confined leadership, which happens in some sectors of the empire; those nobles bow to Nebuchadnezzar, even if they are far away. You would be a *Sakkanakkum*."

"You're talking about either the military or diplomacy. How can you think I'm suited for either?"

"I'm sure you're a talented mechanic, but your test results said more than you were hoping." Oshpenaz sighed. "We need to wrap this up. Last note, you are dressing like the royal court."

"I'm dressing like Samwel!"

"Samwel is a member of the royal court, middle level, not quite at the highest level. Don't think that just because he is taking care of you that he is *kiskattum*. He knows the Kahi language, so I drafted him for the position, even though his talents are much beyond that. You may instead prefer yukatas, lavas, tupenu, or sulus for our hot weather. This month, Sunumunna, and also months Nenegar and Kininnin, are the months of our growing season, though it gets past halfway to boiling sometimes. Our actual hot weather season comprises the months Duku, Apindua, and Ganganna. The other half of the year is dark and sometimes wet."

"Thank you for the information," Azariah said. Oshpenaz knew exactly what to say—the lengthy words and neutral tone cut through Azariah's sharp feelings.

"Ah, I knew you were reasonable. How nice to have my advice heard with no sullenness." This may have been sarcasm. "Tell my assistant I want to see Daniel next. As fun as this conversation has been, my job would be much easier if you were all like Daniel. I have other things to do with my life besides babysitting a bunch of exiles." He waved a finger to dismiss Azariah and flipped through the pages of a book on the tea table.

"Daniel is very special. I don't see how there can be more than one of him in any galaxy." Azariah arose and tapped a panel to alert the assistant but didn't turn off the heat shield and turned back to his new friend. "I have one question if you have time."

"Until Daniel gets here."

"Why aren't any young women here?" He clenched his body, knowing that Oshpenaz's words would hit like a physical blow.

"I imagine you mean young Gospel and Revelation women. It is because Paradise is matrilineal. The best way to break your culture is to not allow any women to have access to anything. No worries, your Gospel young women and other nobles are being well taken care of in the South Pole swamps. You'll meet other young women soon enough. Feel free to hang out with them. It's much too soon to think about marriage, but it's something to keep in mind once your three years of education are over."

Daniel came before Azariah could ask any follow-up questions. Oshpenaz sent him out of the pavilion with a chuckle. Daniel looked at Azariah's face. Who knows what he saw; Azariah felt like his brain was breaking.

"Hey, Azariah, is everything okay?"

"Yes, it's just- well, I'm thoroughly known. That isn't ever pleasant. I'll be fine once I change and drink more water."

Daniel paused. "He? Did Oshpenaz say they are a man? How can you tell?"

"Um." Azariah's brain skipped around for a moment. "Let's ask, asteroid boy." He ducked back into the pavilion. "Hey Oshpenaz, Daniel has been using neutral pronouns to refer to you." Daniel bumped his shoulder. He elbowed him back.

"I am, in fact, a eunuch and use masculine pronouns," Oshpenaz answered with a wry smile.

"My apologies sir, I did not intend for Aza—"

"You are forgiven, my dear Daniel. Ramzi, go away already."

Daniel only had time to give him a pat on the shoulder.

Azariah took a deep breath before he reached the mock orange trees again. *To resist and to return home.*

Later, Mishael, Hananiah and Azariah found themselves at the very top of the Etemenanki palace, the highest viewing tower, the wind whipping around them. Daniel was praying in a chapel or something.

Azariah looked out to the north; the jungle got thicker, and the turquoise river disappeared into the green. He could feel the heat of the desert and the Babylonian blue star on his back. The heat was a heavy presence. The river must be special for the jungle to flourish.

Desert surrounded the palace on three sides. A canyon over the river was on the fourth side, with wide platforms stair-stepping their way down to the bottom of the canyon. The jungle growth fit in wherever it could. The palace was the only building complex fully above the canyon. Even though the vast canyon below held the greatest city of an Empire, Azariah felt alone in the world with his new comrades-in-arms so high up. They weren't Azariah's friends. Azariah didn't *want* them as friends, but he was social and even though he would have been disdainful of nobility on Gospel, here on Babylon, they were his only option.

Their first chat was full of introductory information. Azariah was the youngest at seventeen years old. Hananiah and Mishael were twenty-one. Hananiah remembered from his childhood that Daniel was younger than him and would turn twenty-one during the hottest Babylonian season in a few months, which is the season Azariah would turn eighteen.

"How did things with Oshpenaz go for you two?" Hananiah asked.

"Fine. Daniel gave me a fantastic tip to not insult him to his face. That was so useful." Azariah didn't like the guys much and didn't want to share how he felt. He thought to himself, *I could cry with frustration at how my life was out of my control. How it is these humans and the forces of war and empire expansion and culture and God's will and the idolatry of my former king are affecting my life, its trajectory and the air I breathe and the food in my body. I'm not in the fields, I'm not reading my manuals-* Azariah felt overwhelmed with his emotions and too caged to set them free safely.

"I think they want people they can just show off, and it would be fine if they were only half tamed." Mishael said. "I don't want to learn anything or become an administrator, which they say is the goal. I'll take time to visit the bird races and find the party life, as Daniel allows, of course." Hananiah and Azariah looked at each other.

"I guess that's one attitude," Azariah said. The heat was making him restless, and he waved Mishael off, which annoyed Mishael.

"Yeah, it's not like I need an education, unlike you, I'm sure. Can you read?" Mishael asked. "Your patroness might have picked you just for looks."

"Rude. There's plenty to learn in Zharqua, unlike the bombing and unrest in Darh Dothoma." Mishael's home estate was desert, which allowed for big cities; almost all arable land on Gospel had something growing.

"There hasn't been bombing in a generation!" Mishael insisted.

"Then stop aiming your guns at us."

"Wow, stop it!" Hananiah stepped up to the edge of the tower between where Mishael and Azariah were standing. He leaned with his back to the desert expanse, blinking in the sunlight. "We need real property and assets here on Babylon." Hananiah continued. "We need a united front."

"I will not put my life on the line for estates that look like Gospel," Azariah warned.

"Yeah, you're a peasant. You need to grow out your hair," Mishael said. "I say that as a kind favor. Like Daniel with the food yesterday, this is cultural warfare."

"I'm not going to. I don't feel like changing anything about myself. Just wait three years and then my Patroness will bring me back to Gospel." Back to home, as flawed as it was.

"Yeah, she lied to you." Mishael turned his back on Azariah.

"Hananiah, what did Oshpenaz get out of you?"

"My ambitions are to work in the Royal Archives." He looked over the palace, as if to look for the specific building, but most of that work was done at the South Pole of Babylon.

"What? Ew." Mishael wrinkled his nose.

"Correction, my mom wants me to work in the Archives. It seems like a way to not work for the empire, and to study other cultures."

"I can understand that." Mishael nodded. Azariah understood too but didn't care.

"Another thing. What do you guys think about Daniel?" Azariah asked. "He worships God differently from how I do, but I believe he has visions." So far, Daniel had been the only soothing thing Azariah had found on the planet, and maybe he would be a way to connect better with the other two. Now was the best time to ask.

"I love his prayer. Have you heard of it? He said it to his enclave, and it's been spreading through other exile enclaves. 'If I rise on the wings of the dawn, if I settle on the far side of the sea, even there your hand will guide me.' He's a spiritual leader," Hananiah said. While Azariah wasn't religious himself, he could respect it and liked to see Hananiah's soft spot. Maybe Azariah could consider friendship, but the thought made him grit his teeth.

"I'll be honest," Mishael said, "and I'd rather you didn't tell him, but I know once I say it I can't unsay it, but I'm not sure if God is blessing him with visions. I feel like what's happening to Paradise is predictable: we accrued wealth, we became internally corrupt and unstable, which makes it easy for the Chaldean empire to invade. King Nebuchadnezzar understands how to *not* have plagues, food shortages, useless violence, and so on. It's not like God came to King Nebuchadnezzar in a dream and told him how to run an empire or how to ruin us. Prophet Jeremiah prophesies only predictable forces, but he shows a special intelligence and courage, and I could see Daniel being like that."

"But really?" Hananiah quizzed. "You think Daniel fakes having visions, but is otherwise moral?"

"Hey, my family and I have listened to the prophets. We moved to a small moon when Daniel left for Goethe. My family is smart enough to be in a system with more culture and access to a decent life."

"But you didn't move as many people. I wasn't asking for any complicated reasoning," Azariah said, glaring at Mishael. "I'm asking about this because I think we should support him in the immediate term, like taking turns watching over him if he's in a vision."

"Of course," Mishael retorted.

"Exactly," Azariah said.

"I'd do that for any of you, obviously," Mishael insisted.

"Of course," Azariah said sarcastically. He couldn't imagine Mishael helping anyone.

"Yes," Mishael insisted.

"Me. Too."

"Obviously." He sounded hostile, which was stupid.

Hananiah snorted. "Enough, the two of you. Have you seen anything about Marduk? He's supposed to be the local god. I thought we should visit a temple soon to check him out."

"Did Marduk appear a hundred years ago?" Azariah asked.

"Two hundred. The local gods appeared when the Achaemenid Empire collapsed."

"You make it sound related. There's no reason to think that the veil was drawn back because of that," Mishael said.

"Hananiah," Azariah said, "it sounds like you've researched Marduk. My patroness said there wasn't any reason to, just keep praying to the creator God."

"That's what I've been told too, but now that I'm here, I'm curious. Marduk seems to live in harmony with Chaldean Christianity just fine."

Mishael, unable to help himself, said, "Azariah, don't worry, it's not like you can handle a complicated religious discussion, anyway."

"No, I can't," Azariah agreed, which made them laugh. But he could. He just didn't want to deal with his new friends anymore; he had chatted with old friends on calls while he worked in the field. They talked about a lot of things. One time, he gave someone advice that led to a missile being shot at a Chaldean spaceship.

After Oshpenaz, after talking with his new friends—he would call them friends, even if Mishael was more contentious than necessary—Azariah felt both smarter and dumber. Oshpenaz had peeled back some layers and showed him how smart he was. He also showed Azariah how little savvy he had. How was Azariah supposed to survive with no wits? But he was part of a team, and none of them were to survive alone. His patroness had told him to make friends for political survival reasons. He didn't know if she thought genuine friendship was possible, but it seemed like this was real.

Press Release from King Nebuchadnezzar

I write this so that my subjects may know me, their glorious King Nebuchadnezzar, and my purpose for all that I reign over.

I am creeping toward Aegyptus slowly but surely in one direction; in the other, I would hit a band of the Milky Way—an arm of stars called the Euphrates. So many systems, gold, people, knowledge—what magic might I conquer, what signs of God would become mine, how happy would my army be and continue to worship me? How many people in the galaxy ignore me right now and how many of those will think of me in fear soon, if they think at all? All of this happens with a relatively small bit of work on my hands. I've got the ideas and resources, and everyone else bends to me. My empire will circle around the Milky Way.

We have conquered some truly fantastic, special places. I'm sure they have knowledge they are afraid to share. The sort of thing you can't force out of a person. And yet it must be mine. I have a plan for this. All of these new exiles must stop being exiles and must enjoy my empire—my Babylonia must be their Babylonia. They are not hostages! Who has said this? Anyone who says my new guests are hostages will be put to death! How do I reward my exiles when all they want is to go home, even if home is some blasted crater now? They must stop that and give me their hopes and dreams, and knowledge, so that my empire can reach its heights. I will show them strength and gold, and they will show me their secrets. I'm really quite excited. I've been terrorizing and looting so much, but there is so much to gain, so much still to enjoy. Please, my beloved people, enjoy this with me.

Chapter 5: Daniel

The young men's frustration built up over the next month. They hated how the Etemenanki palace pinned down their futures. Each hour of the next three years was planned for them. For a brief escape, they left the palace and went camping before the hottest months arrived. They would hike through the desert, sleep in the desert one night, hike to Wara Ti'amtum, the salt sea with a luxury resort that served the capital elite, and sleep for as long as they wanted before heading back.

Daniel hadn't ever gone camping in a desert before. He researched and watched what his friends would wear and pack. On the day of, he wore a high-tech inner layer that zipped. Over that, he wore loose white cotton layers and a white keffiyeh. He put in sun protectant contact lenses and used cream to protect any skin the sun might see. Mishael was dressed like him, but Hananiah and Azariah wore only the high-tech gear and hats with brims.

Their preparations took place very early in the morning. They loaded gear into a ground auto and said goodbye to Samwel, who seemed genuinely worried about them.

Azariah was the only one with experience driving. Daniel sat next to him and watched as he played with the controls, the noisy engine making Daniel jump. Azariah made happy noises; his anger wasn't so present any more compared to his first days. Being cheerful in the little things was his natural state.

"Is it supposed to sound like that?" Daniel asked.

"Oh yeah," Azariah said, grinning. "It's not a combustion engine which I wanted, but those are for even richer people. This engine is fine. I checked under the hood yesterday. It sounds good and even if something broke, it would be easy to fix."

Daniel highly doubted that.

"What's the hood?" Hananiah asked from the back seat. And thus started a lecture series from Azariah on automobiles.

They drove along the Turquoise River deeper into the desert and drove across the white Kaspum Mountains; Daniel was shocked that the white parts were sand instead of glaciers and everyone made fun of him. He could not adjust to this planet. He zoned out of the ongoing auto discussion and watched the stars fade and the sunrise.

Daniel had always considered Babylon to be crowded; it was the capital planet after all, but it was full of nature reserves that required permits to visit; luxuries for the elite.

Eventually, Azariah stopped and turned off the ground auto. He had been driving for over five Babylon hours.

"Why are we stopping? We're out in the middle of nowhere." Indeed, the road had been covered in a fine layer of sand for hours. The sun had been above the horizon for a few hours. All Daniel could see were some sparse bushes and the rolling white-lavender sand.

"That is the idea, Daniel. This is the trailhead," Mishael answered. "Obviously. By the way, I never hiked on Babylon when I was here before."

"Yeah, this is the place." Hananiah pointed to a sign Daniel had missed, which had the name of the nature reserve Hunnubum Humtum.

They each had a pack of supplies and equipment. One thing to appreciate, the palace had special technology for carrying water; what would be five gallons of water were in a pint-sized container. Daniel tossed a couple around, still the same weight. Other equipment packed down tight too. Daniel was now fully comprehending how this was all they would have from now until they reached Wara Ti'amtum. He felt panic starting in his stomach. He breathed deeply, breathing it out. *I've done this before, I'm sure.* But still, the backpack that was heavy at the palace seemed inadequate now that he put it on. Azariah helped him tighten the straps.

"Are you okay, dude?" he asked.

"Don't call me dude. I'm fine. Just fine." When that didn't seem convincing, Daniel thought about lying and saying it was the long ride. "Maybe not. I'll let you know if I need anything."

Mishael and Hananiah had joined them and heard that last part. Daniel didn't want to seem weak, so it was unsettling to see their concerned looks. "We should go. I don't want to lead."

Azariah closed up the ground auto and nodded to Hananiah, who put his hat on and took the lead. Mishael walked with him. Azariah put his hat and sunglasses on and walked with Daniel.

The path was wide enough to walk two and two, no one else in sight for them to maneuver around. They set a good pace.

"What was that little panic attack about back at the trailhead?" Azariah asked Daniel.

"Subtle, very nice," Mishael said. He and Hananiah looked back at them but didn't slow down.

"I don't mind answering," Daniel said. "Maybe a bit of agoraphobia. I haven't been under a sky like this since I was ten years old on Gospel. It's different here than in the city."

"Ten years old?? Where've you been?" Azariah asked.

"A Goethe system asteroid," Daniel said.

"I know that's where your shuttle came from, but you've been there this whole time?" Azariah asked.

"I visited a small moon twice. It didn't have an atmosphere," Daniel said.

"Yikes," Azariah said. "And I thought being cooped up on a ship for a month was torture. What did you do?"

"You can't ask questions like that!" Mishael turned around and kicked some sand at Azariah.

"It is very rude," Hananiah agreed.

"Okay," Azariah said, holding up his hands in surrender. "You seem fine now. Except for the bad memories, I guess."

"And good memories." Daniel gave him a small smile.

They walked in silence. Daniel could breathe deep in a way he hadn't for years, that he had forgotten how to. Azariah whistled a hymn for a few minutes until Mishael told him to stop. Daniel started humming it under his breath. He hadn't thought Azariah was being rude.

Hananiah looked back at Daniel a few times, even once he stopped humming.

"What?" Daniel asked.

"So we're having a chat at dinner?" Hananiah asked.

"Yes! Everything is fine," Daniel promised. Earlier that week when they had talked about camping, Daniel had used the phrase "family palaver," which sounded innocent enough, but in his family meant to expect a serious conversation at dinner. At that point, Hananiah had raised his eyebrow, and Daniel had nodded back but gestured to stay quiet. He did want to have a serious conversation away from the palace. And he couldn't have it next to this nice spring. They needed to get to the campsite.

The sun was low on the horizon once they reached the campsite, at another oasis with pine trees, grass, signs of little birds and snakes, and a small creek that they would follow to the Wara Ti'amtum.

Daniel started a fire with wood from an underground cache. Babylon never got cool enough to need a fire for warmth, but his caveman instinct kicked in. He hadn't had one since he was ten on Gospel. Once he got the fire started, he settled down by it and took off his keffiyeh. He liked the flowing feel of the cotton layers and took nothing else off. He got a couple of devices out of his bag.

"Hey, no electronics," Azariah protested, calling to Daniel from where the three were setting up tents.

"What is going on?" Daniel called back, turning to look at what the other three were up to. They had popped six different tents open. They were arguing and kept folding and unfolding tents, which were in boxes about the size of a fist, the fabric would fold up tight into the box on request. The popping noises startled Daniel.

"Azariah was in charge of gear and he's telling us what tents to use and it's not making any sense," Mishael reported.

Daniel decided he was too tired to care. Hananiah would have to mediate between Mishael and Azariah tonight. Daniel turned back to check the scanning equipment. He heard pops for the cots, sleeping bags, lanterns, and a few other things.

After a few minutes, Azariah plopped down next to him, still sulky from his tiff over the tents. Daniel got him to help with dinner and soon enough Azariah's bad mood sloughed off like usual. Daniel was jealous; both his own mood and fatigue felt sticky. Before dinner was even ready, Azariah was rummaging through everything around the fire, cheerfully stirring the food and saying it was incredible, and going through Daniel's pack.

"What do you have here?"

"I want to check to see if we're being monitored in any way. It looks like we're as safe as we can hope to be. No tracking or listening devices got tucked into our equipment, no one is nearby, no satellites." Daniel sighed and put the devices away. "See? No electronics. Not us and not anything nearby."

Azariah took the devices out of Daniel's bag again to poke at them.

"Rude!" said Mishael, settling nearby.

"Oh, I gave him permission," Daniel said, but Azariah put things away tidy and with exaggerated flourishes.

"Mishael, you don't have very many siblings, do you?" Hananiah asked, kneeling to look at the food on the fire. "I would be suspicious if my sisters *didn't* inspect all my property."

"My estate doesn't believe in private ownership," Azariah said. "I'm still getting used to having my own space and all the weird boundaries."

"That's also known as a fascist dictatorship," Mishael said, ready to pick another fight.

"It's not—"

"Oh hey, we haven't been sitting for five minutes and you're at it. So Daniel, what are you calling a family palaver about? Just a minute," Hananiah said, saying a grace and then dishing up zibitum for dinner, the local grain that was easy to transport, like rice from Kaliopi on Gospel, flavored with spicy, dried Babylonian *hasurrum*.

"Oh, this is fantastic." Daniel sighed. He just wanted to eat and sleep.

"What did you say, Hananiah? So this isn't for fun?" Mishael asked. "Makes sense since you haven't enjoyed yourself." He pointed at Daniel.

"I have," Azariah said, enjoying his dinner. "We should do this once a month. There's a bunch of nature reserves to drive to, not all desert terrain."

"I was talking to Daniel, idiot."

"There are a few things I want to talk about and decided I'd feel more comfortable waiting until the palace is less likely to overhear." Daniel started warming *enba* over the fire, a cake with fruit like strawberries that was supposed to be good for camping. "First is Prophet Jeremiah's new letter. There's a part where God is addressing exiles in Babylon specifically."

To all Paradisians, those on Gospel, Revelation, and in exile, Prophet Jeremiah was like a father, a pastor, and an authority figure. The words God gave him were clear and held weight, unlike the confusing visions Daniel had.

"Oooh, I've read that letter," Mishael said. "God is not talking to the four of us."

"I think we need to take the letter seriously," Daniel said firmly.

"I am! Out of the four of us, I'm the most likely to have committed adultery with a neighbor's wife and I haven't! God is talking about specific people."

"That's not the only thing the letter is about!"

"It does mention false prophets. Well, Daniel, do you have a confession to make?" Mishael teased.

"No!"

"We're not Ahab or Zedekiah," Mishael insisted. "We will not be burned in a fire. Next topic. We can talk about Prophet Ezekiel's latest performance if you'd like." Ezekiel, who traveled with his husband, was another prophet who had words from God that were to the exiles, especially the rich, noble ones. His visions of God were different from Daniel's and Jeremiah's.

Hananiah turned and smiled at Daniel. "We can read through the first part together, at least. I'll start: 'This is what the Lord Almighty says to all those I carried into exile from Paradise into the Chaldean empire: Build houses and settle down; plant gardens and eat what they produce. Marry and have sons and daughters, so that they too may have sons and daughters. Increase in number there; do not decrease. Also, seek the peace and prosperity of the city to which I have carried you into exile. Pray to the Lord for it, because if it prospers, you too will prosper.' Well, Mishael, I think that's a little relevant to us."

At the end, Daniel said, "This is the closest I've had to a worship service since arriving. This is important to me." But there was something he secretly struggled with—why couldn't God give him words like this? Daniel was in an even deeper exile living at the palace.

"Being out in nature makes me feel that way, too," Azariah said. "If you feel comfortable being religious only if we're out of the palace, we should definitely explore more."

"The stuff in that letter made me think about our role on Babylon," Daniel continued. "Prophet Jeremiah has a prophecy that there's a ten-year window between attacks on Paradise, and we're in that window right now. Now's the time to prepare before the next attack. We should find a temporary planet to stay safe and not be scattered across several solar systems. We should figure out how to get Gospel back after seventy years; it's highly unlikely God will literally hand it back. Until then, Paradisians will be refugees, so we need policies helping us. I do think this is the work God means for us, Paradisians on Babylon."

"Wow. That's a lot Daniel," Hananiah said, rubbing his face.

"We can't do that," Azariah said, crossing his arms and then waving a hand in the air. "Like, any of it."

"It's important to think about!" Daniel insisted.

"We all have our own goals. You can't just draw us into yours," Mishael said. Daniel had expected his resistance, but not the others.

"Your goal is bird races," Daniel said to Mishael, trying to make it sound like a joke and not a judgment. "Where am I wrong?"

"Let's see, a safe haven planet, get Gospel back, and affect empire policies," Azariah listed. "What makes you think we can do any of that?"

"I'm not saying there's a simple solution! But this is our work here. I'm sure of it." Even with their disagreement, Daniel felt he was right.

"So, you wanted to come out here to talk about this?" Azariah asked. "Why all the secrecy? I can't imagine the palace caring if we have specific ambitions."

"Then you haven't been paying attention to the king." Mishael retorted. "He's violent and paranoid and is definitely spying on us. He'd be annoyed if we had a literal plan to take one of his precious systems away in seventy years, or sixty-five, whatever it is now."

"This is like a self-fulfilling prophecy, isn't it?" Hananiah asked. "We *are* going behind his back now. We could try to actually be trustworthy."

"I've introduced the ideas," Daniel said, raising his hands to placate. He hadn't expected to stir up this much disagreement. "This is a long-term thing. We can stop there for tonight."

"Sounds good to me!" Azariah stretched his arms over his head. "Hey, did you hear that Samwel's wife is having twins? I think her name is Neema. Should we do something? Also, celebrations in general. Do you think we could celebrate Christmas here? Think they'd stop us?"

"We got the shrines kicked out and we're eating food we like. I'm sure we can push for it. What do you think Samwel would like?" Hananiah asked.

"Wait," Daniel said. "There's one more thing. I will not let you get out of this one. I want us to learn sign language. Here," he motioned to Hananiah to hold out his hand and made some signs on it. "That was *the king is stupid.*" It was juvenile, but even out here he didn't feel safe criticizing the king too much.

They laughed.

"Fine, I'll learn," Mishael said. "But not this evening."

"Of course we'll all learn," added Azariah.

Hananiah nodded. "Teach us the dirty words too, *pasisum* Daniel."

Daniel had a bone and soul aching weariness; he had never walked in a straight line for so long. The universe had never felt so empty. He dragged himself to the tents before anyone else. The sun still hadn't set —it was a time of year with long days and if he slept only when it was dark, he wouldn't be rested.

"You missed all the drinking games," Mishael said.

The tent rustling had woken Daniel up. He groaned. He did not care. Hananiah and Azariah were in the tent next to them.

"Shhh," Hananiah or Azariah shushed.

"Shhh," whispered the other.

"Ah, the stars, I hate these stars." Azariah's voice drifted over. "And the moon, if you can even call that a moon."

"Sleepy time buddy."

Mishael chuckled.

"How did Patroness Shelomith *find* you? You keep saying you're a *wheat* farmer. Did you ace some standardized testing?"

"No, my mom hates testing," Azariah gave a short laugh. "My dad took me with him to the wheat silos and I could speak with the Babylonian reps after listening to them for just a bit. My dad and I thought it was just a fun trick. I think maybe they sold me to her so that I wouldn't join the militia. Joke's on them, though. I don't think I can *unfold* and be a good person."

Daniel went to sleep before he heard anything else.

The next morning, Daniel woke up to light from a golden sunrise shining through the tent netting. Mishael was still fast asleep. Daniel crawled out of the tent and walked up a crest of sand to watch the rest of the sunrise, enjoying the cool, tranquil breeze. Azariah joined him, which didn't surprise Daniel, and they sat in the sand. They were both early risers, and Azariah was extroverted enough to follow Daniel around. And he wasn't cranky in the mornings, so Daniel let him. They had watched more than one sunrise together, and he understood Daniel preferred silence until the sun was all the way up.

As soon as it was, they asked each other at the same time, "Are you okay?" They laughed.

"Yesterday was a big day for you," Azariah said.

"Yesterday evening seemed upsetting to you, from what I heard," Daniel said.

"Yeah, that happens. But I thought about everything you asked us. And Daniel," he said, turning to face Daniel, looking alert and at peace. "I'm with you in all things. Whatever you feel like I can do for you, let me know. I'll think about what I can do, too. You're my favorite prophet."

"Thank you."

Chapter 6: Daniel

A month later at the Etemenanki palace…

Daniel prayed for more guidance. Surely, if God had granted him some metaphysical connection, it was for a utilitarian purpose. Not only had Daniel prayed, but he had fasted, had isolated himself, and had abnegated his physical life to the extent possible. He fell into a vision.

In Daniel's vision, first he saw all four parts together—the Eye of the Milky Way, the winds of the galaxy stirred up the stars, and as they sparkled, the four beasts paraded across the galaxy, the lion with the eagle wings torn off with the mind of a man, the bear satiated and on her side with even more ribs in her mouth, the mutated leopard with four heads and four sets of wings that prowled, and the fourth beast that seemed to be part machine and with horns and more destructive than the others; they paraded on the galaxy and yet they were nothing; they were swept away.

A throne room was set among the galaxies; each galaxy sparkled in its place, over, under and on every side of the throne room. The throne burst into living flame; the wheels, like Ezekiel's wheels, were also ablaze. Onto this throne sat a vision of the Ancient of Days; his clothing was white as snow; his hair was white wool. Surrounded and seated on flame, a river of fire flowed, coming out from before him. As he looked out among the galaxies, his throne room filled. Ten thousand times ten thousand came and the throne room wasn't full. The court was seated, and the books were opened. The beasts of Daniel's vision had been swept away only to the side, stripped of their authority, their temporary, weak nature fully apparent. The fourth beast was slain and its body destroyed and thrown into the blazing fire.

Into this court came someone who seemed to be human, coming with her own majesty as represented by the nature of a human world, like clouds and lightning; this was a different power from the living flames and river of fire. The Ancient of Days gave her authority, glory, and sovereign power; the full court of tens of thousands times tens of thousands worshiped her, as did all the worlds of the galaxies. Her dominion was an everlasting dominion that would not pass away, and her kingdom was one that would never be destroyed.

Daniel, in his own weak nature, did not understand this.

"Is it truly happening? What type of vision is this? I can barely stand it." His mind was disturbed. He spoke this to someone in the tens of thousands. They looked at him with all benevolence.

"What about the four beasts?" Daniel asked the courtier.

"The four great beasts are four kings that will rise from the earth. But the holy people of the Most High will receive the kingdom and will possess it forever—yes, for ever and ever."

When Daniel asked about the four beasts, they said those were merely from his own galaxy and were only kings from there.

"Representative of kings? A four headed leopard wouldn't actually rule the Milky Way."

They paused to look at him and look at the beasts and said, "The true nature may not be apparent. If your galaxy has kings that look like you, then that is what kings are. But it doesn't matter, the Most High is beyond time, and will rule, and is worthy of worship. The holy people of the Most High will receive the kingdom and will possess it forever—yes, for ever and ever."

"Is the fourth beast also truly a king?" Daniel asked. "It is so different; surely that represents that its rule will also be different. How is it that you, one of tens of thousands, can understand? How much more is there to be revealed? How much do I not yet understand?"

"The fourth beast is a fourth kingdom that will appear in your galaxy. It will differ from all the other kingdoms and will devour the stars, trampling them down and crushing them." The courtier continued to speak of the fourth beast, but their words left Daniel deeply troubled. The courtier concluded, "The Most High is already among you; his kingdom is an everlasting kingdom; yet you do not realize it and are still in exile. How can you escape exile this time? How often will it happen again?" They asked these as questions, but also Daniel saw they had the answers and were only marveling at how strange he was.

So Daniel woke up. His friends were sleeping around him; Azariah was dozing on a pad on the floor of his little alcove. He could see Hananiah and Mishael without even lifting his head. They were on the couches and cushions of the living space. Azariah woke when Daniel moved a bit. Daniel was too weak to sit up.

"You have been in your vision for a day."

"I have had the interpretation."

Daniel was glad it was him; there was no accusation or worry; his faith in the prophecy was true. Daniel clasped his hand and then slept a more natural rest. After a time, he was stronger, but the world still seemed transparent.

Daniel wrote in detail everything that he had seen. This prophecy differed greatly from Prophet Jeremiah or other prophets. He didn't have a warning, message, or anything that seemed useful; neither the Ancient of Days, nor the Most High, nor any of their messengers spoke to him or asked him to pass some information on. He did have more information on the four beasts but nothing that would help his people. Even so, he passed the prophecy onto his mother Sherah for her to disseminate as she saw fit.

His spirits were depressed, but once he took care of his physical body, he tended to his other duties.

Daniel communicated with the Empire Judicature on behalf of Sherah, Hananiah's mom, Patroness Shelomith, and the Darh Dothoma Negus. He didn't think he could do much, but Sherah pointed out in a letter that the access he had was way beyond what any other Paradisian had, and even more than what many empire citizens had. Daniel could do only a little and had invited him to speak today to a council in person. This was important since the Judicature had rejected all previous requests.

"No, absolutely not. This is ugly and appalling," Daniel said sharply to Samwel when he held out the ensemble for Daniel to wear to the Judicature. Daniel snatched it out of his hands and threw it onto the bench. Samwel spoke to him soothingly but was interrupted by the other three coming to the door of the clothing room, which was the size of any regular room with mirrors and benches to sit on and lots of natural light, everything in white to show off the colors of the clothing.

"Daniel! You were yelling!" Azariah said, leaning into the room from the doorway.

"I've never heard you yell," Mishael said, stepping all the way in.

"I did not yell," Daniel replied.

"You shouldn't speak to Samwel like that," Hananiah said, sitting down on a bench near the door. Azariah joined him.

"My apologies, Samwel," he sighed and gave Samwel a small smile.

"Ah, my dear Daniel, you are as sweet as an *ursanu pasisum*. I could never feel bruised by your words. But this is your burden, and you must bear up under it." Samwel picked the ensemble up off the bench.

Daniel wanted to take the pants and jacket out of his hands and throw them out the window. His friends didn't leave; Daniel was in a mood, and they wanted to watch.

"I don't even know how to put these clothes on."

"What? It's just pants?" Azariah said.

"It's just a suit!" Mishael agreed.

"You go then," Daniel retorted. This was probably the first time they had agreed on something. Daniel was so happy he could bring them together. In fact, this was one of the first times he'd seen all three in a good mood together. Too bad he couldn't join them.

"No, they are expecting you," Azariah said.

"The suit won't fit me." Mishael said at the same time.

"It doesn't look like it will fit me," Daniel said, pulling at the blue fabric of the jacket Samwel was holding. He wished it was green.

"It is to your measurements, I assure you," Samwel replied. "It is only a cut that you're not used to."

"Fine. What do I do first?"

"Pants."

Samwel helped, but he didn't like them at all.

"You should like those pants. Your ass looks great," Azariah said.

"I like only ladies and I appreciate your ass." Mishael agreed. Daniel was once again bringing them together.

"Your work at the gym is paying off," Hananiah said.

"All of you are very embarrassing." Daniel made a face. "Samwel, how does the jacket even go on? It looks too tight in the shoulders."

"First, what goes under—"

"It's a button shirt, right?" Daniel asked. "I hate buttons. I don't want to wear it."

"You must wear it," Samwel said. "I will button it for you. But first a thin layer under that."

"Three layers total! And they all look tight! This is torture."

"This is what it takes to do a good deed," said Samwel, suppressing a smile.

"Instead of going to the Judicature, you could be like Jesus and walk among the poor and give them food and be best friends with a scampering orphan," Azariah said.

"I can't imagine Daniel willingly touching a bunch of strangers."

"Or walking on dirty streets."

"Sweating."

"Stop it! I'm right here!"

Daniel got everything on and the two shirts tucked in properly, his hair done in a tight roll, and the tie on, which he didn't mind as much. He had been practicing knots, and then socks and shoes that pinched.

He left the palace and traveled across the city in palace transportation. He entered the Judicature chambers where the Babylon *dayyantu* would give him an audience for his short list of items that were inconsequential to an empire. The *dayyantu* were three people in suits at a bench and table of white wood a few arms' lengths away from him.

A thought popped into Daniel's mind, a line from his vision. *How will you escape exile?* His visions were always with him. The Judicature had the reality of ghosts when he thought about the Ancient court.

"Your Honors. Thank you for meeting with me. I've been part of the Etemenanki palace educational project. The Treasury set aside funds to provide for servants, food, clothing, supplies, travel, and so on. An examination of the records will show the educational project is anticipated to use only a third of the funds set aside. The participants and I would like the other two-thirds of the funds to be used differently." Daniel had provided information ahead of time.

"What type of project?" A disembodied voice asked the question. The *dayyantu* weren't speaking but checking information in front of them, a set up where Daniel could see them gesture but nothing else. The voice had a perfect Babylonian accent, which made him conscious and uncomfortable of his accent; he had no idea what type of image he projected.

Their evil deeds have no limit; they do not seek justice. Daniel thought to himself before speaking aloud. "King Nebuchadnezzar of the Chaldean empire has, in his wisdom, instituted a Proclamation for the planet of Babylon. Since its institution, it has been found that those of lesser means cannot enjoy the planet as he intended. In an effort to more fully carry out the king's intention, we would like the educational project funds to be given to the Babylon Municipal Mahazum Ruzelum."

That organization helped people with excellent causes who had enough resources to get to Babylon and then had nothing left. These people were easy prey for scammers and illicit trades that needed destitute people. These people only needed a little to move forward, like a place to stay and food.

"You have explained what, but not why," the voice said.

"If this is our money," Daniel answered, "we should be able to do what we wish."

"You don't want to assist your own refugees, Ahab or Zedekiah? They are in prison here, and a few like them."

"No," Daniel said, thinking *watch out for false prophets.*

"We deny your request," said the voice. "The only legally approved use is for your own benefit; while the phrase 'your own benefit' has been defined to include a community, this does not apply to the organization you wish to donate to. If you don't spend the money for your own benefit, the funds will be absorbed back into the Treasury. There is no reason to break established precedence. What is your second issue?"

Daniel hated every moment of this, his jacket pulling at his shoulders, and the bright whiteness hurting his eyes. *You have made us a reproach to our neighbors, the scorn and derision of those around us,* he thought before speaking aloud.

"My family wishes to purchase a moon named Axima in the Goethe solar system around the gas giant Poeninae. As their representative, I must be sponsored by a Chaldean citizen in order to move the request forward, and citizen Samwel Chande sponsors me."

"Do you have proof of available funds?"

Daniel passed the sensitive information from his disc to the room's data storage and projector.

"The purpose of buying the moon?"

"Economic development in service to King Nebuchadnezzar and residency for up to two hundred million people."

"What are the obstacles?"

"The first is that more than one party claims to have legal ownership so we don't know who to buy from. The second is that if a certain private company is the legal owner, they are refusing to sell; we believe they wish to extort."

"We are willing to research this further. Please check in with us in six months."

"Thank you."

Daniel came home discomforted, exhausted. He didn't know enough about the Judicature to know if "six months" was reasonable or a polite refusal. The other three were in the dining room to the right of the entryway. He could hear them yelling about something and slipped quietly to the left into the common area to get to the clothing room.

Samwel was sitting on one of the white upholstered benches, reading a book. Daniel was so sick of this entire planet being white. It wasn't real and it hurt his eyes.

"Ah, excellent, you still look very sharp," Samwel said, taking off Daniel's jacket.

"Is that what this is? I do, in fact, feel sharp. I'll have to remember that." Daniel sat down, removed his tie, shoes, and socks, then started unbuttoning the shirt, his fingers not proficient.

"Please, *pasisum*." Samwel wincing. "Please be careful. Don't tear any of the buttons off."

"I won't, I'm sure. I have some questions for you. While we certainly can't embezzle money, we can be more generous. We can increase your pay and if you or your wife have anyone who needs some kind of nominal job, we'd be happy to help. If you need to care for your children, we can see about having a nanny on site."

"I see you weren't able to give up the palace riches as you'd hoped. Your suggestions are very kind, all of you have made similar offers. Putting that to the side, I do have a request. Can you double the clothing budget? I've been having a lot of fun creating wardrobes for the four of you and now that I know all of you better, I want to buy more, including bespoke items for more prominent engagements."

"I will triple the clothing budget because there is that much money. Azariah has expensive taste, whether or not he realizes it."

"I noticed as well. He likes me to pick outfits for him. Hananiah is very basic, Mishael is very picky and expensive; those two seem to be opposites of each, one with a quiet life and I'm sure Mishael will go the furthest of you. My pardon, except for how your visions may influence your future. Here, my dear *pasisum*, I picked this *rabatum* robe out for you. It is the softest material in Babylonia, and a lovely green color."

"Thank you." The robe was plushy. "I have my own request. Can you do something about this room so it's not so white? Some kind of redecorating?"

"Certainly. Now you look much more relaxed. Please go join your friends. They love you very much."

"Daniel! Finally!" Azariah said when Daniel entered the dining room. "I saved some raspberries for you. If you'd taken five more minutes, I would have eaten them. They smell delicious. And taste delicious, but

I've eaten my share and keep smelling yours."

Daniel sat next to him, picked up the bowl of raspberries and hugged it while leaning back in the chair. They were bright pink, smelled like Gospel summer, and had the perfect crisp taste of sweet and tart.

"The kitchen found us something similar to beer. It's called *kas*." Hananiah gave him a cool drink. It was a red color and tasted thick.

"Thank you."

"First of all," Mishael said, sitting up straight, "I want to know why you're so set on giving up all our money. There are no Kahi churches we can tithe to. I personally feel like charitable work differs from just throwing money at an organization. If I understand you better, I can help better."

Daniel sighed, feeling downcast and not really wanting to be open, but understanding why he should. He pinched the bridge of his nose to keep from crying. "In my vision, I spent time in a heavenly court. Coming back here and having to endure this flawed worldly court just feels like too much. I don't want to benefit from anything Babylon offers. Even though the organization I chose doesn't help Paradisians directly, it helps people in similar need. It's funding the policy part of my goal. But you make a good point that funding differs from actually developing and implementing economic and social structure changes."

"That's very beautiful," Mishael said matter-of-factly. "I'm sorry you're stuck here. So, we knew—excuse me, *I* knew—that you wouldn't succeed. So we have been brainstorming what we can do instead."

"For instance," Azariah started, "I could pretend to lose money betting on the bird races, but we actually give the money away."

"No," Daniel replied, chewing a raspberry. "It's too much lying, and we'd develop a reputation for being gamblers, which isn't acceptable."

"We can hire more servants and send them out to do stuff in the community," Hananiah suggested.

"Maybe. We'd have to be careful. People hired as Etemenanki palace servants expect to have the honor of working in the palace."

"Another idea that's not quite money laundering: we develop hobbies that just take up a bunch of resources and let other people use those resources." That was Mishael.

"Yeah, the right hobbies could work. We're not empire citizens, so that limits a lot of our power and ability to own anything, especially in Babylon."

"I mean, your hobby is obviously trying to give money away. You could probably create a charity and become the administrator and say it's a hobby."

"My hobbies," Azariah interjected, "would be extreme sports. I'm now willing to indulge in all the activities only nobles enjoy, like skydiving, sandboarding, ship racing."

"Yes!" Hananiah agreed. "Finally. I'll introduce you. The equatorial canyons have the best rafting from what I've heard."

Mishael made a face at Daniel, who nodded in agreement. Only the other two were adrenaline junkies. He only liked sailing, wave surfing, and star surfing.

Daniel just listened, sipping more of the red kas, and once the conversation died down said, "Thank you, my friends. These ideas are good starting places."

"Could we buy a bird to race?" Hananiah asked.

"Absolutely not." He pushed a few berries around. "But we could rent a nice watch box."

Was this enough?

Chapter 7: Azariah

Nine months into their time on Babylon, the darkest time of the year, it was time for a city-wide party. For weeks, Azariah had been excited to party, the first time he'd shown interest in anything cultural. But the day of the party, he was unusually quiet and curled up on the common area couch with a book. The day was exceptionally humid, the Turquoise River combating the desert heat.

"What are you studying?" Daniel asked Azariah. "It seems like something different every time I look over your shoulder."

"Yeah, Oshpenaz is in charge. It really is something different whenever I open this, which, by the way, I hate." He closed the textbook and it disappeared. He flipped his disc in the air and then projected a full-sized spaceship engine in the middle of the common area. The image held for a second before blinking as he flipped the disc. He made the image transparent and rotated it, then just turned it off. He still didn't care about spaceships but he could reluctantly admit that the engines were fascinating. He sighed. "Yesterday it was dead languages and empire history. Tomorrow it's going to be military strategy." He looked at Daniel with a certain vulnerability. "Is it really okay for me to learn that kind of thing? I can see where they're going with this. My education is not random at all, and I don't think I like it."

Daniel sighed with him in commiseration. Azariah had driven himself hard to learn as much as possible; he'd learned more than the three others combined. He had a part-time job doing manual labor somewhere and would come back tired and sweaty. They had been on Babylon almost a year, and Azariah hadn't heard from his family on Gospel. Communications had to go through the Gate that was in the orbit of Revelation of John, and there was enough rebel militia activity that the Chaldean empire had a communications blackout over

Paradise, unlike the exile populations who could still send messages through Gates, which was why Daniel could still receive messages from his own mother, Sherah. This life was grinding away at Azariah. He would tease Daniel for his ascetic decisions, but he made similar choices in some areas.

"I thought the party would cheer you up," Daniel said.

"I'm cheerful enough," Azariah said irritably, and then laughed at himself. "But still, can you answer my question? I promise I'll be in a better mood in two minutes."

"Is it okay for you to learn? Of course. And what will you do?" Daniel asked.

"What should I do? You tell me, I'll obey."

"Become a future warlord?"

Azariah didn't smile at that.

"See, you know what a bad decision looks like. You can trust yourself more than you think. I mean, Azariah, it's not easy for anyone."

Azariah raised an eyebrow.

"I sometimes think about my time on the asteroid in the little dark room I would sleep in, and how I still get dizzy. But I can't not unfold. It's important to try, isn't it? You can't just stay nothing if God expects more from you."

Azariah gave Daniel another look—Daniel's relationship with God was different from everyone else's.

"Stepping back," Daniel said, answering Azariah's look, "Oshpenaz has plans for you. Patroness Shelomith has plans for you. You've got your own plans to go back to Gospel. Now, on top of all that, you're coming to me and asking what plans I have for you? I mean, I've asked for help with those three goals, but I guess that's different for you?"

"I trust you the most." Azariah shrugged and didn't elaborate for a minute. "I feel like the ends justify the means, but maybe there's a different way. And how can I know that I'm choosing the right 'end' to work toward?"

Daniel studied him in silence. "Has someone asked you to do something, and you don't know if you should follow through?"

"Oh, I'm not answering that. Maybe I shouldn't be asking my own questions," Azariah finally said. "We've never had the same choices to make."

"I have in many ways lived a safe, peaceful life that you haven't. We haven't had the same options. I left Gospel before the violence arrived;

while you call yourself a farmer, life on Gospel means danger for everyone. You're asking about your education and what it might lead to. My answers aren't your answers. I feel like anything I say is going to sound like impersonal preaching, but we can talk more. I could give you Bible passages to read. The words of Christ?"

"Daniel, thank you for your infinite patience. I think- I think I want to just put all of this aside. Talking about Christ-like behavior, I need to help with something." He leaned out behind Daniel. "Hey Mishael and Hananiah, it's time to do your hair for the party."

Daniel ran a hand over Azariah's buzz cut.

"Are you sure I can't do your hair too?" Azariah asked, giving Daniel a hug and rubbing his hair against Daniel's cheek until he pushed him away with a laugh.

"Don't you dare touch it." Daniel had only one hair style, the roll at the nape of his neck.

"Hey, Daniel, listen," Azariah said in a brighter tone. "At the party, I'm planning to talk to as many people as possible to see if there are systems we don't know about who would be good safe havens." He rolled off the back of the couch.

"Aza, wait," Daniel said, and Azariah stood next to him. "I don't want you to feel as obliged to me as you do to everyone else. You don't have to," Daniel said quietly and a little lamely. "Just do whatever you want." It was quiet enough that Azariah didn't respond, just patted his shoulder. For the next few hours, Daniel watched from the couch, reading his lesson and listening to his friends, while they bickered over hair and clothes. Each had a different idea of what type of image they should project. Azariah knew that their bickering was an outlet, but it always put Daniel on edge, like he personally needed to resolve their conflicts. Usually Daniel would go back to his lesson, but he was watching all three friends with a worried expression.

"Daniel, you doing okay? You're the one who needs to cheer up now," Azariah bent over the couch and spoke in a low voice.

"None of us like policy."

"Not what I thought you'd say, but yes, we hate it with the utmost hatred."

"Hatred is the correct word. But it's important. It's one of my goals. So I need to follow through."

"Oh, I get it. I know what I can do to help." Azariah took Daniel's disc, tapped through to his scheduler, and with Daniel's permission dropped Daniel's poetry and classical *sagarrum* courses. He then sent a message to the scheduler to find Daniel an internship with someone political. By the end, Daniel looked like he wanted to cry, but shook off the mood and smiled at Azariah.

"That's a quick, clean cut. Thank you."

"I only did this so that you'd stop thinking about it. Maybe you'll have fun at the party now."

"I'll try."

"Okay Daniel, stop distracting Azariah. We're all busy. You need to help with party prep!" Mishael clapped his hands twice. "I know you don't want to go to the party. But I want all of us, including you, to wear outfits that show off our tattoos." They each had an estate tattoo on the back of their right shoulder. Azariah's was a twisting, flowering shaft of wheat. Daniel's was a cluster of grapes and a grape vine.

"I can't," Daniel said. "Oshpenaz wants my shoulders and arms covered." All three looked at Daniel for an explanation, which he didn't offer.

Mishael moved on. "Daniel, bring outfit options from the closet. The rest of us have figured things out. We will do Gospel proud."

Chapter 8: Azariah

Party time. Azariah was excited to turn his brain off and party. Actually, he wanted to turn off everything, heart, soul, mind, and let his id take over.

The first party, the Jolly, was right before a Babylonian centric holiday named Dannatum Kussim for the dark month of Sigga. So lots of green *papasu* birds and *urri ajarum*, morning-light flowers, in the decor, people wearing *gabaziim*, bleached white clothing if that was your tradition. The attendees would be the richest people from the most powerful planets in the empire. Events filled the entire month, like the Chaldean Empire's final bird race. Today was the kick-off night. People had been filtering in for a week. There was a welcoming performance for entertainment, but not many got as far as the palace theater. Azariah had a vague idea of meeting someone cool, maybe a couple of cool people, and hanging out with them for a week or month before getting back to his studies, work, and everything he was talking to Daniel about.

The four young men joined the Jolly party when it was in full swing, standing at the entrance looking everything over. People were filling a huge palace atrium, everyone greeting everyone else, eating, gossiping. Oshpenaz gave Azariah and friends only broad guidelines, trusting them with a long leash; he and his attendants were busy with preparations.

"Who's everybody dancing with?" Mishael asked.

"Young men," Azariah answered.

"Young women," Hananiah answered.

"You?" Azariah elbowed Mishael.

"Anyone fun and useful. Daniel?"

"I don't want to."

Mishael and Azariah looked at each other and smirked.

"Hey Daniel, you know what sex is, right?" Azariah asked. "Sexual attraction? Or did your asteroid education fail you?"

Mishael and Hananiah snickered. Daniel gave him a look that said he would kick Azariah if they weren't at a party.

"So we have to split up, right?" Hananiah asked.

"We all have goals to accomplish," Daniel replied.

"Does having a goal help you? It doesn't help me." Azariah didn't think they *had* to split up, but he wanted to. Seeing the crowd made him less nervous. It looked like a big party in his home city on Gospel, just lots more gold jewelry. He knew what to do at those parties and enjoyed the energy.

"I am looking forward to meeting a few people." Hananiah enjoyed *gullatum* sports-ball, something that all four played but were not obsessive fans like Hananiah, who had done his research and found out which players, managers, and owners might be there.

It was easy to let the energy and flow of the party take Azariah over and sweep him away from his friends. He wandered around the right amount, complimented the right amount, and found the group of young attractive men all attracted to each other, and who various other attractive men in the wider atrium party would stare at. He sped through introductions. There were representatives from five different planets, which meant at least ten different ways to handle sexual and gender minority orientations (two insisted there were no hierarchies in anything, someone asked how their planets' breeding was going, someone else said that was rude; Azariah wanted out. These guys were too old for him). These were important people in the empire. This was the first time outside of his university classes that he was mingling and fitting in with the empire, and he found that maybe Babylon and the Chaldean empire weren't so bad. While joining the gossip as he pleased, he looked for cute guys in the atrium, found a good candidate, and left his new friends with a promise to give them a tour of the palace later.

Azariah waved to his new guy, who was bare chested with his hair in a yellow wrap. Azariah had no reason to not be obvious about his interest. If he wasn't interested, Azariah needed to know so he could move on. The new guy waved back with a wry smile.

"Hi," Azariah smiled, "first question, and I'm sorry this is going to sound a little weird, but are you of age? I'm not." Again, a question to weed out who Azariah could *spend time* with. He grabbed his shoulders and looked him straight in his pretty eyes.

"No! I can only *spend time* with other people who are not of age. That's why I'm over here. That group you came from is too serious for the evening!" His teeth flashed white in a big smile.

"Yes! Thank you God. Wow, this party! And the politics! No politics please!"

He sighed with relief. "I agree with no politics but full confession, in case it's a deal breaker, I was just talking to the Babylon issiakkum. She's a friend of my dad's. I hope you're not looking for an introduction, because I'm trying to stay away from those people."

"Understood. She's only an issiakkum-mati, anyway." The -mati governors controlled only parts of solar systems. The asteroid belt of the Babylonia solar system clung fiercely to their independence, and the king felt a united Babylonia solar system under an issiakkum-samsi would be too powerful. But still, Azariah looked in the direction he pointed, and made a note of the woman in a flowing blue robe. "This is my first big Babylon party. I just got here—"

"No you didn't."

"What?" Azariah asked.

"I've watched you make this big circle around the whole room." Nitati made an attractive swooping motion.

"Ooh, you were watching! I'm flattered. It seems I found the right person to talk to."

"It's your hair." He tugged at it a bit and made a face to show he didn't like how short it was.

"Is that an insult? I'm not flattered anymore." Azariah smiled and pouted.

"It's quite a statement. It's easy to be fashionable."

"If guys like you keep looking at me, I'd call it a win. Anything good to drink?" Azariah asked.

"The local wine is my favorite." The new friend held up an empty wine glass. "It's nothing as fancy as some of these drinks."

"No wine! I want liquor or something to smoke! Have you looked around the palace? Do you know other places to drink?"

"I don't know! This is my first time!"

"Let's get away from here."

"What's your name?"

"Nitati. You?"

"Aza." First names only. They could both be a little mysterious. Azariah wouldn't try to remember if Nitati's name was on the guest list.

As soon as they were out of the big party room and in a dark outside hallway with a colonnade, Nitati pushed Azariah against a wall and kissed him. Azariah kissed him back eagerly. He tasted like wine.

"Hey, if you want wine, we can get wine," Azariah said. He felt like being an accommodating host. "We don't have to drink liquor or do anything stronger. The Charax Spasinou is good."

"That's my favorite! But no, where's this other stuff?" Nitati tucked Azariah's arm under his.

They found something from a small bar in another wing of the palace that tasted like gasoline and got them both buzzed immediately.

"We have to stay together. Why aren't there more people our age?"

"You mean, why don't the powerful adults let their precious impressionable children near orgy and drug central?"

"You're here! There are others! We need to find them and rescue them."

"That's right, they belong to us."

They went from party room to party room, gossiping about who was the cutest and the ugliest. They didn't find any new friends.

"Oh, it's time! We can see the king right now," Azariah said and pulled Nitati along. A high walkway went around the perimeter around a party room where the king had moved his high court for the Jolly. Party goers were allowed to walk around on the walkway and be blessed by the king's presence. That was how the guards phrased it when they checked the two young men out and warned them to take only five minutes. The walkway was crowded, but guards kept people moving along.

When they entered, they were able to watch the climax of some kind of performance with strobe lights, noise, and acrobatic performers. Azariah was surprised that there hadn't been a warning for sensitive people and was about to say something to Nitati when he remembered that no one with sensitivity to strobe lights would be allowed on the planet. The tests and decontamination procedures came flooding back into his memory. Following the memories was a shock of emotion — he missed his family and his home planet even more in this moment, the care, the community. Helping and being helped glued them together, and he was suddenly unmoored.

The performance ended, the noise and lights stopped, and the world felt even emptier.

King Nebuchadnezzar was fully visible at the center of a dais. Every eye on the high walkway had turned to him, and he lifted three fingers to them. He had black hair down to his waist. His beard was carefully sculpted and had swirl designs shaved in the cheeks and chin. He was tan with the usual amount of makeup for a royal court. He was in good shape for his forties and seemed ageless; he was a noble who had pursued fame and power in the military until he was stationed in the royal court and anointed the successor to Emperor Nabopolassar. At this particular moment, he was quiet with a calculating look. Azariah made a note of the people closest to the king. Military, diplomacy, a few he couldn't identify.

What could Azariah do in the face of this power? Patroness Shelomith's instructions seemed like a dream. He remembered his talk with Daniel, that he was alone in his choices. Azariah hardly knew what he wanted, except for impossible things like getting back to his family. Acting on the love of Christ—whether or not Jesus was the son of a creator God, his rules of morality seemed good enough, and Daniel, whom Azariah trusted, affirmed that. But what did morality have to do with spaceships and powerful kings, with the good of his family cut off?

But this was too complicated for the night. Azariah turned to Nitati, who was absorbed in his own way, but who was ready to follow Azariah's lead back into the parties. The crowds were giving Azariah energy, but after a while, Nitati needed a break. They hustled over to a garden alcove. Nitati sat down on a ledge while Azariah walked around and pulled at the leaves, wondering if a monkey was in any of the trees.

"Hey, get back here. Are you trying to walk off?" Nitati waved a hand at his face for a breeze.

"Ha, no. I just wanted to let you relax. I don't want you to think I brought you out here to hook up."

"What if we just kissed?"

Azariah was happy to oblige. But first, "Who are you really?"

"Oh fine. Nitati Sagdullu from the Umtebu solar system. I'm the son of the issiakkum-samsi whom the great King Nebuchadnezzar has appointed. You?" He let the littlest bit of condescension shine in that one word. His tone and the fact that he looked like his father convinced Azariah.

"My home planet is Gospel of John, but I've been living here for almost a year as a guest of the king. I'm participating in his educational program." Azariah made a mental note of Nitati's home system for further research.

"Now I'm impressed. You might be an issiakkum-mati in a few years if you play your cards right."

"So I've heard, but I'm more mechanically inclined."

"Do you like the new spaceship engines?" Nitati asked.

Azariah loved the question and sat down close to his new friend. "Of course! I could crawl inside them all day."

"You'll like this: I traveled to Babylon in a ship captained by the famous Captain Maria Sifontes Uzcategui."

Azariah paused for a moment to place the name and was impressed. She had made a name for herself in some important military maneuvers and, instead of chasing after powerful positions, had left to work on top-of-the line ships, some of which went as far as Tyre in the dangerous space seas.

"Is she really here on Babylon?!" Azariah asked. "Do you know why?"

"Oh, so you are excited. But no politics, remember?" Nitati leaned in closer.

"It's not politics, it's technology and adventure," Azariah insisted, leaning in, too. "It's blood and sweat and grease—"

"Do you get your hands greasy every day? Not for me. But as far as what I do with my hands—"

Now they were even more into each other and started kissing when Azariah got a buzz.

Azariah had programmed his friends' discs to keep track of their vitals, so he would know if they were drugged or scared or needed help in some way. This buzz was from Daniel's disc, no message from him specifically.

"Oh hey Nitati, looks like I need to get to a …. Vesper's service…."

"What? You can't leave me like this." His voice had a note of authority.

"Don't you have best friends you would die for?" Azariah pleaded. "I definitely want to spend time with you. This is not me running away because I'm feeling weird about this."

"Yes, I know, we just met, whatever." Nitati was the sulky, entitled kind of heir. Azariah didn't want to make an enemy, so kissed him a little more and he could tell he wasn't going to be an enemy. Nitati was complaining to keep up appearances, but he was intrigued enough. Like the factory boss's son back home, and Azariah handled that fine. Sort of.

"Here, come on." Azariah held his hand and dragged him back to the party, straightening their clothes and his hair wrap on the way, and grabbing a couple of glasses of wine. When they got back to the side entrance, he looked around for the original group of new friends. "Okay, see the guys in the northwest corner."

"Northwest?"

"Near the lion fountain," Azariah pointed. "There's a guy with a bulky sweater that has gold medallions attached to it. His name is Marzihu. He's only a little older and seemed sweet. He wasn't making fun of anyone like the other guys."

"Oh, but that ultramarine ugly sweater."

"He's probably boiling hot. Get it off of him, teach him some style."

"You know, I like you. This energy isn't necessarily transitive." He nuzzled his neck, which made him melt a little.

"You're here for a month? I'm sure we'll find each other again, plus I want friends, not just a one-time thing."

"You're into the horizontal diplomacy method? I've got some tips. I'll look you up in the palace feed. What you can help me with: the Empire is growing, you've got a close-up view on what new opportunities there might be. I want to quiz you. If we don't see each other here, there's an Ishtar temple in downtown Babylon where apparently we meet up," he indicated the group of guys, "and they said they're usually a lot more expressive there. No politics allowed."

"Perfect." Azariah gave him a kiss on the cheek and a squeeze before running off to see what was so upsetting about a religious service that Daniel was setting off alarms.

Azariah finished his glass of wine and blessed himself with holy water before entering the Chaldean chapel. The palace was full of desert architecture: ziggurats, mosaics, and beige-colored onion-shaped pillars everywhere. The Chaldean chapel was a different world, a complete whiplash—Gothic gray with lines in the architecture to lift one's eyes to heaven and make a congregant feel small. The pews were about a quarter full, everyone spread out evenly, the kind of people you'd expect to attend a midnight vesper during the empire's biggest festival week, boring and plain looking. Daniel was in a pew off to the side, looking like a rich monk with his hair pulled back tight and wearing his black kimono. No one was close by. The service was a mass, so followed a script, no surprises. Azariah sat next to him, gesturing for what the problem was.

"The atrium was overwhelming," Daniel whispered, and then signed into Azariah's hand, *There are powerful people here. Stay respectful.*

Azariah signed back into his hand, their hands on the seat of the pew so they wouldn't bother anyone. *What else is there?* Azariah was going to sign more, but Daniel held his hand to get him to stop. His hand was cool and sweaty.

After a few minutes, *you don't have to stay.*

I know. Azariah held his hand. After a few more minutes, during a song, Mishael showed up and stood between them and held their hands.

I've got this. You can go now, he signed to Azariah as they sat down after the song.

Piss off. I'm sure Daniel needs us, don't know what's going on. In front of us is Zuziba'at. He was an ambassador with his spouse from Zuza'al. Azariah had noticed those two walking in and knew Mishael would be interested. Their daughter was known for flashy parties.

After a few more minutes, Hananiah showed up at the end of a prayer, knelt next to Azariah, held his hand, and whispered, "Why are we holding hands?"

Daniel is sad and we have to be respectable.

I was kissing a very nice lady when I got your message.

I left behind a very nice man. We'll survive. Azariah then signed to Mishael, *Did you find anyone to kiss?*

Yes, a very nice lady.

Azariah laughed a little as they sat back on the pew. *We need to expand our vocab beyond "very nice."*

Ask if Daniel kissed anyone, Hananiah signed.

Tell Daniel we were all kissing people, see if he has, Azariah passed on to Mishael.

He passed on the message with the smallest smirk. Azariah watched Daniel out of the corner of his eye. He got a severe expression on his face, lips pressed together, wrinkles on his forehead. He couldn't take a joke or have fun. He pinched Mishael's hand, let go, and things got boring again.

After the service was over, Daniel stayed seated and wouldn't talk to his friends, but they were there for him, so they weren't going anywhere. Azariah wanted to take him back to the atrium party.

Within a minute or so, other congregants lined up in the pew in front of them to be blessed by Daniel. First, it was just one couple who spoke to Daniel for a minute, confirmed who he was, and then asked for a blessing. Daniel could bless only informally since he wasn't a Chaldean citizen. Apparently, staying in a pew was the predetermined compromise. People noticed. Whispers were passed around. The first guy was getting messages on the feed, and he was answering them while still in the chapel. Rude. Azariah had looked over party invitees and recognized several important people; he didn't recognize several of the most boring people, so he decided they were the most important. These people weren't flashy like the king. This was a different source of power.

It was a little unsettling to see Daniel treated this way, but he seemed used to it. In fact, watching him bless over and over again, watching person after person be happy to be blessed, Azariah started to really see the prophet. He got goosebumps to think that his best friend, who got agoraphobic and was picky about wine, was also someone God spoke to on a semi-regular basis, and that changed his place in the world. Somehow, these people saw or respected something about him that Azariah hadn't taken seriously before.

Azariah joined the line when there were only a few people left.

Daniel blessed him like he was anyone else; waiting a moment to see if he had anything to say, like a prayer request, then touching his forehead and shoulders while saying, "May the Lord bless you and keep you."

Azariah bowed and really looked at him. He was tired and holy. The chapel was about empty but just in case, he signed into his hand, *is this what you were upset about, that you were told to do this?*

Yes.

Is this the first time? It didn't seem like it.

This has happened with Paradisians. Paradisians, he signed. *I'm getting dragged deeper into the royal court, and I don't want to. It's nice to have you here, but the only thing you can do is just sit with me. There's so much we need to do.*

Azariah held his hands tightly. One party, one vesper service, wasn't going to ruin things. *Mishael is building his own alliances and who knows what Hananiah is up to. Yes, I'm sure you feel alone, but in a way we're all alone, but then all come together. The responsibilities you've given yourself feel heavy just in this moment.*

I care about all Paradisians. Daniel signed back, with a frustrated look on his face, like he couldn't articulate his unhappiness better.

Azariah looked at him with interest. He saw himself as a Paradise-only prophet, despite everything. He joined the three again in the right pew, his spot between Hananiah and Mishael. They seemed much more blase. Daniel was sitting and leaning against Mishael.

"I'm glad you guys were here, thank you," Daniel said aloud, in some acknowledgement of Azariah's encouragement.

One last congregant entered the pew, about their age and pretty, with long blue-ish braids. When she reached Daniel, he stood up. They shook hands. He even bowed over hers. The person looked at the friends and asked to meet privately. Daniel waved goodbye and left with his friend.

"Huh," Hananiah said.

"He's going to get more action than any of us, isn't he?" Mishael mused.

"I will take that bet," Azariah said. "The night's still young, only an hour or so past midnight."

"We don't gamble."

Once they were out of the chapel, Azariah got a message from Nitati in his feed. *Hey you, no one is on my dad's ship right now if you want to take an elevator ride. Oh, and that guy in the sweater. He's a freaking monk who doesn't even kiss anyone. Where are you? Vespers ended at midnight!!!*

"Guys," Azariah said. "I have a new best friend for Daniel. He's a monk."

Chapter 9: Daniel

Daniel knew Birbirru was going to find him at the chapel, but he hadn't expected to feel so off balance. This was the first time he had been to a non-Kahi religious service. He missed home and felt even more like a foreigner with his accent and surrounded by wealth. He had performed blessings before, but not *like that*.

The guys had also made him feel confused. Azariah had arrived rumpled and smelling like a stranger, and then Mishael did too, and Hananiah was more absent-minded than usual. When Mishael asked who they were going to dance with, Daniel interpreted that as "who do you want to marry?" What Jesus and Paul said about marriage sounded good when he was ten years old and read the New Testament for the first time on his own. Now, eleven years later, Daniel understood the importance of social institutions, but was still dedicated to ascetic ideals. Tonight, his friends were having fun with people in a passionate way that he had never pursued, maybe never had a real chance to think about. He knew many people didn't link passion and marriage together, but the connection was obvious to him.

"Specialist Birbirru, so good to see you again. I'm glad you were able to make it." Daniel gave them a handshake as they left the chapel, and he left all his musings behind.

Daniel and Birbirru headed to a modern wing on the outskirts of the Etemenanki palace complex, winding around trees full of monkeys and little gardens with pools that reflected the stars. They chatted quietly about where they had traveled. He was exhausted, but this was important and he needed them on his side, so he had to play a good host.

"How's your Scythian doctor's training going?" Daniel asked.

"I'm done," Birbirru shrugged. "That's why I'm here now. It's fun.

It's like a little hobby, and it doesn't help me with any of my goals, but it's interesting."

"Plus, you're helping people."

"I don't make decisions based on something like that." Despite the harshness of the words, Birbirru was smiling and overall much less antagonistic than when they had examined him on Cottiae.

"You're helping friends?"

"That's a bit better." With the way they were looking at him, Daniel was pretty sure they were adding 'powerful, attractive friends' to that statement. He met their gaze for a few extra seconds, then looked away and felt his face get warm. The guys' teasing earlier was getting to him.

"You can use *she* pronouns," Birbirru said. "I'm pretty sure you've been using neutral behind my back. That's Goethe for you."

"Thank you." Asteroid culture: people wore bulky suits and helmets often enough that it was hard to determine gender by sight and they didn't care to create some artificial signal. This meant they used neutral pronouns until otherwise specified as a sign of friendship. Daniel hadn't even realized how odd his way of thinking was, but by now had mostly adjusted to Babylonian culture. It was nice for Birbirru to remember where he came from.

Daniel ushered Birbirru into the medical clinic and down to the examination room that he had prepared with the equipment she'd requested. One sleepy nurse was there waiting to help them.

Birbirru did a bunch of light touch physical examinations, testing his nervous system, things like did his uvula tilt to the right or left, what about pressure at the nape of his neck—she suggested a different hairstyle. After that portion of the Scythian examination was complete, she took scans, including one of the special bio-proto scans. Daniel put his kimono back on and dozed in the examination chair while she went through all the data.

"Thanks for letting me do a check up on you." She swirled in and sat on a rolling stool near him.

"Thank you. I certainly appreciate it," he replied, rubbing his eyes.

"I want to do a more in-depth comparison, but it looks like your brain is just as healthy as before. I don't see any reason why you might have stopped having visions from a physical point of view." She pushed the stool to press it against his chair. She was very close, and he didn't move away. After she was done going over how healthy he was, she put the screen aside and held his hand.

Daniel rubbed his thumb over her fingernails, which were painted blue. She swept her hand up his arm, under his kimono sleeve. He could feel her nails skimming his forearm. He looked at her. She had a small smile, so he kissed her.

"Well, that was something. Glad we tried," she had a laugh in her voice. At his confused look, she said, "Come on, you didn't feel anything."

"It's not something I've practiced much." Daniel held her hand lightly. He didn't quite know what she meant.

"That's very polite to say. It's fine if you don't want to, that's what I was getting."

"But I should know how to kiss, right?"

She laughed a bit helplessly. "No, but I'm happy to help, I guess. Let's get out of here. Let's find one of those little gardens *without* monkeys."

The next morning, Oshpenaz woke them up. All four had made it back to their very own beds. They were bleary-eyed and on the couches in the common area when he walked in, chipper as ever.

"Busy day for me!" Oshpenaz said, settling on a low seat. "This needs to be quick. I'm here to talk about marriage! Thankfully, none of you were involved in activities that would lead to a baby being made, but we can't allow for wild oats to be sown." He emphasized we—this wasn't just his idea. "Who wants to get married?"

They all shook their heads no.

"Okay, none of you met the love of your life yesterday. What about marriage within the next five years?"

"I'd be fine getting married once I'm settled in a position," Hananiah said. "I'd want her to have similar work to what I do. Preferably Paradisian, but I don't know if that's allowed."

"We'll see who you meet and how generous the king feels. Next." Oshpenaz pointed at Mishael.

"I'd like to marry someone from Dalmaisha, Baetica, or Arachosia," Mishael said. "I've liked what I've seen so far."

Oshpenaz seemed to know those two were easier to deal with and asked about children and faithfulness and monogamy. They were happy to serve the empire in all things. He then took a deep breath and turned to Daniel and Azariah.

"Please no," Azariah said.

"The king has a firm expectation that people blessed to be educated by him should pass down such blessings."

"What about donating to a fertility temple?" Azariah asked.

Oshpenaz sighed. "That is more complicated than you think. Any thoughts on a political marriage?"

"You can't be serious. If I donated to a temple, or even if I didn't- I mean, regardless of children, would the king allow a marriage to a man?"

"To be frank, no."

"What if my husband was really powerful? Like a -mati or -samsi? Or what if I was?"

"Ramzi, let's stick to possibilities. While the blessed King Nebuchadnezzar legally recognizes and encourages all sorts of relationships, including romantic and lifelong ones, you four are not citizens, and he will exert his control. He's planning for a significant empire expansion over the next few decades and will allow only relationships intended for propagation. If each of you have three children and raise them here, then in about twenty years, the empire will have a dozen admirable, trustworthy administrators. Get used to the idea. Next and lastly, Daniel."

"Prophets don't get married," Daniel said. "I've planned to be celibate since my first vision. Jesus never married. Paul never married and says: 'Now to the unmarried and the widows I say: It is good for them to stay unmarried, as I do. I wish that all of you were as I am.'"

"Ah yes, I am familiar. But if you develop an irresistible passion, Paul does allow it."

"I'm in control of myself. I don't think I'm the type of person to develop an irresistible passion for a woman."

Oshpenaz raised an eyebrow at that. If he had anyone eavesdropping on Daniel last night... well, he wasn't lying. "Even more than the other three—if you say that, but then turn around and have little liaisons, you're going to get in trouble. If you insist on having little culture battles like over food, if you want any access to Paradise, you'll win only if everything is above board."

"He's the least hypocritical person I've ever met or heard of!"

Oshpenaz ignored Azariah. "It was very useful to us to have you give blessings in the chapel; it was instructive to see who is listening to the king. But if those congregants hear that you were kissing the Scythian doctor you were seen leaving with, we would look bad."

Daniel nodded once sharply.

"We'll let you be celibate only if you're actually celibate."

The room was tense. Hananiah was bright red.

"What about a political marriage?"

"It would depend. I'd rather not. Are we done with this?"

"This is for all of you. Any other king in any other time in history would castrate all of you and allow you to live as eunuchs. In his kindness and grace, he is willing to subsume your nobility into his own instead of cutting it off as the threat it is. You are worthy of children and families, and the king will give them to you. If you don't behave, we can obtain samples and then castrate. Thank you gentlemen, I'll see you at the fancy dinner tonight. Scythian *sarabara* formal wear is expected." He looked at Daniel significantly when he said this.

Daniel gave him a short nod.

When Oshpenaz left and closed the door, Azariah picked up an empty water glass and threw it at the floor where Oshpenaz's seat was. Hananiah leaped and caught the glass before it smashed.

"We're studs that the king wants to breed." Azariah spat out a string of curses. Daniel covered his ears and glared, so he stopped.

They were silent for a few minutes. Daniel thought about saying a couple of things, but it didn't seem to be the right moment.

"Oh, just spit out whatever stupid thing you want to say." Mishael snapped.

"We just made some diplomatic mistakes yesterday, me the most apparently. It's nothing that bad. It doesn't sound like he'll actually ever drag anyone to the altar or carry out his threat. We're slaves, so whatever."

"We're not slaves, don't be overdramatic," Hananiah gently repudiated, but the criticism still stung.

"Thank you, Daniel," Azariah bowed. "Your stupid thing was, in fact, entirely articulate."

Daniel threw a pillow at him. Azariah should have had an attitude of *This doesn't affect me, I'm out of here before the king can try.* But he didn't.

They didn't look at or talk to each other. Samwel arrived soon. He was sensitive to the mood and puttered around with tea and breakfast. He usually didn't let them eat in the common area.

After a while, the tension eased and Hananiah broke the silence first. "Daniel, what was that last comment aimed at you about tonight? Scythian clothing?"

"You know I hate that clothing. Shirts and pants. The kind of shirts you have to pull on and off over your head. I didn't wear the outfit yesterday that he wanted me to wear."

"You've got the weirdest hang ups," Mishael said around a mouthful of sweetened zibitum.

"I remember, but I didn't understand why. I thought you were just in a bad mood that day," Hananiah asked.

"They're uncomfortable, like tight at the waist or shoulders, and I look stupid when I'm taking them on or off. I mean, everyone does."

"What!?" Azariah stood up and took off his shirt and threw it at Daniel. "What's wrong with that?"

"You had to wiggle around. I mean, okay, put it back on." He threw the shirt back. When Azariah was pulling it over his head, Daniel said, "See, you wiggle your arms around like a jellyfish."

Azariah got an elbow stuck in a sleeve.

"It's not very graceful," Daniel said reprovingly.

"What about pants?"

"You have to sit down to put them on, otherwise you're hopping around on one foot. That's so embarrassing. I'd rather die. Plus, the waist size that fits when I'm standing isn't comfortable when I'm sitting, especially with the cuts we're expected to wear tonight." Daniel nodded and got up. His friends were kind, but he wanted to be alone now.

Azariah followed him. "Sorry! What are you going to do now?"

"Take a bath, I guess. In private."

Azariah followed him into the bathroom and knelt on the floor as Daniel sat on the bathtub edge to turn the water on to the right settings.

"I'm really sorry," Azariah said, "You're in a bad mood because of Oshpenaz and I should have been more thoughtful."

"You're fine. I'm not mad at all. I'm just feeling overwhelmed with everything. As bad as I feel here, my family is still on the Martigny asteroid. I'm here for them more than anything else. I was getting pulled into all the little political games. And being a little selfish."

"It's not selfish to want to kiss someone," Azariah said.

"I didn't want to kiss Birbirru. I mean, I did kiss her willingly. She's here because the king invited her. I wanted more information on that, and she seemed interested in me." Daniel splashed at the water.

"Hah, and I was defending your character to Oshpenaz. You're a bit cold-blooded, aren't you? Did you get anything?"

"No. Sounds like I need to keep my distance from her. And I'm done playing stupid games. I will trust that God will give me the information I need." Daniel took a deep breath and kept his eyes on the water. "I guess there is something that's bothering me. I saw the way you reacted in the chapel yesterday. I don't want you treating me differently."

"I'm not! What are you even talking about? Wait, let me think." Azariah went silent for a moment. "All three of us have tried our best to support you in your role as a prophet. We haven't had to do much, you know? Especially public facing things. But after yesterday, I understand better what that means now."

They stared at each other while the bathwater ran.

"Daniel, why don't we do something fun? If you stay here, you're just going to sulk in the bath, and you'll still be in a bad mood."

"And then you'll call me cold-blooded again." Daniel turned off the bathwater. "What about a swim at the bathhouse? I think that would loosen me up and my thoughts won't bother me so much."

"I'd like to spend more time with you." Azariah smiled and stood up. On their way out he asked Daniel, "How much did you learn about mining and geology when you lived in the asteroid field? Also, if you're in the mood later, there's a party at the Ishtar temple I want to go to. You could meet my new friends, especially Nitati! Or Hananiah and Mishael are going to the North Pole parade."

Daniel let the words wash over him.

Chapter 10: Nebuchadnezzar

Over a year later…

Press release from King Nebuchadnezzar of the Chaldean Empire:

I, your king, am secretly miserable. Being your king is what I love the most. I love my reign, but secretly the burdens have become great in the heat of the day, when I take my longest nap.

May my Chaldean empire, in all its blessedness, understand and know their king in his glorious entirety as he serves you and the Babylonian Marduk.

I have had a strange recurring dream. It doesn't feel like a dream. It also makes little sense. My sense of reality is warped when I sleep; I wake up and don't feel rested. But I nap after evening court and that helps. I am wise enough and strong enough in body that no one notices my weakness.

With my perfect hair, my perfectly sculpted beard, my glowing skin, the softest fabrics against my skin, the most beautiful music in my ears, the best wine on my tongue, and yet I am the one who suffers the most. I don't say this about myself, but I have heard it a few times from those who love and know me.

I have the greatest capacity to enjoy life; to then be brought down to agony is a greater fall than anyone else alive can understand. I feel the softness of the finest silks more than anyone. I enjoy the music more than anyone; to then not be able to enjoy it at all is a travesty.

Anyone who can solve this suffering, who can tell me my dream and why I'm having it, will be exalted and rewarded beyond the capacity of their imagination.

"King Nebuchadnezzar, it's time to get up," a disembodied voice chimed. If I were a bad king, I would order them to die.

My dream was plaguing me. I blamed my disorientation and absentmindedness on the new elixirs that popped up during the holiday season that ended months ago. It was hard to judge the bird races, stay up three nights in a row, change clothes five times a day, bounce back and forth between the poles, and be serious with the rich, boring people.

Today I was meeting yet another specialist who may have a boring medical reason for my visions. I didn't tell her I was having visions. That was secret information for now. Oshpenaz found her months ago. She had been hanging around, excited to see me, of course. She had plenty of cross training, including Scythian training, which was useless. Other than that, Birbirru's credentials were as impressive as anyone could want; a minor patrician family, just poor enough that they had to fend for themselves; connected enough to receive the best education and best positions, whether or not they actually deserved them. And it seemed like this person did in fact deserve them and used her access to resources to develop a new 3D image of the brain. Even more importantly, she had treated someone who had visions.

I was excited to see a picture of my brain, which must be the best brain in existence; I'd have to dissuade Birbirru from using my brain as an ideal, as the archetype, as the perfection against which everyone would be measured. She would be very tempted. She would probably want to make my brain scan into a work of art; I was sure it would be beautiful enough, but would I really want my brain on display like that? Yes, I would. Perhaps some special art museum where only my most proven worshippers could come and venerate without actually bothering me. Also, we could sell small models across the galaxy, perhaps as part of their shrines dedicated to their king, the best king they could imagine having. My brain in every household, as it should be.

Specialist Birbirru visited me in my innermost chamber, the white clean one. She was professional enough. We had already set her equipment up.

"Your Majesty, the scan is complete. I've studied it, and it is indeed perfect as we expected."

Getting the scan done was easy enough, as I would expect from someone smart enough to be allowed in my presence.

"Tell me, are you able to reconstruct memories? Maybe memories of dreams? Are there little images nestled inside my brain? Could you piece together the memory neurons or whatever and see what I saw in a dream?"

"Your Majesty, that is an incredible idea. You are truly the wisest man I have ever met. It has never occurred to me to think of such a thing. It is a subject I would need to study further. Your kingdom is vast and perhaps there is technology on some planet."

"Exactly, you say many truths. I've heard you have experience with visions. I don't have visions, but it is a topic I am slightly interested in. I'm always curious about my subjects, to learn more about them in order to serve them better as their king and to perhaps find ways in which they may serve the empire better. Have you scanned their brains? Are their brains different? Whoever these people are who might have visions. I mean, if visions even are a real thing. Who is there to say any god speaks to their subjects via dreams? Marduk certainly doesn't. It seems like if anyone were to have visions, it would be me, the king of the galaxy, but there's no telling who might receive visions. Well, speak up already. You have answered none of my questions."

"I have scanned one brain of someone who claimed to have a vision."

"Hah, no one has visions. How could they prove such a thing?"

The specialist described the Paradisian culture, the prophets that answered to kings, what prophets were like, what signaled they were having a vision and not a dream, and why the people didn't think that the prophet was faking it.

I didn't have my own prophet.

"Did kings have visions but no interpretations?" It was time to drop the pretense.

"That has happened in their own recorded history; before slaves escaping Aegyptus settled the Paradisian solar system, the Aegyptian king was having visions and only the advisor could interpret. But Aegyptus denies all of that. It happened thousands of years ago, before this part of the galaxy was colonized, before the beauty of Babylonia and your vast empire blessed the Milky Way, reaching from Mauretania Tingitana, to Arachosia, to Berenike and continuing its ever-bounteous growth."

To think that perhaps that a powerful god saw me and my empire as on level with Aegyptus from thousands of years ago. It was quite thrilling. I had known for myself that I was just as successful if not better than Aegyptus, but it was nice to have a god agree with me.

"Tell me more about this person. You've scanned their brain. What was it like?"

She hesitated, "Your Majesty, just as you can trust me to keep your own health and examination secret, I am also discreet about all my patients' information."

I waved my hand, pushing that objection away. "Feel free to share my information with the entire empire. They should see how lucky they are to have me as king." I stared into her eyes. "Tell me about Daniel." Because yes, I knew about Daniel, and was gathering more information.

That was a very useful conversation with Specialist whoever. I gave her permission to be special wherever she wanted to be, including my court. She was grateful and told me what she was going to do, but I don't remember. I had stopped listening. She had confirmed my positive opinion about Daniel.

I was now developing one of my incredible plans, the kind that can't fail.

Daniel must interpret my dream like his ancestors before him helped the pharaohs.

My own Joseph, my own Joseph, sent from God Themself. Themselves? Who was this creator God?

One reason I talked to the specialist was because I wanted to make a good impression on Daniel; if he was going to be my Joseph, I wanted him to be happy to lean into the role and give me every special little word God gave him. If he could do it; if not, he would be an embarrassment and I'd have him killed so he could never embarrass me again.

I started thinking about my clothes. What style would Daniel respond best to? How could I ensure his first impression was perfect? I'd give myself time to plan. He also needed to make an impression on the high royal court and I needed to draw this out so they'd notice. Also, as with all perfect plans, there would be at least one other purpose: I had desperately wanted a reason to pare down my advisors without offending anyone. Their loss of status would be their own fault. I wanted my own people scared. Daniel would help in more than one way, whether or not he liked it.

The first step of my plan was a series of demands presented to every layer of the royal court every day for a week.

The courts were important, but not my favorite part of my Chaldean empire. I had built a vast army and enjoyed using it; they were so efficient that I could easily hand empire building over to the lieutenants and enjoy my empire in whatever way I wished. Or so you'd think. I had to spend time in my high royal court. This was party time for all the eccentric and unpredictable, powerful men and women who kept my empire strong. Their own worlds and solar systems could be in half chaos but still produce massive wealth, with no desire for harmony or efficiency. Along with these annoyances, they foisted *sangum* priests, *zazakkum* officials, *kakkabum* astrologers, and *hassum* wise men and women as advisors on me. I got rid of the worst as fast as possible, but the ones who seemed good quality still constantly failed me; what was the systemic problem that my efforts to surround myself with quality people kept failing? How could I build an everlasting empire with such flawed advisors?

The only advisor I could stand to have nearby was one astrologer, Dabu'us. She was the last person left capable of Jumping with any accuracy. It seemed like magic. She could Jump to a strange solar system without a Gate and then Jump back to me with information, as long as the Jump destination wasn't too far away. Incredible. Unfortunately, the combination of science and faith that made this possible only worked a couple times before astrologers were never heard of again. Dabu'us, had Jumped five times, and I had retired her, kept her close to me.

As a lead up to the special presentation, I had written special press releases, created a special song; the day of the presentation was full of special pomp and circumstance. I summoned all the specific people I wished to get rid of, and there was otherwise a large audience.

I entered the high royal court and sat on my throne overlooking the best and worst of my kingdom. Famous Rainbow Eucalyptus trees between the windows framed the throne room. They acted as arched supports and were bright pink and green right now and peeling; they stretched up to the cathedral high ceiling. The decor, such as curtains and cushion covers, matched the pink and green. When the trees peeled and changed color, the decor would change again.

The petitioners sat up front. The power players sat in the middle and acted like every day was a party day; they had their little cliques while their servants brought food and drink as desired and talked as loudly as they pleased. The very back of the throne room had no seating, and those people were always the happiest to be in my presence.

I addressed the high royal court directly.

"I have had a dream that troubles me and I want to know what it means."

"May the king live forever! Tell your servants the dream, and we will interpret it." Ma'angi said, a vile person who was routinely chosen as the spokesperson for the vilest advisors.

"This is what I have firmly decided:" I replied, keeping my voice low and casual. "If you do not tell me what my dream was and interpret it, I will have you cut into pieces and your estates turned into piles of rubble. But if you tell me the dream and explain it, you will receive from me gifts and rewards and great honor. So tell me the dream and interpret it for me."

"Let the king tell his servants the dream, and we will interpret it."

"I am certain that you are trying to gain time, because you realize that this is what I have firmly decided: If you do not tell me the dream, there is only one penalty for you. You have conspired to tell me misleading and wicked things, hoping the situation will change. So then, tell me the dream, and I will know that you can interpret it for me."

"There is no one on earth who can do what the king asks!" Ma'angi said. "No king, however great and mighty, has ever asked such a thing of any *sangum* priests, *zazakkum* officials, *kakkabum* astrologers, or *hassum* wise men and women. What the king asks is too difficult. No one can reveal it to the king except the gods, and they do not live among humans."

What a perfect note to end this on. She played into my hands. Once Daniel gave the dream and interpretation, my standing would improve as God would visibly be on my side. "Such a back and forth is useless. I order the execution of all the wise people in the Babylon city."

Chapter 11: Azariah

Azariah was upset beyond belief. The four young men came home from a camping trip, and palace guards confiscated their travel bags and shoved them into a prison. PRISON! With no charges or human rights, of course. They weren't the only prisoners—the king's own courtiers were in prison with them!!

Hananiah spoke to as many prisoners as possible. Some advisors had been in prison for over a week. Apparently, they were at risk of execution. EXECUTION!! Executions were being scheduled! Azariah and his friends were nothing like these people.

Mishael sat in a corner reading. Daniel seemed as stuck in disbelief as Azariah, who was chilly for the first time ever since arriving on this blasted planet that really was going to kill them. All four of them were in swimming gear from the camping trip. Mishael and Hananiah were smart enough to grab shirts but there Daniel and Azariah were, half naked, taller, and honestly, much more handsome than any of the other prisoners. They got a bunch of looks. Azariah glared, wishing he knew more. Daniel wasn't paying attention, and he didn't have the street smarts to understand some of those looks. That's right, those other people would assume Daniel and Azariah were from the high royal court, as the most favored of the empire routinely went bare-chested as a sign of status. The prisoners would soon be drifting over to ask for favors. No. Azariah got the guard to get them *kiskattum* pants, shirts, and sweaters.

"Don't ask how I got these clothes, thanks. Have you talked to the king?" Azariah asked Daniel. "Did he reject you, and that's why we're all here?"

"No. He doesn't know I exist." Daniel took a sweater from Azariah's arms, shook it out, and looked at Azariah, who helped him put it on, like he was his brother Raimi, who was two years old when Azariah left Gospel; or as if Daniel was a noble who needed an attendant for difficult things like clothing that went over the head.

Azariah scolded him the whole time he was helping. "You are a freaking proven prophet! You have prophesied while in his freaking palace!! Of course he knows about you if he's looking for someone to interpret a vision! Why else are we here!? This mass incarceration is about visions. We are in prison because the king had a vision. Not to be overdramatic, Daniel, but *visions*. Why the hell aren't you on top of this?"

"Don't talk like that to me. All people designated as wise are here in prison. He's never asked for me."

"It would look like he was colluding with you. I'm sure you are expected to do your duty to both God and king." Azariah continued scolding him. "We are being trained to be *administrators*! We are not 'wise people' or advisors. Are you telling me that every administrator in the city is in prison? As far as I can tell, only people with certain qualities are here; we—*you*—are on a list somewhere."

Daniel couldn't deny it. He walked over to a window and looked over the Turquoise River near Mishael, who ignored them at first. (It was the cushy part of the prison, delightful views.)

Azariah followed him. "Have you had visions? Do you know what this is about? Have you even tried?"

"No."

"Why aren't you trying? I know it sounds like I'm the one who is dramatic, but you're the one who waited until *executions* were scheduled and even now you are being weak."

Honestly, it looked like he was going to cry. Azariah gave him a hug and then took a minute to put on his own sweater.

Mishael turned his book off and listened while we spoke. "Daniel, I agree with Azariah." He paused for their astonishment. "The puzzle pieces are coming together to form a certain picture. A Paradisian prophet is at the king's right hand while we are in exile. I'm sure that king Nebuchadnezzar of the Chaldean empire will listen to Daniel and respect Daniel better than any Paradisian king or queen respected Prophet Jeremiah."

Azariah nodded in agreement. Hananiah joined them and they caught him up.

"I know my visions have set me apart," Daniel said, "but I have seen myself as a small echo of Prophet Jeremiah. I'm in exile while Prophet

Jeremiah is still on Revelation of John. Mishael, what you're describing isn't a Paradisian prophet, it's more like Joseph at the right hand of a prosperous pharaoh. That can't be accurate?"

"Of course that's you!" Azariah whispered-yelled. Their two friends shrugged and nodded when Daniel looked at them.

"Think it through," Hananiah encouraged him.

"Years ago, I would have preferred to stay in the Martigny asteroid. But I had to leave to keep my family safe. Wanting to know more about my visions also motivated me. The actions I've performed while in Babylon—I've given blessings like a priest. I have helped people if they thought they had special dreams or visions. I've prophesied and received an important interpretation while here. I shared that interpretation only with Paradisians, but it wasn't considered useful. But it wasn't supposed to be for them. I had the interpretation here. I should have shared it with the leaders here. We have our goals to help our people. Maybe there is another way I hadn't considered." He was hyperventilating a little. "This is very new to me. I want to think about it on my own. Was there anything else?" They didn't have anything else to say, so he laid down on a utilitarian bed.

Azariah laid down on the bed above him to make sure people would leave him alone. Azariah decided to just be honest with himself and admit that he was angry with Daniel. Oblivious, useless humility, attachment to Paradise that they didn't deserve, wishing for direction from God and getting so much more than anyone else ever, and still blind.

After a day (five more executions were scheduled), Daniel asked a guard for Erioch, whoever that was. Azariah stayed at his elbow and knocked his shoulder against Daniel's, which was at the same height. Erioch Pubalum—ugh, Daniel was on a first name basis with the commander of the king's personal guard, however that happened.

"Finally," Erioch said as he approached them in the hallway leading, giving Daniel such an annoyed, *I'm disappointed in you* face. Azariah totally agreed. Daniel was getting a bunch of people killed.

Azariah was still scolding Daniel under his breath when Erioch took pity on Azariah. "Don't worry, I killed the ones who deserved to die first." He patted his arm. "And if I have to kill you, it will be painless, okay? Daniel, are you ready to go?"

Chapter 12: Daniel

The king had a high, hard test: what was his vision and what was the interpretation.

The king had an understandable desire to cleanse his court of anyone useless.

The king was having fun with this. He was that kind of leader.

Daniel's heart sank, but he asked Erioch if he could sleep and meditate in his usual quarters, and if his friends could come with him. This would help him seek the answers from God, as he had received before.

Erioch didn't allow his friends to leave prison. He probably guessed Daniel's plan to have them leave for somewhere safe.

Daniel meditated until night, fell asleep, and God or their messenger changed his sleep to a vision almost immediately, and the interpretation was also granted immediately; this is what God wanted for him. The vision repeated the second night, and his fugue state was light. Things were easy in a dreadful way. Daniel remembered the last night of prayers with his mother and sisters on the Goethe asteroid, the last night on Gospel of John with his father. He had been leaning heavily on his three friends. Just as his father and family had dropped away, he was now feeling like his friends too couldn't follow where he had to go.

Daniel watched and re-watched the king's court display. Now with this vision and interpretation, it felt like both God and king were herding him into a corner, and how could he assert himself and gain some control?

Two weeks ago, Daniel and his friends were deep into their training. It felt like God's purpose was for them to work on their goals to take care of Gospel. Daniel had no more visions; little did he know God was giving them to the king at that moment. They were on their way to thriving in exile; each of them was on separate paths to important positions and continued to impress Oshpenaz in their own ways. Daniel was pleased. But that was over for him now.

While Daniel didn't have his friends, Samwel was always hovering nearby, with Oshpenaz available at request. Mid-morning the second day, Daniel said to Samwel, "I will be ready to request an audience with the king tomorrow if he pleases or any time that suits him."

Daniel had to look the part of a Babylonian courtier, that it was reasonable for the king to trust and respect a young foreign man.

Daniel didn't *want* to play the political game. Before today, he had *chosen* to be a passive player; God and king wouldn't allow that anymore. He had no idea how he was going to play in a high royal court and be a good person.

Oshpenaz outlined how he wanted Daniel to present himself in front of the king and court. Daniel agreed immediately, and Oshpenaz sighed heavily in relief.

First was Daniel's hair. That would take the longest. He shocked Oshpenaz when he unrolled his hair—if the curls were straight, it was long enough to reach his waist—as he had always kept it in a tight roll at the nape of his neck and Oshpenaz had never seen it down before. Sherah was vain about his hair, which was as curly as her own; his nanny worked on his curls every day on Gospel. By the time he was old enough to style his hair, he was also vain and would have only the old ends cut off occasionally, but it was too much work for any other style until today.

Daniel twisted a curl around his thumb and let go, "This is the size of curl that is natural but I'm not sure exactly what the trend is right now, it seems like defined curls are going out of style."

Oshpenaz nodded slowly, "We need two stylists for your hair to be done on time." They arrived quickly enough. Their names were Uati and LaMeu.

Azariah came in and Oshpenaz asked, "Have you ever seen his hair?"

"When he washes it. He always smells like a coconut." He made a face at Daniel. "Hananiah is praying and Mishael is talking to people."

"Hmm. It's quite wonderful." Oshpenaz mused, still thinking about Daniel's presentation. "I can't believe he's been here for two years and I only know now. Samwel should have said something."

Azariah made another face. He was still in a mood and didn't feel like talking.

Daniel looked at him with a *please help* expression. Other prep work included polishing—his fingernails, toenails, skin, face. Daniel was deeply uncomfortable with so many strangers touching him, though he'd seen his own parents go through preparations for special events.

Azariah nodded. "I could help with your hair."

Uati moved to apply makeup instead, while Azariah flipped Daniel's hair and tugged at it to watch the curls bounce. Babylonians considered makeup masculine but was something strange to him. Uati put a thick line of kohl around his eyes and tinted creams on his skin, and other things for his eyebrows and lips.

Daniel changed into his royal court outfit, which was a white schenti, made of luxurious fabric folded into stiff pleats, and gold sandals. The attendants wanted to rub oil on all the skin that showed, but that was just too much.

Post-vision, Daniel never cared much about spatial-temporal reality. His physical self was fine. Hananiah helped him with a weight lifting routine more than a year ago. Daniel wanted Azariah to help too, but he said to join him at his foundry job, which sounded disgusting. It was a matter of pride to look strong and healthy, considering the fit Daniel had about eating the right food the first evening. That was the kind of thing an enemy would pick up on, and he had to prepare for anything now.

Azariah was rubbing cream into his hair and saw something change in his expression. "Daniel, are you really going to be happy like this? In this outfit and so styled? The king might expect you to be constantly at his side, looking just like this for the rest of your life. I'm sure you won't like that."

"Oh no, of course not! That is not the king's way," Oshpenaz protested.

"Are you sure?" Azariah asked. "It's fine if going forward he always has his hair rolled up and he constantly wears head to toe clothing in gray and brown?"

Everyone smiled at this image. Even Daniel did, though it was unfair because he wore plenty of green.

"What you are saying is that Daniel knows when to dress up, and does it well, but otherwise prefers to stay quiet in the background and has a reputation like a monk."

"Yes," Daniel said softly. "But I understand that if today goes well,

I'll answer to the king about anything he chooses. I do understand what this means, Azariah."

"Perfect! Fantastic!" Oshpenaz said. "This is, in fact, exactly what the king is looking for. Surely you can see this."

"Daniel," Azariah interrupted, "what do you mean by 'if today goes well'?"

Oshpenaz interrupted with a flurry of emotion, "Are you unsure of the dream? Or interpretation? Did I not ask you that directly? What did you say to Samwel? This is serious and if you have doubts, I won't allow you into court."

"I know what the dream is, and I have the interpretation," Daniel said flatly.

"Oh good, you had me worried, or Azariah, you don't worry me either, the both of you."

"And you're planning to tell the truth, right?" Azariah asked.

Daniel was silent. Lying or saying nothing or threatening or making a deal were small, deep ideas he was still fighting.

"My dear *ursanu pasisum*," Oshpenaz said. "I say this in all kindness. You and your friends will die if you embarrass the king. He doesn't even fully realize it himself, but he has complete faith in you."

"Ooh Oshpenaz, that's not going to help. Oshpenaz, my own dear friend, while I know Daniel won't ask for anything himself, may I ask on his behalf if he were to become an advisor, would he be allowed to invite his mother and sisters to Babylon?"

"I could invite his mother and youngest sisters just on the weight of today going well."

"No." Daniel interrupted firmly. "Stop it, both of you. My mom wants to stay with our enclave. Oshpenaz, I don't intend to embarrass the king. LaMeu, please continue. I'm going to go over exactly what I'll say to the king in my head right now and need everyone to be quiet." Daniel closed his eyes. After a moment, he opened them. "I need help with some Akkadian grammar." Oshpenaz gave Azariah and Daniel their discs back and monitored what Daniel looked up.

A half hour later, Azariah, Uati, and LaMeu were done taking care of him, including his hair.

"Thank you. My mother couldn't have done better."

"If you need help afterwards, please let us know," Uati said.

"Yes, it would be our pleasure," LaMeu added.

"If you ever want to explore what's outside the palace, we can sneak you out," Uati said hopefully.

Daniel bowed politely. Azariah gave them hugs and compliments.

It was time for the last step, the jewelry. Sherah had sent some of the family's best pieces. Daniel picked out a wide belt inlaid with gold and emeralds in a stripe design with curlicues, and a necklace of three square emeralds on a thick gold herringbone chain.

"This is a very fine piece," Oshpenaz said, tapping the largest emerald. "If the king notices it, you may have to present it as a gift. I hope it's not an heirloom!" Oshpenaz looked through the collection and encouraged Daniel to wear all the gold.

Daniel combed through Sherah's jewelry and gave Oshpenaz two earrings, emeralds set in a gold design. "I want to keep the gold settings, but you can prepare the emeralds as a gift to the king." The emeralds matched his necklace.

"You are very kind. I will do so," Oshpenaz said, tucking the earrings away.

Daniel had a tattoo of six lines around his left biceps, one line for each of his dad's island clans, and wore two gold cuffs above and below the tattoo. His left forearm had a Martigny identification tattoo. He had two grapevine tattoos around his right biceps and wore a gold cuff with a vine design that fit between them. When he was twelve, he wanted a sleeve tattoo like his dad, but now there weren't any Unu'utele artists.

His dad, Sefa Ravauviro, had been a third prince from the equatorial island estate Unu'utele, where it always smelled like the sea and he could surf all day. They would spend all their vacations with his dad's family.

Sefa moved from his wife's estate Valla Varra to Unu'utele to fight the Chaldean empire. At the same time, Sherah, with three kids and a pregnant belly, abandoned their Valla Varra winery manor just before Chaldean representatives landed to take over, and moved to Martigny.

Now Sefa was dead from fighting for his island estate and Sherah was in charge of two million people in the foreign Goethe solar system. She was still getting her people out of Valla Varra the best she could. Daniel could still help.

Next were six gold rings. He had thought his dad's jewelry too gaudy, clunky, the exuberant part of his dad's culture he hadn't understood — but his mom had packed it anyway with a sad smile; today it felt perfect. Azariah recognized the rings and gave Daniel a small smile. Was it dangerous to wear them?

"It is time," Oshpenaz said before Daniel could overthink.

"I am ready."

Azariah gave him a small hug and then clasped his hand in both of his and looked him square in the eye. "You are our prophet." He bowed over his hand and then smiled. "You look very intense right now. I'd believe anything you say."

Daniel held onto his hand for longer than he meant. There was something about his expression—they were both just two scared young men far away from home.

"Go get your friends," Oshpenaz said to Azariah. "Get some proper clothes on and stand at the back of the court. I've arranged for it. Just stay at the back. Mishael and Hananiah will understand. Daniel will want to see you."

Chapter 13: Daniel

The king had granted Daniel an audience. This meant that he would be allowed into the high royal court throne room, not that he was guaranteed an opportunity to speak.

Oshpenaz left Daniel to make the walk alone. As he walked, he asked himself, *Am I anxious? No. Am I scared? No. Am I feeling any emotion? Yes, angry, since the first day, it's always been there like the heat. Will I do anything with this emotion? Not today.*

Daniel was halfway through the high royal court chambers on his way to the throne room when his friends came through a side door. They all looked handsome and appropriately rich, with Azariah wearing a formal shemagh head covering and turning his disc screen off now that he found Daniel.

"Hey, should I put this over my face or under my chin?" Azariah asked. Daniel played with the expensive scarf for a moment. It was embroidered with a zebra pegasus. He tucked the corner and edge in both ways and decided on under the chin.

"Leave him alone!" Mishael scolded. "You look fantastic, Daniel. You'll fit right in; I promise."

Daniel nodded several times. He had already seen a handful of people dressed and styled the same way. It was reassuring to hear from Mishael, though.

"We'll stay in the back the whole day if we have to," said Hananiah. "We can order snacks and take bathroom breaks, so if you see one of us leave, we'll be right back."

"I'll stay with you," Daniel replied.

"You can, but we have to be at the back. I don't know if you'll want to stand there. Don't decide until we're there," said Mishael.

They walked into the throne room and found a place to stand at the back. The walls, furniture, and decor were gold, as expected. The eucalyptus trees were beautiful but unexpected, their sharp smell filling the air. It was like the world was here to watch; not just the people of the empire, but the entirety of this universe's nature was represented and watching.

Watching the king, not me. But that felt like a lie. *I'm supposed to be here.*

The recordings hadn't shown how long the room was. Daniel did not want to walk to the king starting from so far back. Mishael knew this. "Your invite means you can sit anywhere, the very front, on the side, whatever you want."

Daniel nodded.

"Hey, there's someone with blue hair. It's not braided though."

Daniel didn't know anyone with blue hair, but he looked in the direction Azariah indicated.

"Her hair is purple. That's a purple color." She was much, much closer to the front, sitting down, with a space next to her. She turned enough that Daniel confirmed she was Birbirru.

"Hey Daniel, are you doing okay?" Azariah put his hand on Daniel's shoulder.

"Don't touch me," Daniel snapped. His nerve endings were too sensitive.

Azariah snatched his hand back like he'd been burned.

"I'm sorry," Daniel said. "When is the king going to be here?"

Mishael answered, but Daniel didn't hear.

"Okay, I'll go sit with Birbirru. I didn't know she was going to be here." He looked at each of his friends before walking off. His life would be different after today, one way or another.

He sat down next to Birbirru, who did a double take and dropped her doctor's stylus on the floor. He let her pick it up before greeting her.

"A mutual friend suggested you might find me today," she said, still flustered, tucking her hair behind an ear. "It's good to see you. It didn't occur to me that you might want to blend in. I've been looking for a monk."

"Yes, this is my first time here," Daniel smiled. "I imagine I'd be drawing a lot of attention if I wore one of my robes. I don't think the king allows monks anywhere near this room."

"With your hair and smile, I'm sure you're allowed anywhere. Are you here about the king's dream thing? It's causing quite a stir."

"Yes. I've watched the recordings. Do you know of anything else happening?"

"Someone was supposed to be executed last night but got a day-long stay. I don't know how. It seems like they'll die tonight, anyway. The staging around the king is usually filled with advisors, and it's almost empty today. The entire court is very subdued. I suppose you wouldn't know that. What are you here for again? I don't think you have the status to just observe."

"I'm here because I have the vision and interpretation."

She dropped her stylus again.

The court started soon with the king's arrival. Occasionally a herald, shaved bald and with a swirling face tattoo, would announce for certain expected people to come forward. The king never addressed anyone. The court wasn't ever fully silent, though the people closest to the front were the quietest, watching the king carefully.

Birbirru patted Daniel's hands. He was clasping them so tightly together that his knuckles were white. He let go, stretched his fingers, and held her hand. He wished— any of his friends were right next to him. He looked back. Mishael and Hananiah were chatting. Azariah was looking right at him and smiled, waved, and signed *brother*, all discreet, especially for him. Daniel gave him a small nod and turned forward.

Each matter of discussion had its own music. Birbirru must have been familiar with the cues. She tapped his arm when a certain one started. After the cue was over, the herald said, "In the matter of the king's dream, does anyone have anything to say?"

Just like Oshpenaz said, Daniel knew what to do. He walked to the front, a very brief walk. No one noticed much.

Daniel approached the herald and bowed politely.

"What is your name?"

"Daniel Rosefinch-Ravauviro. What's yours?"

"My name is Hasdrubal Gullubu," they smiled. "While it is understood that petitioners always ask for things, you can't say your piece in a way that demands some kind of dialogue. The king will say whatever he wants whenever he wants."

Daniel nodded his understanding.

Daniel stepped up close to the throne dais where he could speak at a normal volume and the king would hear him fine. Daniel bowed and kept his eyes on the dais stairs.

The herald announced, "Daniel Rosefinch-Ravauviro, of the planet

Gospel of John, on the subject of the king's dream."

Daniel wasn't supposed to wait for any further signal.

"Your Majesty, I request that if I serve you well today that all the wise people will be spared execution."

King Nebuchadnezzar tapped something. The next words Daniel spoke were louder due to some voice amplification, which hadn't happened to anyone else.

"Your Majesty, no *sangum* priests, *zazakkum* officials, *kakkabum* astrologers, or *hassum* wise men and women can explain to the king the mystery he has asked about, but there is a God in heaven who reveals mysteries. He has shown King Nebuchadnezzar what will happen in days to come. Your dream and the visions that passed through your mind as you were lying in bed are these:"

The king leaned forward.

"As Your Majesty was lying there, your mind turned to things to come, and the revealer of mysteries showed you what is going to happen. As for me, this mystery has been revealed to me, not because I have greater wisdom than anyone else alive, but so that Your Majesty may know the interpretation and that you may understand what went through your mind."

Daniel took a deep breath and glanced up. The king was unreadable.

"Your Majesty looked, before you was the Milky Way, near the Eye, and there before you spun the biggest, brightest star ever seen; enormous, dazzling, awesome in appearance. From this star grew a perfect planet. You watched it form. The innermost part was iron and baked clay; over that was laid a thick layer of iron; over that was a layer of bronze; next, a mantle of silver and then the most outermost layer was made of pure gold. This beautiful, perfect planet spun around the star, both the most dazzling ever seen. On this planet was an enormous, dazzling statue, awesome in appearance. The head of the statue was made of pure gold, its chest and arms of silver, its belly and thighs of bronze, its legs of iron, its feet partly of iron and partly of baked clay. While the gold planet spun, a large asteroid was thrown into the solar system. It struck the gold planet and smashed it through the gold, silver, bronze, iron, and baked clay layers to the very center. The perfect planet was smashed so that it was merely dust circling around the star. The asteroid grew and smashed into the star, causing a supernova."

At that point, he leaned back; it was the end of the vision. He knew it was the end; Daniel had seen the dream. He made firm eye contact with the king for the first time, but otherwise, their expressions didn't change. The court was completely silent. Daniel continued with the interpretation.

"This was the dream, and now I will interpret it to the king. Your Majesty, you are the king of kings. The God of heaven has given you dominion and power and might and glory; in your hands he has placed all humankind, the solar systems, and the nebulae. Wherever there is life, he has made you ruler over them all. You and your empire are that outer layer of gold. Beneath you is another empire, inferior to yours; when the gold layer erodes away, the silver is next. Next, a third kingdom, one of bronze, will rule over the galaxy. Finally, there will be a fourth kingdom, strong as iron—for iron breaks and smashes everything—and as iron breaks things to pieces, so it will crush and break all the others. Just as you saw that the innermost core was partly of baked clay and partly of iron, so this will be a divided empire; yet it will have some of the strength of iron in it, even as you saw iron mixed with clay; this kingdom will be partly strong and partly brittle; the people will be a mixture and will not remain united, any more than iron mixes with clay."

The majority of the vision had nothing to do with the Chaldean Empire. Daniel didn't know how the king would respond to that. So be it. Daniel continued.

"In the time of those kings, the God of heaven will set up a kingdom that will never be destroyed, nor will it be left to another people. It will crush all those kingdoms and bring them to an end, but it will itself endure forever. This is the meaning of the vision of the asteroid that broke the gold, silver, bronze, iron, and clay, which then caused a supernova. The great God has shown the king what will take place in the future. The dream is true, and its interpretation is trustworthy."

Daniel bowed, indicating he was done.

The king rose from his throne and gave Daniel a small bow. The king's voice was also amplified as he said, "You have reported my dream as I myself have dreamed it many times without sharing it. I pay you and your God all honor. May we present you with an offering and with incense?" A few young men were on standby next to the king. One gave Daniel a signet ring to wear, and the other lofted frankincense around him. "Surely your God is the God of gods and the Lord of kings and queens and a revealer of mysteries, for you were able to reveal this mystery." He made a gesture, the next words weren't amplified, and he walked down the dais stairs, "Ah Daniel, it is such a great pleasure to meet you. Let's have some refreshment in private. Oh, and don't worry, none of your friends are at risk of execution anymore." He laughed and put his arm around Daniel's shoulders and led him to a side door.

Chapter 14: Daniel

King Nebuchadnezzar ushered Daniel through a series of introductions, a tea ceremony, and a medical examination.

During a free moment, Daniel got his disc out of the one small pocket his outfit had.

To his friends: *I'm fine. I don't know when I'll see you again.*

His friends responded with a group message: *We love you dearly.*

Daniel's feed already had new accesses and a detailed map of the palace with his new quarters flagged, which had a note from a new assistant named Sigazibi that all his belongings were being moved. There were new schedules and calendars to review. The king was perhaps taking Daniel seriously. Beyond what kind of control the king would place on him, this was a special position. He hadn't forgotten his three goals: find a safe haven for Paradisian exiles in the immediate term before the prophesied second war, prepare to get the Paradisian solar system back in seventy years, and implement empire policies according to God's wishes. Daniel meditated on this until someone retrieved him for dinner.

The weight of what he had done pressed down on him, like a galaxy shaped lion had a paw on his chest; it was only during uncommon eras that God lifted the veil between the physical and metaphysical.

Daniel was the last to arrive at the king's dining hall. The king, sitting at the head of a table, indicated for Daniel to sit at his right hand. Behind the king was a hundred-foot-wide gold and blue stained-glass window. Due to some trick to the physics of the room, the king was above everyone though table was level. Oshpenaz was at the king's left hand and introduced Daniel to everyone. He knew Birbirru and Te'oma and had heard of Dabu'us and the king's military leader

Hammu-Rapi, who was also the king's best friend. The rest were strangers.

Daniel let the information flow over him. He hated the king. He hated being here. His friends didn't talk about their circumstances much, that any kind of success or comfort depended on a man who had brought such violence on their people. They'd never had to confront the hypocrisy in person the way Daniel was now, to be pleasant while full of loathing. He remembered what his sister Magdalene thought of this, to prefer physical death to any concession like he was making. But then he remembered his visions and that Magdalene, his mom, and his other sisters needed his protection.

The woman next to Daniel, En-hedu-anna, who was as round and pretty as a rose, and a socialite and cousin of the king, asked Daniel a question, and he shook off his mood and answered politely.

As servants brought out the first course, the king asked, "Daniel, that is such an exquisite emerald necklace. Is it something special?"

"It's a family heirloom." Daniel looked at Oshpenaz, who passed a small box to the attendant behind him, who then walked around and handed it to the attendant behind Daniel, who then handed him the box. It was ridiculous. The table was narrow enough that Oshpenaz could have handed it straight to Daniel, but the pomp caught the king's attention. Daniel rose from his chair and, with a formal bow, placed the box near the king. Erioch, who was standing by, took the box, examined it, then handed it to a senior attendant, who then handed it to the king. It was embarrassing. His little gift was not worth the attention.

"Ah, these are quite nice, a matching pair to your necklace, I assume?" He chuckled. "Never fear, I shan't take your necklace." He picked an emerald up and examined it in the light, then placed it in the box and gave it to the senior attendant.

"They are Aegyptian emeralds that have been in my family for five hundred years."

Gasps and repeats of "Aegyptian" drowned Daniel out. The senior attendant immediately placed the box on the table as if it had burned her. The king opened the box to look at them again but closed it after a second and placed it carefully to the right of his plate setting.

People leaned to look at his necklace.

"Your Majesty, I apologize. I did not know they were Aegyptian!" Oshpenaz glared at Daniel, who only sipped his wine.

The royal court had an obsession with Aegyptus. Daniel hadn't wanted to make an impression of wealth and power, but he had stepped right into it, and didn't want to appear as if he was stupid as to the worth of his gift, so he stayed silent.

Once the murmuring died down, the king spoke. "I can't believe you are walking around with Aegyptian emeralds. They are too great a gift for me to accept today. Remember me when you want something." He tried to hand them to the senior attendant, who refused to touch something so valuable and sacred. "Oh, fine." The king leaned forward and placed the box within Daniel's reach, who set it beside his plate.

En-hedu-anna cleared her throat and rustled a bit in her seat. Daniel smiled and opened the box for her view. She flushed bright red and murmured, "Formed in another arm of the galaxy. What history they must have." Birbirru on the other side of En-hedu-anna leaned forward and didn't look at the jewels but smiled at Daniel. He was grateful for the little kindness and nodded once to her.

Daniel directed his next comment to the king. "They've been on Gospel for millennia and were set in Ophir gold until recently."

"Oh yes, that beautiful yellow Ophir gold. Those asteroids are mine now, you know. Are there any more Aegyptian jewels on Gospel? Or Revelation?"

"My family has a set of rubies. I know there were rubies and sapphires in Darh Dothoma, but I don't know if they are still there." Daniel looked the king in the eye for a fierce moment before averting his eyes; the Chaldean empire had bombed the chief city recently. He clenched his fists in his lap.

The king said nothing.

Daniel ate a bite of food after a moment.

"Excuse me Daniel, but can you prove they are Aegyptian?" asked Hammu-Rapi the general, who looked like a skinny eagle, like he grew up in the wrong gravity.

"Yes."

The challenge loosened up the table.

"Your Majesty, I direct this question to you, though it does concern Daniel as well; how do we know that the performance today was for real?" asked En-hedu-anna, with an apologetic smile.

"My dear friend, I hardly know how to convince you if you decide to not believe. Feel free to examine any records or journals or whatever."

"I have had visions before," Daniel stated flatly. "After spending a day in prison, I prayed to God to reveal this mystery. I was given the same vision and interpretation two nights in a row and reported the vision and interpretation as God gave me."

"Come now, Daniel, don't be so intimidating. Duanna, your lack of faith is noted," the king said without allowing time for follow up comments or questions.

Birbirru turned to En-hedu-anna, "I certainly believe that the king's dreams have been disturbing him." She leaned to address Daniel, "I know who you are, but no one else does. Where did you come from? You've popped up out of nowhere."

Daniel answered literally. "I came to Babylonia two years ago from Martigny, the Goethe asteroid. I've been a part of the king's Etemenanki palace educational program."

"You grew up on an asteroid." Birbirru stated.

"That sounds like an insult," Dabu'us said. "You shouldn't think that."

"Only since I was ten," Daniel replied. "Before that, I lived in Valla Varra on Gospel of John, where my mom is prime minister of the estate, though she's now in exile." Was his tone bland enough?

"Daniel Rosefinch-Ravauviro—you're that family?" Hammu-Rapi asked.

"Yes."

"Interesting. That's an inherited position, isn't it? So you're not a nobody out of nowhere, really," Hammu-Rapi said bluntly.

Off in the shadows sat a man with glittering eyes. Daniel had kept his eye on him, and now that he wanted to change the subject, Daniel raised his wineglass to him and took a sip.

Everyone turned to see who had Daniel's notice.

"Te'oma, pleasure to see you here at the king's table," Daniel said. "I didn't think you would belong."

"Twenty," was all he answered back.

This was hardly the place, but everyone was eccentric, so Daniel followed suit. "Ten. What about the mineral rights?"

"There aren't any minerals."

"So you'll include the rights just in case?"

"Fifteen, surface mineral rights."

"I'll have Samwel get in touch with you." Daniel didn't trust Te'oma, but maybe he wanted to show off to the king. But would he scam or do Daniel a favor? Daniel searched Te'oma's ugly face. He looked pleased. Samwel would take care of it.

"Is this about Poeninae?" Hammu-Rapi asked.

"The moon Axima." Te'oma and Daniel said at the same time. Axima orbited Poeninae in the Goethe system.

"Oh, you're talking money. I should have known. You're that Daniel too?" asked En-hedu-anna. "I suppose there's only one Daniel in the entire galaxy, and you're behind everything he does."

"You're very kind," Daniel said with another smile, which made her blush. He stopped smiling.

Daniel was here, at this table, because God wanted him to take care of Gospel the best he could, and he could do a lot of good work for Gospel in this position. For Revelation, too; for the entirety of his Paradise solar system and the exiles. Te'oma's antagonism reminded him of that. Daniel had been trying to meet with him for years and now this two-minute conversation was enough, maybe.

"We have heard enough from Daniel. Now it is time for us to tell Daniel plenty of things." The king's voice was quiet, but everyone obeyed. He smirked. Preened. He was happy that this dinner impressed Daniel.

They talked to Daniel about the recent purge, the empire expansion plans, what they expected of him, the general purpose of everything, and so on, way past his usual bedtime.

Daniel was dreading his new quarters. He wanted to climb into his old bed but wasn't brave enough to disobey the little note in his feed. The new quarters were fine, similar rooms to what he shared, but on a smaller scale and with a view of the sunrise. Someone decorated the rooms in a way that said, "I think this is who Daniel is."

Daniel found the personal bathroom and his clothing. Among the different greens and browns hanging in the closet, there was a soft gray robe he recognized but wasn't his. He set the emerald box aside and put the robe on. It smelled like Azariah. Daniel couldn't believe this was still the same day that he kissed his hand and signed "brother."

Daniel used his new access to video call his mother, Sherah, for the first time in years. Martigny had a Gate about ten light-minutes away, so the delay in the signal was insignificant compared to how far away she was. This was the first time Daniel had seen her since he left. She gave him a big smile, which crinkled her face like it wasn't used to smiling. Daniel explained what had happened and asked for guidance.

She shook her head. "This is you, Daniel. God and king have given you power. If anything, I will come to you if I need Babylon's help."

Keeping that in mind, Daniel reported his short conversation with Te'oma regarding the Axima moon. After that, he still wanted guidance: "But what about Paradise?" He meditated during the ten-minute wait for an answer.

"You need to pray and meditate on your new position. Let's talk about other things. How are your friends? I've been keeping in touch with their families the best I can."

Soon they said goodbye until next week. Daniel climbed into bed. His feed had messages, nothing he felt like answering. Azariah had messaged "I'm still up" about once every ten minutes for most of the evening but had stopped over an hour ago. Daniel sent a goodnight-good morning message with a picture of him in the gray robe, queuing it for when Azariah woke up. Daniel went to sleep less sad than expected.

Daniel slept only a couple hours before it was time to arise and prepare to perform his first Chaldean religious service at the palace chapel. King's wishes which were life-and-death orders.

Ever since the king started having his vision, he had daily prayers with lots of pomp and a retinue. Daniel was not allowed to refuse just because he was baptized into Kahi Christianity, not Chaldean. Did anyone understand his visions came from the creator God, and not from a local god like Marduk?

Daniel dressed in the simplest Chaldean robes Tiffany, a clergy member, could offer for his new position and he washed his face, eschewed makeup and jewelry, and kept his hair in a tight roll. He had hopes that an ambitious bishop or someone would push him off to the side, convincing the king he wasn't ready. The king had imprisoned the worst of the clergy with the other "wise people" and subsequently shuffled off the planet or was still in the process of shuffling off. This left leadership gaps and only the kind, decent clergy behind.

When they were in the palace chapel, Daniel asked Tiffany if she really felt like he was the appropriate clergy member. She and the rest all nodded yes, that he had a genuine connection to God and it would shine through any human rites, and indeed they could see it even while we were practicing, and also the king insisted and they definitely listened to the king. Tiffany, with a tall, broad shouldered, serious mien, was their ringleader. Daniel kept her nearby the whole service.

Daniel spoke the shortest homily ever. The first person he blessed was the king.

"This is unacceptable," he whispered, waving a hand around his face. "We will talk about your presentation later. You look like you just rolled out of bed."

Daniel moved to bless people in a general line, just like he did at that first festival during his first year. He was now standing at the head of the church and had a much longer line of people waiting. After an hour, Daniel stepped away for a moment to drink some water and asked Tiffany next how much longer.

"Basically, until you call it quits. I don't want to tell you how many people, but I'll say that we will not run out."

That feeling he had in prison—when he couldn't recognize his fate—that pressure was still there. He was a destination on a pilgrimage now. He couldn't ever step away from that.

"Once the newness wears off, I'm sure it won't be so bad. I'll pull you out if you look too miserable. We have to look good for the king!" She patted his shoulder with a heavy hand.

Daniel stepped back into place to bless again. Assistants on either side kept people moving along. These people were rich, complacent, and diverse. He looked at them closer to see what planet or continent they were from. Who might be more amenable to hosting Paradisians, to creating a safe haven? Would they do it to please Daniel? How could he find out? Should he try to talk to people behind the king's back?

Daniel spent at least an hour evaluating people like this before he realized he was not behaving appropriately in the house of God. The last time he saw his own people on the Goethe asteroid, they had asked him to pray. Now this new group of people were also asking him to pray, and he had no prayer for them because they were Chaldean. But God said to pray for his enemies, so he would pray for them from that perspective. Taking a deep breath, he released his unhappiness. Taking a break to eat also helped. He wished he could bless Paradisians. When twilight deepened, he said to not let anyone else in the main aisle. Daniel would give a general blessing to the remaining crowd after he was done with the line, if Tiffany thought that was appropriate.

He did so and finished the day. He went straight to bed.

Chapter 15: Daniel

At the end of the month of Duku, when Daniel had been with the royal court for three months, he accompanied the king's entourage to yet another event.

"I want to talk to you about the census," Daniel said to Sigazibi, his main palace assistant.

"Do we have to? Today is supposed to be a day off," she said, wrinkling her nose. "Enjoy the view."

"I'll let you enjoy the view," he mumbled, but joined her at the rail. They were at the bathhouse, the competition part with enormous pools, high diving platforms, and stadium seating. The air was warm, humid, and smelled like chemicals. The light from the sky windows trembled off the blue water. Daniel and Sigazibi were with King Nebuchadnezzar and his entourage in his special viewing box. Daniel watched the next round of swimming, the butterfly stroke. None of the competitors were from Paradise, so he cheered on the people from the Lagoon Nebula since they were the closest to home.

During a break before the high diving rounds, Birbirru appeared at the railing next to Daniel.

"I heard you ask about the census," she said. Birbirru's place as a minor patrician meant that she didn't have access to any government money or resources, but she had insinuated herself deep enough into the king's court that if she wanted to know about something or get something done, she knew it and made it happen.

"Did you know the census was my idea?" Daniel asked. "I know I'm not getting official credit and I'm not fighting for that, but I imagined a limited religious census, not this huge thing." He meant for the census to track Paradisians who were being sent all over.

"I wondered about that," she said, bumping his shoulder. "Everyone hates the census. Just categorizing all the solar systems was a monumental task, and this is so much bigger. I didn't think the administrator in charge was really creative or ambitious enough to think of such a project."

"None of the data they are gathering is what I want, which is what I was asking Sigazibi about. Or are you offering?" Daniel asked.

Birbirru said something, but the first high diver distracted Daniel. The diver flipped and twirled through the air before cutting into the water without a splash. Daniel wondered if gravity was different in that part of the bathhouse and leaned into the rail.

"Daniel, did you hear me?"

"No, my apologies." Daniel turned to Birbirru.

"You find the high divers attractive? It's nice to know you're at least a bit human. I like their little swimsuits. I hate this chlorine smell, though. Now that the new empire is strong and stable, we should implement better technology."

"My humanity does not depend on my sexuality," Daniel said coldly. "Did you have something to say about the census?"

"We'll talk later. This is too much fun. You are not made for the high court," Birbirru said with a smile.

"I serve the king as he sees fit," Daniel said coldly, but then immediately warmed up. "As do you, my friend. We won't compromise each other." That last line might have been some naïve hope.

Birbirru glanced at the king and gave him a brief nod. Daniel looked at the king, who waved him over. He introduced Daniel to the people in his entourage today and had him go through the dream and interpretation again. Daniel once again repeated, as he had over and over to different courtiers, the king correcting him if he deviated from the script. He did not consider this a day off.

Later, one of Erioch's guards came up to the rail a few paces away and cleared their throat. Daniel looked over at Erioch, who was always next to the king. Erioch looked at Daniel straight in the eye and then glanced off to the side. Daniel casually looked over his shoulder. Azariah was nearby, standing on the other side of a protection barrier. Daniel immediately walked to him without looking back.

Two guards were at the entrance. The barrier was clear and not soundproof.

Azariah looked wonderful. Seeing a true friend, and his best friend at that, made something blossom in Daniel's chest. Daniel had been coping with some serious unhappiness, but just seeing Azariah was enough to make all the irritations of court life fade into the background. Daniel hadn't seen any of his friends since he joined the high royal court.

"Azariah," Daniel whispered, but it was loud enough for his friend to hear.

"Daniel! It's so good to see you," Azariah said in Kahi with a big grin.

A guard near Daniel got out a screen that would translate Kahi into Akkadian.

"I can't let you in," Daniel said. "And I can't come out."

Azariah looked at the barrier and shrugged. "At least we can talk. I've missed you a lot."

"Yes. How have you been?" Daniel asked. Azariah poured out a flood of words that washed over Daniel. Just hearing his voice made Daniel feel better, no matter what the words were. The blossom of happiness in his chest spread and soothed all his wound-up nerves.

"—And so that's why I'm here today. I didn't know there was going to be a competition but I still want to swim with my friends. And lucky me, I get to see you!" Azariah smiled and ran his fingers through his hair.

Daniel still didn't want to talk. Conversations were hard sometimes and just looking at his friend felt like enough communication. Azariah was indeed in a swimsuit, no friends in sight. His hair was the longest it had ever been. He looked more like a man than what Daniel remembered, with chest hair and bulky with muscle from his foundry job.

"Hey, Daniel, are you okay?"

Daniel shook himself out of his gaze. "I'm fine. You're looking good."

"Thank you!" Azariah said. "Tell Samwel that. He says I look sloppy and should shave more than once a week."

"Whatever you want," Daniel said. He liked Azariah with long hair.

"Actually, there is something I'd like," Azariah said, looking more vulnerable.

Daniel nodded, listening. He wanted to give Azariah everything.

"We missed celebrating our birthdays together. But I'd like to do something with you," Azariah said. His happy chatter had dropped into a serious tone.

"Of course. We can spend time together. I can do that. I want to do that," Daniel said, his hand going to a long chain around his neck. Azariah had sent a birthday gift to Daniel, a niobium chain and cross. "I wear your gift all the time."

"You do like it? I thought you'd be sick of gold," Azariah said, still downcast.

"Yes. I didn't forget you. I promise I have a birthday gift for you. The Library is having a hard time finding it," Daniel said.

"A book? Whatever, it's not about gifts," Azariah said, waving his hand. "No one else is like you."

"You need me to try harder," Daniel said. "I can do that. I'd be happy to. It'd be good for both of us."

"If you're sure. I don't want to get you into trouble," Azariah said.

"Azariah, I should have been making the effort before. I'm sorry." Daniel wished he hadn't missed celebrating their birthdays. He had been worried about the king stopping him, but he had enough courage to try now.

"We've all missed you. It would be cool for all of us to hang out together again," Azariah said with his arms crossed. Daniel wanted the cheerful Azariah back.

"No, Azariah—I love the others like brothers but you are my best friend. I don't think I've said that but it's true." Daniel was starting to get a stomach ache.

"I thought you might be done with us. I should have had more faith in you. For what it's worth, you're my best friend, too." Azariah had tears in his eyes that he was blinking away. He looked away at a swimming pool. The light reflected in trembling streaks on his face.

"We'll celebrate your birthday however you want," Daniel said after a minute. He wasn't used to having this effect on people, but their lives had been bound up for years and neither of them wanted to unravel their friendship.

"A hug," Azariah pointed at him for emphasis. "You come over, say hi to everyone, and we'll see what there is to do."

"Your conversation has been long enough," a guard said.

Daniel's relief and happiness came crashing down. He bowed to Azariah and went back to the entourage. He and Azariah used to live together, get up at the same time, go on vacations together, and so much more. But they didn't have that anymore and wouldn't ever again. The loss hit Daniel hard. He hadn't grieved for his old life at all. Going forward, if he was going to be friends with Azariah and the others, he would have to work hard. He got out his disc and gave calendar access to Azariah, and any other permission so Azariah would know what was going on in his life.

When Daniel got back to the dais, the king said, "There you are, Advisor Ravi. What were you talking about with that swimmer?"

Daniel's mind went blank.

When he didn't respond quickly enough, the king gestured to the accompanying guard, "What were Daniel and his little new friend talking about?"

"About the swimming competition," the guard said.

"Yes, Daniel, you do like the swimmers." The king smirked. When the guard said nothing else, the king dismissed him.

Daniel glanced at Erioch. The guard would not have been so discreet without orders. Erioch knew very well who was at the barrier, so Erioch was protecting Azariah from the king, or something.

Daniel went back to his seat, Sigazibi on one side and Dabu'us on the other. She had recognized Azariah and asked questions in whispers when the king was busy. Daniel wrote messages to help his friends and quietly watched the rest of the swimming competition. He did especially enjoy the diving.

Press Release from King Nebuchadnezzar

Press release from King Nebuchadnezzar of the Chaldean Empire:

I, your king, as appointed by all gods as the greatest king, wish to create for you, my people, the best empire ever. We all deserve not only the biggest, strongest empire but also one that excels in the arts and sciences. I've been talking with some physicists, engineers, artists, and others, and we're going to create a truly fantastic art installation, a magnum opus, a wonder of the galaxy. Just to give a hint, I'm going to need a lot of gold.

This is another reason Daniel's God has given me all of Paradise. The asteroids in their Ophir belt are solid gold. And they were just sitting there! The Paradisians had a ritual where once every ten years they would take an asteroid, carefully set it in some special area like on a mountain or an empty space in a city and carve a temple to their god from the asteroid. There was so much gold in the Ophir asteroid that the sculpted building would shine and sparkle. It's cute they think that the rest of the universe would let them just keep their sparkly asteroids with no interference. There are to be no more temples in Paradise. People will worship as I please.

Chapter 16: Daniel

To the Chaldean King Nebuchadnezzar, to the exiles from the solar system Paradise, and to the continued residents of Paradise:

God's messenger came to me in a vision.

I was again in the throne room of the Ancient of Days set among the galaxies; each galaxy sparkled in its place, over, under, and on every side of the throne room. The throne was a living flame; the Ancient of Days with woolly hair was on the throne. A river of fire still flowed before him. He looked out onto his court of ten thousand times ten thousand and did not see me.

Out of the river of fire came a vision; the archangel Gabriel arose and came to me, her face golden and her wings and clothing living flame. She carried a large basket on her left shoulder, supported with her left arm and hand; she carried a second basket under her right arm. Gabriel approached me and I fell on my knees and face in veneration. She told me to rise and placed the two baskets before me. One was full of very good figs, like those that ripen early. The other basket had very poor figs, so bad they could not be eaten.

From the river of fire arose another messenger, the archangel Michael. She drew from a sheath a sword the length of two arms and held it across her body; the sword glowed like iron from a furnace. She had the same appearance as Gabriel; she had a golden face, with wings and clothing of living flame, and wore a silver crown in her hair.

Per Azariah's request, Daniel was doing his best to make friends with Marzihu.

"To move forward, can't we just say that the war of Elam 525 was not based on the prophecy of Christ?" Marzihu said with preciseness. He had recently become a postulate in the Chaldean Church and was diving deep into eschatological history.

"I don't know, that only works if you don't take the sermon on the mount literally, which is ridiculous." Daniel drummed his fingers on the table, tempted to bring up the copy he kept in his feed.

"The lens you're using is stricter than anyone else I've heard." He leaned back in his chair with a smug look.

"Are you really saying," Daniel asked in disbelief, "that you can use the Bible to justify slavery, poverty, oppression? How else did the Achaemenid Empire build their wealth? Didn't they even work on the Sabbath?"

"The Chaldean Church takes a different view."

"*I* am the Chaldean Church," Daniel said, sounding more cranky than convincing. Every time he and Marzihu talked, they bickered. Daniel couldn't believe that Azariah thought he could be friends with someone who thought that the wars over baptism weren't necessary.

Daniel could not, in fact, break millennia of theology and tradition, to no one's surprise but King Nebuchadnezzar. He was a chaotic element and didn't yet understand that even with the purge of the worst religious people, there were still strong, intolerant religious clergy who looked the other way at innocent blood being shed in empire wars, who wouldn't help the orphans and refugees of those wars, and so on. With this type of Christianity, Daniel didn't care if people turned to Marduk. Both were false gods.

Daniel watched Azariah from across the room. He watched everyone watching him. They were at a graduation party for Azariah and his comrades, not a religious conference. Marzihu and Daniel were sitting at a table in a corner. Erioch was hovering somewhere in the shadows behind them, ostensibly to guard Daniel but excited about recon on university graduates.

Azariah was wearing coveralls like all the other graduates. The outfit at first glance didn't seem appropriate to a party but looking closer, the insignia over the left breast showed the Jump engine program with Babylon University, which was impressive. Plenty of these people were impressive and impressed by Azariah, like Xa Le of the Urartu Star Cloud University. Azariah talked to Daniel so matter-of-factly about his education that Daniel hadn't thought of the prestige, reputation, or contacts. He smelled an Oshpenaz scheme. After thinking about this for a moment, Daniel turned his attention back to the crowd and couldn't find Azariah for a moment. He panicked but then saw him. A blond woman was hanging off Azariah as he talked to a few people. She was his language teacher, Brigette Beck. Her behavior was inappropriate and making Azariah uncomfortable.

Daniel made a note to look into her. It was one way he could take care of Azariah.

Finally, Marzihu left Daniel alone to greet a cousin, and Azariah came over.

"Congratulations," Daniel said as Azariah approached. Daniel was a little nervous but stood up and gave him a brief, light hug. Something tight in his chest relaxed.

"Thanks." Azariah showed him proof of his certification with a flourish. He had graduated with an excellent understanding of Jump and propulsion engines.

"Oh, here, I finally have your birthday gift for you," Daniel said. "I think it fits as a gift for today, too." The two young men had celebrated Azariah's birthday together. When they had met at the diving competition, Daniel had realized he wanted to give Azariah anything he wanted. But when they had met for Azariah's birthday, Daniel had realized he couldn't give Azariah anything. They were still working on a new friendship, and Daniel had developed a whole range of awkward feelings. There was a bunch about the birthday party Daniel was trying to forget.

Azariah smiled wide like nothing was wrong and opened the gift box to find a bright pink book the length of his forearm. It had platinum trimming. He opened the hardcover and flipped through the pages.

"At my request," Daniel said, "the Library found this old Jump manual that no one's seen before. Some people were fighting over it, which is why I didn't have it in time, but it's mine to do what I please."

"Wow!" Azariah exclaimed, "This is incredible, Daniel. Fantastic! The University has only ever been able to find one. Daniel, this has information no one at the University has seen! I don't think you understand how serious this is. How did the Library have this, and we didn't know?" Azariah asked.

"The Library is better than the University and I have access to the Library resources to whatever extent I want. I asked them to find Jump manuals and my request apparently jump started a huge expedition months and months ago. I had to fund part of it, like five million tetradrachms. No one had ever asked them. They were shocked that they could find only one. So this is good, right?"

Azariah laughed. "Yes. We don't have time today, but be prepared to have your ear talked off the next time you can spare an hour. What does this say about quantum paths? I've been working on understanding Jumping theory and technology." He skimmed through the book.

"That's what you're good for," Daniel said. "That's what Paradise needs."

Azariah froze. What Daniel said had hurt him. Azariah's face looked like his heart was breaking. He turned off the book and sat down hard opposite Daniel, his back facing the room.

"I'm sorry, you're a lot more than that," Daniel said. But the words were out there. Like he was a tool in a toolbox to be picked up for only a specific use. Like what Patroness Shelomith and Oshpenaz wanted to do, what Azariah wanted to avoid. "I didn't mean that's all you're good for…" but that's what it sounded like. What were the right words? "My love for you is not based on your utility." Daniel sounded so flat.

They sat in silence. Daniel wasn't sure what he could give Azariah. He reached out a hand for Azariah to hold, but he didn't reach back.

"We talked about sacrifice when we celebrated our birthdays and you're sacrificing yourself, your goodness," Azariah said, not making eye contact. "You are becoming less kind. God can't possibly want this for you." He reached for Daniel's hand and squeezed. Daniel rubbed his thumb over the fingernails and knuckles of his best friend.

"It could easily be a lot worse," Daniel whispered. *I could use my Chaldean Church appointments to trade favors. I could make friends with war criminals so that they'd sell me military ships.*

"I'm done with this. I'm done talking with you about yourself. If you're going to stay, you have to chill out or warm up and be nicer."

"You want me to talk to people? I can try. I mean, I'll get up and walk around and be nice." Daniel did that all the time for the king. He could do it now.

"I don't want penance." Azariah sighed, rubbed his face with his hands. "Let's try to salvage this. Yes, I did all of this work to help you." He looked over Daniel's shoulder. Daniel looked, Erioch was nearby.

"Erioch knows about our three goals," Daniel said calmly. "He thinks they are silly, and he'll let us blow off steam so we don't feel trapped into doing something worse."

"Screw you too, Erioch," Azariah mumbled. "Anyway, so that means you're working on policy? That's what you are good for."

"It's been a struggle to translate what God told Prophet Jeremiah into enforceable policy."

"That makes sense since God told those things to Prophet Jeremiah about the Revelation of John and exiles in general, not to you about Babylon."

"I'm blessed to be here to help Paradise," Daniel said.

"If that's what you want, then it doesn't seem like God is stopping you," Azariah said, letting go of Daniel's hand.

"What do you want?" That question was too emotional. Daniel regretted saying it and followed it immediately with, "What will you do now? What are your days going to look like?"

"If I need to get a job to support myself, I might go back to the foundry. Probably go swimming more. A couple professors might have internships coming available, though competition is stiff. I'm meeting with Oshpenaz in a week."

"What are the professors' names? Maybe I can do something for you. If that's what you want—as far as me pulling strings, I mean."

"You can pull strings. It's the way things are done. The info is in my feed." Azariah stood up. "I'm done with this. I've got to go." His energy had changed. Daniel was saying stuff that was pissing him off.

"Can we still have lunch together tomorrow, like always?" Maybe then Daniel would know what to say.

Azariah leaned over Daniel, putting a hand on the back of his chair so he could look him close in the eyes. "I'll come." And then he was gone with the book in hand, lost in a crowd of friends who wore the same coverall uniform, back to that other impenetrable self. Daniel found all of this, his entire life, extremely dissatisfying.

Chapter 17: Azariah

Azariah felt Daniel's love—brotherly love—in his daily life. Daniel had never stopped thinking of his friends. He got them daily bathhouse passes and better teachers. The Chaldean elite invited Mishael to more posh parties because Daniel had access to the right diplomats. The Chaldean government invited Hananiah to speak with galaxy-renowned anthropologists because they answered to the high royal court. Azariah still had his hodgepodge of subjects from Oshpenaz, but his teachers were of an even better caliber. He took a two-week-long trip on a ship with a new type of Jump engine because Daniel stood around the high royal court with the king's astrologer. Daniel would video chat with his friends, apologizing for missing events and things. His earlier avoidance really was a self-inflicted punishment; the king and court never stopped him.

The time Daniel spent with them changed. The type of people he had to interact with just closed him up and it would take an hour for him to unwind and open up, and he hardly ever had that time, between high court, required parties, petitioners, living on his own, and his own projects. This made him possessive of what time he had available and also withdrawn. He needed to constantly know where Azariah was, and then once he found him, would only sit and read or listen before he had to run off again. Azariah kept track of him via his feed.

Two months after Azariah graduated, he was still wrapping up a few classes. After a day of math and physics—good for the mind but his body needed to stretch—he was on his eighteenth of twenty laps in the bathhouse pool when someone swung their legs in and dangled them. Azariah popped out of the water. Daniel was right there.

"Two more laps!" Azariah called and swam away. He was pretty sure Daniel was mad about something new and he wanted an extra couple of minutes.

That was the plan. Instead, Daniel jumped into the pool after him, expensive court clothes and gold jewelry included. So Azariah stopped swimming and turned to him. Daniel immediately pushed a wave of water at Azariah and started yelling.

"I'm furious with you! How dare you!" Daniel sent another wave of water with his arm.

"So it's finalized?" Azariah asked. "Or it's not completed, and you just found out some other way?"

"No, no, I forbid it. It doesn't matter because you're not going! You can't leave!"

Azariah swam to the edge of the pool and held on to catch his breath and to drink some water from a container while Daniel continued yelling at him for the first time ever. Azariah was usually mad at him. It was thrilling to have him mad instead. Azariah was happy about it, even.

"Ever since Duku, I've spent every moment I could spare with you!" Daniel continued yelling. "I've done my best to look out for you and you paid me back by going around my back and using your connection to me to get what you want, which is to leave me for four years."

That was incredibly unfair and so out of character for him.

"It's too dangerous!" He continued. "Dabu'us says there's no chance the *Klipspringer* will make twelve Jumps when the record for any ship is five."

Azariah turned his head away from him to smile. *Klipspringer.*

"No, no! Stop turning away, stop running away! This could be forever!"

Azariah turned to him, of course. Daniel was holding onto the wall with one hand and facing him.

"Please stay," he said. "You always give me what I want. I don't want you to go. It's obvious you should stay."

"No, it's not," Azariah smiled. Daniel sounded haughty, like Mishael.

"Don't smile. This is serious. I'm a representative of your God and king, and you think you know better!" Daniel kept his voice raised and slapped the water to emphasize his point.

"I'm going, Daniel. This is important enough to leave you." Azariah looked him firmly in the eye, copying how he looked at people.

"How! How could this stupid, dangerous empire expansion project be important to you? I thought I knew you!"

"You do, you do, I promise. You found out about this like five minutes ago, right? Can you just stop and think for a minute?" Azariah walked them along the pool wall until the water was shallow enough to sit in, near a waterfall.

It clicked with Daniel that his emotional state was out of control, and he breathed deep. He half laid, half floated with his eyes closed in the shallow water, which was an artificial beach, with his buff-colored court outfit floating around him and wearing his gold jewelry and his gold belt with emeralds, and still soaking wet, with no self-consciousness, pulling the look off easily, and with people watching. Honestly, his outburst wasn't surprising.

Azariah checked his disc to see what position he had on the *Klipspringer*. No info.

Daniel sat up and faced Azariah. "It hurts a lot to know that when I thought you were chatting about every single thing, you were hiding a big secret." Daniel splashed Azariah a little. He was probably expecting an apology or something.

"You never answered my question," Azariah said instead. He would not convince Daniel he wasn't hiding a secret.

"I forget."

"There's no information on my feed. So is anything actually finalized, or did you just hear people bouncing my name around?"

"Look at my feed. It's under general announcements for the king to sign off of." Daniel laid back down in the water.

Azariah Ramzi was next to one position, King's Envoy. He was disappointed with the diplomatic role but kept his face blank. The king had signed off on the whole crew. He thumbed through the names. There were a few people he didn't know. He wanted to meet the head cook ahead of time. He didn't recognize the person in charge of space phenomena. Also— well, now wasn't the time.

"Thank you," Azariah said with a small smile to Daniel, who was pouting.

"Azariah, I want to know why you're going. I promise to listen."

"Let's go closer to the waterfall, so it's harder to eavesdrop." After they moved, Azariah faced him with his arms crossed. "You've got your three goals, right? *Our* three goals. I could *find* a planet on this *gerru*! I could get Jump tech! Isn't that what you want? If we're going to claim Gospel again, then we need hard and soft power, and this is a chance to make that kind of connection with new worlds. Even if I don't do a good job, they will know we exist. Isn't that important?" Azariah raised his voice. "The king signed off on this. You're only his advisor. You aren't my connection to my God! I can pray and She can tell me something you don't like. I decide! I'm not asking for guidance or commands this time." Azariah stopped. Trying to answer all his little bites wouldn't help.

Daniel turned away for a minute. When he turned back, whatever emotional response he had was off his face.

"If I were to give you anything," Daniel said, "absolutely anything for you to stay, what would you ask for? Anything. Whatever it is that makes you not want to stay, whatever would make you happy to stay, what would that be?" He was referring to a conversation they had when they celebrated Azariah's birthday, which hurt to think about.

Azariah looked him in the eye and said slowly, "I'll stay here if you give up your three goals, if you give up on helping Paradise."

Daniel physically recoiled, turned away for a moment again, then faced Azariah with a stern expression. "No. You're asking me to choose between you and God."

"I don't see it that way. To put it one way, if you sacrifice yourself, then I'll do the same. This is either worth the sacrifice or it's not. For both of us."

"Is there anything else I can do to make you stay? What about becoming a consort or *harmu*?"

"No. I deserve better than this." Azariah gestured to him. Daniel was still so mad he wasn't listening properly. "I'm going. What I want is for you to be there when I tell Hananiah and Mishael. What I want is for you to not be mad at me for the next entire month before I'm gone for four years. I want to tell my best friend that I am scared, without you trying to talk me out of it."

Daniel flinched at the words *best friend*. He took a deep breath. "Okay."

They got back to Etemenanki palace, to home, and Azariah was right on time for Samwel's dinner. He had taken a chef's course recently. Azariah was the only one with a predictable schedule, so he got the special meals. Today was Garki fish, which Samwel liked to make on days Azariah went swimming. They had created this dish together over several conversations about what Azariah considered an edible fish. Daniel had ceased eating meat altogether in protest of the extravagant parties; his ascetic life continued unabated. But he was fine with a zibitum and lentil wrap. It made for a decent replacement for a Gospel bean and rice burrito, according to him.

"Ah, this is so good and sooo beautiful. I'm so hungry and happyyyy," Azariah sang. "Samwel, I have news for you later. First, I have to tell Hananiah and Mishael."

Samwel glanced at Daniel meaningfully. Azariah shook his head no; it wasn't about him, even if Daniel was trying to make it all about himself. Samwel raised his eyebrow and nodded. Azariah looked. Daniel was definitely in a mood. When they were changing, he'd grabbed Azariah's kitu, a Babylonian style hoodie, as a shirt. It was bright white and striking against his skin. He'd taken off all his jewelry, which was unusual for this early in the evening, and let his hair down to dry. Instead of sitting in his usual spot across from Azariah, he sat right at the corner of the table next to him while glaring like a wet cat. Azariah almost laughed once he realized how they must seem to Samwel. Azariah gave him a smile and shook his head again.

Wait a minute. Azariah told himself sternly. *I am twenty years old now. It is time to be honest with myself. I deny that Daniel is the center of my universe, but he, in fact, is. If I'm running away, I can do it to his face.* His relief from getting his way dripped away. Azariah stared at Daniel, who stared back, his face softening from whatever he saw.

"Do either of you require anything?" Samwel asked, sounding like he was far away. "I have dinner set aside for the other two once they get back. I'm happy to stay, but if there isn't anything…"

Before he could finish, Daniel was making shooing motions. "We're fine, thank you. You can leave for the day. If you didn't get my outfit ready for tomorrow, don't worry about it."

"Say hi to Neema and the kids for me," Azariah said.

Samwel gave him another knowing look before bowing to Daniel and leaving.

"What's your schedule for the rest of this evening look like?" Azariah asked.

"Nothing. I had Sigazibi cancel everything for the rest of the day once I saw that communique to the king. I should have LaMeu come by and fix my hair." He twisted a wet lock of his hair around a finger and glared at Azariah.

"This is so fun!! This is the first time that you've had a full evening free!"

"No, I took time off when I was sick."

"That is not the same! Really? So you won't go back to work? You're calmer now."

Daniel handed his disc to Azariah, which he tucked away. "Give it back to me tomorrow morning. Sigazibi can come and get me if there's some actual emergency, which there's never been."

"The other two are at the bird races. We could join them? The races should be over in about an hour unless there are fights."

"No. Aza, I'm sorry for earlier." Daniel laid his hand on Azariah's arm briefly. "Why don't you tell me everything."

Azariah beamed and reminded him of some conversations about the project, or rather, lectures that Azariah had given him. The new Jump engines were so different and safer than whatever his court astrologer got famous for using. The *Klipspringer* had entire teams of people, not just one person. Once they finished eating, Azariah took him to the living room, pushed all the furniture aside except for some cushions, got him settled in on the cushions—Daniel always needed water or a blanket or something (Azariah usually did too)—sat down next to him, and projected a huge 3D model of the new Jump engine, and talked about it.

Right away, Daniel shifted over. "I'd like to be close to you."

"Of course." Azariah paused his lecture while Daniel figured out what was comfortable. He decided to have his arms around Azariah and lean against his chest with Azariah's arm across the back of his shoulders.

"Danny, did you want to talk about anything?" *Because this is new. And unsustainable.* While Azariah could cuddle with his friends without it meaning more, having this closeness to Daniel was special to Azariah in a way that it wasn't to Daniel.

"No, I'm happy to listen," Daniel said. "I can see why you're talking about this, and I can follow."

So Azariah did enthusiastically talk about space engines and math for about ten minutes, and by the time his heart slowed down to normal, Daniel was fast asleep.

Without shifting him off or moving too much, Azariah spread Daniel's hair out so it would dry nicely. He drew a thin blanket over Daniel to ward off the breezes.

Azariah continued looking over the engine for his enjoyment until the other two got home.

"Hmm, I haven't ever seen this before," Hananiah whispered.

"A fresh development," Mishael agreed.

"In case it's not obvious," Azariah said, "I am in love with him, but that's not what he feels for me. That's not what this is about. Sit down, my *talimutim* brothers. I have some news."

Chapter 18: Daniel

The next month passed in a blur.

After living on asteroids, Daniel never took a sunrise for granted, even if he saw only Babylonian sunrises. He usually greeted them with happiness and relief; he understood why their Earth ancestors worshiped the sun. But today's sunrise was excruciating.

Azariah was leaving today.

Daniel had already said goodbye. They had watched the sunrise together one last time and now Azariah was already on his way, at the space station port above Daniel by now. It was too sad to dwell on.

Today was also Mishael's formal introduction into the high court as an Atabek ambassador. This was a game for the king: Would Daniel do his duty to the king, his friend Mishael, and the Atabek solar system and attend court? Or would Daniel forsake his duties again and risk the king's rage in order to spend every moment with his best friend and see Azariah off? Daniel had canceled too many of his duties to the king over the past month. Azariah called Daniel self-centered to think the king would take the time to do this, but he'd seen the king play similar games with twenty people at the same time while making economic decisions that would impact entire sectors. One time the king ruled that a planet's judicial system needed to be wiped out entirely and replaced by the Empire Judicature because the ambassador's dog growled at him.

It wasn't much of a choice. It just meant Azariah was walking to the space elevator station with other friends, which Daniel encouraged him to do. The last three friends had a last breakfast together. It was one of those quiet, boring goodbyes where they talked little so they could be strong for each other.

Hananiah left first for his South Pole Archive assignment. Daniel left for the high royal court at the same time Mishael left for the Atabek embassy, where he would prepare for his court introduction. Mishael, as a bone fide diplomat, made sense—he'd go to parties, be a snob, and politely insult people all day long. Azariah as an envoy still made zero sense.

Daniel arrived at the court on time. The sun wasn't too hot, the rainbow trees were bright blue and yellow, and the king hadn't entered yet. Daniel positioned himself far to the right of the king's dais and behind the other exalted inner circle members.

At the back of the court, Daniel saw Mishael and his team. Mishael had his hair in braids. He wore a deep red robe of a close-fitting style without a collar and a full black cape with red embroidered flowers, reminiscent of the echeveria from home, like the coveralls he wore the first day Daniel met him. On that first day, he flickered between being easy going and intense. The easiness had shed away the last year, leaving a vulpine intensity. He had a politician's laugh and smile, and eyes that saw more than Daniel did.

Mishael walked with the Atabek ambassadors, one in white with a fez, one in white with a turban, down the middle aisle with five lesser Atabek officials in a procession behind. The middle aisle was ill defined, people crowded in groups, their servants going up and down the sides then squeezing over to deliver food. When Mishael walked down the center aisle, people moved past him and talked to his entourage. Even with the loud nonsense, people were paying attention. The king himself never paid much attention to who was approaching him. Nevertheless, the Atabek delegation proceeded with all due formality.

Oshpenaz greeted them before they approached the king. During the brief conversation, Mishael looked around and stopped when he saw Daniel, who gave him a quick bow. The king allowed Mishael to approach the dais, and he was busy with the proper bows and formalities. Hasdrubal gave Daniel a signal to approach. He stepped forward with bonhomie, bowed to the king, to the ambassadors, and gave Mishael a big hug, the kind he hated.

He hugged Daniel back, hissing, "Do I even want your official favor?"

Daniel answered with a smile, "The king has given it to you, like it or not."

Hasdrubal directed Mishael to stand with Daniel and directed the other ambassadors to leave. They gave Mishael genuine smiles. All the politics seemed smooth. Daniel checked the reactions of different people—and was heartbroken that his friendship with Mishael, which had been precious and private, was redefined in an instant.

Despite them being on display, Mishael relaxed when they were standing back in Daniel's little corner, leaning against a ten-foot-tall pot with a sycamore tree growing out of it. Some little girls, nieces or daughters of the king, played in front of them, facing the court and smiling and waving as their governess directed.

Mishael spoke gracefully, his voice still deepening. "I suppose Azariah is on his ship by now. And then his ship will leave the station in about five hours, and then hop through three gates, and then make the first jump tomorrow."

Daniel nodded, playing along with his wry tone. "Yes, let's go over his itinerary in detail. Where will he be exactly at every hour?"

"He is indeed our hero who will save us all." Mishael said this with his sly sarcasm, which always made Daniel wonder what he truly believed. Mishael hadn't tried to talk Azariah out of going, so maybe he believed a little.

"A new promised land." Daniel didn't believe what he was saying and struggled with that. His friends were leaving him today, but for a greater cause? "I can't imagine Azariah ever promising anyone anything."

They laughed.

"I have been speaking with Patroness Shelomith," Mishael said. "Her ship docked at the space station a day ago. The palace has been trying to keep quiet about her arrival, but I think there's a way for her and Azariah to meet before he leaves."

"This is possible because of you?" Daniel asked, looking at Mishael. "That's quite the triumph. They thought they wouldn't be able to meet."

He had the smallest smile. "I wanted to impress the embassy and see how much power I had. Did you know the Chaldean empire considers Azariah and Patroness Shelomith a high risk for causing a disturbance if they work together? I've seen their profiles. If they could make plans without interference, they could cause quite an upheaval."

"Really? So there is a proper reason. The palace isn't just being ornery. Perhaps we can try to replace him, the three of us, since we'll still be on this planet."

"No, we can't. I'm sure the palace will watch us."

He inquired about people in the crowd. They watched Hasdrubal admit an ambassador. Daniel checked his personal screen, and was shocked. Azariah's tracker showed he hadn't arrived at the space station. He was, in fact, at the east palace entrance, just standing there, where Daniel had said good-bye.

"This can't be fun for you." Mishael said, looking over Daniel's shoulder.

Daniel looked up.

"I'm referring to politics, of course," his gaze shifted to the crowd.

"*He* has something planned," Daniel said, referring to the king in a tone they had developed.

"Another invasion? I mean, besides the *gerru*. Is some other solar system at risk?" Mishael said with a faint, political smile, which disguised the concern in his question.

"No, I'm sure it's different from that," Daniel said, crossing his arms. "The vision and interpretation make the king seem finite and beatable on more than just one level. More warfare won't solve that doubt. He's got another project."

Daniel checked the tracker again.

"Do you have to stay all day?" Mishael asked. "I'm ready to slip out. I can see the servants' door."

"We can take brief breaks. We should not be gone at the same time."

"You take a break first."

Daniel slipped out when the king wasn't looking and ran for Azariah.

Daniel grabbed Azariah's hand. "Let's go." They had to hurry. If the king called for Daniel and he wasn't there, he would be in huge, huge trouble. His family's mining contracts could disappear or a Goethite asteroid could blow up. All Daniel could risk was making sure Azariah wasn't alone when he got on the space elevator. Daniel wanted to scold him, that he didn't have to go alone. Azariah could have asked Samwel or Hananiah, or a friend he had outside the palace, or even Oshpenaz, or someone from his stupid ship. But—

Daniel studied him when they were on a smooth part of the path; Azariah had shaved, cut his hair even shorter than usual, and was in a space coverall outfit; he looked so young.

Azariah was scared, which he wouldn't want anyone to know, but Daniel saw it.

"Azariah," Daniel said, a little short of breath but still moving. "We've known each other for almost three years now, right? There's something I've always wanted to say to you but never have. I'm going to say it just this one time." Daniel checked he was paying attention.

"Well? What is it?" Azariah squeezed his hand.

"You need to grow your hair out. Your adoption is valid and recognized. The Patroness Shelomith of the Zharqua estate on Gospel is your mother. You have the estate tattoo and education. You need to present yourself as a noble. It is a power you've refused to recognize. You are not in the *kiskattum* class. Wear the right clothes, grow out your hair, ask for special favors. Please think about it."

"Of all the last-minute advice to give me." Azariah gave a short laugh.

"Do you have your signet ring? I don't see it."

"Yes."

"Wear it. There's something else. From Mishael." The day had been such a mess. "I'll try to remember." Daniel squeezed his hand and pulled him on, running when they could.

When they got to the station, Daniel threw his arms around Azariah and hugged him until he got his breath back. Daniel still had to *climb up* before the king noticed his absence. Azariah held him tight.

"I remember," Daniel said once he could speak clearly. "Your patroness will wait at the space station before you get onto the *Klipspringer*. Or try to wait for her. I want to write to you every day, if that's okay."

"Yeah, of course." Azariah squeezed his arms and leaned back to look at Daniel.

"You'll be too busy, so don't feel guilty."

"*You* are busy and might peter off. Don't feel guilty either."

"Okay, one last thing." Daniel released Azariah and breathed deep. "I want to bless you one last time."

"Of course, that— that's exactly what I want." He smiled faintly.

"With all the saints, I bless you Azariah Ramzi and I ask that you are blessed by Jesus Christ and the promise of his sister, by the Ancient of Days on the throne, by Gabriel and Michael, that they will bring you back to me. Dear God, guide him on his way. We make this prayer through Christ our Lord. Amen." Daniel touched Azariah's shoulders and heart with his right hand and kissed Azariah's forehead.

"Thank you." Azariah gaze Daniel one last solid look. "Daniel, you are my *sudatim* home. I am coming back to you. Now go, don't wait for me to leave."

Daniel nodded.

Daniel climbed the stairs at a decent pace until he reached the first overview of the Turquoise River. Right here was the tree he had leaned against three years ago. Azariah had offered to carry his bags. Once more, Daniel leaned against the tree, the bark scratching his fingers, and burst into tears. Daniel had put Azariah on that ship to die. *Why did I do it? I could have talked him out of it. Did I say anything useful?* Daniel calmed down, said another prayer, and ran back to the palace.

PART TWO

THE SAGITTARIUS ARM

Chapter 19: Azariah

The Babylonian City space station is the biggest and best in the entire galaxy. I'm not the one to brag, other people say that, but it's true. When sector governors see it for the first time, they are always in awe of how wonderful it is, truly amazing technology. This is one small way I serve my people and become the best Chaldean emperor, or so I've heard.

Azariah was dazed and nerveless as the space elevator took him from the Babylonian surface to the transportation space station, passing by other space stations for habitation, research, and shipbuilding. Saying goodbye to Daniel was as overwhelming as the new existence he was stepping into, which first looked like chaos but as he settled down, he could see the orderly, complex dance as he watched sitting near a window in the main node of the space station.

There were different ways to create artificial gravity. One cheap way was to spin the ship around like a wheel and people can stand on the inside edge of the wheel. But if someone couldn't afford the entire wheel, they could still have a bit of an arc that spun around a middle point like a swing on a swing set. If they were careful, these little ships could travel close to the space station without crashing. The ships timed their swings like a game of double dutch jump rope. The more Azariah watched, the more the playground metaphors seemed appropriate. This was where his patroness's ship would be if Daniel was correct.

The main node of the space station where Azariah needed to wait had zero gravity. It was built during a time when artificial gravity for large space stations wasn't easily available, and then the station was so established that no one wanted to update it. Travelers moved by using their momentum to swing between the many handholds as well as long hand rails that ran into the middle space of the station, guiding them from ships down to a big funnel leading to the space elevators. Travelers lost momentum mid-air if they misjudged their movements between hand holds and rails, and station managers did their best to keep order. Spaceships connected to station nodes via long space tunnels, some of them kilometers long.

Azariah pulled himself over to a wall to flip through the station feed. His patroness's ship was expected to dock soon; if he hadn't known to check, he would have gone straight to *his ship* and missed her, but now he would wait. Not that he wanted to hang out for a few hours—bathrooms were always gross in zero g, so everyone was in a hurry to get on board their proper ship, and eating in zero g was just bad manners.

Thousands of travelers moved through the station. The 3D sphere space was filled with clusters and lines, the travelers bouncing from one part to another. The station managers in red uniforms and white turbans with whistles were pulling people into place, or sometimes gently shoving them. Azariah watched, leaning against a space pillar at his wall, not seeing anyone who looked at the patroness or anyone in her entourage. He thought about the kiss on his forehead, like it was a shield to protect him from danger and his fears. He would not fail.

And then Patroness Shelomith was right there! About to bounce off of Azariah, but he caught her using the guards' method and settled her onto the hand holds. Azariah studied her to make sure it was her: late thirties, hair rolled in two braids, petite, doe eyes, and a smile that could twist a dozen different ways. Today she had no heavy make-up, no cumbersome space-ridiculous outfit, just normal coveralls. Incognito. Azariah checked their surroundings. No one seemed to be interested. He didn't think anyone had been idling nearby, but he wasn't used to being aware of people in the corner above and behind him, like a camel spider. He saw those once while camping on Babylon.

"It's so good to see you!" She crowed. "You have grown. It's not something I could tell in the pictures or videos." She patted Azariah's arm. "Have you seen Mishael's introduction?" She showed Azariah a video. "It's amazing being on this side of the Babylon Gate. I have so much information available so much quicker. What little they allow through the gate is a sin." She talked while he watched the video. "Another piece into place." Mishael certainly looked like someone who had the money and power and resources to help Patroness Shelomith with whatever plans she had.

Azariah handed her the disc, raising an eyebrow, "If I'm also a piece, what is my place?"

"To be honest, I have a particular reason to meet without surveillance. If you don't want to join the *gerru*, I can arrange for a ship to smuggle you to Gospel or Revelation."

Azariah had enough respect for his patroness that his shock and anger didn't impulsively turn into sharp words. Azariah took a deep breath (guess who he learned that from) and said, "Thank you for the opportunity, but I reject it. I do believe this is where God intends for me to be, and I intend to board the *Klipspringer* shortly. So, like I asked, what place do I have in your plans?" Azariah waved his hand around, like there was a literal place in the station she wanted him to be.

"My plans were to have you in the military, but that didn't work. Sounds like you're getting your marching orders from Daniel," Azariah didn't correct her, "and I will not say no to him. Plus, he probably checked with his mom. I suppose it was too much to expect a young farmer to be a competent spy." Having given her opinion, she moved on to useful information, such as specifics on what to look for in a solar system and what specific planets to check.

"Yes, ma'am," Azariah said in full agreement; this was what Daniel wanted, a safe haven.

With a slash of her hand, she said, "Do whatever you want on the ship. Your envoy status gives you a long leash even if you don't have the deep security access we were hoping for. Your engineering education and experience should allow some access beyond all the diplomatic access and power."

"Yes ma'am." Azariah's tone was dissatisfied. He still didn't know how he was going to represent the king without it backfiring.

With a shake of her fist, she insisted, "Surely you see how the envoy position is better. You have soft power to develop. It's not direct control, but over four years you can manage things properly. You've grown so much; I've seen your projects." She waved her hands around again. "You need to make your mark on the planets, suggest infrastructure projects. The king is known for that. Get your own name on them too."

"Yes ma'am." Becoming known, having people know the Paradisians existed, was an important step to their safety and finding a safe haven.

"You aren't prouder of yourself. You must have confidence. Do you not see your position? Lean into the expectations. Be lazy, grow your hair out, you must be more undercover. Get supplements and grow and wear your hair in braids." She flipped a hand to his buzz cut.

Azariah started getting annoyed, just a twitch of his mouth, but Patroness Shelomith caught on.

"Or whatever," she conceded. "Do whatever you want. I'll be sourcing infrastructure material, colony supplies, possible transportation, mercenaries who don't mind kidnapping slaves. I need a planet to send Paradisians to."

"You think that's easier for you to do under the king's nose?"

"It's been impossible elsewhere. Plus," she said grimly, "I want to focus on the populations that have stayed righteous, and the palace is keeping track of that, I'm sure. Only the righteous should return home. I'll live outside the city at an estate which is owned by someone who is sympathetic. This estate owner is expecting a formal visit from the Atabek embassy."

"Before you get any further, I have a little gift for you." Azariah got his disc out and transferred banking information to hers. He had come into a large amount of money.

She raised an eyebrow. "This will be incredibly useful. There was something about being an envoy that I wanted to ask you…. Oh yes, why aren't you in the military? It seemed like a useful route, Oshpenaz was for it, and then you wrote nothing more, even when I asked. I suppose it turned out for the best, but why?"

"There was a classified incident and I'm not allowed any military access. I'm not even supposed to talk with the commandos stationed directly on the ship."

"Is this why the *Klipspringer* doesn't have any military escort ships?"

"Because of me? No, not at all. No other ship except the *Klipspringer* can Jump safely. That part of the propaganda is true. I hardly have a good hold on what's happening. I've just been stumbling around the overlapping diplomatic, military, and research-science spheres. Ask Mishael. Don't bother Daniel too much."

"It's too bad you're not in the military. I was looking forward to having a trusted contact. But diplomacy is fine."

"I'm not really a diplomat. I prefer engineering work. The Jump engines are amazing." Azariah didn't want her shaking her fist again, but he wanted to be clear on what she could expect.

"Engineering is useless and will kill you." She poked him in the arm with a finger.

"No! Look into it. Anyway, I'm hoping to get enough information to program an AI Jump." He whispered the last part.

"We don't have ships," she said automatically. But her eyes brighten. "Interesting. Good work. We don't have ships *yet*."

Azariah took a deep breath. This was happening. This wasn't playing strategy with my friends. Patroness Shelomith was a leader with off-world power and drive and focus. Many Paradisian leaders were implementing plans, and he had been delegated his part. Azariah felt capable of doing half of what she said. He looked out the window. Babylon was glowing blue-white, with the north pole jungle under them. He could pick out the capital canyon.

"How's Gospel doing?" Azariah asked.

"Mishael's estate has been blasted to pieces. The survivors are at Grid 16," she sighed, but stayed matter of fact. "The Rosefinch estate in Valla Varra hasn't been bombed at all, but no one may migrate there. My Zharqua cities are broken. Hananiah's estates are slowly falling apart; freezing natural elements are taking over areas that don't have proper residents to maintain infrastructure. Everything else is still destroyed, like when you were there."

They traded specific details, specific names, news about loved ones, anything about the Gospel and Revelation of John. Many little things that they couldn't share through their hidden communications. It was grim. Very grim. And somehow that was enough. That flipped the switch. Azariah finally saw his friends as like himself. Their nobility couldn't save their families, estates, or cities. They were as lost and empty-handed but moved forward anyway. His friends were slaves just as much as he was, and they knew it more deeply. They knew how to wear it better and assert their power—as God willed. Azariah ran his fingers over his buzz cut and regretted cutting it. He would wear a formal head covering for a while, perhaps.

"So you know the plan?"

"So that we may all prosper."

Chapter 20

Three hundred years ago was the height of the Achaemenid Empire. In order to solidify their power, this Empire systematically wiped out all Jumping technology in order to force all people, goods, and information through Gates, by which means the Achaemenid Empire could much more easily exert total control. Jumping from one solar system to the next was already fading out of fashion, and the Achaemenid Empire capitalized on that to destroy the technology. Rebel factions rose up in waves, proving that knowledge could never be erased. The Achaemenid Empire released an anti-Jump AI that learned to move from wiping electronic knowledge to recognizing the knowledge in paper books and erasing it, like burning down libraries, and then finally jumping into people's minds and giving aneurysms to anyone who had outlawed knowledge. The AI could ride in on light and radio waves, so in the end, if anyone knew how to Jump or if anyone had hidden a ship, they could survive only if they stayed in an isolated bubble. Many people started destroying Gates to keep themselves safe, some choosing and some rebel-terrorists making the choice for worlds. Even if the Jumping knowledge couldn't completely disappear, the ability to understand and wield it, to have leadership and initiative were gone.

In response to this total control, the last rebel-terrorist faction rose up two hundred years ago. They destroyed the last known store of Jump knowledge that the Achaemenid Empire had kept in reserve, and destroyed the Gates leading to hundreds of worlds, cutting the Achaemenid Empire into pieces, and causing its downfall as anyone could have predicted. As a consequence, those worlds were also cut off from the Achaemenid Empire and went from being an integral part of an empire to being totally isolated, as no one world was allowed the resources to build their own Gate or even be self-sufficient.

From the chaos rose the Chaldean Empire. Prosperity increased enough and the political fears of Jumping decreased enough that the anti-Jump AI was quarantined and neutered. People were finally able to build knowledge again without it disappearing. King Nabopolassar of the Chaldean Empire wanted to expand his empire and the best way seemed to Jump to these former Achaemenid worlds and claim them as his own, to gather them into the loving bosom of a much better empire. The best empire, even, as Daniel's vision had proved.

That first king managed to find twenty scraggly Jumpers, who against all odds had maintained twenty personal Jumping ships. He gave them full honor and treasure. He sent teams to find and study old manuals, other teams to study the twenty ships, and other teams to quiz the Jumpers who had been anointed with the title "astrologers." Dabu'us was the most famous and favorite.

Despite this work, Jumping continued to be unsafe, and the ships were lost. The Chaldeans had one bit of luck during the reign of King Nabopolassar: Jumping to the Paradisian solar system. One of the original ships successfully Jumped and built a Gate between Babylon and Paradise, defended it against the Aegyptians, and brought Gospel and Revelation into the loving bosom of the delighted king. This was how the Paradisian solar system became a colony of the Chaldean Empire.

The next time that same ship Jumped to build another Gate, it was lost. Around the time Daniel and his friends were born, the original twenty ships were down to five and the Chaldean Empire couldn't build replacements; the best way to not get lost was to not Jump. Nevertheless, the empire expansion plans were well on their way under King Nebuchadnezzar by the time Daniel and his friends were at Babylon.

Jumping technology improved while Azariah was getting his education; he helped build prototypes. Azariah's particular empire expansion project was to accomplish in twelve other solar systems exactly what was done to his home world.

Out of the hundreds of solar systems lost at the end of the Achaemenid Empire, twelve were chosen carefully. They would not have a strong military presence; they would not have fallen apart to the point that they would be a burden on the empire; they possibly had special qualities that would serve the empire. The empire could not in fact handle twelve more military expenditures like the Paradisian solar system. The king wanted easy prey, docile children, whatever phrase suited him for the day.

The king had wanted access to these worlds since he was a child, kicking at purple-white sand. He demanded ships to start Jumping immediately as new engines were designed and built. A few would Jump back with reports but those were small ships that couldn't carry materials to build Gates, and would eventually be lost, assuming something went wrong with a Jump—calibration, coordinates, something they didn't quite understand yet. The *Klipspringer* would be the second ship large enough to carry Gate supplies (the first was the one that Jumped to the Paradisian solar system) and the first of such a significant size that it could carry out a long *gerru* campaign. Other ships like it were also being built. The king didn't care too much if the *Klipspringer* was lost; there would be other chances soon after. This was another reason why the crew was based on merit—no one really wanted to pull a favor to get on this particular ship.

The king was sending the crew on a *gerru*. A *gerru* was his vague term for this endeavor—a military campaign, a religious procession, a royal road, a caravan. The *Klipspringer* with a crew of 256 people was only the first. Azariah's firsthand experience with the Jump engines gave him full confidence that the ship and the crew were capable of twelve successful Jumps. He didn't understand Daniel's fear on his behalf or how hard it was for Patroness Shelomith to put on a brave face, to send him to his death instead of kidnapping him and stowing him away somewhere safe.

Chapter 21: Azariah

My dear Daniel,

We are about to Jump for the first time!

I wanted to let you know that I do think of you often. I'm worried you'll keep to yourself too much. You should ask the king to send you on some spiritual tour of special worlds or something and take a friend with you, a real friend. A different kind of gerru.

Last night, one of the last things you said to me was how I had been a much better friend to you, that I've pushed and guided you and protected you more than anyone, more than you've done for me. I didn't have a chance to disagree and now I'm glad I can put this in writing so that you can't pretend you didn't hear or understand me correctly. Being with you is like being alone out in a wheat field, after I've turned off the video chat and I'm watching the stars come out. Surely you understand how important it is to have a friend where you can just exist as yourself. You have been an inexorable pressure on my spiritual and moral self. I wouldn't even know who I am without your prayers. I will think of you fondly as you suffer surrounded by luxury. We both have our burdens to bear.

Remember how I felt like a fish out of water when I first arrived on Babylon? The non-noble in a palace? It's happening again, but the other way around where I am the palace, with palace manners and a palace accent and I accidentally complained about the food once and I wear my headdress, so I just come off like a snob. I'm sure you're proud of me. One thing I'm truly looking forward to: I've never worked with propulsion engines, so I'm going to spend my free time with Professor Alejandra, or whatever I'm supposed to call her.

Jumping into a solar system is the beginning of a cycle. That's terminology that everyone is using now. Jumping away is the end of that cycle and the beginning of a new one. Twelve planets over four years means that we expect each cycle to last three months, mostly from traveling, like I've explained.

Only three months! We'll get to hear from each other every three months. That's not bad at all. You'll get a diary from me of about a hundred Babylon days each time.

Love much, Aza

Lughamstone, Sumer, Idmari.

Those were the names of the three solar systems that Patroness Shelomith thought would be friendly to the Paradisian cause based on records from two hundred years ago.

For now, it was time to focus on the *Klipspringer,* which was docked in the diplomatic-military space station node, and scheduled to leave at the end of the day, Babylonian time. *Klipspringer* was the most modern spaceship in existence, a sphere with perfect living conditions and an ultra-modern ring around it to create a Jump bubble. Azariah was late to check in, but they would not have left him behind.

As soon as Azariah boarded the spaceship, he went to the commissary and got a proper, formal turban appropriate to the gravitas of his position as king's envoy and exactly what Daniel and Patroness Shelomith would wish for him. Azariah also got everything else he needed from the commissary. The ship crew were allowed only very limited personal items, so Azariah brought only his disc and a couple blank ones.

He first stopped by his little office. He was one of five people who had their own private space. No one but the captain had individual sleeping quarters, so the office was his personal space. He turned on his disc to project a crucifix, which was a hologram work of art from Mishael; he made a canvas painting version for Daniel and a sculpture version for Hananiah.

Azariah put on his turban. That improved his mood. He felt like he could boss anyone around. He could talk to Captain Maria Sifontes Uzcategui and tell her he should always be at her right hand. The right turban was amazing, and he was going to grow his hair as fast as possible so he could stop wearing it.

Right outside Azariah's office was a large work room with a high-tech display table that could project a 3D model of the ship and maps of space using real-time data and processing. He shared this work room with the Jump team, a group of four people that were part of the Engineering section but had significant Jump-algorithm duties. They would write the Jump manual to make Jumping more safe as they figured that out. For now, the work room was empty.

Next stop was the dormitory area, meeting technicians along the way, and that's where Azariah found his colleagues. His assigned dormitory had three sets of bunk beds, with its own set of showers and toilets. The Jump team went silent when he entered the room.

"Hello, looks like I'm the last to arrive." Azariah nodded to Bounthavy, the space phenomena expert he had been curious to meet ahead of time.

"Hi! This is your bunk," someone said, patting a bed nearby. Their features were round and plain. Unlike Daniel, Azariah was usually comfortable assigning someone a gender right off the bat and then let them correct if needed, but this time he really couldn't tell. "You can choose top or bottom. Both are free. Because you are the special envoy, you won't have to share the bed."

"Thank you."

"Sure. I'm Sa'almaum, but you can call me Sal." They gave a half wave, half bow that was common for colonists.

"Nice to meet you." Azariah looked around. Everyone had the same haircut and was wearing the utilitarian uniform and looked very androgynous. But they were a range of shapes, sizes, height, skin color. It's not like he was going to get people mixed up. His friend Bounthavy was the oldest and smallest. The other trio were standing together at one bunk, including the person who pointed out his bunk.

"I'm Wamiri. You are the envoy, right? Azariah Ramzi?" asked a stout young woman with short wild curls and leaning on a beautifully carved cane with a second cane in their other hand.

"That is correct," Azariah said with a smile.

"Are you really an envoy? Have you really met the king? You seem too young to have diplomatic experience."

Ah yes, what his friends made him practice to assert his position. Azariah said in a flat tone, "I've dined personally with the king. I've attended six royal parties in the last month. The king required me to sit with astrologer Dabu'us every day at the dais during high royal court for the past week and his main spiritual advisor gave me an in-person blessing." He threw in that last one. Despite being the *king's* envoy, Azariah hadn't ever actually met him.

"What do you mean, at the dais?" asked a man about his own age and rangy, relaxed, and with brightly colored hair. "By the way, my name is Razumdingir but you can call me Din."

"Hi, Din. I sat at the right hand of the king. Honestly, it was very boring, though of course I'm honored and will do my best on the king's behalf." *Despite my age.* Azariah's diplomatic training told him to leave out the catty remark. "I know I'm not a part of the Jump team but I'm very interested in your work." Which was why he arranged to have their work room and his office right next to each other, and also made the dormitory arrangements, though that was in part because he didn't really want the large suite he was assigned and the cooking staff would otherwise have to sleep in the kitchen. They really were packed in. His bunk might have the only free bed.

"By the way, envoy," said Wamiri, "you may have noticed a few of us have mobility devices. I want to remind you that *we* are here on merit, no matter what visible or invisible defect might be keeping us from Babylon or the royal court. I hope this won't be a problem for you."

"I'm sure you have accounted for *all defects* and been assisted to the extent necessary in order for you to complete your duties," Azariah said, heading for the door. "I saw for myself that the king signed off on all the crew and I will certainly respect his wishes. It was great to meet everyone. I look forward to being roommates. I need to meet the rest of the crew now."

Down some hallways, Azariah found the executive meeting room where Captain Sifontes and communications officer were waiting for him.

"Captain. Ma'am," Azariah said, bowing to the captain and nodding to the comms officer, Brigitte Beck. Azariah was going to be stuck with a creepy lady for four years. He was pretty sure she wouldn't try to sit in his lap in front of the captain, who was former military and was going to run a tight ship. Azariah received a reminder of the general rules and his personal responsibilities. Beck kindly hinted to the captain that Azariah wouldn't flirt with any of the women, so wouldn't be disruptive in that particular way. Azariah refrained from commenting on Beck's comments about his sexuality. She was embarrassing herself enough. Both women faintly praised some of his skills and accomplishments. He kept his mouth shut and excused himself to Engineering.

Another walk through more hallways and stairs, meeting more techs doing last-minute checks.

Engineering, where the two beautiful engines were located, one for Jumping and one for propulsion in a solar system at 1.5 billion kilometers a month. Azariah had access to the floor, but not to any consoles or equipment. Yet. Looking and watching were enough for now. Eventually, he looked around at the people. The head of engineering had two people reporting to him, one for each of the engines; the propulsion engine leader was a former teacher, and the Jump engine leader Keo was who Azariah interned under. He had been so, so hopeful that he'd be stationed under her, but he didn't qualify. In his opinion, the person they chose, Noy whoever, was too cautious and she definitely hadn't memorized the hardware and software to the extent Azariah had. Noy was also in charge of the Jump team and he didn't envy her for that duty.

"Keo!" Azariah waved.

She walked over with a big smile and gave Azariah a hug. "Call me Engineer Lee for now, Envoy Ramzi. It seems like formality is important to Captain Sifontes Uzcategui and Walter is taking that to heart. Excuse me, Head Engineer Marxer. Make sure to stress the head part."

"Speaking of the captain, I asked her for a favor right away—if I could be in Engineering for the first Jump, just as an observer."

"We are always happy to accommodate the captain. I'll arrange it with Marxer."

After introducing himself to as many people as he could find, and after the ship had broke from the space station, he went to his office and wrote one last letter to Daniel before they Jumped and wouldn't have a way to communicate until they built and opened the Gate. *Dear Daniel, This Jump will be the easiest. We have made this Jump there and back home. The planet just doesn't have a Gate yet. Love, Aza.*

He attended to his other duties and then spent time in Engineering. An hour before the Jump, it was time to get into place and put on space suits just in case something went wrong.

All the engineers and technicians were at their stations. Azariah stayed out of the way near the door and watched the complicated little dance. They checked the engineering table one last time; it was lit up with all possible quantum paths *Klipspringer* could take, and then the computer started erasing dangerous paths. The computer identified several safe paths; this is where the Jumping team came in. Wamiri and Din were present. This was why Jumping was considered an art form because how did you choose what path? How could you be certain that you fed the computer the correct data? This particular Jump to the solar system named Ecbatana-Hamadan was easy because they could compare what the computer identified as safe with prior Jumps that had been successful.

After the last minute check, Engineering turned off all electricity in the ship, including propulsion and gravity. The propulsion engine went silent as Azariah felt himself floating. He grabbed onto a handhold. There were plenty of bars as part of the molding on the walls and ceiling, and hand holds that could pop out of the floor if necessary. The crew confirmed the momentum of the ship, making sure they knew exactly where *Klipspringer* was down to the nanometer, in reference to the Eye of the Milky Way.

Keo ignited the Jump engine at the Bridge's signal. Engineering was at the very bottom of the ship. The Jump engine had a ring going all the way around the spaceship, like a stripe on a ball. The ring was embedded in the floor of the engineering room and started to pulse and glow with a bright white light five feet wide.

A Jump moved everything in the bubble from one physical point to the next. The ship didn't move through physical space, but forces, such as those from black holes, would disrupt the bubble if the quantum path took the ship too close. There were an infinite number of quantum paths between two points. For a long time, as the empire was re-creating the technology, they couldn't choose the quantum path, which is what made Jumping dangerous. While most of physical space was empty, the way quantum properties and forces interacted beyond physical space meant that it was pretty likely that the quantum bubble would be ripped apart. That's what they assumed happened, based on theory, and that no lost ship ever returned. The breakthrough: they were finally able to choose the Jump path. They could choose the safe, empty space route. They had the theory and the technology, and the *Klipspringer* was the first ship with both.

They Jumped.

According to everyone but Azariah, this was a successful Jump. That was dramatic.

Engineering performed the initial scan. *Klipspringer* was in the correct place. Everyone cheered. Gravity was turned back on and Alejandra's team got propulsion going. They were at the edge of the solar system. They would travel for three months to get to the populated inner planet where they would set up the Gate in their orbit.

Why was Azariah concerned? *Klipspringer* technically didn't land in the correct place—it was two meters off where they expected to be. They Jumped such a huge distance and two meters was too much for

Azariah? Yes. Two meters might seem like an incredibly small amount compared to the number of meters *Klipspringer* Jumped but it wasn't infinitesimally small, which meant something happened. And next time something happened, it might be worse.

What did "two meters off" mean? The heart of the Jump engine had a very small calibration point that was aimed at a specific point *Klipspringer* was Jumping to. The two points were expected to line up exactly at the end of the Jump. Their ability to measure, calibrate, and move made that possible. To Azariah, either they did it right, or they did it wrong and were lucky to be alive. The only definition of doing it right was for those two points to overlap. Why didn't they overlap? It bothered a couple of other people too, but at the moment, the celebration of being alive took over. As the ship sailed for the Ecbatana planet, that was the question Azariah asked over and over, with various amounts of support. Keo was worried too, but had her attention divided in different ways. She gave Azariah permission to poke around. Noy brushed him off completely. She had a different theory about the calibration points, which was wrong, so there's no point in explaining it.

After a month full of lengthy letters to Daniel about "why didn't the two calibration points overlap?" and explaining in detail everything Azariah thought of and recounting every conversation, Beck told him to do his actual duties; she depended on him for languages. He buckled down. Time to learn how to make friends with people who the king was probably going to bomb in a couple of months. He wrote a letter to Daniel about his feelings about this.

Just to move forward, they built the Gate successfully, sent their mail and reports through, got mail in return, and then Jumped away immediately.

Again, the calibration points were off—this time by three meters.

"Why didn't the two calibration points overlap? Why did this happen again?" The engineering team was useless; it wasn't a mechanical problem as far as anyone could tell.

So if it wasn't a hardware problem, it was a software problem. This was where the Jump team came in, perfecting everything, watching over everything, all of them truly masters. Were the equations good? Were the numbers good? Was the theory correct? Who can double check? If Azariah's question was "why," then they knew how to break that question into pieces.

It was Noy's job to manage and direct this team. She saw it more like personnel management—get them to act as a team—instead of directing them to solve problems. Not to be too hard on Noy. She was good at the front-end implementation, not the back-end clean up and analysis. She trusted the Jump team fully, which is cool. Azariah was gracious.

And he couldn't blame her or anyone else. He could see how it felt like they had finally made Jumping safe. They were within "parameters" which was a bunch of bullshit, sorry, because no one knew yet what safety margins were, but engineering leadership was happy except for Keo, and that's probably because Azariah would sit next to her at each meal and talk her ear off.

Once she got sick of him, he started talking to the Jump team. He was making friends with the cook, Conceição, and got her to give him some special treats and something besides tea to drink. He had picked up over the last five months what everyone liked. Once they were well fed and comparatively quiet, he asked them his question, "Why don't the two calibration points overlap?"

"Yeah, we know you want to know," Wamiri said, crossing her arms.

"This is the first time you're actually asking us," Sal said, steepling their fingers.

"I bothered Keo and now I'm bothering you! I obviously didn't forget you." Azariah pulled apart one of the last bappiru.

"You're skipping over Noy," Wamiri insisted.

"Yes." Azariah replied. "She and I have different theories on Jumping, have you heard that? What theories do all of you have?"

"We do not have a group mind decision on that at this point," Sal said, glaring at Wamiri before she could answer.

"We don't need to." Din leaned on Sal for a moment and then straightened. "We can write the manual without references to theories."

Terrible manual, in my opinion. Azariah almost said that out loud.

"Aren't you just the envoy?" Sal asked. "Maybe your question about the calibration points doesn't have any merit."

"Speaking of merit, we're the ones here on merit." Wamiri said. It's like she had to get a dig at Azariah every chance she got. "You're the only person actually appointed by the king instead of getting here on merit."

"That doesn't invalidate my question! So what if I'm not the best suited to answer the question? I can still ask. You might be the best suited to answer. Do you really think this is invalid, or is there another reason you don't want to try to problem solve?" He had a very hard time addressing the group as a whole, but if he tried to take one or two people who were on his side and separate them and, like, pit the group against each other, he would get in trouble. "I'm not your boss. I'm just asking. And I'd be happy to help problem solve. I can bring more snacks. Okay, I'll go prep for Lughamstone. See ya at dinner." Azariah left the Jump work room to go exercise.

He had planted that seed the best he could.

Chapter 22: Nebuchadnezzar

I'm pacing back and forth, back and forth. Back and forth. Back. And. Forth.

I'm on the best military ship, the *Dakaku*, the best anyone has ever seen. I heard the Aegyptians saw pictures of my ship and were like, amazing, that guy knows how to be an emperor. I didn't say that, but it's a good ship.

As stupendous as this ship is, it's in the wrong place and it's having a hard time getting to the right place. I'm at the Gate waiting for the Gate on the other side to finish so I can go through already. Why is it that Azariah's ship got there so easily but my ship, which is the best, isn't there?

"Why is Azariah's ship taking so long?"

"Your Majesty," said General Hammu, "while Azariah is your representative, the captain of the *Klipspringer* is Captain Sifontes Uzcategui. Azariah is a slave and can't own any ship or give any orders."

"I could give him a ship. Saying he can't own a ship overlooks my goodwill and power, and what my possible wishes are." I kicked over a chair. "This blasted Ecbatana-Hamadan! How dare they destroy their Gate! How dare they cut themselves off from the benefice of the greatest empire to have ever existed? They are doing just as they please, even if it hurts me, hurts the galaxy, just as Azariah is challenging me. I'm sure this delay is because he doesn't wish for me to take control of a planet the way I took control of Gospel. The entire ship is following him, I'm sure."

"Your Majesty," Erioch interrupted me. I ignored him.

"I will make him and all on that ship prove themselves. Have no worry. I will make that planet bow and I will make all citizens of all planets bow. Doesn't Daniel's creator God say something like that? Why don't you draft up some possible assassination plots for me please? As a kind favor?"

"Your Majesty," said Erioch, not answering my requests for now, "I have received a report from Babylon regarding Daniel."

"Ah yes, the proof he is rising up against me from inside the palace, just as Azariah is against me from within my own ship."

"No, in fact, the report shows he is not rising against you; the communique to his mother was entirely innocent. He has made new friends, but there is no change in the balance of power. The advisors and courtiers all think of him as they have been. Surveillance footage —"

"How dare you say no to me? Fine, fine. Now tell me, have the golden Ophir asteroids from Paradise been moved? What's the gold import level at right now? What about those artists? Perhaps I will let this planet worship me properly."

"We have a signal, your Majesty," the captain said.

"Excellent, take us through," I said.

After a few moments we finally went through the Gate. I graciously allowed the captain to take over. Oshpenaz guided me to the viewing room, only us, Hammu-Rapi and Erioch.

"I want to talk to that ship, and I want to see the planet. I want to see all the mail they're going to want to send through. I want to find out what the top five largest cities are and bomb them flat and then we'll talk with the rest about why they destroyed their Gate. And fire on any space stations or inhabited moons on our way in."

"Yes, Your Majesty," Hammu-Rapi bowed.

"The *Klipspringer* will Jump in a half hour if it pleases you," Erioch said. "They stay only to receive mail and parts for the next Gate. Did you have any questions for them?"

"No." For the moment, I was quite, quite pleased. We would force civilization on people, and they would worship me for my bounty. Their very own Gate! At their doorstep! I was the one to make this possible; I was the one to say that non-Gate Jumps were still possible; I was the one to choose who would take the risk for the first tentative Jumps, and who would lead in the first big ship. Their success was mine; Azariah's success, as my slave, was even more mine, as was all the nobility.

"Erioch, I know you favor Daniel. Tell me more about this report."

He came over and found a certain part of the report. "As you can see, we put him to the test. He passed with flying colors."

"You gave him the true locations of all twelve planets! If you had been wrong, this is very sensitive information," I huffed.

He raised an eyebrow. "I trust our containment measures."

"Now, about the plans I mentioned earlier."

Chapter 23: Azariah, Lughamstone

The second solar system on their *gerru* was Lughamstone, the first planet on Patroness Shelomith's list of planets to watch out for. Azariah needed to keep his head down and look for opportunities.

Klipspringer Jumped to the outer edge of the solar system, still the same two meters off, and set sail for the inner planet. The crew deployed a one-percent scanning-communications drone. One percent of the speed of light was fast enough to get the data *Klipspringer* needed before arriving at the planet. For instance, if the solar system had more weapons than expected, the crew would just hold tight, build the Gate right where they stopped even if it was still months from the planet, and let the Chaldean empire know before Jumping again. Prepping for the next Jump was always a priority, so that *Klipspringer* could get out of the system as soon as possible if needed.

Azariah got to know the propulsion engine better and how the one-percent drones worked. Alejandra, the perfect instructor, took one apart for him. He made friends with the Jump team the best he could. They were the only ones to see Azariah without his turban and one of them, Sal, helped Azariah keep his hair cut tidily so that it didn't look like just a grown out buzz cut. Azariah and the team shared the 3D table in the workroom, and he overheard them when they wanted to take a break from the Jump manual. Azariah held his breath, hoping they'd be interested in his question about why the ship Jumped two meters off. But no. The first data from the drone was coming back, and the team decided they should build a Dyson sphere or swarm out of an iron moon. Eccentric.

A Dyson sphere was a perfect infrastructure project. Azariah would have been delighted and excited to work on it, but his other responsibilities called him away.

* * *

Lughamstone acknowledged they still knew the old Achaemenid Empire language, Elamite, which, big surprise, Oshpenaz had insisted Azariah learn. The planet also had their own language and sent information along. Azariah would keep half an eye on the Dyson sphere, half an eye on the Jump info, and an eye on learning a new language.

Soon enough, *Klipspringer* passed the iron moon and the space stations. At the edge of the planet's gravity well, the *Klipspringer* dropped off *Phidippus* with Captain Sifontes, Beck, and Azariah, with a couple of protection officers, and then headed back to where it would construct the Gate.

The little ship lowered itself into the atmosphere at the sunrise mark. Azariah looked through layers of fog filled with the roars of their fighting birds and reptiles. Once *Phidippus* landed, they met with the officials appointed hastily to be the chief representatives of the planet. An entire room of reps for all the different states was waiting for them. Colonists had settled the world five hundred years ago, so not quite enough time to colonize all of it, especially when cut off from empire resources for two hundred of those years.

The Lughamstone clothing and furnishings were of dingy colors and voluminous materials showing wealth, with anything electric rare and on display, like a physical touch screen strapped to the outside of an upper arm or a portable computer in a transparent case. The reps spoke in a subdued manner. Captain Sifontes did *not* have a "we're here to take over, here's the tax you have to pay" speech but a "greetings, how can we mutually benefit each other" speech; people relaxed a little. Azariah had studied this planet and while there were some basic, boring reasons why the king *said* he chose the planet, he would not make a basic, boring decision. The bird and reptile fights were supposed to be special, which were not to be confused with the bird races of Umm el-Marra.

Azariah wanted to know more about the fights to see if he was right about the king and he needed to know more about the world for Patroness Shelomith, both of whom he honored in all things, of course.

First step: talk to people. After the speeches, Azariah turned to a representative named Leander Prudence Windlass in a gray boring jacket with pale hair the color of the fog. Azariah flashed him a smile and started happily tripping over awkward words. They had to speak a little loudly because of all the animal chittering and roars in the background. Azariah hadn't seen any animals yet but was getting a feel for them.

"It is a great honor to be your guests. Thank you for having us."

"Verily, your appearance surprised all our factions because we don't have a Gate."

"Understandable."

"Your appearance is also unsurprising since obviously someone would check what happened to our Gate."

"Also understandable." Lughamstone was one of those cultures with complicated double speak, garnished with gloominess. "Dost thou dine with me and my comrades this night?"

"Nay, but I must introduce you to those who may."

"That is of most excellence, I thank you."

An especially loud roar shook the glass windows, like something could be right outside the building. Azariah looked aghast at Leander, who gave him a big grin.

"Thou shalt see a sight this night after sup."

Azariah nodded politely, tamping down the visceral fear that the roar had woken up. It was still quite early in the morning, so if he was going to hear roars like that all day, he needed to get used to it.

Captain Sifontes and Beck were handling more sensitive topics. Azariah was supposed to chit-chat and make a good impression and represent the king to the best of his ability. He made note of any pet animals for the king to be displeased about. Attendants in sleek outfits led animals around that looked like a cross between porcupines and dogs. The meeting hall had a hundred-foot-high ceiling with reptiles of all sorts carved into the concrete walls, with strips of neon lighting filling the carved grooves. A yellow alligator was on one wall, a brown pterodactyl on another, and a blue lizard with a long tail that curled around carved plants.

The time went by nicely enough. Before long, it was time to move on for lunch. The Lughamstone citizens were proud to drive the *Klipspringer* group through the city. It was all very gray, brown, neon, and Gothic.

The entourage arrived at their lunch destination, the dining room of a resort hotel balcony with eery, beautiful views into the layers of fog. Leander notified the *Klipspringer* group ahead of time that they would be meeting with some special people. So far, they had met the basic power players, political, economical, and all the people that get attached to them.

"We wish for your spiritual edification," Leander said with a flourish. "It is our duty to present God to the emperor. At least, that is how some people on this planet view it."

Azariah followed the captain and Beck politely.

Leander introduced them one by one to a line of people, the last of whom was the most beautiful woman Azariah had ever seen. She had long curly hair, a black satin dress with a full skirt, which was richer than anyone else's. She reminded Azariah of Daniel, so he wasn't surprised when Leander introduced her as a priestess.

"It is a pleasure to meet you, Envoy Ramzi. I am Priestess Wilhelmina Justice Cholmondeley," she said serenely, holding out a hand bare of ornamentation except a ruffled sleeve.

"It would honor the Chaldean empire to have a *pasisatum* such as yourself." Azariah bent over her hand and kissed the back. She snatched her hand away.

Whoops.

While no one, including the priestess, *said* anything, there were all sorts of looks and poking, and Beck glaring at him. As they walked from the atrium to the balcony with the tables, there was some bustle. Leander whispered that there were some last-minute seating changes, so Azariah wouldn't be seated next to the priestess. Azariah was mortified, but the best thing he could do was to stay quiet and collected.

Azariah sat near the middle of the long table. Unfortunately for everyone, he was still an honored guest, so it wasn't like they could banish him to the end of the table. But they did surround him with old men, which was kind of funny, honestly. One older, handsome man introduced himself as Colonel Enoch Temperance Askew and chatted with him about geography and geology. This seemed safe enough.

"I've heard it said that the king likes gold," the colonel said.

"Verily it is true. To the king and gold!" Azariah raised his cup of tea. "If you desire to present a gift to the king, gold is always welcomed indeed."

"What do you say to this?" The colonel drew a device out of his pocket and showed it to Azariah.

"This looks like a watch," Azariah said, running a fingertip over the smooth surface.

"It is more than that, but I ask about the presentation of the gold."

"The etching design of the gold is beautiful." Azariah asked a few questions about their process.

"I say unto you, you are most knowledgeable about an art that is truly an unknown art here," the colonel smiled.

"Thank you. I grew up with the Ophir gold asteroids right in my backyard, so it's hard to not know a little, but nothing compared to a genuine artist."

"Gold asteroids?"

"Ah, yes, they've always been famous to me, but they are brand new to the empire." Azariah explained about how much gold his home solar system had, how Paradisians had melted a couple down and paved the streets of Otero Linda, but that was very special. No one else ever did that. Gold was rare in plenty of parts of the empire.

"But truly, you could do that and still have asteroids of gold left over?"

"Indeed, indeed. But it's not just about the quantity. If your world has special artistic skills, that would be invaluable to the king. I say this in my office as the king's envoy."

"Thank you kindly," the colonel nodded his head and abruptly turned to talk to his other neighbor.

Azariah wasn't sure what had put him off. He had enjoyed talking about home for a moment, and that was something Patroness Shelomith had told him to do. He turned to speak to the gentleman on his other side, who wore a top hat and a glass eye that had projection technology. They spoke about hats, cloth, and mustaches for a minute and then he bowed his head to Azariah respectfully and made some kind of farewell gesture.

Azariah just enjoyed his food for a bit. It was mushy and flavorless, some kind of tuber, but altogether different from ship food. Not that ship food was ever bad. The tea was mushroom-earthy, which felt comforting.

"Envoy Azariah Ramzi, please come this way." Beck was hissing at him from behind, her lips close to his ear. He flinched away. Yuck. He wiped his ear and got up to join Beck, who looked pissed off. The captain stood nearby consulting a report, her usual stern mien in place, the protection officers out of earshot. Azariah looked around and noticed quite a few of the people were leaving, their food half eaten.

Azariah looked expectantly at the women.

"We have decided to send you back to the ship," Beck said. The captain joined them but stayed quiet.

"What! No!" Azariah said. "Please, I really want to stay. What happened?" Besides the priestess, apparently.

Beck answered with a sneer. "Your little story about the Ophir asteroids is getting around and tanking the price of gold which their economy is based on, so everything is crashing. It's breaking down supply chains for reptile food immediately."

"I caught myself! I then made sure to emphasize that gold has a lot of worth to the king and that they had artistic skills that would be invaluable! I wasn't even lying!"

"They don't believe that part!" Beck hissed at him. Azariah was aiming his remarks at the captain. She listened but let Beck do all the speaking.

"This feels like a set up, right?" Azariah asked. "I bet anything we say could have been twisted into a disaster, if that's what someone was looking for."

"No! You do not understand diplomacy. How could you have been trained by the Etemenanki palace?" Beck said, swiping her hand as if that would remove him.

"The damage is done, and I'm sorry for my part. Can I stay the rest of the day at least?"

"No!"

"I really wanted to see the dinosaurs!" He should have waited until tomorrow.

"You child." Beck sneered again.

Here the captain smiled the tiniest bit and said, "They aren't dinosaurs. You'll just have to come back in the future. Perhaps by the time the *Klipspringer's gerru* is over, there will be reptile fights on Babylon. This will just have to be a learning lesson; I was keeping an eye on you and you should have been suspicious about why he was showing you the watch. Take the shuttle back to the *Klipspringer* and have Park Haet Bit bring it back." She was second to Beck.

"I obey you in all things, Captain Sifontes." Azariah bowed respectfully. "But I do have one request, that you take pictures if you see any dinosaurs."

His Lughamstone adventure was over. *For now.* Azariah looked towards the roars. Hopefully, they didn't get too hungry.

Chapter 24: Azariah

Azariah was in timeout for the rest of the Lughamstone cycle. He wrote his public report with many favorable details for the king, more than might have been expected from an envoy, with the intention that Patroness Shelomith would find the details she needed.

Azariah found plenty of other things to do, such as planning birthday parties. The ship didn't have a fun time coordinator, but it made sense for the envoy to figure something out. He could be an envoy to all the cultures represented on *Klipspringer*. The crew had different preferences; some loud and colorful, some like a tea ceremony. As he planned a party, he got to know the person—eight months in and he knew everyone on the ship. Azariah knew what it was like to be away from home and he saw that reflected in the crew, who were all talented people in disfavor with the empire.

Klipspringer crew prepped the Jump to the third solar system named Old Taxila, where they expected to find a working Gate that led to the small Sheba Empire. Two hundred years ago, a Sheba military population had an outpost on an Old Taxila ice planet. There were stories that one of Sheba's planets had a Gate connecting to the greater galaxy. The king was confident in his strength enough to open his empire to the risk of new connections. Indeed, their success so far was proof of the empire's manifest destiny. *Klipspringer* wasn't sticking around to explore the Sheba Empire; they would still Jump down the Sagittarius Arm once the Gate to Babylon was built. If the Sheba Empire was still active, other ships and people from the Chaldean Empire would deal with them.

Klipspringer Jumped to Old Taxila. The calibration points were three *kilometers* off! People in Engineering did not cheer as loudly. Keo finally prioritized this and immediately ordered Noy to order the Jump team to focus on solving what happened before planning the next Jump.

Once Azariah and the Jump team were out of their spacesuits, Azariah was hanging out on the edge of the Jump team in the shared work room.

"Let's be thorough, team," Wamiri said, sitting in a chair and clapping her hands together. "While it's not like we have a hard deadline—"

"If we can't solve this by the time we reach the planet," Din broke in, "we risk executive staff sticking their noses into the Jumping business and making decisions."

"So yeah." Wamiri nodded aggressively, "three months is a hard deadline." She stared at Azariah until he went into his office.

Azariah was still persona non grata among his immediate group. The Jump team turned inward and didn't want outside interference. Wamiri glaring at him was the last contact he had with the Jump team as far as Jump business went.

This whole situation was dangerous. It felt like they were on the cusp of finding out why no one made it back home. Azariah wanted to figure this out himself, but it was out of his control. The Jump team was smart enough that he decided to just leave the matter in their hands.

Once Azariah put those concerns aside, he focussed on his assigned duties: *Klipspringer* contacted the guard on Old Taxila who was welcoming enough, so they started a three-month journey to travel across the solar system to set up a Gate. Azariah wondered if in-system Jumping would ever be possible. In the meantime, Old Taxila's dominant language was tonal, so he worked with communications officer Park Haet Bit.

Soon enough, *Klipspringer* arrived at an icy, snowy planet with only a thin strip of habitable area. Beck didn't want Azariah to go down at all, but it would be too big of an insult for the king's envoy to snub any new acquaintances. Captain Sifontes decided Azariah would go down for the basic duties and then go back up to the ship. So that's what he did; greeted everyone, handed out gifts, received gifts, and then left before any proper conversation or policy discussion started.

When Azariah got back, Engineering and the Jump team felt like they had solved the problem, that it had been a hardware calibration problem and also that the Jump team had provided incorrect information on the last Jump.

The Jump team moved on, starting the Jump preparation process so that *Klipspringer* would be ready to Jump once the Gate was complete.

Azariah's space phenomena friend, Bounthavy, was depressed. He thought at first that the stress had gotten to her. He made sure she ate and slept and walked around the ship with him, but she was still depressed.

"My dear *ummasu*, please tell me what's going on." Azariah swung an arm around Bounthavy's shoulders for a hug as they walked down a wide leisure corridor that was lined with plants and art. Azariah did not like his friend in this state. She was still working fine with the team, so no one else worried about her mood. No one thought enough about her, in Azariah's opinion. He pulled her arm into his; leaning against him while they walked would be as good a support as the walking stick she used. "You're depressed because of the last Jump, right?"

"Not depressed. Guilty. But I shouldn't feel guilty. There were plenty of safeguards, even if I made a mistake. If we were three kilometers off, then it's all of our fault."

"So why isn't that good enough for you? I know you're completely reasonable."

"As the expert on space phenomena, I take measurements and provide data. I'm sure that it was my data that caused the error. The rest of the team agrees, but I don't understand why. But analysis and quality assurance are other people's jobs, mostly Wamiri and Din. So I just walk with you and say why, why, why with each step." She gently knocked her head against his shoulder.

"Tell me more about the error."

"So Jumping is like riding all the rapids of a river in the same instant —"

"No metaphors, please. You know I know what you do. I can handle the math."

In short, she measured, among other things, gravitational waves, which could emanate from different space phenomena.

"Black holes are important ones. They are like trash compactors that dump into dimensional—"

"Again, no metaphors. Let's hear the math."

Bounthavy's history: over the course of the last five decades, she had traveled to most of the solar systems connected by Gates and taken measurements of all sorts of space phenomena. This included using a high-tech interferometer to measure gravitational waves. She had the best real time map of how all the gravitational waves of the galaxy were constantly rippling out and colliding with other waves. Universities and research centers had certified her map, the most important being the Urartu Star Cloud University. She was the master. In recent decades, her knowledge had become invaluable because of how it related to Jumping.

"I took measurements while in the first two systems we Jumped to. I updated my map significantly. Using that information, I was, in fact, able to model a Jump where your two calibration points overlapped."

"You remembered my question! And you answered it! That's fantastic!" Azariah crouched down so he could give her a proper hug.

"No, no, you move too fast. I provided data for the third Jump, and something went wrong. My data wasn't correct, and that's why we were so far off. Even though I was able to model perfect Jumps, it didn't work like that in real life. I ruined it. I could have landed us somewhere dangerous."

"I don't believe it. *You* don't believe it, otherwise you could come to terms with your guilt."

"If I could see the mistakes for myself…. This team, it's funny how sometimes everything is shared and also how sometimes things are so fragmented."

Azariah gave his friend another hug. She was an example of someone who got onto the ship because of pure merit and knowledge. She was the opposite of ambitious or assertive.

"So you want to go over the numbers for yourself?"

"And in a perfect galaxy, take some more measurements with my interferometer. Alas, I am destined to be quiet."

"Let's change our walking route." Azariah steered her to the doctor's office.

"Ah! Excellent! Patients!" Doctor Parivrajaka ran over to them. "No one on this ship gets sick enough. I've never been able to devote myself to my research so thoroughly." They sighed. "I should be happier. What can I do for you? Did you have a stroke?"

"My friend here is feeling depressed and fatigued. She needs a quiet place to rest for about a week."

"Indeed, and is your friend so weak as to be unable to speak for herself?"

"Honestly, I want her to do some work for me and she can't when she's in the Jump work room. I think a change of scenery would be good for her."

The doctor's face went through several emotional changes. For some unknown reason, they didn't like the other three members of the Jump team. Because of that, Azariah thought they might be amenable to sheltering Bounthavy. The doctor took Bounthavy's arm and led her to a back room with a nice bed, meant for long-term patients.

"What do you need?" Azariah asked, following them.

Bounthavy flinched a little. He coaxed a list out of her and ran off.

First stop, Engineering to talk to a friend. Azariah ran down a hallway and found him alone, sitting cross-legged on the floor and reaching into the wall, having taken off some wall paneling to access the Jump ring for maintenance.

"Hey Kilzan, I have a favor to ask. Well, a future favor. I might need you to do something for me in a week, and if you do it, I'll give you a kiss."

Kilzan Rincones flushed bright red and threw his screwdriver at Azariah. "Nitati is my boyfriend. You can't go around saying stuff like that to me."

"Well, you should stop turning red, and then I'll stop teasing you." Azariah caught the screwdriver and gently tossed it back. Azariah and Nitati had stayed friends after their first Babylonian party, and Azariah had introduced him to all kinds of *kiskattum* people. Nitati's family was so upset about him falling in love with Kilzan, a commoner, that they got Kilzan stuck on this *gerru*. A chance to earn his honor or die.

"Seriously, what's going on?"

Azariah explained what he wanted.

Kilzan groaned. "If we weren't both in love with other people, I'd absolutely demand a kiss as payment. Are you serious?"

"Yes, tell me now. If you don't have the nerve, I need to find someone else. You're the first person I'm asking for the record."

"Fine. I mean, what are they going to do, kick me off the death ship if we don't Jump on time? Oh *no*, not that."

"I wouldn't ask if I thought that was a possibility." Azariah gave him a look. The king was clear on how he'd punish anyone who didn't want the glorious purpose of serving on the *Klipspringer*.

"You and your confidence," Kilzan called after him as he rushed off to his next stop.

"This isn't a death ship!" Azariah called back and ran off to the working room to get Bounthavy's equipment and master map. Sal was there. They were pretty chill, so Azariah told them what was going on and that the doctor would not allow much visiting.

"Did you need my assistance?"

"Well, Bounthavy also needs stuff from our dorm. Would you want to carry this stuff or do that?"

"I think out of the two of us, Bounthavy would prefer for me to poke through her personal items."

Azariah handed the items over to the doctor, who wouldn't let even him back to see her, in order to be consistent and not favor him. They exchanged looks; Azariah obviously owed them one now.

Bounthavy had four days.

Captain Sifontes would be back from the planet and would expect to Jump within an hour of arriving. So Azariah had a very narrow window in which to get this done, but if Bounthavy would come through, he knew he could do it.

Chapter 25: Azariah

Bounthavy: *I figured it out. Long story short, they replaced my most up-to-date, accurate data with data off one of my old maps.*

Azariah: *Excellent! Thank you. Please get ready to explain this in person to someone.*

Bounthavy: *I'd rather tell you and then you tell people.*

Azariah: *No. You are the most qualified. You can't be a scared* arnaba *rabbit for the whole* gerru.

Bounthavy: *Will you be there with me?*

Azariah: *Of course! Wouldn't miss it for the galaxy.*

While messaging Bounthavy, Azariah was running off to the shuttle bay to intercept Captain Sifontes.

He made it and was on time to bow as the captain exited *Phidippus* wearing a very rich, beautiful gray cloak and a fuzzy ushanka. He was out of breath. So embarrassing.

"Captain, it's a pleasure to see you back safely from the trip. That is quite a nice winter outfit. I wish I could have seen more snow. Make a snow angel."

She gave Azariah a *look,* which she gave him all the time and meant *you talk too much.*

"I request an immediate meeting," Azariah said in a firm Daniel voice with his own look that threatened to pull Envoy status.

The captain raised an eyebrow and nodded, inviting him to her office. Azariah nodded in reply and walked next to her.

He messaged Kilzan. *Hey, grab Bounthavy and bring her to the captain's office.*

Kilzan: *Order confirmed. The hour countdown to Jumping has started.*

Azariah: *Good thing I have you.*

Kilzan: *Alert Doctor P. so I don't have to fight with them about stealing*

161

Bounthavy away.

Azariah did so.

He and the captain arrived at her office. It was a level immediately above the Jump work room, the same shape and size. She had her own 3D table and a tea table instead of personal workstations, the walls decorated with silk tapestries embroidered with antelope in honor of *Klipspringer*. Her desk was in the same area as Azariah's desk, which drove home his status. Suddenly, he wished he had spent more time on the planet instead of sulking. But no, he needed to be here to support Bounthavy.

Azariah sat and began a simple tea service, setting four places, as Captain Sifontes settled in. This tea service was a creamy golden color with thick plates. He was nervous—about Jumping, about Bounthavy being convincing, about being with the captain alone, about his responsibilities that he didn't fully comprehend.

The other two arrived and sat to tea. Bounthavy handed each a physical printout. Azariah skimmed through the first few pages. It explained what she found. The first pages were so full of math that he didn't blame the other two for setting the printouts aside.

"My dear Bounthavy, I hope you are feeling better," the captain said.

Bounthavy flushed. "You are too kind, Maria. But as you may know, while my spirits were low, I was isolated in order to work on a project alone at Envoy Ramzi's request."

The captain sipped her tea.

Bounthavy took a deep breath, walked over to the 3D table. She displayed the three Jump paths *Klipspringer* had taken so far and also gravitational waves which started as concentric circles around objects; as the circles spread out, they interacted and created patterns that were pretty to look at.

"My apologies for the orthographic projection. It's too mathematically simple, but it's a good start for this explanation. Here are the algorithm parts in question. The data I provide compensates for the shear transformation to the path of the quantum bubble because of gravitational waves from nearby stars, black holes, and other phenomena. My apologies, but I've never liked the word Jump. Path isn't better, though. And *shear* has greater meaning within this context. Sorry, I'm jumping around now, no sorry, I didn't mean that pun…"

It was Azariah's duty for now to watch. The captain and scientist were two small older women with gray buzz cuts, and yet they were so different. While Bounthavy's hesitant manner differed from the captain's straightforward manner, the captain respected and was listening intently.

Despite this, Bounthavy wavered more as she explained her mistake, or what she initially thought had caused the three-kilometer discrepancy. She looked at Azariah for strength and he nodded encouragingly.

"I think I found the real error. However, it hasn't been reviewed by anyone yet. I'm uncomfortable with presenting this, but I understand we are under a pressing deadline." She gave Azariah a pleading look.

He completely trusted her. He completely believed he could read her printout and agree with everything. The captain noticed this and indicated that he should take over the presentation.

Azariah smiled at his little audience. "I believe Bounthavy has proven to our satisfaction that once she had more up-to-date scans of this part of the galaxy, she could retroactively predict the correct Jump path to greater accuracy. She then supplied data for the third Jump. As you can see, if you dig enough into the equations, *this* is the data she reported for the third Jump, but the Jump team QA and Engineering used *other* old data. The decision to use the old data was made because of a quality assurance argument over a negative sign, and concern over using a different map than the Urartu Star Cloud University certified gravitational wave map. Bounthavy didn't know any of this until she studied in private. Her new data predicted a more accurate Jump; while it is understandable that QA and Engineering want to use a certified map instead of untested, unverifiable data, this is in fact the reason why Bounthavy is here, appointed by the king." Azariah had been summarizing so far but added that last as his own commentary. He flipped to the next page. "Bounthavy believes that if Engineering uses her old data, we will Jump into the solar system's sun." Azariah looked at her aghast and shook the printout at her. "This is information you lead with! Is anyone else aware of this?! Oh wait, this report says they are aware but calculate the risk differently and believe the risk is within acceptable *parameters*," he sneered at the printout and smiled at Bounthavy. "Your new data can predict with greater certainty. Have you not mentioned this to Keo at all in the last three months?"

"I told Noy."

"Surely you believe Bounthavy, Captain Sifontes. This is why I'm coming to you, so you can order them to use her data!"

"How do you know it's just this one thing?" The captain asked. "There's a hundred things that go into a Jump."

Bounthavy's voice wavered a little. "I know my part. I know when my part of the algorithm is in harmony with the rest, but I'm not supposed to have confidence until it's verified. The information has been sent through the open Gate, but it will take days or weeks to re-certify the master map."

"In my opinion," Azariah inserted. "I do trust that everyone has mastery over their own section of the Jump algorithm and only Bounthavy has had any concerns."

"Bounthavy, I have complete confidence," the captain said. "Two follow-up questions. Why is Technician Rincones here?"

Azariah answered that. "All the Jump duties are partitioned enough so that no one knows the whole algorithm for security purposes, as you know. One side effect is that we absolutely can't Jump until Kilzan is at his workstation. He's here for insurance. After all, the Jump was scheduled to be complete about fifteen minutes ago."

"I canceled it before then."

"How was I supposed to know that?" The captain and Azariah exchanged a look. Was he an equal or annoying? Rincones was giving the opposite wall a military stare.

"My next question is to Bounthavy. It sounds like you were prepared to die and have the entire ship die because you're more scared of your group dynamics than of death. Is that correct?" The captain said this with a small smile, which Azariah didn't appreciate.

"My apologies. I think I also trusted Azariah. As something that I believe to be the truth and also as a favor, I ask that when you pass this information to Engineering and the Jump team that you give Azariah full credit."

"Because of the group dynamic," the captain said, "I'll allow it, but I'm putting Azariah in charge of the Jump team now."

"What! Do I get a say in this? Because—"

"No, you don't. Don't waste my time any further. I don't ever want a last-minute dramatic emergency like this again. All three of you need to respect the hierarchy better, discomfort or disagreement notwithstanding."

"Wait, wait. I *insist* that there's at least some official private acknowledgement—"

"Fine."

"Because I've done nothing."

"Fine. Continue doing nothing. Go away, all of you." She turned away from them, rubbing her face.

Azariah was serious. He wasn't legally allowed to do what he wanted with Bounthavy's information: to program an AI. In his opinion, Bounthavy's scanning technique and map updates should be an automatic part of the process, not this excruciating process that depended on several people with master-level knowledge. But overall, he was also ecstatic. Now that he had a couple planets tucked in his belt and his concerns about Jumping addressed, he could more fully focus on what Daniel needed and get back to him as soon as possible.

Interlude: Daniel

My dear Azariah, brother in Christ:

I've been telling you all the little worries of the day, but there's something good and new in my life that I haven't mentioned. Some good, new people too.

I found a small vineyard. It's walled off, between the palace and the desert. It gets beautiful morning sunlight. I've prayed there in the mornings when I can get free. Since our brothers left the palace, I've been almost every morning. The gardener is a good man. He knows the soil and the weather; he enjoys experimenting with diverse growths. I learned about Babylonian soil and fertilizers. When the vineyard grew grapes and smelled like home, I would sit for hours and meditate.

When the gardener's wife was sick, I asked if I could help and he said no; I didn't have enough experience, not the right experience. He didn't trust that I knew how to water correctly. He had his six-year-old granddaughter do it, and she didn't let me follow her around. She took my hand and led me back to the bench where I sat and prayed. I hope you have children someday. Is that okay to say? I have a bit of peace, where the vine-covered walls block out the sand, where the blue sky in the morning is like the blue sky at home.

I bought a telescope, took it to the vineyard in the darkest part of the night, and looked at the stars. As I write this letter, you are at Dunhuang; when you read this letter, you will be at Sumer, so I look at both every night. Gospel and Revelation of John still twirl around Paradise, and I can't see all the trouble from Babylon. The Goethe system isn't visible from this hemisphere. I found most of the other stars you are supposed to visit.

I miss you terribly. You want me to make new friends, so I'm meeting new people; I promise. I knew I would be sad when you left, but I didn't realize how much I would struggle. You were my safe haven, my bulwark. You were the manifestation of my emotions. I could feel them and understand them by watching you and talking with you.

There is something new going on between God and the king and our Paradise solar system. Everyone I love is caught up in it; I'm delivering the messages, but I can't tell what's going on. I'm sure it would be obvious to you. Where should I go to find a friend that will help me in this way?

Much love,

Daniel

To the Chaldean King Nebuchadnezzar, to the exiles of Paradise, and to the continued residents of the Paradise solar system:

God's messenger came to me in a vision.

I was again in the throne room of the Ancient of Days, who was again on the throne of living flame. Archangel Gabriel again showed me the baskets of figs.

I have received the interpretation. This is from our Lord God, not of my own understanding, but from the God who gave us the Gospel and Revelation of John, that we may prepare for his Daughter.

"Like these good figs, I regard as good the exiles from Gospel, whom I sent away to the solar systems of the Chaldeans. My eyes will watch over them for their good, and I will bring them back to this land. I will build them up and not tear them down; I will plant them and not uproot them. I will give them a heart to know me, that I am the Lord. They will be my people, and I will be their God, for they will return to me with all their heart.

"But like the poor figs, which are so bad they cannot be eaten, so will I deal with Zedekia, queen of Revelation, her officials and the survivors from Otero Linda, whether they remain on Revelation, Gospel, or live in Aegyptus. I will make them abhorrent and an offense to all the solar systems of your galaxy, a reproach and byword, an object of ridicule and cursing, wherever I banish them. I will send the sword, famine, and plague against them until they are destroyed from the land I gave to them and their mothers."

When I awoke, I was very weak. I prayed, fasted, and meditated, in great confusion that God would allow any of us to be cursed. God's messenger, Gabriel, answered me, as I am a good man and his prophet.

Gabriel brought me again to the throne room of the Ancient of Days. Gabriel was before me with her baskets of figs, one basket of good figs, one basket of poor figs. From the river of fire arose another messenger, the archangel Michael. She drew from a sheath a sword the length of two arms and held it across her body; the sword glowed like iron from a furnace. She had the same appearance as Gabriel; she had a golden face with wings and clothing of living flame and wore a silver crown in her hair.

This is what she said to me: "The Ancient of Days has handed all solar systems over to his servant, King Nebuchadnezzar of the Chaldean Empire; even the wild animals of the worlds are subject to him. If any solar system will not serve Nebuchadnezzar, king of Babylon and the Chaldean empire, or bow its neck under his yoke, God will punish that nation with the sword, famine, and plague until it is destroyed by his hand. So do not listen to your prophets, your diviners, your interpreter of dreams, your mediums, or your sorcerers who say you will not serve the king of Babylon and the Chaldean empire. They prophesy lies to you that will only serve to remove you far from your worlds; God will banish you and you will perish. But if any solar system will bow its neck under the yoke of the king of the Chaldean Empire and serve him, I will let that nation remain in its own land to till it and to live there."

I was given this interpretation seven nights in a row that I might tell you.

I am the servant of God born on Gospel and exiled who was brought before the servant of God, Nebuchadnezzar, king of the Chaldean Empire, and was given by God the King's dream and interpretation, which has proven me a prophet; before this, when I was an exile with my mother on the Goethe system asteroid, I was given the dream of the four beasts, showing the favor that God has given me for seven years now. I say this vision and the interpretations as God has given them to me.

Press Release from King Nebuchadnezzar

I have the favor of the gods. With their might behind me, I will make Revelation of John suffer.

Their only hope is to bow and beg for mercy, but as their own God has called them, they are hardhearted and happy to spill innocent blood in their most sacred places. Their Queen Zedekia, appointed by me and now having betrayed me, holds no promise sacred, and welcomes destruction for a little more power.

It is my place to purge their evil, to corral them and keep their poison from spreading; their exiles may yet be innocent, and to keep them so, we must eliminate all who are left. The exiling started twelve years ago and look how far some of them have come, and look at how far others have fallen.

Interlude: Erioch

King Nebuchadnezzar paced on the bridge of the *Dakaku*. He paced back and forth for two minutes until Erioch pulled him off onto the palace floor, which took up an entire level of the ship.

"I was getting some real work done!" The king said. "I'd forgotten how being at the front lines is so invigorating! This foggy world with the Dyson swarm and their economy crashing and how we're rescuing them, and we get to be in charge. I'm living the dream here! And there are several worlds to go!" He turned and looked at Erioch seriously. "I do not want to return to Babylon. Don't tell me I have to."

"Sir," Erioch said, unwilling to humor the king, "we have reports that there may be an uprising on Revelation of John."

"Queen Zedekia?" The king turned to him.

"We have reports that she has raised a militia and contacted Aegyptus. Also, there's the other …. stuff. She promised to be a better person to her people, making covenants before their God, and she's breaking those too."

"A traitor through and through."

"If these reports are true."

"And what do we do to traitors who break their word to us, to their God, and try to run to Aegyptus?" The king walked up to a window and gazed into space.

Everyone on the palace floor remained silent.

The king sighed and cursed. "I'll stay here a couple more weeks to wrap things up and to see if these reports are true. I will examine divinations and consult with Marduk. Erioch, I want you to get me the Paradisian Queen Zedekia, may she be the last of the name."

Erioch and his team stopped by their glorious home, Babylon, to replenish not only supplies but their souls, and to pick up a different fleet and to say *I love you* to all their loved ones, especially the children. Erioch sacrificed beer, milk, and ghee to Marduk, but he was leaving Marduk's solar system, so Erioch didn't know how useful the sacrifice was.

Off they went.

For Lughamstone and the other new planets, Erioch and his people knew they would probably bomb them but maybe not; the fleet they took to each planet reflected the open possibilities. This time, their mission to Revelation of John was narrow and severe. This time, the small fleet was like an intelligent and trained pack of dogs, hounds for the hunt. King Nebuchadnezzar had their leashes and was happy to goad them on. The small ships created chaos from the king's personal space station to the Gate.

With a hop, hop, hop they were at Revelation, whose sister planet, Gospel of John, was on the other side of their sun.

"You." The king pointed at Erioch. "It's time."

Erioch nodded and left for the bay where his elite team was waiting. He loaded everyone into the ship and was the last to get settled. They were packed in like sardines.

The ship went smooth and silent through space and then through the atmosphere of the planet.

Queen Zedekia was expected to be at her palatial estate. King Nebuchadnezzar was planning to have a video conference with her at a specific time. Once that was under way, Erioch's team would be in a position to interrupt. They stayed hidden. Once they got the signal, they moved in. Short and sweet, the team wasn't surprised, they were doing the surprising. They weren't expecting to see any children, but if they did, they would leave them alive; everyone else would die.

Queen Zedekia was holding her video conference deep in her Revelation palace with several layers of protection. When the team got to the last layer, they killed the communications people first to make sure they wouldn't cut the broadcast. King Nebuchadnezzar wanted to watch. The team stationed themselves at each entrance. By the time they were in place, Queen Zedekia knew what was up, but she couldn't escape. They slaughtered everyone around her. Erioch had read up on the prophecy from Prophet Jeremiah; killing and murdering damaged the soul, but their God wouldn't punish Erioch and his team any further. They took the queen captive, and Erioch checked in with King Nebuchadnezzar.

He was cackling with glee. "Excellent, excellent. Hello fellow royalty, it will be a pleasure to strip you of the title. There is no one worthy on your two worlds. There will be no more chances, no more kindness, no more hope. Each world is so special and sacred, and you have defiled your holy worlds three times over. They can be purified only through destruction. Do you feel the weight of your responsibility?"

"This is not the end as you would have it!" Queen Zedekiah insisted. "The Aegyptians are coming. They will take up quite a bit of your attention!"

The king waved his hand, and Erioch gagged the queen, who was now a prisoner.

"I am not interested. You are interested only in yourself, and they won't be here in time to save you, so please do go on."

The team killed some more officials in hiding and captured the queen's children. These were the last of the descendants of the Paradisian queens and kings. It had been a bloody few decades for the generations to narrow down to these two teenagers. Erioch patted them on their heads, gave them food, loaded them with their mother, tucking them in a bit more comfortably.

The Gate above Revelation of John was moved to the orbit of Gospel, which was too important as a breadbasket world to be harmed.

Revelation was promoted to a great siege, violence, and warfare. A wing of the Chaldean fleet bombed it flat and let the entire world burn, aiming to relocate at least ninety percent of the population before nuclear winter hit hard. After that, they would bind the planet into isolation, completely cutting it off from the God-blessed bounty of the Chaldean empire.

Interlude: Daniel

Azariah: I've got this memory. I don't really know if you remember. You said you didn't, but maybe you were embarrassed. When we were camping in the painted canyon on the Atabek world, it was Hananiah and Mishael on one bed and you and I on the other bed, which we'd done a half dozen times before. But that time, instead of us sleeping back-to-back, I woke up on my back with you sleeping on my shoulder and your arm wrapped around me. You were on my arm, which is what probably woke me up. I got my arm free and just tucked it around you, on your back, and I went back to sleep. You were already up when I woke up for the day. I ask you if you remembered curling up closer than usual and if you were okay, but you didn't seem to remember, and I was feeling embarrassed enough. So I'm telling you this because I definitely remember and it's a very comforting memory, and it's the type of memory I've clung to in the past few months with all the news about Paradise. But it's like I'm using you for comfort and you don't even know, so I wanted to mention it. I'll write more later. Daniel.

Daniel stood in the middle of the Hunnubum Humtum desert with Patroness Shelomith, Hananiah, and a team of Hananiah's people; the Archive was to preserve non-Babylonian artifacts, after all. Four ships landed in sequence, each dropping off a fourth of the Otero Linda golden temple. On invading Revelation, the Chaldean ships had cut it into four pieces and stored them in the cargo bays for transport to right here. It took two days to land the pieces properly. They had set up a temporary camp but were also making arrangements for longer term stays, like drilling a well. Daniel had seen the temple before in its rightful spot—on Revelation of John. It was quite, quite out of place here. It was hard, hard, hard to be grateful it still existed at all. Maybe that was part of the point.

After a few days, Daniel dragged himself back to the Etemenanki palace, where even more trauma awaited. The king had a new storehouse built immediately for all the treasures from Revelation. Along with the treasures, the deposed queen Zedekia arrived with her children. Daniel was there when Erioch slaughtered her children in front of her and then gouged out her eyes. *When the deposed queen dies, that lineage will finally be dead. God did not want us to have queens or kings in Paradise.* Daniel wrote to Azariah everything in his heart.

Chapter 26: Azariah, Sumer

Azariah found himself about to jump out *Phidippus* into the thin air of a planet named Sumer. His survival instinct kicked in.

What am I doing? Why was I chosen to do this? Now that his life was on the line, it felt like he was waking up for the first time in weeks.

Azariah had learned about the Revelation bombing when the Dunhuang Gate opened. Then *Klipspringer* had Jumped close to the inner planet Sumer thanks to the new accuracy. Azariah had only a few weeks to grieve before the ship was in orbit of this new planet. His grief had overtaken him. The Sumer plans had swept him along. Only now, at the last crucial moment, was he wondering what was happening.

Below him was a mass of stormy, swirling clouds. That was the worst skydiving weather.

Why is the mission skydiving? Why am I skydiving? What was the decision-making process? Azariah wondered to himself. As *Phidippus's* door opened to the howling wind, his conscious mind scrambled for details his unconscious mind might have absorbed while he was grief stricken.

The crew had no contact with anyone on the planet below. The planet residents were probably low tech, but possibly high tech and hiding it. A small, focused mission was called for.

Why weren't the commandos called in? They had specific infiltration training, etc. The answer to this was more convoluted and Azariah wasn't sure what had happened, except that Azariah had useful experience. If the residents weren't hostile, his diplomatic skills would be important. And if the residents were hostile? Azariah had the sinking feeling he was expendable.

Phidippus and other shuttles couldn't navigate the storms well, but

Azariah could with special tech. Looking down, surviving that storm seemed unbelievable. But stealth was important—even if the shuttle made it through the storm, they didn't know what was waiting for them on the other side of the storm, and *Phidippus* could be shot down.

His survival instinct was still screaming at him to not jump into that storm, but logic was creeping in and taking over—he didn't have a choice. This was happening.

Movement next to him caught his attention. Someone in a flight suit and a helmet with the visor down was next to him. Azariah put his hand on their shoulder and recognized the shape—Sal, of all people, was next to him, suited up to sky dive with him.

Azariah turned on the comms inside his own helmet.

"Why are you here? Don't you need to program the Jump?"

"Now you care? It's too late, buddy." Sal had never sounded like that before—actual emotion in their voice, a mix of grimness and laughing at imminent death. Or Azariah was reading too much into that. "Wamiri can handle it," Sal added dismissively.

"One minute," the *Phidippus* pilot called.

Azariah's training kicked in. He'd done this plenty of times with Hananiah and made a quick check of his gear, something he'd already done twice. A device for a high-tech landing. A parachute for a low-tech landing. Other equipment with anti-gravity tech was attached to his harness, something he'd need once he landed on the planet. He visualized the plan—get through the storm and to the landing spot, a wide beach at low tide.

Don't worry about anything else. That thought freed him. His life was a mess. He was away from his closest friends while the king was destroying their people, but he'd survived so far, and he could focus on surviving this next thing.

Once he was done checking his equipment, he swung to outside *Phidippus*, holding onto the outside bars, the wind trying to whip him away, but he fought back and held on, moving down to make room for Sal, who swung onto the bar, a little hesitant.

"Have you done this before?" Azariah asked.

Sal gave a shaky laugh. "Skydiving into a storm? Can't say I ever had a death wish."

"If you hurry, you'll make it down before the rain starts." That was Beck over the comm, sounding pleased and excited. "Once you hit the clouds, we'll lose contact until you've landed."

Again, another detail that made little sense, Azariah's conscious mind swam through his unconscious, looking for more information and coming up with only confusing mission debriefings.

"Now," the pilot called.

With permission, Azariah let go, falling backwards, *Phidippus* getting smaller and smaller as he fell and it pulled up, Sal in the middle distance. Azariah swung around to face the storm. The planet curved out of sight in every direction, with no break in the cloud cover. Sal was now behind him. Azariah could imagine for a moment he was alone in an expansive universe, and wondered if this was how Daniel felt in some of his visions. And in a flash, there was a sharp pang in his chest that he had been hiding from.

They had jumped from so high up it would still be another minute before they hit the storm.

Azariah twisted to look for Sal and found them close to his shoulder. Azariah arched to move away.

Sal grabbed Azariah's upper arm with more force than expected.

Out of the corner of his eye, Azariah saw a dull glint of metal in Sal's free hand. As that hand slashed up to Azariah with great speed, Azariah flinched up, away from Sal. The knife in Sal's hand was meant for Azariah's throat, but cut through a strap on Azariah's chest, through his suit, and scratched his skin.

As Sal prepared for another slash, Azariah called out on the radio and grabbed their wrist and applied a quick thrust on the wrist pressure point and a snap meant to break their wrist, but Sal was wearing a cuff for protection and Azariah's first defense failed.

No one from the ship answered his emergency call and Sal had cut off their comms.

Azariah wrenched his upper arm from Sal's grasp. The storm was coming up fast. He held the knife hand away, his own strength easily overpowering Sal, but Sal fought back, focusing on controlling their knife hand.

Azariah, with his free hand, pulled at the straps on Sal, habit guiding him to pull at one release and then another, and Sal's parachute pack came free, so Azariah pushed it away. With a few more pulls, the high-tech landing gear loosened enough for Azariah to wedge in a foot and pop the engine section out of the harness, and spin that away hard in a separate direction.

This took only a couple seconds and by the time he was complete, Sal registered what he was doing and frantically struggled, letting go of Azariah.

With Sal preoccupied, Azariah could focus on the weapon. Before Sal could choose what equipment to chase down, Azariah took Sal's knife hand in both of his and slammed it on his knee with a satisfying crack.

Sal let go of the knife and it hung in the air next to them, falling with them.

Azariah took it and hurled it in yet another direction, far away from Sal's equipment, into the storm, while Sal, free of Azariah's grip, swung toward the parachute pack.

Sal grabbed their parachute backpack and put it back on. Azariah watched them fumbling from a distance. What had Sal been thinking when they had been above Azariah like this earlier? No projectile weapons allowed. One quick knife stroke. It shouldn't have been that hard. Azariah patted his chest where the knife had cut through his suit. The tears in the layers of clothes were razor thin. Now that he took a second, he could feel blood running down his chest. The waterproof layer of his suit had kept the blood from blooming onto his front, and only a few drops had escaped the cut in the cloth. Nothing he could do for now.

Before Azariah could process the assassination attempt, he hit the storm. He held himself in a streamlined position so the tech would keep the winds from buffering him around, keeping Sal in the corner of his eye.

The storm clouds, the part that worried Azariah the most, were easy. The complex technology kept Azariah safe from strong winds and lightning. On the underside of the clouds, there was no storm. It wasn't even raining yet. Also, no sign of advanced technology. Assessing the view, the famous rainbow palace and cathedral were on a cliff nearby, still far under him, sparkling even without sunshine, and the beach, their destination, spread out in front of it. The ground was coming up fast.

Sal opened their parachute way too early. Azariah's heart fell a little, but didn't open his yet. They were supposed to do a low altitude opening for safety reasons, and clearly Sal didn't have the skills. Azariah didn't want to be anywhere near Sal when they both were on land again and felt a red-hot flare of anger and indignation. The assassination should have been successful. Azariah had been free of suspicion, open to attack.

Azariah performed a low-altitude parachute opening and landed on the beach, thanking Hananiah for enjoying the extra adrenaline rush of a parachute landing, which had given Azariah plenty of practice.

What was going through Sal's head? Were they going to try again? What was their motivation? Azariah looked up at the drifting parachute. Sal didn't hate him as far as he knew, but Azariah had been thick-headed before.

He took off his helmet and ran a hand through his hair. As a defensive measure, Azariah had stopped wearing a turban and had started wearing his signet ring. His hair, a fine straight texture and past his chin, was long enough to give him an air of authority. Tucking his hair behind his ears, he unpacked the survival kit, put a knife at his belt, and cleaned and healed the cut on his chest. It felt like the knife had scraped his breastbone.

Sal landed in the trees a kilometer down the beach from the chosen landing point in front of the rainbow palace. Azariah debated just leaving Sal to their fate. But Daniel would help if Sal had severe injuries. So Azariah went down the beach, cursing the kindness in his heart, monitoring the trees where he saw the parachute disappear. Before he had jogged down all the way, Sal came crashing through the underbrush onto the beach, stumbling and falling to their knees once they reached the sand. Azariah stopped. They were within yelling distance. Azariah jogged closer to the trees for defensive cover. Going after Sal was the worst idea ever, but he couldn't turn his back on them now, if only for personal safety reasons.

Sal didn't see Azariah right away and screamed at the ocean and threw their helmet and fistfuls of sand. They tried to get up, but their leg or ankle was injured and they flopped back onto the sand, crying.

After a few minutes, Azariah called out, "Hey, Sal! What is going on?!"

When Sal saw Azariah, they wiped away their tears and called back. "You can come closer. I have no more weapons. You can scan me."

"You know how to fool a scan, which begs the question again, what is going on? First of all," Azariah said indignantly, "why didn't you wait until we were on the ground?! Trying an assassination attempt while skydiving is ridiculous!"

"I was losing my nerve! I had to try before I lost it completely. I mean, I haven't been able to find the nerve to kill you on the ship, and the captain said I should kill you in the air, that that's when you would be the most defenseless."

"That's several layers of ridiculous!" Azariah yelled, aghast. "I don't believe the captain would tell you anything like that!"

"It doesn't matter." They cried some more but continued, "I used to be an assassin! I got an order when the last Gate opened."

"You're kidding me! I never would have suspected—which I imagine is a useful quality." Azariah crept closer so they could hear each other without yelling.

Sal continued, "I'm not an assassin any more. It is considered an honorable profession to some, but I was becoming more and more mercenary, so I asked a doctor to wake my conscious up and he woke it up too much. It's not all bad. I went on a journey of self-discovery and then back to school where I met Wamiri and Din. They helped me realize I was non-binary. I'd do anything for them, and I think they'd be sad if I killed you."

Azariah believed Sal to a certain extent. Sal laid down on the sand, spent. It made sense that the empire was Azariah's true enemy, not plain, quiet Sal, even if Sal was carrying around some big secrets. Plus, Din and Wamiri had always been more transparent, and they wouldn't be friends with someone evil. With that decision made, Azariah jogged back to the precise landing point, looking over his shoulder frequently. He'd get every bit of the mission perfect so the king would have as little to complain about as possible. It was the best he could do to ensure his survival, but he felt young and incompetent.

At the landing point, Azariah cleared a space in the sand that was six by six meters and then took a fist-sized cube, the one with the antigravity tech, from his harness and set it in the middle of the area. He turned off the antigravity and the cube sank halfway into the sand under its correct weight. He left the six-by-six-meter area and then used his disc to trigger the cube. It exploded into its full shape, a rectangular base that filled the area, two meters high, and on top of the base was a huge instrument that looked like a cannon pointed to the sky. Azariah took a canister, the energy source, off his harness and attached it to a valve on the cannon. He ran down the beach and turned the machine on. The cannon shot pulses of energy into the clouds—calibrated, special energy that would dissipate the storm clouds right overhead to allow shuttles to come through. It would take a while to work.

Azariah settled on the beach halfway between Sal and the cannon. Sal appeared to be sleeping. Scans showed they weren't in any danger. Assassination attempts took a lot out of a person, apparently. Azariah still didn't feel safe, and wouldn't until he could talk to the captain about what happened. He was a little tempted to disappear into the forest at the edge of the beach, but there was no real hiding from the empire.

For now, he looked again at the rainbow palace. It was architecture that the king was interested in, so Azariah wrote notes down on his disc. King Nebuchadnezzar would chortle like a little child that he had a new shiny world added to his collection.

As it rained, as the world went quiet in all the different ways, Azariah's grief flooded back. It wasn't the colors of the palace that he noticed but the crystalline texture of everything, of how each spot of water was like a diamond that could cut him and his grief, where reality turned him into a nothingness shadow.

During his silent contemplation, Azariah's warning system went off. People were coming down the beach, wearing loose handwoven clothing. Judging from the way they were waving their hands over their heads, laughing in the rain, spreading out, some walking in the water and kicking it around for fun, and the lack of visible weapons, they weren't hostile. Azariah turned on his disc to record whatever would happen next.

"Who art thee?" They called out from a safe distance. "Art thee from t'other side of the world? Thou hast no insignia. Hast thou food? Didst thou bringeth friends? Art thou friendly?" Each question came from someone different in understandable Elamite.

Azariah bowed while the group was still at a distance. "I'm a representative from the Chaldean empire, which replaced the Achaemenid empire. My ship is in orbit. We Jumped here from a nearby solar system."

At this, before he could go further, all their faces lighted up in understanding, some dropped into prostration, bowing to him from their knees. Others ran up to him and then dropped to their knees, with tears running down their faces.

"Thou hast saved us! Thou art our savior! We shall honor thee above all people!" They each said.

Azariah's heart sank. This was not an introduction that would put him in the good graces of the king.

Someone close to him asked, "What is thine name? Mine is Baeru and I am a lowly medical doctor, imputed with political power for a time. This is a most wondrous honor of many generations to meet thee."

"I am Envoy Azariah Ramzi on behalf of King Nebuchadnezzar."

"Thee shall go down in history as our savior, Azariah Ramzi. We shall sing your name forever."

"And also the king's name, King Nebuchadnezzar. I do nothing without him."

"Is he here?"

"No, not yet." Azariah's heart sank more. The king arriving meant nothing good for anyone. But his own survival was at stake, and the king would do whatever he wanted, no matter what Azariah said. "Sing not my name. I am merely a representative of King Nebuchadnezzar, who will provide you with a Gate."

"A Gate! Thee giveth us a Gate! Shall thine blessings never cease? Thank you, Azariah Ramzi." Baeru shook Azariah's hand.

"Again, it's not me. I am not the only one here. My friend and I are both here only as the first before the proper representatives and diplomats."

The crowd looked over to where Sal was still splayed out and sleeping.

"We shall help your friend. But thou, Azariah Ramzi, need not our help, thou art the savior of us all! What is the machine?"

Azariah explained, and that started another round of prostration. Between surviving an assassination attempt and a weariness from grief, he was having a hard time stopping their too-complimentary comments.

"Azariah, thou hast saved us from the storms!"

"The technology is a gift from the king. I only pushed the button to turn it on."

"Thee did push the button! It truly is thee who has done everything."

Azariah was panicking a little. Everything he said was making things worse for himself.

"Please tell me about yourselves." Azariah sat cross-legged in the sand and they followed suit, a few tending to Sal, who Azariah decided to not worry about. The less he spoke, the better. He learned that there was a medical conference on Sumer when the Gate was destroyed, and they had done their best to preserve and advance medical knowledge. On the other hand, there were cannibals in the icy northern regions. The survivors in the luxury winter resorts had been driven to extremes after the first isolated snowy seasons. The tropical region, where Azariah had landed, was cut off from them because of the storms and blizzards.

A few hours passed, which included a meal that Azariah provided.

His survival pack included a week's worth of protein bars and fresh water. The miniaturization technology and his sharing earned him another round of prostration.

Finally, his comm system came to life with a greeting from the captain that the shuttle was in the atmosphere and would land soon. Azariah had never felt so much relief. Despite Sal's story, and all the implications, Azariah still trusted the captain. So far, she had conducted most of the *gerru* the way she wanted. If there was no choice but to let him die, then he would have already died; she was talented and efficient enough.

The shuttle landed, the captain and real diplomatic team made the real first contact, with Beck interrupting them every time they tried to praise Azariah, who had never been so thankful for Beck's selfishness.

At the first free moment, Azariah and the captain went off to the side of the primary group. With much indignation in his voice, Azariah reported what had happened while skydiving and what Sal had told him. The captain didn't show any surprise, just winced twice.

"Well, Captain Maria Sifontes Uzcategui, what do you have to say to that?" Azariah asked in a tone that was incredibly, completely respectful.

"I'm very proud of you for staying alive. I did my best to keep you alive."

Azariah huffed at this.

The captain continued, "This mission was going to be dangerous no matter what, but skydiving was an unusual choice, as you might remember. Looking at your file and Sal's, I decided this was the best way to keep you alive. Your experience would give you the leg up you would need. I told Sal that this was the one attempt I would allow."

"My experience almost wasn't enough. They still surprised me."

"How could you not be aware of the danger?! You—" the captain cut herself off, avoiding a lecture. "Sal was the only one with assassination orders this round. We can say that they tried and are not in a condition to try again. I believe I can keep you safe on that front. However, we have an additional problem: Beck is almost certainly going to report you for treason because of how the Sumerites keep offering you obeisance and veneration."

"I've done my best to discourage it." Azariah was thankful to have the captain's support, but her power was limited.

"Go back to *Klipspringer* in the shuttle right now and write the best report you can. The entire thing, assassination attempt, meeting the local population, everything."

"I have a recording that will help. Sal should come with me."

"Are you sure?"

"What I'm sure of is that I want this *gerru* to be over as fast as possible and that means Sal doing their proper work to get the Jump ready. I'll stay away as much as I can. Maybe I'll hang out in Engineering."

"Or you could work from the bridge," the captain said mildly, "with the rest of the diplomatic and communications team. As your Jump team leader responsibilities allow."

Azariah winced. "Thank you for the reminder. I will be the best envoy possible."

Once Sal was at their regular duties, the algorithm programming for the next Jump to a nebula village named Leuke Kome continued much more smoothly. With the improvement in Jump accuracy, Klipspringer would shave a year off the *gerru*.

The Gate was ready before the Jump, but the captain refused to let the Gate be opened, grumbling about bureaucracy and running from the real diplomats and that they were fine on their own. Even so, the Gate opened a few extra hours early.

Within minutes, Azariah received a video chat request from Daniel.

"It's so good to see you," Daniel said, rubbing his eyes from waking up.

"Oh, this is such a relief! I know this sounds terrible, but you look better than I expected." Azariah felt tears in his eyes. Not just from seeing him but speaking Kahi to someone for the first time in over a year. "Did your sister Magdalene survive? You don't say."

"She did. She's with my sister Hippolyte and the Queen of Sheba, of all people, stirring things up. She's much more impressive than I ever thought she could be. I love her very much, but she doesn't believe me. I'm sure there are reports. Hananiah is married!"

"What? To who?"

"Piama. She's—"

"I know who she is! Wow!"

"That's a whole story. I wrote it out for you."

"Thank you. I'm going to write to her. What about my family on Gospel?" Azariah played with the controls to get a better picture, but Daniel stayed fuzzy.

"Nothing," Daniel answered, looking more awake. "There's no

reason to think they are in danger. Gospel is too important as a breadbasket world."

"I wish I could be there with you."

Daniel asked how are you feeling at the same time Azariah asked what are you doing. They laughed, and then Azariah cried.

He couldn't feel if Daniel wasn't with him.

"The Gate opened so fast," Daniel said. "I don't know if I've written everything I want you to know. When you wrote one month in your last message, I thought you mistyped. An hour ago, the entire court was shocked to hear you'd Jumped safely in such a short time. You were given more credit as the king's envoy."

"Did you write more about what happened with the heirs of Queen Zedekia? I know that must be eating you up inside."

Daniel's expression, which has been severe with grief, crumpled. "No, I didn't write. It's not the thing to write about. Or talk about."

"I'm glad we're talking right now." Azariah huddled closer to Daniel's image. "I know you well enough to know what went through your mind and how detached you were, and how once it was over, you were horrified. Was anyone else there with you? I mean another Paradisian."

"No one else was there. I just let things happen. I should have tried. It seemed so right for the royal lineage to be destroyed that I didn't realize what violence would be necessary until I was in the moment. What does that say about me that I didn't even want to try?" Daniel asked.

"I know Daniel, I know you. You were there. The Paradisian queen's last two heirs didn't die alone. You… you were there for burial rites. That is a different bravery." Azariah would have tried to save them, but that wouldn't be helpful to say at this point. He was angry at himself and their people. "You shouldn't have been alone."

"I have been detached from everything since then. You're right. What is the point of being here if I can't do what's obviously good? Or what action isn't futile? Sorry, this is hard." Daniel wiped a couple of tears from his eyes.

"One thing about your visions that we've talked about, how God views time differently from us, like how all the kingdoms are destroyed at once by the asteroid, or how all the beasts are in the heavenly court at the same time, despite being consecutive rulers. So when God or a messenger says that you are a good man, they are looking at your whole life, not just who you were up to a certain point.

I have great faith in you that you can move forward. In the past, you've prayed 'my transgressions are only before you, oh God.' You know what that means now."

Daniel was wiping tears away the whole time Azariah talked. "I love you very much, as my best friend. Why aren't you here? I'm sure I'd sleep better if you were next to me."

Their conversation after that got very personal. Din knocked on Azariah's office door to give him the half hour Jump notice. Azariah noticed a flashing alert that Mishael was trying to get ahold of him. Mishael was on a ship on this side of the Gate!

Azariah said goodbye to Daniel and connected to Mishael, who berated him for talking to Daniel for so long about their feelings. He spoke Kahi with a strong Akkadian accent.

"You were listening?" Azariah said incredulously. "Rude! How did you even break into the connection?"

"Obviously I wasn't literally eavesdropping. I just know both of you. And before you say anything else, I didn't know about the heirs even being at the palace, much less Daniel being a part of that fiasco. Daniel didn't tell anyone until after they…died."

"Yes. I know. He does this to himself. Which is why you have to be proactively in his face about everything!"

"No one has time for that!" Mishael waved his hands.

"I'm so happy you made time to see me," Azariah flicked his hand back at Mishael's image.

"Yes, I believed you when you told Daniel a month. Predictions were that this world would be more needy, and I was right to follow up on that too." He gave Azariah a look, like, is Sumer a promising world?

Azariah shrugged. "You'll be able to read the state of the world in my report. I'm sure they'll appreciate anything." Azariah sent him contact information for Baeru and other Sumerites and then realized that maybe he shouldn't have done that.

"Your mission is legitimate, right?" Azariah asked.

"Yes, signed off by the military and the chancellor of the state. I'm here in my official capacity as a rep from Atabek." Mishael checked something off screen. "The first ship with food to feed two million people will be here in an hour. I asked for that."

"Um, we're Jumping really soon." Azariah grabbed his space suit and put it on over his daily uniform.

"I'm looking at your report," Mishael said. "Do you think Sumer can accept people who need medical help?" There was a change in his tone, from casual to urgent and emotional.

"You should wait for official permission before bringing any refugees, but I think it's okay to plan for it. Anything else?" Azariah slipped his legs into the space suit.

"The Revelation evacuation ships are old, overcrowded, and not suitable for treating people with mass radiation poisoning. The Revelation citizens don't have the status of refugees. They are registered as slaves. I know the four of us complain about our status, but while we haven't been full empire citizens, we have some rights."

"Sumer's pressure point is that they want to please the empire," Azariah said. "If you can frame it that they're doing the empire a big favor by accepting the refugee ships or something, I don't know. You're better at that kind of strategy."

"I am better at strategic thinking," Mishael agreed. "Please stop trying. I'm sure you caused some big diplomatic faux pas again."

"Two. Someone tried to have me assassinated!"

"Oh, of course. I can't believe it's the first time. I'll do my best to clean up after you. But thank you for the list of resources and contacts. Now, Azariah, how are you really doing? Pretend I'm Papa Hananiah."

Azariah wanted to sob, but he sat down again and translated his emotions into words. No time for tears. "It's too late to find a safe haven. I wanted to find a good quality place for a couple billion people, or at least a couple million. That's impossible now. It was naïve of me to think that I could do such a thing. But for Daniel's sake, it was important to try. I didn't know this is what war looks like when our people have no power." Mishael stayed silent, so Azariah talked himself through. "I'm stuck on this *gerru*. What am I here for? What can I do? Never mind." There was more he could say, but it was stuck in his throat.

"Thanks for sharing," Mishael said awkwardly. "I hope you feel better now because I don't. I imagine you'll get yourself killed at some point, but for Daniel's sake, don't throw yourself into danger."

They gave each other small smiles. "I love you too. I've got to go."

Sumer, as a place to welcome refugees despite their own need, was doing what God had called his people to do. Paradisians had failed and now had to be taken care of though they wouldn't care for others. He thought of all the different ways Prophet Jeremiah said they had failed. How his home worlds had failed him. If it weren't for the Chaldean empire, he would still be an under-educated farmer.

Chapter 27: Azariah, New Godaniya

Sumer was the fifth cycle. By the time *Klipspringer* started the eighth cycle, Jumping to a solar system named Godaniya, Azariah was more or less normal again; a new normal. Five Babylonian months had passed since they had Jumped away from Sumer. Azariah had communicated back and forth with his friends enough to feel like things were stable, that other events were taking precedence, and he could more or less do his job as he saw fit.

In fact, Azariah sat with Captain Sifontes and other crew on the bridge for the Jump to Godaniya. While he was still the leader of the Jump team, he had been spending more time on the bridge since Sumer, but it had never been so busy or focused as it was now. He hadn't ever seen the captain in her space suit. She kept her rigid posture and had an eye on everything, even with her helmet blocking some of her vision.

The bridge was like the captain: small, functional, and with surprising style. Azariah had an assigned seat, which he knew but hadn't ever cared to look at after the initial introduction to the bridge. He was behind the Engineering station. It was interesting to see commands given from this end, to see the Jump activated, the Jump ring curving at the very top of the bridge ceiling.

Klipspringer Jumped to Godaniya. It was fine. They did their on-site scanning and deployed a one-percent drone. Unlike elsewhere on the ship, nobody removed their suits. Checking out the new area took precedence, though a few were free enough to remove their helmets, so Azariah did too.

"We're picking up a transmission," Beck said from her station. "According to the pings, it's been playing for about ten Babylon years. The one-percent drone is following the direction to find the source."

Beck was listening through an earpiece. No one else could hear the transmission. Her eyes darted around. "It's in Elamite and repeats in a dialect of Oghuric. I'm listening through again."

Everyone paused and watched her.

"Envoy," Beck said, "since you're here, I'd like you to confirm."

She played it over the speakers. Azariah translated in his head as he listened to the old Elamite.

Verily oh visitors dost thou presence bestow much fortune upon us.

The inner planet Godaniya experienced catastrophic war. The healthy populace of the entire solar system is congregated, densely packed on space stations twinkling, surrounding the gas giant moon, New Godaniya, under the auspicious gaze of the jellyfish aliens. Please come with glad tidings.

The message repeated in Oghuric which he hadn't mastered yet.

"I think that's clear enough." Azariah raised his eyebrow at Beck, who looked away.

"Envoy," the captain said. "I caught some of that, especially the first sentence. Can you translate the entire message?"

When Beck didn't jump in with an insult, Azariah recited his translation.

"Na'adu'um sakikum?" The captain repeated the Elamite words.

"That absolutely means jellyfish alien. I prepared special notes on this and can show you."

When Beck and the captain still looked doubtful, he unlatched his space suit enough to get his disc out and projected a book of notes for the captain to flip through on his research showing several instances of Achaemenid citizens having encounters. Beck shrugged her shoulders when the captain asked for confirmation.

"How soon can we get scanning information on the inner planet?" Captain Sifontes asked.

"A day perhaps," Kilzan answered the captain. He had gotten a promotion to the bridge.

"*Phidippus* will go to the inner planet now to verify the message while *Klipspringer* will go to New Godaniya. If the scanning data shows the inner planet to be dangerous, *Phidippus* can return at that point. The drone following the source of the message is heading towards a gas giant that presumably has a moon?"

"Yes," Kilzan confirmed. "The gas giant is significantly closer to us than the inner planet. We should receive scanning information soon."

The crew were restless, especially Security Officer Juma, who had a lot to say. There had never been positive experiences with the na'adu'um sakikum. The aliens colonized gas giants, so over the thousands of years of space travel, humans and aliens left each other alone. Humans had never had a complicated level of communication with the aliens. Just *if you hit me, I'll hit you back*. And now *Klipspringer* was flying straight to them.

The next day, Captain Sifontes called Azariah to a meeting in her office. When he arrived, he was the only one there, and the captain had set up a tea service.

"I've sent Beck, Park, and the commando team in *Phidippus*. Considering how socially unstable the inner system appears to be, I'm sending the main part of the diplomacy corp that way." The captain said this like it was supposed to mean something, but it didn't, except that Azariah thought he was a member of the main part.

Azariah sipped at the green tea, served in a delicate cup with a blue pattern. The tea smelled like a flower but tasted sour.

"How's the Jump team?" The captain asked. "You've taken on a leadership role; how much guidance do they need? How is Sal?"

"They're fine. Thank you for saying that I'm in a leadership role, but I don't do too much. I spent a lot of time on languages on the seventh cycle." A solar system named Shabwa of Hadhramaut; the population spent most of their time in a virtual reality which the king would destroy as fast as possible because he still didn't trust AI.

"To our benefit, thank you. As I've said, Beck and Park will be gone when we reach New Godaniya. So I am putting you in charge of diplomatic relations on the moon."

"What? That sounds like a terrible idea. I'm not good at diplomacy. It's very different from being an envoy."

"No it's not. You've been more than adequate over the last few cycles." The captain put her tea cup down, ready to convince Azariah.

"Wow, high praise for someone you want leading first contact procedures." Azariah also put his tea cup down as a challenge.

"I know it's not what you enjoy. You may feel inadequate compared to the diplomacy of Etemenanki palace, but you now have significantly more first contact experience than anyone there. I'll support you, but there are formalities I don't have time for. You perform different risk assessments, and while you stick your foot in your mouth all the time, you are great at gathering data. Plus, you know the languages much better than me. The king saw fit to call you Envoy, so be it. We haven't received any further assassination orders if that helps."

Azariah nodded slowly. He would do better without Beck breathing down his neck. The captain had won this round. He finished his tea with a gulp.

"Just as a heads up," the captain continued, "the Gate cannot open until we're ready to Jump. We're going to build it in the gas giant's orbit, but there's a chance we'll have to dismantle and rebuild at the inner planet's orbit. We need to do a full risk assessment and I don't want to deal with the empire. For now, I need you to write a message to the moon."

"Do they seem hostile, cooperative?" Azariah asked as he rose from the table and rinsed the cups and dishes in the sink. "We've checked out their message the best we can. What I've seen would justify *Klipspringer* staying out of reach until Beck has done her assessment, but unless the space stations and moon hostile, I want to go forward with first contact protocol." *Oh look at me, the power is going to my head immediately.*

The captain made no indication that Azariah had taken over quickly, despite his protestations. "We've done this enough times that out of our experiences, Beck and I can say that we do not know if they are hostile. Good luck, get out of here. Stop doing my dishes, you're going to break something."

The New Godaniya moon responded in good time, with a good amount of information, and seemed all politeness. *Klipspringer* would probably not get blown up. The moon had two unpowered ground-to-space missile launchers. The outermost space stations all had offensive and defensive capabilities, which made the crew wonder about continued civil wars, political-economic power disruptions, or the aliens. *Klipspringer* passed an alien jellyfish-shaped ship, the tentacles wrapped around the body tightly, no sign of power or life; they were probably deep in the gas giant. An entire space station State was safe and happy this close to an alien colony. Azariah had been through more than a half dozen solar systems by now, and he had never been responsible for any of these things. He was sweating.

The innermost space stations were like a tropical coral reef community. Little blue ships with spikes like sea urchins floated between the brightly colored community space stations that were stuck together like different species of coral. Tugboat ships pulling sections of stations together looked like brown spotted sea slugs. The citizens had plenty of one or two person space vehicles and started following

Klipspringer like a school of fish, twinkling their lights and calling the crew over the communications, though no one had time to do anything but wave an acknowledgement. Azariah spoke a little with a Vice President named A'ishe Khatun, who was posted on a space station.

Klipspringer pulled into a close orbit over the New Godaniya moon. Captain Sifontes, her aide Khamla, a couple of protection officers, Azariah, and Kilzan as his aide traveled to the moon's surface via the small shuttle *Qamlet* with their new entourage following. Azariah was heady with nervousness; he was not yet accustomed to a leadership position, with no one between him and important decisions. Wamiri had given him a warm wool cloak, and he had to resist pulling it tight around himself. This was his metaphorical Zero-G throw up experience, and he might get his Scythian pants and button shirt messy. Contradictorily, he had full confidence in his skills.

Landing, exiting, and meeting everyone was chaotic with all the small shuttles landing and disgorging their people. The diplomatic greeting was not as formal as usual. New Godaniya officials tried to provide security to keep all the nosy and noisy people from pressing up tight against the crew.

After a minute of chaos, where Azariah found his footing in the low gravity and tied back his hair because it was floating too much and people were touching it, the crowd backed off, like a wave receding back to the ocean.

A man was approaching with the presence of someone in charge. Not only was he surrounded by aides and protection, he was tall, swarthy, and broad with a regal bearing even in the same coveralls as everyone else. Everyone responded with a low call when he smiled and waved. The man had a bushy beard and his smile showed white teeth. He said something in Oghuric about respect and made shooing motions for the crowd to back off. They obeyed and were soon several paces away from the *Klipspringer* crew.

Captain Sifontes and Azariah prepared for a proper introduction. As the man approached, with his shoulders held back, he gave them a cool, appraising look without losing his smile, but it didn't have the same happiness.

"This is President Wahap Seyfiddin," one of the initial diplomats said in accented Elamite, and rattled off a list of honoraries and titles that asserted he was the rightful ruler of the entire solar system.

The president and the captain traded greetings in Elamite. It was Azariah's turn. He would almost wish for Beck to do this, except that he hated her. Azariah spoke his greeting in Oghuric, much to President Seyfiddin's delight, and he gave Azariah a more genuine smile and offered his hand to both the captain and envoy for a shake.

The next few hours were the careful, tedious dance of initial contact. The *Klipspringer* crew, the president's entourage, and everyone else moved to a newly built plaza a short distance from the shuttle port. The moon's chill didn't bother the crowd and instead of dispersing, they set up a party in the wide space around the raised pavilion that the diplomatic teams were on.

For other solar systems, they had acted on a tight time schedule. Now that *Klipspringer* was waiting to hear from Beck and her team, all necessary conversations and negotiations could take place at a relaxed pace. The president and his people didn't consider this a problem, and everyone fell into easy chatting soon enough. Tomorrow, the moon and stations were hosting a formal gathering when more political representatives and power players would be available, and they would all trade gifts and give speeches.

After a meal of brined vegetables and fish, both stringy, the President Wahap invited the *Klipspringer* crew on a tour. The captain stayed at the plaza, which Azariah expected; there were some topics that were easier to broach with the head of state away.

"President Seyfiddin." Azariah started as he led him away. Behind them were Kilzan, a protection officer, and a few New Godaniyans, including the President's top aide, Lieutenant Zikirulla Moydun.

"No, please, call me Wahap. I insist," he said in Oghuric, taking Azariah's arm, and looking him in the eye. He had bright, light-brown eyes, like a tiger's eye. "And I will call you Azariah. You must indulge me, as I'm not allowed to interact with many people as equals. I must beg forgiveness for requesting the privilege."

"Wahap, where are you taking me first?" Azariah gave him a charming smile and locked his arm with his. This was a fun political game. And by fun, he meant terrifying. Beck always insisted on distance and formality, and while he saw the point, he didn't mind doing the opposite.

"This diplomacy pavilion we invited you to is a brand-new area. It's quite a distance from our current capital city. We are thinking of creating a new capital right here. It's one of my new projects. It will be not only the center for politics but also for education and commerce. We are *planning* more. So now I am taking you on a tour of all the nearby highlights of our society." He paused between each sentence.

Azariah had a feeling the president was simplifying an entire speech to Oghuric Azariah could understand. Azariah's hold on a language always improved with complicated conversation and he would push for that later.

"Our sports are very important," Wahap said gravely, with a twinkle in his eye, leaning in close. They were at a sports center that looked like it could hold all the people in the space stations and all the crowds Azariah had seen so far. "The people on the space stations live at regular gravity. Some moon buildings have regular gravity. So it is fun for everyone to play at low gravity here. We are living outside the Gold Locked zone of our solar system. We have limitations, but we adapt."

"Indeed, Wahap, your moon is more developed for independence compared to most moon colonies I've seen," Azariah said as they continued their walk. "The gas giant in the sky and the low gravity are the only things that make it obvious we aren't on a typical planet. What's the name of the gas giant?" The fractal-like swirls of the bright planet were hypnotic at this distance.

"Khoshkhar Muiz. It belongs to the na'adu'um sakikum." He gave Azariah a side glance at this.

"I don't have protocol for aliens." Azariah admitted.

"Well, Azariah, there's not much to say. They showed up decades ago. No understandable communication. They disappeared into the gas." He paused, like he was gathering his thoughts, and smiled. "Next stop is our schools. What are the education fads in the Chaldean empire? How do you use technology?"

After the schools, they walked to the factories and then to the fields. At that point, they went from walking on the paths that were on top of the moon's natural regolith to walking on terraformed soil, with plants growing on every surface possible.

"I've seen nothing quite like this," Azariah said once they arrived at a field. The crop was a blade of cobalt blue eelgrass but on a huge scale, so he felt smaller than a little crab shuffling among seaweed. He reached up to touch a blade; it felt as hard as stone with no give, but also slimy. When he took his hand away, blue algae covered it. "Oops. I hope—"

"You're fine. It's not dangerous to you and you didn't hurt the plant," Wahap assured Azariah. If he had comments about strange diplomats and common sense, he kept them to himself. Lieutenant Zikirulla held up a clean cloth, which Wahap took before Azariah could, and he wiped his hand. The touch surprised Azariah, and he gave Wahap a look before glancing at the lieutenant. Should he walk the intimacy back? What if he was fine with this? Once his hand was clean, they continued the tour, walking deep into the fields. Azariah asked farming questions about soil composition, the growing season, what type of harvesting equipment they used, genetic work, and so on. It was very pleasant.

"This bright blue *kurak* is ground up to form solid surfaces. There are other kinds of *kurak*," Wahap said, walking and gesturing to an icy-blue version. "These are molded into shapes for construction. Another kind is translucent for windows. Others are used for textiles. These *kurak* over here are modified to be radiation resistant." He paused. "The atmosphere is thin, but you are safe from radiation poisoning. We ignite an artificial sun once a month, which is enough for the *kurak*. The crops for eating are still grown on the space stations. Not yet here." He grew quiet. They had reached an edge of the fields. "I have one last stop."

A cliff loomed large over their heads, five hundred feet up, and in front of them at ground level were carvings on the cliff, with significant religious markings and signs of sacrifices, though no blood sacrifices. Azariah saw a shrine to Sultan Satuq Bughra Khan, who he had studied in preparation, and other shrines or tombs he couldn't identify.

"We have a religious mazar culture that is especially important to our solar nomadic tribes. These cliffs protected us from physical disaster, and we continue to approach them for other forms of salvation, where we pour out who we are and ask for what we need, to treat disease that is beyond medicine, to save our souls, and even have parties for pleasure." Wahap spoke seriously and gripped Azariah's arm.

Azariah met his gaze and nodded. This was the heart of who they were; the religious vessel which held everything important and therefore would be a target for destruction if the Chaldean empire wanted to enforce a hegemony. Azariah clasped Wahap's arm in return as he thought about Darh Dothoma and Otero Linda bombed flat.

Wahap already trusted Azariah to a surprising extent, beyond their surface-level communication. Besides the religious import, he was saying that the civil war had been between the Achaemenid colonizers and the pre-Achaemenid population, which Azariah had already guessed. Wahap's own native Godaniya population had won the war at the expense of their home world; freedom from the colonizers had been that important. Azariah wanted to turn their conversation to safer ground.

"In the Chaldean empire, in the last hundred years, we've experienced a metaphysical veil being drawn back; the Babylonia solar system has a local god named Marduk. Have you had this mazar or others built for local gods or metaphysical events?" Data gathering like this was usually Beck's responsibility.

"I don't know," Wahap answered slowly, "how to answer that. I'm not sure if I understand correctly. Is this something I can read about in the database you've given us?"

"Yes, Wahap. Let's go back now."

Azariah would report on everything he had seen, so the less he saw, the better. But— "Let me tell you about where I'm from." Azariah spoke in a low tone and Wahap picked up the hint and they walked far enough from their staff that they wouldn't be overheard.

Once they were back at the diplomatic pavilion, Azariah found out that the captain had arranged for quarters on the moon so that they could be on site for the duration of this Jump cycle. *Phidippus* was still heading towards the inner planet, which was eight hundred million kilometers away.

Wahap beamed. "This is perfect. I will show you your quarters now."

He took the crew on a short walk across the plaza. They were lodged in small, ground-floor apartments that overlooked the plaza. The rest of the *Klipspringer* team looked as tired as Azariah felt, and the captain agreed to a break before accomplishing more before the moon-day was over.

Wahap and his aide followed Azariah to his apartment. "Lieutenant Zikirulla will be next door to you. My dear Azariah, if you go anywhere, I'd like you to take him with you," Wahap said, with such a complicated tone, seeming to say that yes, this was monitoring, but it was necessary.

Azariah nodded his compliance and the lieutenant left to settle in next door.

"Is there anything else I can do for you, Azariah?" Wahap asked, spreading his hands wide.

Azariah took off his cloak, and Wahap showed where to hang it up. Azariah was tired but wanted to keep Wahap around to learn more, and also it had been a long time since he had a charismatic man to chat with. Azariah's interest and exhaustion loosened his tongue as he explored the apartment, with Wahap following. "Wahap, if possible, I would like other crew on the *Klipspringer* to come down for leave, for day trips and also for longer stays." The bedroom was small, with only one bed. The textiles were woven from delicate *kurak* while firm, translucent *kurak* made the outside facing wall. "It would be good for morale. Wahap, this apartment is a tremendous luxury." Azariah knocked on the cobalt-blue surfaces in the bathroom and checked how things worked. "What's the water situation? This is the first time in my life that I have a living space that I don't have to share with anyone. I can move from the bed to the bathroom to the couch with no one else in the way!" Wahap stepped out of his way with a laugh as Azariah walked to the main living space, which was his and not a communal space. "I'll be here long enough that I will decorate for Gospel Arrival Day. Are there shops that sell supplies I could use? I can pay, don't worry." Azariah placed a hand on a wall as sturdy as concrete and wondered about decorating; the wall was painted but he could feel the texture of the radiation resistant *kurak*. Khoshkhar Muiz emitted enough radiation that he did indeed need protection, whatever Wahap had reassured him about earlier. One side of his apartment opened to an outside patio with a walkway leading to an open field and canyon. Azariah paused at the door to enjoy the view and breathed deep. He even had his own air.

"If everything is to your satisfaction, I should leave now, Envoy Ramzi," Wahap said.

"Of course. President Seyfiddin, it has been an honor. I am at your service." Azariah bowed, willing to end on a formal note. Once he was gone, Azariah wrote a long letter to Daniel, begging his forgiveness in advance if he needed to kiss Wahap for diplomatic reasons and then reminding Daniel he could kiss whoever he wanted because Daniel was still wedded to his goals, and also wrote that he looked super gorgeous in his new cloak and glowed in the light of the gas giant. And then Azariah erased it. As intimate as he and Daniel were, Daniel had been clear that he wasn't interested in a romantic pairing, or would give into what Azariah wanted with only deep reluctance. But maybe Azariah would write that out again, just in case. For now, he took a nap.

Chapter 28: Azariah, New Godaniya

After a few weeks, the diplomatic teams were settled into a routine. They spent part of each day just learning about each other; Azariah talked about the history since the fall of the Achaemenid Empire. The New Godaniya people spoke about the current state of their solar system. They spent part of each day on informal negotiations. Once the Gate opened, the diplomats with the power to create and sign contracts would come and do as they pleased.

On this day, Azariah had talked through religious expectations. He and Wahap had ended earlier than usual, frustrated with each other.

Once Azariah had an evening meal alone at his apartment, he decided to take a walk across the field out his back door. He wrapped himself up in his warm wool cloak and knocked on Lieutenant Zikirulla's door to let him know.

Azariah walked across the crunchy moon grass, leaving the work day behind, breathing the chilly, thin air. This was the first inhabited planet or moon he had ever been to that wasn't in the Gold Locked zone—where the planet or moon was the right distance from the sun and with the right ingredients that life was easily supported. This moon was in a Silver Locked zone and felt on edge, wild, much more alien, even without the literal aliens nearby. There was never a sun in the sky. There wasn't enough natural atmosphere to diffuse the starlight or Khoshkhar Muiz's glow.

The moon wasn't in tidal lock with the gas giant, so they had bright and dark times of the daily moon-cycle. Right now, a long curved edge of the gas giant was sinking at the edge of the horizon and stars were popping out. A perfect time of day for introspection. At home on Gospel, twilight was when Azariah would turn the machines off and ride his truck back home and go slow if he needed to think anything over. Twilight thinking was a habit he kept while on Babylon and he was drawn to it again now that he was on a planet. He felt uncaged.

He crossed the field and sat on a rock outcropping near the edge of the cliff, watching goats spring from rock to ledge on the cliff face across from him, the low gravity stretching the arcs of their jumps. The ranch they belonged to was nearby. Lieutenant Zikirulla had followed from a distance and had settled down on a rock of his own with his back to Azariah, facing the city. It was enough privacy.

What would Daniel think of me? Azariah wondered. His work as a diplomat was over for the day and it had gone terribly. Not that he needed an excuse to think about Daniel, but the day made him wonder what Daniel would have done. Wahap and Azariah had talked about having refugee Paradisians settle in the Godaniya system. His government didn't oppose the idea but thought they could support only a few hundred thousand settlers; fewer if the refugees were destitute. This was not the solution Daniel or Patroness Shelomith were looking for.

Before Azariah could think too much, Wahap joined him, laying a comfortable blanket down, which was a nice layer since the rock was cold. Lieutenant Zikirulla moved further away to be out of earshot, still facing the old capital city.

"Now, Azariah, we may speak in friendship." Wahap said, his bright eyes sparkling. The earlier frustrations had passed like a quick storm for Wahap.

Azariah sighed. "You can't possibly want us here. Why haven't you destroyed us yet before we build the Gate and bring the empire down on you?"

"I won't say it hasn't been suggested. You are convinced that the empire is inevitable—"

"I have said no such thing," Azariah retorted.

"You do not have to say it. Beyond that, some factions are curious to see if your other diplomatic team could somehow bring unity and healing—"

"That is ridiculously naïve to the point of suicide," Azariah interrupted.

"My instinct says to trust you," Wahap continued, "and it hasn't been wrong yet. Maybe a local god is giving me nudges. My dear Aza, I trust you specifically, hmm? And you've been honest enough in these matters? You are okay with me finding you trustworthy."

"As long as you remember, I am inexperienced and have terrible gut instincts. My degrees are all in Engineering."

"You are not an engineer. You are a diplomat. Your training, as such, exceeds all others. You think you wear your diplomatic role as a cloak, out of self-preservation and anger, but that is not true. Your successes come from deep inside you, who you really are."

"I'm no diplomat."

"Who else is saving solar systems from cultural genocide? Are you not a friend to kings and presidents? Who else on *Klipspringer* can be friends with the captain, Jump team, the doctor, the mess hall, and engineering? You take good care of all of them."

"That means nothing, not what you are suggesting." Azariah shook his head. Wahap held his hand, and Azariah shifted closer to lean against his shoulder. It was like leaning against a bear. Wahap took a device off the utility belt of his coveralls and set it on the ground. It blinked a yellow light and then a brown light and would protect them from eavesdropping.

"Come now, I've read reports from the other planets, and I know what your life on Babylon was like. This present moment might be the only time you can talk about it openly. Do you want to overthrow the Chaldean empire? Do you want to give up and be cut off and stay here? Or free Gospel? What is it you really want? If you've never talked about this, maybe you don't know."

"That's deep, my friend, as deep as your canyons. I think the truest answer is that I wanted to run away from all of that and more. But I'm dedicated to working towards what Daniel wants. How is that not an obvious, satisfactory answer?"

"Because it's what Daniel wants. It's his answer. Loving him is not the same as having your own goals. And goals are too immature a concept for what a full, lush life should look like."

"No, I don't allow that." Azariah took his hand back but didn't shift away. Wahap locked their arms together.

"My apologies. You're all over the place. Are you allowing different people to pull you in different directions or is there an underlying strength of purpose I haven't divined yet? But you haven't thought about this seriously."

"Wahap, you know me well enough by now that if you think I haven't thought about it seriously, then that is true. I am a good engineer and I enjoy the work. But if I were to see this from your perspective—my engineering classes gave me relief from the serious political machinations going on around me. I am good at the work but

I'm smart enough to be competent at whatever I try, and I've never mastered the engineering concepts or technology to the extent of the others. Many of the breakthroughs I've been credited with have been because of my relationships with people, and that is where any excellence has come from." This was all rushing out of Azariah. "This is very hard. I was happy with that work and now you're taking it away from me! Pouring myself into complex diplomacy— does anyone want me to— I'm already pretending. This is temporary. This is the only way I can get through."

"You do not have a clear purpose." Wahap took over gently. "You've kept yourself safe so far."

"And so how am I going to move forward and how can you use me?" Azariah said drily, after taking a few deep breaths and calming down.

"Let me see your hand again," Wahap said. They unlinked their arms. Azariah had been holding himself tight and took a moment to stretch before letting Wahap hold one hand in both of his. "This is not the hand of a farmer or engineer."

"Anyone's hand is going to look small and delicate in yours."

Wahap chuckled and rubbed his thumbs over Azariah's knuckles and calluses, and at the half-moon indents in the palm from his fingernails biting into the skin. "You do have people pulling you this way and that. It won't end after your *gerru*. But you can leave that all behind. You don't have to go back to the Chaldean empire or participate in the expansion. You could stay here and help me save this one solar system from colonialism. In return, I can protect you in more than just one way."

Azariah wanted to be mad at him for how self-serving he was being while pretending it was kindness. Azariah's anger fought with another reaction. Relief. Staying here would cut the Gordian knot he had made for himself. Even if Wahap didn't really like—

"Aza, I am lonely too." His voice was husky. They stared at each other for a moment. This whole moon was like a heady daydream, but he grounded Azariah firmly.

"I can't answer that right now," Azariah whispered.

"No one says no to me," Wahap said with a small but confident smile.

"You need to get used to it," Azariah answered. "What do you think the Chaldeans will be like?"

"Which is one reason I want to keep you close. But for now, the

Khoshkhar Muiz twilight is gone." Wahap knelt for a moment, a moon version of an evening prayer. "The ranchers are wrapping up for the day, as should we."

Azariah looked across the cliff where Wahap gestured. The ranchers herded the goats into an enclosure. If it was time for them to go inside, then he would too.

Chapter 29: Daniel

Revelation of John had been bombed at the beginning of the year, during the month of Baragzaggar. Daniel had spoken with Azariah six months after the bombing, during Duku. It was now Segurku, the last month of the year and with the shortest days. Azariah had just Jumped to the Godaniya solar system. Azariah had been gone for almost two years and it would be another year before he came home if he stayed safe. The events of Baragzaggar had consumed the whole year. Daniel was still full of grief, without a way forward.

The only time Daniel had directly asked God for anything was about King Nebuchadnezzar's first dream interpretation. Now, his grief was making him selfish enough that he asked for guidance. Daniel began a traditional mourning ritual where he ate simply and meditated while still living normally. He asked God to have mercy on his people. Surely they wouldn't endure slavery for seventy years. They were now assuming that the seventy-year countdown in Prophet Jeremiah's prophecies referred to the destruction of Revelation, not the relatively smaller scale violence that started a decade ago. After three weeks, Daniel was given a new vision.

Daniel received the vision when he was awake at an oasis near the Otero Linda temple in the Hunnubum Humtum desert. He was the only one who saw the vision; he had no strength left. His face turned deathly pale, and he fell into a deep sleep, his face to the ground.

Daniel looked up and there before him was a woman dressed in linen, with a belt of fine Ophir gold around her waist. Her body was like topaz, her face like lightning, her eyes like flaming torches, her arms and legs like the gleam of burnished bronze, and her voice was like the sound of a multitude.

A hand touched Daniel and set him trembling on his hands and knees. She said, "Daniel, you who are highly esteemed, consider carefully the words I am about to speak to you, and stand up, for I have now been sent to you." And when she said this, Daniel stood up trembling.

Then she continued, "Do not be afraid, Daniel. Since the first day that you set your mind to gain understanding and to humble yourself before your God, your words were heard, and I have come in response to them."

Daniel sighed in relief.

"I have been on the other side of your galaxy, which is why I didn't come right away. A chief prince called Michael came and helped me since I was detained with the king of Hecatompylos." Suddenly, the woman stood up. "We are not alone."

Gabriel, the archangel Daniel had seen in the earlier vision, came in swift flight about the time of the evening. She gave Daniel a complicated prophecy, saying, "Daniel, I have now come to give you insight and understanding. As soon as you began to pray, a word went out, which I have come to tell you, for you are highly esteemed. You wished to know about the seventy years. Consider these words and understand the vision: Seventy 'sevens' are decreed for your people and your holy city to finish transgression, to put an end to sin, to atone for wickedness, to bring in everlasting righteousness, to seal up vision and prophecy, and to anoint the Most Holy Place. Know and understand this: From the time the word goes out to restore and rebuild Jerusalem until the Anointed One, the ruler, comes, there will be seven 'sevens,' and sixty-two 'sevens.' It will be rebuilt with streets and a trench, but in times of trouble. After the sixty-two 'sevens,' the Anointed One will be put to death and will have nothing. The people of the ruler who will come will destroy the city and the sanctuary. The end will come like a flood: War will continue until the end and desolations have been decreed. She will confirm a covenant with many for one 'seven.' In the middle of the 'seven,' she will put an end to sacrifice and offering. And at the temple she will set up an abomination that causes desolation until the end that is decreed is poured out on her."

While she was saying this, Daniel bowed with his face toward the ground and was speechless. Then the woman touched his lips, and he opened his mouth and began to speak. Daniel said to Gabriel standing before him, "I am overcome with anguish because of the vision, my lord, and I feel very weak. How can I, your servant, talk with you, my lord? My strength is gone, and I can hardly breathe."

Gabriel didn't speak further. The woman touched him again and gave him strength. "Do not be afraid, you who are highly esteemed," she said. "Peace! Be strong now; be strong."

When she spoke, Daniel was strengthened and said, "Speak, my lady, since you have given me strength."

She said, "Do you know why I have come to you? Soon I will return to fight against the prince of Iréchikwa, and when I go, Abisare, the prince of Larsa, will come, but first I will tell you what is written in the Book of Truth. (No one supports me against them except Michael, your prince. And in the first year of Cazonci Tariácuri, I took my stand to support and protect him.) So then, let me tell you what is happening..."

The words she said were to be rolled up and sealed until the time of the end.

Daniel had the vision again and again, the woman of the vision continually catching him at bad times. Once he was on a pleasure cruise with the king viewing the Tigris Nebula. She made Daniel thankful for Gabriel and other messengers who came only when he was sleeping. He couldn't decide if the woman was the Daughter, like a heavenly interpretation. It was a very confusing vision, and he didn't share it with anyone.

Daniel didn't have a way to verify her information; she said she was coming from battle but were those battles concurrent with his time? Without giving specifics, Daniel asked the king if the next Jumping ship, the *Skakavac*, could be sent to gather information. He was delighted with the idea.

After a couple months, as Daniel memorized it, he stopped having the vision.

During Gusisa, a month with short days, Daniel received a message from Prophet Jeremiah that he was going to come to Babylon to check on the deposed Paradisian royalty, Queen Zedekia. Daniel was eager to meet him and obtained permission to do so with Oshpenaz as a chaperone.

They waited at the space elevators. Jeremiah was unmistakable in his Revelation style coveralls with a Revelation cloak and long beard. Daniel knew enough about life in court to recognize and appreciate the display, even if Jeremiah represented a now-destroyed court.

Daniel bowed and introduced himself and Oshpenaz. They would speak in Akkadian instead of Kahi for Oshpenaz's benefit, though Daniel was pretty sure he had mastered Kahi in the last few years.

Jeremiah scowled at both men and sneered at Daniel's robes and general appearance. Daniel's robes were dark and modest but rich; he didn't look like a Gospel prophet or like he belonged to the Chaldean royal court either—or perhaps he was fitting in. Daniel was indeed indulged and given real political power compared to Jeremiah. Queen Zedekia had thrown him into prison more than once.

They started the walk up to the Etemenanki palace. Within five minutes, Daniel was lagging behind and it was clear that he was in the worst shape.

Jeremiah glared. "I thought we might talk about your vision on the walk so I could go straight to the deposed queen, but I suppose you can't say anything while you're gasping for breath."

Oshpenaz threw Daniel an exasperated look. This was Daniel's fault for wanting to wear formal, heavy robes on a hike under Babylon's sun, which was still warm even during the constant twilight.

His visions had worn him out more than he had realized. Between them and his formal grieving, Daniel hadn't eaten well in a long time, and before that he hadn't been taking care of himself. The woman's encouraging words hit him anew.

They eventually arrived at the palace. Oshpenaz led the prophets to a pavilion with a view of the Wara Ti'amtum mountains. Daniel drank half his weight in water and citrus juice. The two men had polite conversation with horrible biting undertones. As soon as Daniel could —

"My vision" —*whoosh*, he had their attention like two birds of prey hunting a *huljum*. For the first time, Daniel shared what this vision was, telling them everything, getting his disc out to check his notes on some of the specifics.

"So you asked your God about the next seventy years, you asked for mercy, and Gabriel and this woman, who may be the Paradisian Daughter, tell you about the next seven times seventy years," Oshpenaz said with a chuckle.

"Is this what you wanted to talk to me about? These visions have nothing to do with me." Jeremiah scowled. "Why are you asking about this? Why are you bothering me? Go off and do your own thing with your visions. I'm here to see the deposed queen. You've clearly made your home here with the whore Babylon. Do you have anything to do with your native people? I've never seen a sign."

"That's not true," Daniel said in a quiet voice, trying to hide his emotion. "I'm a hostage more than any other Paradisian. I'm in exile just as much as any of them. Haven't I been working the best I can for our people?" Daniel felt punched in the gut. He respected Jeremiah and didn't know what he had done to be so dismissed. Daniel knew within his heart that he was true to his roots; Jeremiah's words were about their people abandoning Daniel, if anything.

"What we see is that you are at the right hand of the king who is happy to have you there. You serve the whore Babylon. I doubt that is the kind of prosperity God calls us to." Jeremiah added in a tone a shade kinder, "What is it you want from me? We've had nothing to do with each other."

Daniel answered in Kahi, "I wanted to speak to my people's prophet. I wanted to know what I'm supposed to do. You are still my spiritual leader." His Valla Varra accent got thicker the more he spoke, rolling his r's. "What does any of this mean? How can any of us move forward? Who is our God even?"

"Your answers are not my answers," he answered back in Kahi. "We have nothing to do with each other. What is blocking you from seeing something so obvious? Clean up your own house, you young, rich, spoiled thing, with your web of lies—"

"I have not lied! We have not lied! No one is hiding the children. They are dead. I helped carry their bodies away! Have you had the literal blood of children on your hands? You were the one to fail our people as much as you accuse me now."

"Daniel, no one has accused anyone of failure," Oshpenaz interrupted smoothly, Jeremiah scowling at his Kahi. "I am sure, Jeremiah, now that you are here, we can provide proof that the lineage is dead but for the deposed queen. Perhaps it is time to visit."

"Maybe you are not lying. My apologies."

Daniel stood up. "I visit the deposed queen once a week. She is fine. The quarters are this way."

Jeremiah's "web of lies" comment was directed to the general belief that since Daniel was a good man in a politically powerful position, he therefore could not have possibly allowed the last royal children to die. From there, several conspiracy theories blossomed. One rumor was that Daniel sent them to Aegyptus—possibly setting the stage for clones to appear in a few decades. Daniel was tired and his emotions were lost in reliving some very bad memories.

Visiting the deposed queen didn't help his mood, but he was composed enough to assist when appropriate. Daniel never talked to her; his idea of doing the right thing by the deposed queen was to just show up and make sure she wasn't being actively tortured. He thought about Jeremiah's words. Daniel didn't belong to Paradise anymore; they were done with him. But he certainly didn't belong to the Chaldean empire. Neither were his. So where did he belong? God gave him visions, but that wasn't who he was, nor what he did in his day-to-day life. Right now, all he'd done was repeat the vision as a mouthpiece. But there was more to do. Helping Paradise hadn't been working; an intelligent man would find something that did work. This is when Daniel would fall on Azariah and weep and then try again, but Azariah had taken himself away. Why wouldn't he stay? But no self-pity.

From the start, Jeremiah had planned to stay at the North Pole for only a few hours. Daniel and Oshpenaz walked him back to the space elevators when the twilight was deep. At the station, Jeremiah stopped him.

"Daniel Rosefinch-Ravauviro, I will say this to you, which you have been told before and have been deaf to: God has given you, more than once, galaxy politics for the next five hundred years; God has given you unprecedented access to an emperor whose empire is only growing; God has not condemned you personally but has said the opposite; God has told you and your friends to prosper outside of Paradise, yet you continue to look back like Lot's wife. God has led you to your destiny. You must choose to move forward in peace. You asked God for mercy and God answered you; if you are confused or think I can advise you, that's your problem. I'll see if I can think of another metaphor on how stupid you are. Until next time." He bowed to both and, without waiting for a response, was away.

Chapter 30: Daniel

Daniel was exhausted. Oshpenaz left him behind. Daniel went straight home to his palace quarters, cleaned up for bedtime, and said his evening prayer, adding, *please don't bother me, please let me sleep well.*

His sleep became a lucid dream.

Azariah was leaning against me at a tropical beach. The smell and taste of salt in the air and the sound of the waves and the saturated, pastel colors of everything made a perfect heaven, much better than the stupid fire throne room.

I looked out over the green waves to the horizon.

"Have we ever been to the beach together?" I asked.

"No."

"Have I told you I like to surf?"

"No, babe."

"My father surfs. That's how he lived with his family before marrying my mom. We would go surfing almost every vacation."

Azariah was quiet.

I looked out over the green waves to the horizon.

"Have we ever been to the beach together?" I asked.

"No."

"Have I told you I like to surf?"

"No, babe."

"There's still so much that we don't know about each other. How could we spend every day together for years and still not know things? And now we're apart and might be forever."

"You're my best friend."

I looked out over the green waves to the horizon.

"Have we been to the beach together?" I asked.

"No."

"Have I told you I like to surf?"

"No, babe."

I could stay here forever.

Time passed in a funny way.

I looked out over the green waves to the horizon. I looked at Azariah, which I hadn't done before. He was how I remembered him, short hair, well-trimmed beard, deeply tan, almost as dark as me, well-muscled and leaning against me, and wearing sunglasses and a swimming suit.

I looked out over the green waves to the horizon.

"You've looked at me funny before," I said.

He was quiet. My thoughts were sticky like honey.

"Prophet Jeremiah said things and you've looked at me the way he's said those things."

"You're my best friend."

"Have we been to the beach together?"

"No."

"Have I told you I love to surf?"

"No, babe."

Time passed again.

I looked over the green waves to the horizon.

"The first time I blessed you." The memory clicked. "We were in the Chaldean chapel. I was upset, and you were surprised. Do you remember that?"

He took off his sunglasses and looked at me with interest.

"Yes, like that. What were you thinking?" I held his face in my hands.

He smiled but didn't say.

"Fine, I'm asking in a letter when I wake up."

Time passed again.

I looked over the green waves to the horizon.

"When I was about to enter the high royal court for the first time." The memory clicked. "I was tucking in your shemagh, and you were so proud of me. I remember your expression. Do you remember that?"

He took off his sunglasses and looked at me with pride.

"Yes, like that. What were you thinking?" I held his face in my hands, his beard wooly.

He smiled but didn't say.

"Fine, I'm asking in a letter when I wake up."

I looked out over the green waves to the horizon.

"Have we ever been to the beach together?" I asked.

"No."

"Have I told you I like to surf?"

He held my face in his hands. The sunshine made his brown eyes shine like jacinth. "Daniel, we will always love each other."

When Daniel woke up, he re-read all of Azariah's letters to see if he said anything like what Prophet Jeremiah said. He found nothing. He would continue to think about this.

Chapter 31: Nebuchadnezzar

"I, in my magnificent benevolence, shall allow the Paradisians to heal at Sumer before being sent off as slaves." I handed the permissions off, delegated, etc. and turned to the view for a bit of fresh air. I was, in fact, at that very moment on Sumer. My personal shuttle had landed on the top of an old building at the edge of a hygrophyllic forest. Gigantic monoecious winewood trees had taken over this city. Quite fun to see. A thunderstorm was threatening in the distance, which only added to the beauty.

"'The world is charged with the grandeur of God. It will flame out, like shining from shook foil.'" I breathed deep, throwing my head back and stretching my arms. "'There lives the dearest freshness deep down things.' I would have made the galaxy's best poet if I had put my mind to it, don't you think, Erioch?"

"Yes, Your Majesty."

"Next topic, I want to spend ten minutes talking about Envoy Azariah Ramzi." I looked around me. Hasdrubal and Oshpenaz were at my right hand; protection officers were the only other people in earshot. "He is accreting a significant amount of soft power and is not giving me enough credit. I am clearly the best person in the entire galaxy, anointed by Ramzi's own God, and yet Ramzi has not instilled enough respect or fear for me in my new subjects. He has informed the leaders of these various worlds on how to assert their own sovereignty. Envoy Ramzi should be only an extension of me, his king. How has this happened?"

"He met the technical qualifications for the position, and I encouraged him to volunteer," Oshpenaz said. "People who enjoy being envoys don't enjoy taking on the risk that this *gerru* was judged to have. The *Klipspringer* wasn't ever expected to be this successful."

Hasdrubal held a screen for me to view, showing me Ramzi's qualifications.

"I can't believe they've been so successful. I can't believe it's annoying me! I love these worlds! But *Klipspringer* is proving me wrong. I don't like that; why are they so successful now and not the last ten years? Wait, don't answer that, this time is for the envoy." Hasdrubal made a note of my question. Good woman. "His latest report on Shabwa of Hadhramaut indicates he serves me in an active, positive way. But does that outweigh the negatives? No. If he knows me, then he knows how to work against me. He's telling me about these vacation spots to distract me from all the stuff he's hiding from me. It's enough to make any king furious. And you're right about the risk. Why would Ramzi take the risk? What's his profile?"

Hasdrubal flipped to the information.

Erioch answered, "According to the psych profile and what I've seen for myself, he's in love with *pasisum* Daniel, who may not love him back, and so Azariah wanted to get away."

I made a blessing sign after hearing Daniel's name. "Awww, that's very cute and tragic, but it doesn't negate that he's making a mess now. He was always going to marry a woman, anyway. My breeding program, you know. This is what I want to talk about. Maybe it would be better for him to just never come back from this *gerru*, or perhaps have him die soon after so that he's not doing anything with all this power he's gathering. It would send a message to the new worlds. Erioch? Besides being in love, what's wrong with the envoy?"

"I don't have access to his internal dialogue to know if his true motivations are different from the observable evidence."

I sighed. He and Hammu weren't done investigating and wouldn't tell me anything. "I suppose I'll ask Birbirru about her research. I want to see all the little thoughts in people's heads. Some observable evidence: he is stirring things up—the *gerru* worlds have courage to protest against us—but they are sentiments we would have dealt with, anyway. Now it's like one clean bombing, one clean purge, and they are under our control more fully." I had my doubts about so much violence, but I was such a softy. My benevolence and mercy were worthy of worship. "He will need to die at the end in order to complete this picture." Erioch nodded politely in agreement, which was a relief.

"I don't think there is enough evidence to take such an extreme measure," Oshpenaz objected.

"It's not that extreme. People die every day. You know my feelings about that."

Oshpenaz closed his eyes like he was in pain. He was annoyed with me but couldn't say anything. If he fought for Ramzi, that would prove my point. If he didn't fight for Ramzi, then he risked me delegating another assassination order. In hindsight, the first one was obviously going to fail. My people failed me regularly, but I was merciful.

"Perhaps he can still prove his loyalty." I said encouragingly. "I'll give him until the end of the *gerru*. But don't tell him that. Overall, this should be a learning lesson for all of us on who gets to be an envoy. Okay, that's five minutes on him. Anything else?"

"To get everything out in the open," Oshpenaz sighed, "he is being accused of treason, something that happened on Sumer."

"My God! I told you! Hurry up, Hasdrubal, let me see this."

"It's a report submitted by the main communications officer, Brigette Beck," said Erioch, and summarized things nicely. It's why I kept him around.

"Excuse me, your Majesty," Oshpenaz interjected. "You need to see the recording Azariah made. It's been sealed against tampering."

Hasdrubal played a passage of Azariah interacting with the natives.

"Ah, I see. They do try to worship him, but look! The envoy referred to me several times. I am reasonable, the most reasonable; of course that isn't treason. If I have him executed, it won't be for this. Have you read the reports? He's terrible at this job. Maybe he's okay. Re-reading his report in light of the treason accusation, things make more sense. Brigette Beck.... I feel like I've heard her name connected to something else. I try to stay away from the Beck clan. They're a bunch of alligators."

"You referred to a breeding program. Beck has requested Azariah father a child for her. She wishes to get pregnant soon after the trip, to perhaps *start things* while still on the ship. The request came through on the last batch of mail. We didn't hear anything from Azariah."

"The same Beck? She sent a treason report *and* a formal breeding request at the same time? And it's not for marriage." I checked.

"The request came on a later cycle."

"This is too much drama. Is she making some personal, controlling play for him? What do you think?"

"Do you want to expand the scope of the conversation to Beck? Dig up her psych profile?"

"No, just the envoy. What do you think? Oshpenaz?" I raised an eyebrow.

"He's handsome and charming with no vices. I'm sure half the ship is in love with him. It's part of what makes him a good and bad envoy. Based on previous knowledge, he won't want Beck to have his child. It's within the realm of decisions you have delegated to me, and I was going to allow him to reject her if that's what he wants."

"And you say he's in love with Daniel? My Daniel?"

"Indeed," Oshpenaz answered. Erioch and Hasdrubal both nodded. "He has been very resistant to marriage to a woman."

"Who? Ramzi or Daniel?"

"I was referring to Azariah. But Daniel is resistant to marriage to anyone."

"I knew that." I thought about it for a minute. If the envoy was allowed back, he would be very interesting. The potential, entertaining pathos. "Who's cuter? Daniel or Ramzi?"

Oshpenaz glared at me.

"Well? Erioch, who do you think is cuter?" I asked. Hasdrubal flipped between a couple of pictures.

"My wife—I'm attracted to my wife."

"Ah, no fun. Hasdrubal?"

"Daniel. Have you noticed he's changed recently? There's something different."

"Yes, but this is Ramzi's time. Focus. He's fantastic. If I have to assassinate or execute him, this might be the only chance to get his progeny, so let's set assassination plots aside. That one committee already approved Beck's request, so Ramzi has to fulfill his part. How do embryos do with Jumping? Time to find out. Don't have them wait until they get back. I still can't believe they might make it back. I'd written them all off. Also, if he or Daniel ever seem friendly with any Chaldean women, fast track those marriages. But Azariah doesn't have to have sex with Beck. It can be artificial. In fact, it should be. Sexual morality is important to me now. You can say that when you deny his request. Actually, don't wait for him. Send a response he'll receive immediately that I proactively deny any request to refuse and he shouldn't delay, per my own request."

"If I may offer an alternative plan, or perhaps an additional plan, we could let Azariah and Daniel get married. Daniel's sisters could have Azariah's children. Maybe we find a royal or noble donor for Daniel to have biological children, and they can raise their children together, or perhaps let the mothers raise the children."

"I want three children each."

"I know."

"Do you see those two raising six children? Or voluntarily having their progeny raised outside their households? They can marry women and still love each other. Does Daniel love him back? Is that why he got all weird? Don't answer that yet," I said. Hasdrubal made another note. If Daniel was in love, that would be a wrench in my plans, because there was no way I was going to screw around with Daniel's life while he was blessed by his powerful God.

"Azariah has ten brothers and sisters, so yes, he might be happy to raise six children."

"Delightful idea. This is in addition to Beck's child. Ramzi can have children with whatever sister is the most culturally Chaldean, probably the youngest." I had Hasdrubal scroll through Daniel's sisters. "WHAT is this?! Daniel's sister Magdalene is *THEE* Magdalene? Why have you never told me? This is an egregious mistake. Why? Erioch, you favor Daniel too much. This is almost too far. I wouldn't have hurt him too badly to get to her." I made another blessing sign so that Daniel's creator God knew I was telling the truth.

"Your Majesty, we told you," Erioch said with a polite bow. "But he was in especial favor with you at the time because he gave you the Aegyptian emeralds."

"Ah, I remember. Very clever of him."

Hasdrubal tapped the time.

"I obey you in all things," Oshpenaz said to wrap this up, "but in order to mitigate the risk of execution, is there anything I can do? Any orders to rein in Aza?"

"No to all questions. Why do you care? Didn't you send him on this *gerru* to die? Don't answer that and don't say anything to anyone. We'll see. Last wrap up note, if Daniel loves him and I decide to not execute him, we should have a big wedding for them, like delegations from all of my worlds. Would Babylon be big enough? Maybe have a few months' wedding feast on a luxury planet? So what's next? Has the next batch of Ophir asteroids been delivered? Get me off this planet before the cannibals get me. We've wiped out the frozen region cannibals, right? We think the people at the tropics might be cannibals. Let's just wipe them out as a proactive measure. That will leave room for more hospitals! I like the idea of multiple sanatoriums. What are you standing around for?"

Chapter 32: Azariah, New Godaniya

Azariah's time on New Godaniya had reached the half-way point. Beck and her team were communicating with the inner planet and sending confidential information back to *Klipspringer*; Captain Sifontes, Wahap, and others disappeared into meetings. Azariah was happy enough to stay out of it. One of the monthly "lightings" was about to happen and he was helping to make it a bigger party than usual, with shipmates coming down to enjoy the food and music. This festival matched with Gospel's Arrival Day: a few weeks after a quiet Christmas in the Godaniyan tradition and a little before Babylon's Dannatum Kussim holiday. Azariah suddenly felt old; He had enjoyed the Dannatum Kussim hedonism as a teenager, but now it seemed too crass, with no soul or purpose. What were bird races compared to lighting a sun to help crops grow? He was happy here.

On the day of the party, Azariah found a new balance between engineer and diplomat. He wanted to see how the artificial sun worked and wanted to know the pros and cons for why just one day a month was good enough. Many people from the United Station States of Godaniya were arriving with food, and he wanted to talk with them as well.

The actual lighting of the sun took place early moon-morning when Khoshkhar Muiz was just peeking over the horizon. Azariah was with Lieutenant Zikirulla, Kilzan, and the captain's aide in the chilly morning, standing shoulder to shoulder with the technicians right under the sun, on a small platform surrounded by New Godaniyans and the seaweed *kurak* towering over their heads. The searing burst of light from the sun brought all the textures and shapes around them into great detail. Azariah cheered with the rest of the crowd in the *kurak* fields, and they paraded on a short pilgrimage to the nearby mazar and then back to the plaza, though some of the crowd parted off to go on a longer pilgrimage to other mazars. Today was dazzling.

Usually, the lighting ceremony ended there; everyone got back to the plaza and then back to life. However, this was the month of a big harvest, so the pavilion of the plaza was full of musicians. Half of the plaza was full of food carts. They wandered around and after eating breakfast, Kilzan and Khamla went off in one direction while Lieutenant Zikirulla and Azariah went in another, where he saw people from the USSG. Azariah memorized names and facts as usual when the lieutenant introduced him. This time, all the information felt weighty.

Wahap hadn't asked Azariah to stay again, but he was folding him into this life, and Azariah wasn't pushing back. Lieutenant Zikirulla's introductions had *intent*. Azariah had written many long letters to Daniel about Wahap and New Godaniya, trying to work things out for himself but not succeeding. Daniel and Azariah had talked several times over the years about choices made in order to survive versus having the ability to pursue self-fulfillment versus sacrifice, and Azariah was having those conversations again with Wahap. What did survival even look like?

Before Azariah could get too confused again—introspection was not his strong point—Wahap found him.

"President Seyfiddin," Azariah said, bowing, with the lieutenant smirking nearby, "I've been honored with an in-person introduction to the Vice President A'ishe Khatun of the USSG. She will give me a tour of the outermost military post soon, which I'm looking forward to."

"Excellent. Indeed," he said, stroking his beard. After a few minutes of polite conversation, he excused himself and Azariah away and whisked him to the food carts again. They lost the formality. "I had one of my favorite vendors prepare a special treat for you. I hope you're hungry."

"It's lunchtime! It feels like I just enjoyed breakfast, but the entire morning is gone." Azariah held his hand out to the sunshine. "Does the light dim, or will it just turn off? It doesn't move, so I don't feel the passage of time."

"The mathematical relation between luminosity and time is beyond me. I will find a scientist for you to talk to. But here we are." He greeted the vendor and handed Azariah the food, as proud as if he had made it himself. "A shish kebab. This is what you eat for your Arrival Day, no?"

"It's perfect! It smells and looks divine." The shish kebab layered meat between his favorite vegetables, skewered and grilled to perfection. Azariah took a small bite. The hot fat and bitter vegetables tasted perfect. He bowed to the vendor. "Thank you. New Godaniyans have this a different time of the year, though."

"Which is why it's a special treat for you today. It's goat meat, which I know you can eat, and no, not the goats you are friends with." Wahap took one for himself and they wandered, everyone happy to see him and still curious about Azariah. This might be the last lighting festival before the empire arrived and changed their hard-won equilibrium. Wahap took Azariah to another vendor that had chocolate pressed into starship shapes—another Arrival Day tradition that made Azariah smile. After that was one more surprise but it was meant for kids. "I thought you could demonstrate and they will enjoy the rest. We've never seen balloons before, so I don't know if this is right." Wahap led Azariah to a gigantic bouquet of balloons that looked perfect.

"Ah! I know exactly what to do!" Azariah grabbed a balloon, shook it, heard a proper rattling, and brought it to a stout, unafraid looking little girl named Khadijah wearing the heavy, ubiquitous utility belt. "Do you like loud noises?" She gestured yes solemnly. Azariah showed her his skewer and then used it to pop the balloon. Khadijah jumped and then smiled when he showed her the toy inside, a mini replica of the moon. "This is mine. You can pop one balloon for yourself." She and the children nearby had a fun time for a few minutes, much to everyone else's consternation, which was perfect.

Azariah gave Wahap a big smile, and in return, Wahap gave him a very tender look. "There are fireworks for later."

"I helped with those! Do you have the handheld ones? I said those were important." Azariah waved his hand in the air to mimic a sparkler.

"No, they sound too dangerous," Wahap said, cutting the air with finality, which made Azariah laugh.

"For now, this is the time of day when I debrief with Captain Sifontes at my apartment. You are always invited, but if you have other things…"

"I will come," he smiled and held his elbow, looking around to make sure Lieutenant Zikirulla was nearby, and they wound their way across the plaza. Kilzan and the captain's aide Khamla were with Captain Sifontes as well. Good, they would have a proper meeting.

"Lieutenant," Wahap frowned, "where are the aides for Kilzan and

Khamla? Have the utility belts come in? They need to be wearing them."

"Captain!" Azariah waved, and when they were close enough, he bent down to give the captain a brief hug. She stayed stiff but patted his back twice. Azariah stood up and—

Chapter 33: Azariah, New Godaniya

Two things happened at once.

1. Azariah received a message that a bomb was incoming.

2. Over the captain's shoulder bloomed an enormous explosion with a mushroom cloud.

Wahap, on the other side of the captain, saw too. He took her arm and pulled her to Azariah's apartment entrance. Lieutenant Zikirulla took Azariah's arm and pulled him and Khamla. As soon as Kilzan cleared the threshold, Wahap hit a switch next to the door and a thick emergency shield slammed down over the apartment entrance and windows. From the explosion to entering the apartment was less than five seconds.

"Not yet," Kilzan yelled. "We can save more." The shockwave hit and they all fell to the ground.

They stayed quiet on the floor for a moment.

"Open this up, we've got to see—" Kilzan said. Azariah helped the captain to her feet.

"No, not yet," Wahap said, removing his communicator from his utility belt.

"There were children!"

"They were all near buildings or shelters like this one," Wahap answered. At a nod from Wahap, Lieutenant Zikirulla went to Kilzan.

"Emergency protocol," the captain said to Azariah and Khamla.

Khamla nodded and reached into one of his coverall pockets. He pulled out two emergency communicators, one the size of a pill and the other a disc, handing the pill to the captain and the disc to Azariah. Wahap moved to the other side of the living room and spoke quietly and urgently. Lieutenant Zikirulla was still whispering to Kilzan while digging into compartments in Azariah's apartment walls.

The captain set her pill-sized communicator, which was an emergency message set to transmit to the Gate above Babylon. She clicked on the small buttons, and it floated in the air in front of her. It created a true vacuum around itself—not just free of air but from any force that could interfere with a communication Jump. Azariah had seen only a couple. Sometimes they floated and sometimes they didn't. After a moment, the pill fell into the captain's hand. Presumably the message had been successfully sent. Besides the transmission tech, it had only five quarks, six settings per quark, each with a spin, which allowed for a significant number of coded messages.

"I chose the pre-set message: *nuclear bomb, unknown casualties, Gate open in five hours*. We need to Jump."

Azariah nodded. He was already talking with the ship. Several bombs had originated from a stealth ship. The inner planet took credit. Most bombs had been intercepted. A space station that had been guarding the *Klipspringer* was destroyed. Azariah told the crew to get the Gate hooked up and that they would Jump as soon as possible, which was the emergency protocol. Security Officer Juma said that both would be ready in two hours.

"So we're leaving Beck and her team behind?" Khamla asked, interrupting the plans Captain Sifontes and Azariah were discussing.

"If they make it back here alive," the captain said, "they will catch up when we open the next Gate. Good to know it will be only two hours instead of five." Her forehead wrinkling was the only sign of emotion.

Wahap joined them, looking sick, with the same information they had received from the ship. He addressed Captain Sifontes. "I can report from my military that the threat has been destroyed. Even so, the military ships and stations are moving to create a better barrier to protect this city. We're safe from another attack." Azariah squeezed his arm, and he rallied a bit.

The captain took Azariah's emergency communicator to make some specific orders.

Azariah hustled Wahap off to the side. "We've been improving the empire's radiation healing technology. I don't know what yours is like, but let me give you what I have." Azariah transmitted info from his personal disc to Wahap's personal data storage.

Wahap scanned through it. "It's different, not necessarily better, but different options are always good. Here." He transmitted information on their type of treatment. He motioned to the couch and pulled the cushions off. "Here are the special radiation suits. We need to put these on before we go out." Lieutenant Zikirulla was helping Kilzan and Khamla.

The captain and Azariah grabbed one each. She motioned to Azariah, and they moved to his bedroom.

"Interesting that they had that kind of emergency door and these suits. I didn't know about any of it," Azariah said.

The captain frowned. "You didn't come to any of the proper meetings."

"Someone should have told me about this threat. Are you sure about Jumping so soon?" Azariah asked as he slipped his legs into the suit.

"The threat being so dangerous is obvious only in hindsight. Protocol doesn't say I can't Jump and if we don't, we might get bogged down for half a year writing reports. We wait for the parts for the next Gate to be delivered and then Jump." She lowered her voice further. "If anyone has died, which seems likely, we leave their bodies here, which is borderline against protocol. I trust that President Seyfiddin will be respectful. The only people going back to the ship are the ones who can do their duties. Do you have anyone who's absolutely irreplaceable?"

"We're ready for this Jump. For the next Jump, to plot and program it, the people I truly need are on the ship. We'll be fine with the updated algorithm if.. um… if… Din and the others… can't make it back. For other duties, there aren't any irreplaceable specialists."

"Can you back me up on what I'm saying?"

"This is… I'm glad I don't have to make decisions. I don't think anyone will be able to object until it's too late." Azariah sighed. "If there are survivors with broken bones or internal injuries due to the shockwave, they should stay behind. While the ship could treat them, the Jump would be pretty rough."

"Thank you."

They put on the suits. Before Azariah put on the helmet, Captain Sifontes grabbed his arm and looked him in the eye. "I saw you exchanging info with President Seyfiddin. You cannot do that. You can't be so independent. I'm saying this to keep you safe. Exchanging tech behind the king's back is going to get you into deeper water, both you and your friends, as I'm assuming you're planning to pass any new radiation healing tech onto them. Use official channels only. I'm warning you. Also, you said something about an updated algorithm. You better not be working on AI; that is highly monitored and still hasn't been approved for this mission. In fact, what you said is enough that I'll be making a thorough search of your belongings, electronic information, office, and person once we're back on the ship."

"You won't find anything, but I understand."

After this, they joined the other two, who were ready. Lieutenant Zikirulla, with Kilzan's help, had piled all the emergency supplies near the emergency door in readiness. The captain and Azariah glanced at each other to acknowledge that this one apartment contained a significant amount of supplies.

"Just to prepare you," Wahap said, "my people have personal protection fields to protect against such a shockwave." He showed them a device in his utility belt. "If the shockwave wasn't too strong, and my people were close to any of your crew, which they are supposed to be, a personal shield could probably protect one other person."

Azariah looked at the captain to see if she had known this. She raised her eyebrow. The implications.

Wahap opened the emergency door. The destruction was total, the food carts tumbled, Azariah's patio and the pavilion were crumbled, with the musical instruments shattered. Azariah couldn't see far, but a few people were walking around, checking out people who weren't walking around. Everything was gray, the air still thick with dust.

Per emergency protocol, it was Azariah's duty as second in command, which he unfortunately was, to make the official on-ground report and be the liaison between the ground and ship. With permission from the captain, he dictated a report to Wamiri on the ship so that he could walk around and help people.

Azariah described the nuclear blast. He explained the personal shield on the moon citizens' utility belts. He summarized how he and his companions were able to escape damage from the shockwave. The part of the city they were in was clearly prepared for such an attack. The minor damage sustained indicated the buildings would have survived anything except a direct hit. A triage area was already being set up. People in line had huddled together on grass-like growth at the edge of the ruined patio. Other people were dead or too injured, the shockwave overloading their shields, and were still out in the plaza, though they were being treated or covered up one by one respectfully. Azariah checked on the group of children he had played with less than an hour ago; they were safe. Their parents had protected them and now they were washing the radioactive dust off in a community shower.

There was a search in the extensive field on the other side of Azariah's apartment building. He dictated more of his report as he walked, helping to search the field. He named the crew he saw alive. So many survived thanks to the personal shields, but so many were still unaccounted for, and a few already known to be dead, which should have hurt. But Azariah was in shock.

The first person he found was a moon person. Their personal shield seemed to have been overloaded during the shockwave; while they were alive, the force of the shockwave had broken bones, they had decided to lay quietly instead of calling for help. Once someone arrived, Azariah continued his search. He found Din unconscious and with several broken bones and burns; he had been alone and appeared to have taken cover against a rock. Azariah reported it to Wamiri, describing his injuries. Wamiri cried.

"Wamiri, have you been writing this down?"

Azariah only heard crying.

"Wamiri, you can cry. I understand the need to cry, but you need to cry and write. Have you been completing the report?" Azariah asked coldly.

Bounthavy replied. "Sorry Azariah, it's hit her hard. The last line is — is describing Din. It looks like she's got everything you've been saying. We've all been listening."

"General announcement, people, get back to your work *now*. Bounthavy, send Wamiri to the dorm and then go into my office."

Once Bounthavy was settled in she said, "Sorry sir, just with Din down and a few others dead, we're all a bit shaken but we're prepping for the Jump."

"Understandable. Let's move on." Azariah asked if Engineering was getting ready to Jump, Bounthavy confirmed they were, so he continued his description of the damage while waiting for someone to take care of Din.

Azariah's search area went to the edge of the cliffs. The farm across the cliff was flattened, as were all the structures in any direction. Movement in the ravine caught Azariah's eye. The goats were leaping from ledge to ledge like nothing was wrong. The shockwave didn't go into the canyon. At this point, five of the crew were still unaccounted for. Hoping against hope, he jogged right to the very edge, sliding down a slope and calling out.

"Azariah! Here!" That sounded like Conceição, the cook.

Azariah projected a flashlight from his disc. Thirty feet below on a ledge were two of the ship's cooks.

"There's three more of us," Conceição said when he found her with the light. "They fell down a lot further. There's a moon farmer too."

"Hold on!" Azariah called, putting Bounthavy on hold to contact help.

"Hey Aza," shouted Aparecida, the other cook, "I heard how you liked the goat meat, so I was talking to the rancher about getting some meat to take back with us, or maybe a couple goats for milk, how does that sound?"

"Thank you for thinking of me. The captain has other orders. Maybe we can get goats on the next planet." This was the last straw on the camel's back. Azariah felt tears gathering in his eyes and blinked them away.

Azariah opened a private channel to the captain, who was back on the ship, that the cooks could be rescued in a half hour, but the others deeper in the ravine would probably take hours.

She saw what he was getting at. "We can wait until the cooks are rescued. I'll make them a priority. You and them will be the last on the ship and then it will be time to Jump. Azariah, listen to me, I will Jump as soon as the shuttle is on board, okay? By the way, now that we know who survived, do you want to make a last-minute request for replacements? They will arrive at the next Gate we open."

"I don't know how to make that decision right now. If Din can't make it back, someone to replace him, I guess."

Azariah clambered back up the slope. Wahap was waiting and Azariah collapsed onto him for a hug. He held tight. *I could stay here. This* gerru *could be over for me right now. I can get the cooks in place and easily not step onto the last shuttle. I could help Wahap; if he's here right now, he needs me.*

"About the radiation tech," Wahap whispered. "Captain Sifontes Uzcategui said something, but how do I help you? You need it for your people on Sumer, yes?"

Azariah leaned back out of the hug and wiped tears from his eyes. "Donations of knowledge to the planet as a service to the empire would be welcomed. No one would look askew at that."

"I am so sorry, my dear Aza—"

"You have done a good job protecting your people. This was not the disaster it could have been. I need to leave soon. But I'll write to you, okay?" In the heat of this emergency, they had not forgotten each other, but they clearly had separate priorities; Azariah was still a part of the *Klipspringer* crew, even with such a strong friendship with Wahap. And beyond that, Azariah still loved Daniel and all that meant, including finishing the *gerru*.

"You can come back anytime you want. You are always welcome here."

Azariah nodded and hugged him tight again. "Good bye for now."

As soon as he and the cooks were aboard, the *Klipspringer* Jumped.

Chapter 34: Mishael

Mishael was exhausted. He usually lived on a Babylonian space station completing missions to other solar systems, but for a little while he was spending time in the Babylon capital city helping Daniel.

Daniel was a mess after the Revelation bombing and, of course, just as he was finding balance again, God gave him another exhausting vision. Mishael thanked God every day for sparing him from anything metaphysical. After meeting with Prophet Jeremiah, Daniel became more compliant with what the palace wanted and, therefore, was empty and overworked. After dealing with sad Daniel for a few days, Mishael insisted he accept Hananiah's invite to the Gospel South Pole Arrival Day party so that he could rest.

Daniel and Mishael packed for a week, boarded the space elevator, and made it to Hananiah's home in good time. Daniel was in a tired daze, and talked to Mishael about how stupid, boring, ugly, and meaningless everything was.

A few hours into the party, Mishael received an urgent communique from the Office of the Chancellor of the Chaldean Empire. They had received an emergency Jump communication from *Klipspringer*. Nuclear bomb, unknown casualties, Gate open in five hours. Mishael panicked for five seconds. Then he looked around. No one else seemed to have noticed his reaction and also no one else seemed to have received the same news. Mishael especially kept an eye on Daniel, and he didn't reach for his disc at any point. After freezing for another five seconds, extremely tempted to hide the news for a few more hours, he first pulled Hananiah aside whose first thought was to pray. Hananiah's second thought was more useful, to leave as soon as possible.

When Daniel saw the message an hour later and came over to them panicking, Mishael and Hananiah were ready.

"I have to leave. You can't stop me this time," Daniel said. "I have to be there when the Gate opens."

"We're not going to stop you," Hananiah reassured him.

"We've got a ship, and I packed our bags," Mishael added.

When Daniel paused for a second, Hananiah said, "Of course we're coming with you! We're worried about Azariah too."

Daniel headed for the front door. "Did you get clearances?"

"I've been working on it," Hananiah said. "I've had things lined up for my team, so we're just piggy backing off those. With Azariah—it's not the worst-case scenario. *Klipspringer* can still open a Gate and they can do it fast."

"What if this is the end?" Daniel asked. He was silent in a way that said he was about to fall apart. They all knew what nuclear bombs could do.

"I have a hard time believing that. Could our Azariah Ramzi not make it through?" Mishael gave a morbid chuckle. "God has blessed him more than any of us. He could throw himself off a cliff and God would find a way to save him."

"*Even if I go to the ends of the earth, you are there,*" Hananiah quoted.

"Exactly."

"Let's go."

They went through the Babylon Gate to the Ecbatana-Hamadan solar system, where there was a set of five new Gates. As they approached, Mishael's disc buzzed, indicating messages from Azariah. The Gate had opened early! Daniel got up from his chair so fast it spun around, and he paced while he brought up his own messages.

Mishael's first messages from Azariah were typical responses to whatever Mishael had written to him. Mishael skipped to the end. The last message was that he and his new friends were arranging a Gospel Arrival Day celebration, which sounded like a terrible idea. And that was it. Nothing else.

They still had hours to wait until arriving at the Godaniya system. Hananiah flew the shuttle for an hour to the Gate leading to the Leuke Kome nebula and used their combined royal court statuses to cut the line. At the nebula was another set of new Gates, the latest already activated from the Godaniya end.

Hananiah flew them in line, talking to the right people.

"Does Azariah mention President Wahap Seyfiddin in any of his letters?" Daniel asked. His tone was unreadable, but he was still pacing.

"President? Of what? A football team?" Hananiah asked.

"No," Daniel snapped. "Of the solar system."

"Oh, like an issiakkum-samsi. He's made friends with another one! So I'm sure he's fine." Hananiah nodded.

Mishael kicked Hananiah and gave him an urgent look. This was not going to de-escalate Daniel. Sure enough, the color on Daniel's bronze face was heightened.

"Of course he's best friends with another guy like that. Or more than that," Daniel frowned and read his letters intently.

"You really think you're not his best friend?" Hananiah asked.

Daniel stopped sulking. "He can have a new best friend as long as he's alive." Now he might cry, which was just as bad.

Whyyyy aren't you here to handle his moods? Mishael said silently to Aza. *Of course, you're the one who causes most of them.*

Their turn came soon enough. The newest Gate did indeed open into the moon's orbit, as the report said. But the report also said that bombing casualties were low, which seemed impossible. The space station State and the moon were overflowing with ships, both their own and Chaldean. Between the three young men and their empire accesses, they got through to the moon pretty easily, especially since they had landing capabilities. Sumer had taught Mishael to arrange for that, which was a long story involving decrepit space elevators. As they approached the moon, Mishael could see the center spot of the nuclear bomb, right at the middle of the city, everything flattened. It was hard to look at.

They landed the shuttle as directed at a new ship landing area at the edge of the city and were requested to wait until an escort arrived. Daniel paced up and down their shuttle, the lighter gravity tripping him. Mishael sat, stretched his legs out, and relaxed, looking out over the field of *kurak* to the gas giant Khoshkhar Muiz. Soon enough, an aide named Lieutenant Zikirulla Moydun led them through a gray disaster area, past wounded who were headed to shuttles to receive treatment on a space station, to Azariah's apartment that was now a central meeting spot. They could see only a bit of the damage and injured moon citizens. Mishael was sure that the report had lied and the death toll had been higher. Lieutenant Zikirulla ushered them along and soon enough the young men met the president, who had everyone else in the apartment leave.

"Hello, my dear friends. I do consider you dear friends, as Envoy Ramzi speaks about you all the time," President Seyfiddin said in Elamite. "I am unsure of the formal reason why you are here?"

"You know Azariah personally," Daniel said flatly. "He's alive?"

"My dear Advisor Daniel Ravi, of course! He isn't here. He left on the ship. Did you not know that? Did you come here with the intent to speak to him?"

"His name wasn't on the roll call of the official *Klipspringer* report," Mishael said.

"Ah, my dear Ambassador Mishael Kahalani. I assure you as well that the envoy departed in good health. He probably wasn't on the ship when the report was sent through the Gate, as the ship Jumped within a minute of him boarding. You see, he stayed until the very last to help rescue two cooks, and he did leave. This happened only a few hours ago. I haven't forgotten."

"Are you sure?" Daniel was glaring.

"Perhaps there is something that is making you feel unwell. Did you get the inoculation against the fallout?"

"We've been inoculated," Hananiah answered.

"Yes, Advisor Ravi, maybe you want to lie down for a little?" The President pointed to the bedroom, and Mishael led Daniel there. He climbed into the bed.

"It smells like him." Daniel hugged a pillow.

"You are so dramatic," Mishael said, leaning against the doorway.

"Did he leave anything behind?" Daniel opened a few drawers in a night stand and found some jade in a silky pouch, which he gave to Mishael to hold on to. Daniel also found a disc, which he tried to access.

Hi Daniel! You're close, but that's not quite the right access code, spoke a voice from Azariah's disc.

Mishael snorted.

Daniel tried again and got access. "Go away. I want to look at this in private."

Mishael rolled his eyes and left. They were getting themselves into so much trouble.

Mishael joined the president and Hananiah in the living room. They were having an earnest discussion about recent events and expectations. The president was going through a moon fridge for drinks.

The decor caught Mishael's attention and made him furious. "Why is this apartment decorated like this? It's like a Gospel Christmas and Arrival Day!" He started tearing down the paper stars and bulbs and ripping it all up. He pushed a spaceship toy and a nativity set into the trash. The president watched in silence. Hananiah helped half-heartedly. Mishael glared at the president. "Have the *real* diplomats seen this? Sophonisba is the king's true diplomat and will see through everything and extract exactly what the empire wants from you."

"No, Sophonisba and her team have opted to stay on a space station they think is secure," the president said. "I'm intending to join them after a nap. Surely you don't need to destroy this." His genuine sadness that Mishael was throwing out Azariah's stupid knick-knacks didn't help Mishael's mood.

"If you want something like this," Mishael held up a red glass bulb. *Red.* Gospel's Christmas colors. He threw it away. "You can go to the Otero Linda temple on Babylon and get something from the gift shop." Mishael snatched a throw blanket off the couch and threw it away. "Do you have a textile printer? I'm assuming you do."

Hananiah and Mishael printed out a Chaldean empire flag to hang up.

"This is purple and gold. Aza would think this is ugly," the President said, a shadow passing over his face.

Mishael calmed down and the three of them sat down. "Are we in your way? We can leave. It feels like we should leave."

"No, not at all. This is useful. I told my people I would rest to please them. They do not understand I cannot yet rest. I talked with Hananiah before you became a tornado around this room. His teams will be on their way soon; Envoy Ramzi mentioned them. I will enjoy writing to the envoy that I took care of Daniel for him and that Hananiah and I are on good terms."

Fantastic. Aza will get us all killed. No one understood discretion or how to stay on the king's good side.

Mishael went to the bedroom and grabbed the disc from Daniel. "I think you've read enough of his diary for now. Read anything interesting? New boyfriend?"

"Nothing I didn't already know. Mishael, I've come to my senses. Let's head back to Babylon after I talk with Wahap."

"Why? Why do you need to talk with the president? Please be polite." This was enough of an international indiscretion.

Daniel ignored Mishael's outburst and held out his hand for help to get out of bed. Mishael pulled him up. At a discreet moment, if the room was being surveilled, Daniel signed into his hand *incomplete AI—* Mishael pulled his hand away before he could sign anything else and Mishael groaned inwardly and almost cursed again. Azariah did *not* work on an AI Jump and then just leave it behind. Mishael could *not* believe the messes he was making. Azariah had no way of knowing the disc would land safely in their hands.

Daniel made a beeline for President Seyfiddin and shook his hand like they were just meeting. "It's a pleasure to meet someone who has taken such good care of our Azariah." Daniel was still frowning and unpleasant.

"It's a pleasure to meet Envoy Ramzi's best friends. I thought I'd have to wait until the *gerru* was over," the president said coolly. They were glaring at each other.

Oh no, oh no, oh no, you did not actually get this guy to— the system president and the king's advisor were not, after a nuclear explosion, fighting over stupid you—

"Envoy Ramzi enjoyed his time here," the president said. It sounded like a challenge.

"It is easy for Aza to enjoy anything. He makes friends everywhere." Daniel crossed his arms.

"I know. He gained the trust and *affection* of my people easily." The president nodded to Hananiah as a reference to their earlier discussion. He turned back to Daniel. "I've heard how the king might be displeased with Aza and I've made it clear he will always be welcome here."

"He has plenty of powerful friends on Babylon. He will stay on Babylon."

"If that's what he wants." The president waved his hand.

"Of course."

"I need to get back to my people." The president stood up and led them to the door.

"Thank you, President Seyfiddin," Mishael said. "I'm sure you will see the envoy again. I look forward to spending time with you under more official circumstances."

The president nodded politely.

The three young men left the apartment, with the president waving to Lieutenant Zikirulla to escort them.

"Lieutenant," Mishael said. "I'd like to see more of the damage sustained."

Lieutenant Zikirulla took them to the tallest structure in the area, a sports stadium with a view to the inner city.

"We knew there may be a bombing," the lieutenant said. "For the last half-year we've been relocating to this area. We did have a day's worth of warning, and less than a hundred were in the deadly blast zone. Many of our people are in some safe cliffs." He pointed in the opposite direction.

"I know enough about bombs to know that this part of the city that we are standing in is within the death zone," Mishael said, ready to start an argument.

"And yet, here we are," Lieutenant Zikirulla said calmly. It was enough of an answer.

Mishael was badly shaken, and he almost took his strong emotions out on the lieutenant but stopped himself. President Seyfiddin, everyone on New Godaniya, had recognized the threat of nuclear bombing and had prepared for it, had been preparing for a long time. Mishael was aghast at the differences between how they had handled the threat versus how Revelation of John had, and the differences in results. Despite the report, he had been expecting a wasteland, and now here on top of the stadium, he could see the tens of thousands of people who had survived and the twinkling of space stations where other citizens were safe. He had not been prepared for life and industry and lack of harm. He wanted to be mad at President Seyfiddin for being so competent, for keeping so many of his people safe. Blaming only King Nebuchadnezzar and the Chaldean empire for Revelation's destruction seemed a little harder.

"We're done here," Mishael said, unable to handle his frustration. "Let's go."

"I want to see the aliens," Daniel said calmly, like that was a normal thing to say, and he hadn't been bickering with a president a few minutes ago.

"What the heck, Daniel," Hananiah swatted his shoulder.

Lieutenant Zikirulla gestured to the gas giant and, indeed, the patterns in the atmosphere weren't naturally occurring.

"Nope, not anything we should know about," Mishael insisted. "Let's get out of here now."

Once they were on the shuttle, through the first Gate, away from radiation disaster zones, President Seyfiddin, and the aliens, Mishael could finally relax a little.

"So Daniel, you're feeling better now? Was this worth it?"

"I'll feel completely better once he writes to me again. And he's back on Babylon and I see him again. And once he's happy, of course." Daniel rubbed his face with both hands.

"Daniel, is there some special understanding between you and Azariah?" Hananiah asked.

Mishael turned his attention from the shuttle controls to Daniel. They had asked before in a less direct way more than a year ago and Daniel had shut them down.

"No." Daniel struggled with responding further, tapping his fingers on the armrest. "I think I'd like to try kissing him."

"You do? And you know you do?!" Mishael said. "Never mind." He didn't want to know about his friends' sex lives.

"Have you kissed? I never saw anything, but you were very clingy sometimes, especially the month before he left." Hananiah was too gossipy. He enjoyed that stupid showdown with President Seyfiddin.

"The month before he left? I saw him as my best friend who was going to his death. I did— I did make it clear that I would kiss him and do anything to make him stay. He laughed at me." Daniel's face went so sour and serious that Mishael was pretty sure that wasn't what happened.

"So really, you've never kissed?"

"No."

"Really? Not by accident or in a fit of passion at any point?"

"No."

"You ran off during high royal court to say goodbye again and didn't kiss or anything romantic?"

"I blessed him and kissed his forehead."

Oh, poor Azariah. Daniel sent him off to his death with a kiss on the forehead. That poor man. Mishael would choose a president in the middle of a civil war over Daniel.

Mishael finally broke in, "Daniel, you're asexual, right? Azariah doesn't want that. He's not going to always live with you as a platonic best friend. He's going to find a way, your and the king's wishes aside, to build a romantic, sexual life with someone. This President Seyfiddin really might have the power to protect him, depending on the next few months of integration. This is all contingent on Azariah surviving the *gerru* alive, which still means beating incredible odds. I would never bet on a bird with Aza's odds. Not that I gamble."

Daniel's color heightened again. "I've dreamed of Azariah. He's the only one I've ever dreamed about. I do love him differently from how I love the two of you but my choices are limited. There's more to life than sex. I don't want to think about it," he said, flat and cold.

"You should." Mishael needed to write to Azariah about this so he would know what terms were waiting for him.

Chapter 35: Daniel

Daniel received another batch of letters from Azariah when he Jumped to solar system eleven, Idmari. Daniel read through them once, and looked forward to reading them again soon. The time between responses made him anxious.

The excruciating details of timing, of Daniel obsessively pacing his life by Azariah's cycles: Daniel visited New Godaniya in Sigga, the end of the dark season, right after Azariah Jumped to cycle nine, a solar system named Nippur. After his New Godaniya adventure, Daniel wrote to Azariah a bunch. Azariah received those letters at the end of the Nippur cycle, which was in mid-Nenegar, a growing season month. Daniel didn't receive Azariah's response to those letters until just now, the end of cycle ten, a solar system named Qatna, in Apindua, the hottest month. An entire season. Now it was the eleventh cycle out of twelve.

In summary, Azariah was alive. No only that, Azariah really was almost done. It really was time to prepare for him to come back.

Azariah's latest batch of letters had some passages that worried Daniel.

I hope my dear Daniel that things will be different between us compared to when I left. I still love you very much, but I don't want to fall into old habits. Are you doing things that make you happy? Are you full of peace and joy? Are you still grieving? Is Prophet Jeremiah bothering you anymore? I wish you had a better support system. I'm sure we'll figure something out together, but I want to be honest about what is going through my head.

So Azariah would be calling Daniel to an accounting soon. Daniel had seen Azariah grow in his letters. Azariah had wanted to be Daniel's equal, but now it felt like Azariah had surpassed him. If Daniel thought deeply about what he wanted from Azariah, he became uncomfortable fast, wanting to back away from Azariah again, when he'd done that several times and been so unhappy each time. But could Daniel step forward to him? *If you sacrifice yourself then I will too*—Azariah had said that years ago, and was Daniel's sacrifice worth it? His three goals were useless. His ambitions were in tatters.

"Daniel, can I ask a favor of you? It is quite a serious one."

Daniel woke himself up from his reverie. This question came from Tiffany, who had become important to him as religious and spiritual support. They would gently argue theology one evening a week, drinking tea in her modest quarters next to the palace chapel. She asked this question during one such evening, after the beginning chat. Daniel set his tea down to listen. The cup had a red fractal pattern, which echoed his thoughts.

"I know you bless anyone who asks. You sincerely wish for God to hear everyone's prayers and don't mind giving everyone a boost. However, I know you pray and ask for knowledge and blessings in a different way, where you meditate and seem to go through a physical transformation—not anything drastic—am I making myself clear enough?"

"Yes. I'd be happy to have you join me next time."

"Thank you. My favor: I am quite worried about the spiritual direction of the empire. The king is clearly using religion as one tool to exert hegemony over the *gerru* solar systems. But perhaps your visions could reveal how we can stay spiritually healthy?"

"The king sees me as a personal spiritual advisor. It is convenient for him to say that I don't have any information that applies to how he runs his empire. The creator God has called the Chaldean empire the golden empire; therefore, anything the king wants to do is worthy of that name."

"This isn't about the king. I'm asking you because of your connection to God, not the king. If you could make a specific request in a vision about the empire?"

Her concern for the empire was palatable. Daniel had never seen it before. Had they talked about the spiritual welfare of the empire before? Or only religious services and broader theological concepts, and their specific religions. Tiffany cared about the empire. Something inside him broke. Daniel stood up.

"I need to go and pray on this. Regular prayer, not a vision state."

When he got back to his quarters, he went straight to a little room he had set up as a meditation room.

Daniel needed to think about himself and what he was doing. He wasn't prepared to pray yet. Prophet Jeremiah said that Daniel was looking back at Paradise like Lot's wife, but he hardly knew what to look forward to. If God didn't place him next to the king to protect Paradise, then why was he here? Why was it obvious to Prophet Jeremiah? Daniel wasn't supposed to care about Paradise. But that would leave a blank hole. But talking with Tiffany right now, the image of intercessory prayer in order to take care of the empire, apart from the king—that was new to Daniel. The Chaldean empire had been his antagonist, with its slavery and economic structure and bombings. Of course Daniel didn't want to take care of it. But he was supposed to. Daniel burst into tears at the thought. But his tears were a quick, cleansing storm.

His visions: the four beasts, the king's dream, the vision of a woman and Gabriel. They were all about the power centers of the galaxy, whether they were consecutive or all at once in different parts of the galaxy. Only one vision, the one with figs, had a warning about his home Paradisian solar system. Daniel begged God's forgiveness; if he had cared less about Paradise, it would have been easier for Daniel to save the children.

The next day, Oshpenaz and Samwel helped him prepare for a formal meeting with the king. Uati and LaMeu did his hair and nails. His outfit was not for the empire's high royal court but slightly lower and more business-like. He wore pants. He stifled his hatred for the king.

King Nebuchadnezzar was excited to see Daniel, who hadn't hinted at what he wanted to meet about. Daniel's request was based on research from over a year ago, so there was no trail for anyone to snoop around to anticipate him.

The king invited him to a small throne room where they had had tea before. Today the room held the maximum seven guests, including Birbirru and Te'oma. The way a couple of the gossipier people were evaluating him, whatever Daniel said would go through the palace as fast as the feed could take the information. Thankfully, feeds were disabled in this room.

Daniel drank a cup of tea peacefully, chatting with Oshpenaz on a red cushion that was kitty corner to the king's throne-like chair while waiting for the king to address him. The suspense was making the king shift in his seat and interrupt them with little quips, though he was supposedly chatting with Birbirru. Daniel was calm; he was not emotionally wedded to the outcome of his request.

"Okay, Advisor Ravi, I'm ready if you are," the king finally said, exasperated, as if Daniel were the one keeping him waiting. Daniel stood up and arranged himself for a presentation.

"Thank you, Your Majesty, not only for meeting with me today, but a greater thank you for bringing me into the Etemenanki palace educational program over five years ago. You brought me here to train me as an administrator. I have followed through on that training, even after being brought into your high royal court. I have utility to you beyond that of a spiritual advisor. From what I understand, the current issiakkum-mati of Babylon has been wasteful and there are rumors you've considered replacing her. I wish to take her place." There was a combination of more quiet as the other conversations stopped and also a bit more noise as people reacted. The king smiled widely and nodded. It was the type of mixing things up that appealed to him. "However, before you agree, I wanted to present what I plan to accomplish. This is based on some research I had the library do for me a year ago, but I believe there's been only more corruption since then." Daniel was using his policy education to help Babylonia. He clenched his fist for a moment, only a moment. His Paradisian people deserved help, but he personally couldn't give it to them.

"You've been thinking for that long?"

"No, not consciously. I just knew something was wrong and wanted to find out how deep the corruption ran. The library did an audit the best they could with the information available."

"Ah yes, you got a few library people in trouble," Oshpenaz said.

"They brought it on themselves. But moving on from that, if you appoint me as governor, I do want you to know I'll clean things up, things like slavery, refugees, religious intolerance, and usury. Babylonia, over which I would be issiakkum, accumulates wealth beyond that which it creates. The wealth benefits only a few. I followed this money. Considering what I found, I wish to restructure the Babylonia economy."

"Of course you do. Continue."

Daniel debated internally on whether he wanted to say this in front of Te'oma and the others. "I wish to speak to the king alone."

"We are alone?" He raised an eyebrow. Maybe he could trust the others with his own life and goals (Erioch's presence suggested otherwise), but Daniel didn't trust them with his.

Daniel spoke in Kahi to Oshpenaz, "I have economic plans that could be dangerous, and I want an open, thorough discussion."

Oshpenaz bowed and spoke to the king in a separate language, maybe a dialect of Sumerian. As a result, Oshpenaz ushered out everyone but Erioch.

"You can stay," Daniel called to Oshpenaz in Kahi.

"Ha, not on my life do I want to know this scheme," he called over his shoulder.

Daniel switched back to Akkadian. "It's fine if you stay," he said to Erioch. Both he and the king rolled their eyes. Daniel wanted a witness, and Erioch would be honest enough. He got them food.

"The financial banks established on Babylon would come under my purview. They are already forcing the expansion of solar systems into projects which will require them to pay signifiant debt payments forever. This is a similar model to what is in place on some of the poorest planets in your empire. I will tell both the expansion solar systems and the poor planets to stop making debt payments. It will be a year of Jubilee. I will order the banks to stop accepting the payments. If we are to be a strong empire, this exploitation has to stop. It is all ridiculous and un-payable debt. The banks will say that they have a legal right to demand payment, even after I change the laws. The banks may need to be brought under empire control, which can be seen as an overreach of power. The Judicature needs to be full of *dayyantu* who will support the changes. I need your help to appoint supportive *dayyantu*. That's the main action I need you to take besides generally supporting me. I don't want to take this position without this specific support. I can handle everything else."

"Good God Daniel, you're asking for the richest and most powerful people in the galaxy besides me to assassinate you. Are you sure you can't be happy with something else? What if we stopped rigging the bird races? Or enforced holy days? What you want is a complex economic issue."

"It is an easy moral issue. It is why God has brought me to you."

"God is not the one who decides! The economy is in my hands; if it changes, it is because I say so, not any god. And I do not choose based on visions alone. I weigh many factors. I decide. This is my empire. God has recognized me as the greatest empire. It is mine and therefore the choices I make are mine."

Daniel made a bow of deep obeisance in reply.

"I want something else. I'm sure you have some ace card. I'm sure you have some special sacrificial offering. I'm sure you're keeping something from me. I can tell. I know you. I'm sitting here wavering and you're not worried because you've got something else and are waiting to see."

"You are correct. There's no issiakkum-samsi of Babylonia because of the Ctesiphon Federation," an independent colony among the moons and asteroids of the second biggest gas giant named Belit-ili. "I can unite them with the rest of the solar system once my other changes are underway. You know I am the one to make it happen in a way that is agreeable to you." Daniel instinctively covered the Martigny tattoo on his arm. Babylonian lower classes on asteroids were required to get similar tattoos. The permanence felt like a brand, but Daniel had escaped and he could bring something better to the Ctesiphon citizens. The king wouldn't understand or might see it as a threat, which Daniel didn't intend.

"Indeed, that is quite the ace card. You said Babylonia earlier, and you knew what you were saying. What you are suggesting is more cleaning up than I'd really like, but let's see what you can do. I certainly don't care that much, but it'd be interesting to see how things work if someone like you is at the head. I'll, of course, remove you if it's tiring."

Daniel bowed deeply. The king was giving him what he requested. He felt a much greater sense of relief than he was expecting. "Thank you. If I am successful within the next five or ten years, I expect whatever I create to be applied further than Babylonia, especially if economies on the expansion worlds need to be rebuilt."

"Oh, do you?"

"I'd like to bring my friends into this, especially Azariah Ramzi."

"Our dearest envoy. What trouble might he cause when he gets back, right, Erioch? Daniel, can you bring Azariah and your other two friends to heel? I wish they obeyed me the way you do."

"No, your Majesty. That can't be a condition of my appointment."

"Oh fine. Tell me, Daniel. Azariah is your best friend, but is he more than that?" The king chuckled.

Daniel's mind went blank, and he didn't answer.

"Good enough answer for me. I'll start with the transfer of issiakkum power officially right away so the outgoing regime can't sabotage, and we'll have a ceremony in good time. You'll need to be sworn in as an empire citizen. Oh Daniel, this is fun and exciting. That stupid issiakkum brought this down on herself. The penthouse of the new skyscraper, it's so tall it basically looks into the palace. It's been pissing me off. It was built while I was off planet, and now I have an excuse to keep her from moving in. It might take me a few days to get you the deed, and it's not ready to be moved into for at least a few months. I've been stalling some off-world supplies from being delivered, but I'll allow them now. Are you still afraid of heights? You might be the only person on the planet who won't enjoy that penthouse. Perfect. Don't worry about any of your spiritual advisor duties for now unless you have a vision, but I don't need to tell you that."

"The deed shouldn't be in my name. There should be a trust so the penthouse is passed to future issiak—"

"Oh, shut up. You just have to take it."

"Might I suggest Tiffany as a replacement spiritual advisor?"

"No, ew, boring. I don't want anyone but you."

"You need a better security detail. Don't leave the palace for now," Erioch said, which indicated his approval.

"Excellent, perfect," the king said. "I even sort of believe you, Daniel. This change is good for both of us. Please go. I'm sure you have plenty to do if this is some brand-new idea."

"Indeed, Your Majesty, you are more generous than I deserve."

"One last thing, I'll want you to start having children soon, and no donating. I want you to raise them. Maybe marriage, but I don't require it for you."

"Okay," Daniel choked out, and left.

Daniel performed one last religious service. When he blessed people, he struggled to see his duties differently, to remove the veil of history and social upbringing; going forward, he would be taking care of these same people in a different way. They would be his *issiakkusakin mati*. He had several years of stubbornness and prejudice to overcome.

The transition to his new life—he didn't know what he was expecting. For God to make the path smooth now that he was on the correct one? For everything to be hard and miserable because he had taken so long to figure things out? Daniel definitely didn't expect to have any friends, but plenty of people were happy to show him what rocks to turn over to find the maggots. Lower-level people kept their heads down, protecting their own people, but were otherwise free of graft and incompetence. Other people had been forced to retire or leave because they hadn't wanted to take part in the corruption, and they were happy to come back.

This was overwhelming, but Daniel was no longer subject to the whims of the king on a daily basis and was able to keep a consistent schedule for the first time in years, which was so, so nice. His health and disposition immediately improved with proper, consistent sleep and food.

After a month of settling in, Daniel adored the penthouse and was delighted that he caught the king on a day he felt petty. It had views up the canyon to the ziggurats in the cliffs and the palace, which was above the penthouse despite the king's opinion, and also views down the canyon, where he could follow the Turquoise River with his eye for kilometers. This made him dizzy, but he kept the windows uncovered.

Daniel added a little chapel and Mishael's sculpture and some Gospel art and some other Kahi Christian things, as well as art Azariah had been sending from the various planets. Daniel had a red rug and a *kobyz* instrument from New Godaniya, a painted piece of wood from Sumer, and his favorite, sculptural incense holders from Leuke Kome. Azariah also sent candy and a few books of religious poetry from New Godaniya.

Part of his new life included the king's insistence on babies. The long leash to be issiakkum felt like a bribe.

Hello issiakkum. Do you have any marriage or maternal candidates? Asked a message from Oshpenaz.

Daniel didn't answer. He curled up with a glass of wine on his favorite emerald green sofa near a window with a view to the side of the canyon, layers of purple and white rock, with a sliver of navy-blue night sky.

Daniel looked through the profiles of the Paradisian women on Babylon. He threw his disc aside for a minute and then picked it up again. There was one woman, Amina, Mishael's cousin, who had been educated at the South Pole and now worked in the North Pole, but far from the capital. But it was within commuting distance.

He threw his disc aside again. He walked through some penthouse rooms, wondered if the master suite should be for whatever woman might move in. Then he thought of Azariah, and how the king would probably ask the same thing of him, and what would he do?

This was ridiculous. Daniel wasn't going to ask a woman he had met only a couple of times and had no further connection to besides the cousin of a friend. Daniel picked his disc up and threw it further from himself, and laid on his belly on the couch.

This felt like one of those moral dilemmas Aza would come to Daniel about, how he had to live in a gray area where the options weren't good, and the right choices weren't clear. What would Aza do? He had once been flippant about just donating samples, but later had admitted that he did want to raise his own children. Daniel was angry at Beck but reminded himself to check in with her family again.

So, now, considering the lack of control Azariah was experiencing, what could Daniel do that was within his control for his own progeny? He didn't want anyone else but Azariah raising his kids. He wanted his kids to have Azariah's energy and exuberant enjoyment of life. Ever since he had talked about kids with Azariah on his birthday, he'd built up a brittle shell when Azariah refused, but it felt like it was breaking. Oh wait, this still wasn't within his control until Azariah returned. The idea of raising kids with Azariah felt completely different now compared to the first time they had talked about it. He remembered Mishael asking about romance and sex, and Daniel had answers only for Azariah. He needed Azariah here, and it would happen soon.

Daniel's disc buzzed right then, like it had the answer. Daniel reached across his couch. He felt a scary thrill when he saw it was a quantum pre-set message from the *Klipspringer*. They had reached the three-month mark. *What happened? Where are you?* Azariah had been at Idmari for three months, so about the time the Gate was expected to open. Daniel accessed the message.

Gate destroyed. Jump engine destroyed. Unknown if the planet is inhabited. Unsafe for Jumping. Multiple dead.

The thrill in his hands and heart felt like it was choking him. Daniel cancelled his schedule for tomorrow. He went to his chapel to meditate deeply. It wasn't a prayer to God. Instead of kneeling in front of the crucifix, Daniel sat crossed legged at a window, opening it enough to look over the Turquoise River. Daniel dropped into his deep meditative state.

Gabriel, I know you're there. Please protect Azariah.

It took a while, but Gabriel responded. Her fiery form was only a shadow of what it could be, but blinded Daniel with her brilliance in his little chapel.

Daniel knelt to her and kept his head to the floor. "I don't know what's happened to Azariah. Will you please take care of him? Will you bring him back to me?"

"You are speaking of corporeal danger. Because he is your friend, I will protect him." Her voice echoed deeply through the room.

"Thank you."

Her brilliance disappeared in a flash.

It wasn't quite the reassurance Daniel wanted. It felt like there was some kind of loophole, but it was more than he expected.

The next day he sent a request to the king, which was immediately approved. Daniel sent a letter of introduction to Azariah's family on Gospel and asked for an egg from his sister.

Chapter 36: Azariah

Jump Day had arrived. *Klipspringer* had the next Gate in the cargo bay. The tenth cycle at Qatna was complete. Azariah had received his letters from Daniel and other people. *Klipspringer* was ready to Jump to a solar system named Idmari for the eleventh cycle. The available information wasn't the detailed, high-quality data like usual. The crew could only guess where the major celestial bodies were in the solar system. This meant Jumping to the edge of the solar system. Everyone was used to shorter cycles, a few weeks instead of three months, but they agreed that this was safest.

Azariah was with the Jump team, all in their space suits, zero electricity so floating in zero-g, holding onto the worktable in their workroom near the top of the ship. Wamiri was with Engineering at the bottom of the ship. Azariah nudged Bounthavy next to him and she grimaced; she was hesitant every time they had to Jump and was especially nervous this time. She was the reason why Azariah was here instead of the bridge, as she needed extra reassurance. The rest were chatting to wrap up the Qatna engineering project, something fun with black holes.

Klipspringer Jumped.

Klipspringer's luck ran out.

When *Klipspringer* moved from the quantum bubble to physical space, the ship and the physical material of the space it entered overlapped, like sifting ingredients for a cake. When the Jump finished for Azariah, he felt dust in his mouth and saw small rocks in front of his helmet. A tremor ran through the ship. He punched a button on the sleeve of his suit to prep for an emergency and did an internal check of himself—he could wiggle his toes, his fingers, he could breathe though it was uncomfortable. He could still think, which was great. The emergency scan showed that there was dust throughout his body, but no blockages. Azariah had dust in his brain, even, but the screen said he was fully functioning.

That took only a few seconds. Azariah turned his attention outward. There were rocks floating throughout the working room, from the size of pebbles to the size of his fist. Regular lights hadn't turned on. Gravity hadn't turned on.

"I'm okay, surprisingly," Bounthavy said.

"The scan says I'm intact." Sal said. They and Azariah were basically back to their normal friendship. What was a little empire-ordered assassination attempt between friends?

"My throat is dry. I feel like I have metal shavings in my mouth," Azariah said.

"The scan says I have a rock in my thigh! I can't feel it!" Din yelped.

"Your thigh?" Azariah asked.

"The rock! I feel like I could walk around."

"We're still floating, idiot. Don't try," Sal snapped.

"It's my good leg too."

"Azariah? Can you contact Engineering?" Bounthavy asked, who would usually be on the call to check in with Wamiri.

Azariah gave her a look and clicked the right buttons. No answer.

"Emergency protocol then," Sal said.

"Which is?" Din asked.

Azariah tried regular communications but nothing, as expected. With no general electricity, there was no way for him to call the bridge or anyone. Azariah then tried the shortwave radio and got generic please wait signals from the bridge, engineering, and the sick bay. The Jump team cycled a wireless battery. Communications to the bridge and engineering were still down. They hadn't started the emergency protocol yet.

"Something is wrong with… electricity? With all EM fields?" Din said.

"The shortwave radio seemed to receive signals fine," Azariah said.

"Sure. Whatever," Din said, "But the wireless battery will transmit energy over just a fraction of the distance it's supposed to. And physical transmission connections, like the wiring, aren't working at all." The ship trembled again. Everyone paused for a moment.

"That's not emergency protocol. Get the rest of the supplies out and the team leader checks on the bridge." Wamiri nodded to Azariah.

Azariah stayed long enough to ensure the supplies were fine. Just some dust. His destination was the bridge, which was at the middle-front of the ship. The stairway doors wouldn't unlock when he tried, so he made his way by removing floor and ceiling panels to navigate from floor to floor. He held onto the walls and ceiling handles in case gravity came back. He climbed into a hall and made his way to the bridge. The door was closed and sealed. He knocked the old-fashioned way.

"Who's there?" That sounded like Beck. She, Din, and a few others had caught up with *Klipspringer* when the ninth cycle Gate had opened.

"Envoy Ramzi, following emergency protocol."

"A rock caused the bridge to decompress. We didn't lose anyone to decompression, but a few people are unconscious. We don't have any air right now, so we're not opening the door."

"Ramzi, this is the captain. Two things. One, there's some serious dampening field. It appears widespread and is affecting… a lot. Just a lot. That's all we've got so far. Two, obviously something is wrong with Engineering. They should have implemented some kind of countermeasure or mechanical power or someone reporting here. Nothing is happening, so please go there. Have someone report back here as soon as possible. Doctor Parivrajaka came by, and they were on their way there too. I'm making that a priority over the injuries we have here."

"Do you have emergency supplies?" Azariah relayed the information he had about the wireless batteries.

"Thank you. We're fine, just go."

"Have you used an emergency quantum pill?"

"No, I want a full assessment first."

"There is clearly enough damage to justify. It's not like you can include a full report with one of those pills. What is it, five quarks, you choose one of six types each? You can send something. This is obvious."

"You have your orders. Go now."

Azariah knocked his fist on the wall but left. He didn't know why he wanted to send a message. It's not like anyone could come save them, so he went on his way and pushed off down the corridor.

Azariah entered Engineering from a service door that opened into the main area.

Engineering was a tragic disaster. A large rock has embedded into the floor, the entire length of the room, destroying part of the Jump ring that went around the edge of the ship. Someone had their leg embedded in the rock and was unconscious. Everyone had some kind of injury. Doctor Parivrajaka was performing surgery right in an alcove, with the person strapped to a surface, maybe a wall. Azariah couldn't make sense of the chaos and stayed at the door without moving.

Wamiri found him.

"How's the team?" she asked, pushing her black curls out of the way.

"Absolutely perfect compared to everything else I've seen. What is this?"

"The Jump engine exploded. The shrapnel cut into everyone." She showed him a cut in her suit. Her arm had been bleeding but wasn't now.

"The Jump engine exploded." Azariah repeated that to himself and carried himself over to see. The poor heart of the ship had burst open. Wamiri pointed out how a large supporting strut was gone and then pointed behind him. He turned around. The explosion had pushed the strut through several decks; he could see stars.

"Azariah!" the doctor called. "Help me triage. Everyone here is in too much shock."

"Okay, one minute." Azariah turned to Wamiri. "Get ship communications working."

"No. The explosion sliced some parts, and we don't know what to do about the dampening field."

"Okay, you are going to deliver a report to the bridge."

"But my arm and legs—"

"Shut up. You can handle the journey. I left all the ceiling panels open. If gravity turns back on, I'm sure Sal or Din will happily rescue you." Azariah gestured to Wamiri to bring up her good arm. He brought up the projection in the sleeve, brought up a notepad and pen, and wrote some notes to the captain.

"Hey, both of you! I've got notes for the captain!" Doctor Parivrajaka called again.

They pulled over to the doctor.

"First off, Aza, what are your projection capabilities?"

"I've got a full battery, no damage."

"Good. We've rigged enough batteries to create overlapping fields, as limited as they are. You connect to all of them and don't let your suit leave this room. Access surgery packet two. I'm going to want a bunch of bandages for everyone in Engineering and the amount in that packet will last for two days before the batteries run out. Don't use your suit projection tech for anything else. Wamiri, add this to your notes: I went by the mess hall. The goats are fine, but we've lost our water. It's my recommendation to prioritize finding water. I also went by the Gate section. The cargo bay with all the Gate parts is gone. An asteroid hit the living quarters for the Gate engineering team, which is where they should have been for the Jump. It's possible that there are survivors drifting, so we're in a countdown to finding them. And I guess those are the two most serious issues."

"Go by the sick bay on your way," Azariah said to Wamiri, "and have at least one more doctor come here with real medical supplies, unless things got worse since I was there."

Wamiri nodded. "If the captain doesn't have any orders, I'll go to the team and see about repairing stuff, maybe sensors? Or gravity?"

"Mechanical power, but an engineer should make that decision. Don't turn anything on without the captain's permission." Azariah didn't look to see her leave and followed the doctor's instructions for the next few hours. He learned just how strong his stomach was.

Five people in Engineering needed major surgery immediately, one of them Alejandra. Once she stabilized, she followed Azariah and the doctor as they performed other surgeries and patched up all the deep lacerations and head injuries. Azariah helped keep her conscious as she assessed the damage. Head Engineer Marxer died. Jump engine leader Keo was unconscious.

"We're running into rocks. Can you feel that?" Alejandra asked, holding his elbow and gripping a handle on the wall.

Azariah paused and could feel a trembling.

"We're not out of danger. That needs to stop." She called Noy over and gave instructions to stabilize.

Noy shook her head. "The belt broke."

Alejandra looked at her in disbelief.

Azariah bit his tongue, traded a glance with Alejandra.

Noy took a deep breath. "Okay. Okay, I guess if this is the priority, I can fix it. I can find a spare or find torque from something."

Azariah refrained from nodding in approval. That would be condescending. Alejandra had him prop her up near the Jump engine so he could catch up with the doctor to continue first aid.

Soon, Sal arrived with the hardware to fix the ship's communications. The captain wanted to talk to Azariah and Marxer. Azariah joined Alejandra in her relatively quiet corner, Sal hovering nearby, and she explained the current state of Engineering.

The update was grim. The bridge was still isolated. No further information on the dampening field. Alejandra wanted to send a team to fix the worst hull breaches from the outside. The captain asked about the propulsion engines. Alejandra almost cried and said she didn't know. Azariah checked and thought they could be workable soon. Noy was restarting the clearing and avoidance tech. When Azariah got back, the senior staff were arguing over something he didn't catch—

The entire ship shuddered, and Azariah could hear and feel the scraping along the ship. It seemed to last forever, but only ten seconds.

"Sorry!" Noy called out. "I'm so sorry!"

"What part of the ship is that? Are there breaches?"

"Whatever else, there shouldn't be any more injuries. Protocol is to get away from outside facing bulkheads if possible." Engineering bulkheads were thicker compared to the rest of the ship; Azariah double checked the integrity of his suit, just in case.

"But breaches—has someone checked all the rooms?" Azariah asked. "It's Juma's responsibility, but did he sign it over to someone since he's stuck on the bridge?"

"Unfortunately, now is not the time to do a census," the captain said. "Ramzi, you can't be responsible for everything."

Azariah immediately turned to Sal or someone to order them, but Alejandra stopped him. "We've got something else for you. Though, Captain Sifontes Uzcategui, I'd like to say once more I would prefer him here. With his memory and experience, he knows the engine better than anyone but me, and I can't climb inside for a while."

"I know he's a competent engineer."—high praise—"That is, in fact, an important skill for this mission. Plus, he's the diplomat recommended. Right, Beck?"

"Again, I should be there too," Beck answered. "This is such an important first contact. No one diplomat should be alone. Even I, as the highest, wouldn't want to go alone. This is too important for the responsibility to land on one person."

"You're not going. The bridge will not be accessible soon enough. I want Azariah on his way now."

Azariah felt a chill go down his back. "What's going on? What did I miss? The propulsion engines should be fine, by the way."

"I'm sending you in the *Zayets* to the inner planet," the captain said. "Considering the extensive defensive measures in this solar system, it's a high enough risk that I'm sending only one person and you are the best suited."

"Understood. Thank you for your confidence." The *Zayets* was a new small ship that Beck had brought back. It traveled fast, almost as fast as a one percent probe.

"Ideally, you'll make the trip in two weeks, but it depends on the composition of the rest of the solar system."

"Space is big," Azariah said, stating the obvious like a champ. "Once I'm out of this cluster, it won't be an obstacle course."

"No, we don't know that. Prior data suggests that this entire system might be like this," Beck said.

"It might be artificial as protection. I'm finding it very effective," Alejandra said.

"No shit. It's clearly all artificial," Beck snapped.

"Which is why we're risking only one person," Azariah interrupted, stripping out of his suit. He had his normal uniform underneath. "I'll go now."

"Once you're in contact with whoever lives here, use your skills to bargain for what we need," the captain ordered. "This is of the utmost importance, and I give you a free hand. First order of importance is emergency aid. Second, Gate technology. Third, any Jump technology. If they are as backwards as most of the *gerru* worlds, we may be starting from scratch. Fourth, long-term living arrangements."

Azariah said his goodbyes and made his way to the shuttle bay. Without his suit, it was a dark, eerie journey with many creaks like they were in a water ship. The shuttle bay was pressurized, so it was quick work to prep the *Zayets* with what he needed. He couldn't think.

I'll be back soon, he promised *Klipspringer* silently, patting a wall before heading into the little ship.

Chapter 37: Azariah

Azariah dearly wanted to take an hour to help his crew—look for ice, look for survivors—but he left them behind, understanding the importance of his orders.

The *Zayets* was the fastest ship the empire had ever designed, but it was hard to go fast. This particular solar system was barely past the post-protoplanetary disc phase. It was a baby solar system that hadn't smoothed out yet, full of rocks. Planets had only just been formed. According to the Achaemenid records, the inhabited planet was in the Gold Locked zone. This messiness—how *Klipspringer* Jumped into a rocky cluster—might have been created as a defensive measure or might be a natural consequence of how new the system was. Azariah decided to keep a positive outlook.

The first day was rough; space was never empty enough that he felt safe moving at top speed. He changed his course to head out of the solar system disc where space should be emptier. His attempts at staying positive waned as the dampening field was still in effect; while the *Zayets* could fly safely, he was isolated, unable to communicate with the *Klipspringer,* and unable to scan ahead to the inner planet.

Another day passed; he prepared for the first contact meeting; he even had the textile printer create an outfit. The population during the Achaemenid empire had their own language, but there was no record of it, so not much else he could do to prep.

Third day. Without any busy arrangements left, Azariah was fully feeling his isolation. He started reading his letters, which, instead of distracting him, pushed him into an introspective mood. Wahap had shown him who he was more clearly than he had ever contemplated for himself; *I am a diplomat who hates this expansion and loves Daniel.* And apparently now he was trapped with himself and had to think of this seriously.

What would Daniel tell me to do at this moment? The answer was obvious; meditation, which always threw him off balance. Just like Wahap, it showed him who he really was. This was Azariah's theory of why Daniel had visions: Daniel easily reached deep meditative states; he reached that conscious self-abnegation and death of ego so completely that there was room for God to give him visions.

Not true for Azariah. But he could do something.

His first bouts of soul searching landed on things like, *what did I want to do with my one precious life*? After more than a week, his meditations took him to Daniel. His mind settled on the memory of the last time he celebrated his birthday with Daniel, which was the first time he saw Daniel in person after seeing him at the swim competition, and also the first time he got to hug Daniel since the King took him away. It hurt to think about, but now Azariah's mind wouldn't turn away.

Daniel had interpreted the king's vision, disappeared into the high court, and then Azariah had accidentally seen him at the bathhouse competition. After that, they decided to celebrate their birthdays by going to a dancing show at the temple for Ishtar. They decided to meet up beforehand at their Etemenanki palace quarters where Samwel would help them get ready. Azariah arrived first and Samwel's toddler Fatuma saw him, screamed, and toddled straight to him. She loved Azariah and he loved her. He picked her up and tossed her in the air. She screamed in his face with happiness and laughed when he tickled her.

"Tuma Tuma Tuma," Azariah told her.

"Zaza Zaza," she answered, patting his cheek.

Azariah held her on his hip as he and Samwel puttered around the clothing room, and then handed Azariah a small box and took Fatuma. "I've already given you a birthday gift, but this is something else. No one knows about this, but I want you to have this for one day."

Azariah opened it and wasn't quite sure what he was looking at.

"These are contacts that will correct your color blindness."

Azariah was green and red colorblind. To him, he didn't even notice, and it wasn't a big deal. But it was the type of defect that should keep him out of the palace, and he told Patroness Shelomith the minute she brought him onto her ship several years ago. She had shrugged her shoulders and made it work. Samwel had figured it out because of clothing colors.

With Samwel's help, Azariah put the contact lenses in. The world changed. Samwel showed him a rainbow and named the colors. Brown shades turned into reds and pinks, and that was just scratching the surface. Samwel wanted him to help pick outfits for the night, but the searingly colorful racks of clothing hurt to look at. Azariah looked out a window and Babylon was purple instead of blue. This would be nice for a day. He would save these contacts for special occasions.

Eventually, Azariah heard squeals from the outer room. Samwel put outfits down on a couch. Azariah ran out with Fatuma in his arms again and yes, Daniel had arrived. He hugged him. Daniel laughed and hugged him back awkwardly. It was so good to see him that Azariah could barely even look at him, but kissed the side of his head and buried his nose in his hair.

Fatuma reached out for Daniel too, but Samwel took her away and showed them two outfits, one a beautiful emerald green and one a gorgeous orange that he said was like a sunset, the brightness of the clothing room making them shimmer. Azariah touched both of them. They were both silky kimonos, the orange one a bit more structured.

"Is the green one for Daniel?" Azariah asked.

"No, it's for you. I think Daniel would like to see you in green." Samwel smiled. He always knew what to say to get Azariah to wear whatever he wanted.

Azariah stripped off his white pants and shirt and put on his outfit. Daniel was just standing there watching him. Azariah looked to Samwel for help, who just raised his eyebrows and Azariah helped Daniel undress and put on his robe. Daniel hadn't been in the high court for too long but been with him was new and electric. It felt like Daniel was looking at him differently.

"Can I take down your hair?" Azariah asked.

"Um sure. Yes." Daniel sighed once it was down and Azariah was shaking the curls loose. "I had it too tight. This is nice."

"You smell like coconut oil."

Samwel said offhand, "Daniel, I know you usually like to wear a green because it matches your eyes, but I feel like this particular shade would be fun for Azariah to wear today."

"Wait," Azariah said. "Daniel has brown eyes."

"Anyway, I need to step out for at least an hour. You'll have to figure that out. Bye. Put Fatuma down for a nap soon on this couch." He sat her down on a low couch with firm cushions and a *habarattu* rattle.

"You've never seen the green in my eyes?" Daniel asked.

Azariah dragged him over to the window. "Look straight at me. Open up your eyes wide." He leaned in close and, yes, Daniel did have a ring of green around his pupil and the rest of his eye color was a soft brown, so it's not like Azariah gave himself away. He held his green sleeve to Daniel's face. "I'm not sure if this is the exact sheet of green, but I guess your eyes are pretty enough. This orange is a good color too. It makes you glow." Daniel was vibrant. His face was gentle curves, he was meant for poetry and owning a tropical vineyard; instead, life had made him stern, his lips pressed thin, his makeup severe. Azariah smudged some of the kohl around his eyes. "I'm making it better."

Daniel smiled and relaxed. Their friendship was new again and there was something so different now— before Azariah could think further, Daniel leaned in for a hug.

"This is your birthday present, right?"

Azariah hugged him back fiercely, as tightly as he could and he expected Daniel to go tense because he couldn't remember a hug this tight but instead Daniel relaxed and held him tight too, one arm around Azariah's neck and one around his waist. They stood there forever and ever until their body heat was the same and their heartbeats were the same. Azariah felt so at peace and full of joy for possibly the first time ever, and Daniel was quiet and calm in his arms.

Fatuma tugged on Azariah's kimono and squealed.

Daniel jumped awake in his arms.

Azariah looked down. The little girl raised her little chubby arms and made baby noises to be picked up. So, of course, he picked her up. She was very cute with her little red baby afro. Daniel laughed at her, too. She pouted in Azariah's face and then when she saw Daniel she gave her extra loud scream and tried to dive into his arms.

Daniel held out his arms and said, "I don't mind."

"No, she's going to pull your hair."

Daniel laughed, which made her laugh. Azariah insisted it would hurt.

Daniel took her out of Azariah's arms, and she immediately latched onto his hair with one little hand and patted his nose with her other hand. He winced but wouldn't admit it hurt. After a minute, she let go of his hair, pulled his gold ear cuff off, and bit it.

"I say no to that, though. No baby teeth marks." Daniel held her with both arms while Azariah pried the cuff out of her hands. He tucked the ear cuff into his pocket. She started to whine softly.

"You know what I think? She saw you napping—"

"I wasn't napping."

"—and she ran over here because she wanted to sleep too. I actually do help her sleep. So let's see here." Azariah jiggled her in his arms and walked around the dressing room looking for a blanket or something. He found a soft paisley purple shawl and wrapped her up like a baby burrito with her face poking out. Within a minute she was deep asleep and in Daniel's arms.

"She's so heavy and warm. And smells good," Daniel marveled, like billions of people before him.

"Is this the first time you've held a baby?" Azariah asked, suppressing a smile.

"I've never held one like this."

Azariah took the ear cuff out of his pocket and brushed Daniel's hair aside and put the cuff back on his ear. Daniel leaned into the physical contact, and then straightened, put Fatuma down on her little floor-level couch, and the two young men sat on another couch, one Samwel usually draped clothing over.

"Aza, you said that our friendship, if we were going to work at having one, would be different now. And I want to be clear how important you are to me, and I do want to keep you close. I just had this thought—what if we raised our children together? The king is still insisting on his breeding program, and I'd rather have you raise my children than anyone else."

Azariah felt surprised, deliriously happy, and cautious all at once. "When you say that I'm important to you and you want to have a family with me, it sounds like you're asking for marriage, but I thought—"

"Oh, no." Daniel shook his head. "I'm not talking about that. It was just a thought. I guess it can't happen."

Azariah's heart sank. "I want everything with you. Marriage, romance, sex. My feelings for you are very special. And you've been looking at me differently."

"It's easy for me to set things like that aside. When I lived in the asteroid field," Daniel said softly, "Prophet Jeremiah had these instructions from God that we needed to be fruitful and have children so that we would have enough to fill our home Paradisian solar system again. I decided I would only date young women with the intent of building a family. Then my visions came, and I put that aside. It was a relief. But now I wish you could be the father to my children. I wish we could have a family together. I can see how that would make me happy, how we would be serving God by building a family. But now God asked me to serve him in a different way and I'm sorry. For a moment, I could see us waking up together every morning because a little kid came running in to wake us up. I did want to say something once."

"I love you so much, Daniel," Azariah whispered. "I want that with you. It's being in love, it's physical and emotional intimacy, that's what you're describing. You can't possibly think that if you want something so good like that, that you can't have it."

"It's a sacrifice I have to make."

"No, it's one you're choosing to make. I want a family with you, too. How can you offer it to me like that and then take it away?"

"It was a mistake for me to say anything. I'm just trying to figure out how to move forward with you, but it's not going to be like that. Can we pretend I didn't ask? We can still be best friends, right?"

"Of course." Azariah's love for Daniel was more profound than he had expected. Daniel's words had opened that up, and Azariah couldn't just forget. He didn't even know he could feel like this, like he was breathing fresh Gospel air again. Seeing Daniel in full color was overwhelming. Every part of himself loved him. But Daniel had made his wishes clear. Azariah wouldn't forget how Daniel wanted only friendship and would find a way to live with that.

Chapter 38: Azariah, Idmari

Of course, Azariah did not find a way to live with just friendship. He had to leave Daniel. Now, as he was meditating in the shuttle, dwelling on each vivid moment, holding him, seeing his green eyes, playing with Fatuma together, he thought about how that took place three years ago. A few weeks ago, he had turned twenty-three. Everything now was so different from what he expected. One constant was how he felt about Daniel, though physical separation was still nothing to knowing Daniel didn't love him in the same way. A part of Azariah was fine with being lost.

Azariah was as much in love now as on that birthday when Daniel broke his heart. He had been trying to recover, and now he had to carry this to Idmari, where diplomacy was more important than ever, where he was cut off from Daniel more thoroughly than ever. Having re-lived that memory, a small part of Azariah was relieved that he was cut off. He was stuck far away. The decision was taken out of his hands; indeed, this was the reason why he joined this *gerru.*

Finally, Azariah was approaching the inner world. The inner planet's moons were within the reach of his scanners and the inner planet would be soon. He didn't find anything resembling the society of two hundred years ago, when the system had been a center for engineering and mining.

That is until his scanners could almost reach the planet; he had just caught the edge of an oxygen rich atmosphere when his scan triggered some sort of machine or small station. A mechanical voice broadcasted a question.

The machine spoke in a language Azariah didn't understand, but what he assumed was Ugarit and then repeated in Elamite.

"You have reached Idmari. Are you here for Ordeal or Judgment?"

Azariah didn't answer. That was a terrible question. He scanned the station for biological life. None. He accessed the station to search for artificial intelligence and found something, but he wasn't sure what. He tried to say hello in what appeared to be the coding language, but he only triggered the question again.

"Are you here for Ordeal or Judgment?"

Azariah backed off a bit, which triggered a different question.

"Are you here voluntarily?"

Other station systems were revving up. The *Zayets* had no defenses if those were offensive systems.

"I'm here voluntarily. Can I talk to someone?" Azariah winced. This wasn't going to get him anywhere. He moved the ship closer to the planet to scan for life.

Whether it was his answer or his movement, the station shot something at his ship! One of the two engines was completely destroyed.

Azariah was an average pilot. He could keep his head in an emergency, but hardly had the skills to compensate for whatever happened.

"Computer! This is on you!" Azariah yelled.

The ship trembled again.

"Did it shoot again?"

"Negative," the onboard computer replied. "The foreign station pushed the ship to the planet. Foreign station systems powering down. Prepare for crash landing, which is the best-case scenario. I can't compensate."

Azariah pulled himself around the small cabin, closing all the compartments he had left open, strapping down anything loose, and cycled the emergency batteries before strapping himself in and watching the dashboard. The *Zayets* was supposed to survive an atmospheric entry but had anyone tested properly?

The ship whined and heated up, but they got through the descent. Enough tech was damaged that thermodynamic physics were kicking in, but the *Zayets* wouldn't burn up or fall apart in the atmosphere.

"Aiming for the largest body of water," the computer announced. "Printing underwater mask and supplies."

Azariah scanned and yelled, "No! You're aiming for kilometers from any shore! I won't have support!" When the computer didn't respond or change course, Azariah took manual control, set himself into a terrible spin because he had no idea what he was doing, but didn't let go until he could see a shore. "You can crash now!"

"No, unsafe."

"There's nowhere safe! Stop trying to crash me so far offshore!"

"Acknowledged." The computer took the ship over a cliff—and there was a lava ocean on the other side! It was black, with sharp neon yellow light breaking through cracks in the surface.

The working engine was doing a good job of keeping the ship in the air, but after an hour of the computer and Azariah wrestling over control with hell underneath the ship, the last engine started to break. It wasn't built to fly in the atmosphere for so long, and the ship gave one hard shake before evening out again.

"Are you sure you can't just land? How do we not have the ability to land? When is anti-grav coming back on?"

"Body of water ahead. Prepare for a crash landing."

"I don't see it!" Azariah checked the scans; all he could see was the lava ocean; then he saw an enormous row of black cliffs ahead, silhouetted against a gray sky. Still no water. "This isn't water!" Azariah tried to wrestle back control, but the circumstances were dire enough that the computer didn't allow him to do anything.

The cliffs were approaching extremely fast; the ship was flying low enough, stuttering, that he could feel the heat of the lava ocean soaking through. At the last moment, the ship pulled up enough to fly over the cliff—and then the nose of the *Zayets* pointed almost straight down— pointing at a lake that seemed very, very small. Azariah wondered if maybe the sea had been the best option.

"Is the lake deep enough?" The ship was going so fast the computer didn't have time to respond.

The *Zayets* hit the water hard. The inertial dampeners weren't enough, and Azariah was thrown hard against his restraints. The ship shook hard; it crashed into the bottom of the lake and rolled several times.

The windows of the ship, the weak spot of the structural integrity, split open like an egg before the ship had even stopped. His precious air spilled out of the ship, creating room for the lake water to gush into the ship. Azariah held his breath. He held himself in a protective fetal position, his arms on the back of his neck, gravity pulling at his side, until he was underwater without any strong forces acting against him. He unbuckled and swam to the printer. An underwater mask was waiting. He put it on and breathed deeply. A huge wave of relief flowed through him as pure oxygen gas flowed into his lungs. He held onto a handle on the ship's wall. No bad injuries. The ship wasn't moving anymore. He opened the emergency compartment and grabbed the largest supplies bag. He set the anti-gravity tech just strong enough to be buoyant next to him. He swam out of a broken window and took a moment to gather his bearings.

The lake was devoid of life. The bottom of the lake was rocky; no silt had been stirred up, and Azariah could see the hazy light at the top of the lake. He was far enough down that he would need to rise slowly. As he started to swim up, his instinct to swim as fast and as hard as possible kicked in. His chest was aching from injuries he hadn't sensed right away. But he kept himself safe and finally reached the surface.

Azariah rolled onto shore with the bag next to him, resting just a moment. When he woke up, it was night. His bag was still hovering nearby, a foot off the ground. The two largest moons in waning gibbous phase cast diffuse light through the haze. They were close enough to each other that it seemed like they would crash that night. Azariah pulled the emergency supplies bag away from the shore onto a bed of white flowers, not knowing what to expect from tides, and started prepping a site. Gravity was stronger. The air was warm, he was mostly dry, the supplies were fine. First piece of equipment; was anyone nearby? Black cliffs surrounded him on three sides. He couldn't scan through them. The fourth side was open, and no one was nearby in that direction, only more white flowers. Nothing was above him, nothing interesting below him or in the lake. Moving on, the second piece of equipment; light. Third piece of equipment; water filter and food. Fourth; a tent. As he popped it open, his injuries called attention to themselves. He stripped to the waist. His torso was covered in ugly bruises, and something had slashed through the back of his coveralls and he had bled from a cut about a foot long. Fifth; medical equipment, which he used. Sixth; he found a sleeping bag, crawled into the tent, and slept a much more rejuvenating sleep.

Chapter 39: Azariah, Idmari

Azariah woke up to the proximity alarm beeping shrilly.

His device reported a life-form was about three hours away, given the current velocity and distance. He cleaned himself up and ate.

When the life-form was close enough to magnify, he could see it was someone human in a veil riding an air-cycle. He had time to cut a square from the emergency cloth, tie on a shemagh, and pack everything. He debated leaving supplies out to make tea.

His new friend, an Idmarite for all Azariah could tell, was not in the mood for courtesies and started yelling at Azariah the moment they got off their air-cycle.

Azariah bowed. Not the worst first contact. He could handle yelling.

Azariah said a greeting in Elamite.

The Idmarite stared at him. Their head wrap and veil made their bright blue eyes stand out. They said slowly in Ugarit, "Ordeal or judgment."

Azariah said the Ugarit phrase, "Are you here voluntarily," and then swooped his arm to show my ship crashing into the lake. He walked towards the lake.

His new friend grabbed Azariah's arm, pulled him further away, and started yelling with gestures, flinging their hands and arms to the lake. His new friend had very nice arms. Azariah decided he was a man. He patted Azariah's face and pointed.

He looked.

The lake was boiling. A geyser erupted from the side of the far cliff.

Azariah walked closer to the lake, shocked. He needed so much that was still on the ship.

The Idmarite gripped his arm and pulled him away.

Azariah startled out of his thoughts. If he couldn't access the ship, he should go with this man.

Instead of leading Azariah to his air-cycle, he pointed down the shore of the lake, where it curved out of sight. Azariah got his emergency bag and followed him as he walked along the edge of the lake. His cycle followed. He was quiet during the walk. Azariah was docile.

The Idmarite was very short, not even to Azariah's shoulder. *Is this dwarfism? Malnourishment? Response to gravity and other environmental conditions? If they're hungry, are they cannibals?* Azariah tried talking a few more times, only like five or seven, before deciding to not press the point any more.

The first sign of civilization was a fence, an odd one that wouldn't keep anything in or out, each part of the fence like a house-high tuning fork. His new friend ducked between tines and insisted Azariah follow him. The fence went into the lake in one direction and circled a large area of land before ending at a cliff.

The man led Azariah further from the lake into a field of white flowers. The markings on the ground and the fire pits indicated they were in some kind of campground.

After some gesturing, Azariah understood that he shouldn't go beyond the fence. His new friend, who wouldn't give a name, yelled a lot about that, nothing about ordeal or judgment.

Azariah gestured to his cycle; he didn't want to be left alone. When it seemed like leaving was his intention, Azariah decided to not push, but did pantomime for food.

The Idmarite glared again, but instead of yelling, picked one of the flowers and put it to his veiled mouth.

Azariah nodded his thanks.

He gestured to Azariah's back, said something, and pointed to the cliffs near the campsite. Azariah looked and saw nothing. His pantomime showed he wanted to help with Azariah's back. He thought about how one small favor can make asking for a bigger favor easier and so he let the Idmarite help and then asked to go with him again, which he refused. Azariah was so incredibly disappointed and worried, but all he did was sit on a patch of white flowers and pinch the bridge of his nose.

Even so, his diplomatic manners automatically kicked in. As a parting gift, he dug through the emergency bag, pulled out two oranges, and offered the Idmarite one, demonstrating how to peel, and then handing half the peeled one before eating his half. The smallest, saddest gift he had ever offered, but it was something.

The Idmarite sniffed the peeled half, took the whole second orange, and then left.

Azariah sat on the patch of flowers and stewed for a minute before setting something up to keep track of the water temperature; if there was a pattern, he wanted to go diving to the ship during a safe period. He scanned his new food; safe and healthy. He chewed a few petals; sour and velvety. The leaves would be a good tea. They grew from tubers that looked like good eating. He wondered if his new friend would come back and yell if he started a fire.

Chapter 40: Azariah, Idmari

Azariah's world was now black and white, with a slash of neon yellow from the tent. The sky was permanently hazy. The sun and moons were ghostly white discs. The cliffs were severe black obsidian. The grass and flowers were gray and white. The lake was a colorless void.

Azariah's explorations the next morning resulted in a time-consuming discovery. The Idmarite had gestured to the cliffs, and on the morning's closer inspection, Azariah saw a small building with a low door nestled into the cliff. It shone the black of obsidian.

On examination, the small building was an abandoned monastery full of objects that might be relics and sacred texts for a few different religions. Azariah skimmed through his favorite passages to see what they looked like in Ugarit. Those could be a starting point if he couldn't find something simpler. The monastery had a reading room with shelves of books and seats near the windows. He looked over the books and found the poetry section. The first book he pulled and skimmed through was much too complicated. He set it aside on a small black table near a black armchair.

Azariah flipped through more books. They were all made of *kurak;* every world since New Godaniya had their own versions of the versatile plant. This gave him hope that there was an advanced civilization on Idmari, even though he hadn't ever been able to scan for it once he was within range of the world. Maybe the ship had done some passive scanning, not that the information was accessible.

Exploring the entire monastery, he found a small room with leftover clutter from camping trips. Black pants and a masculine blue shawl with an embroidered pattern in a different shade of blue replaced his ripped-up coveralls. The blues were dull but a surprisingly joyful relief from the monochrome monotony.

Azariah found a children's book section and grabbed a picture book with bees. He settled into his chair near the window and started to read. He preferred learning a language by speaking it, but everything was different now. The children's poetry and songbooks introduced him to their basic metaphors and cultural references, and then he moved on to more complicated subjects until he was back at the first poetry book. He found and used a dictionary.

The old empire had established a population here to focus on mining in post-protoplanetary disc solar systems—he expected a simple, straightforward grammar like subject-verb-object and simple vocabulary—one word for water, one word for door, maybe even one word for all of clothing. Instead, he found that the grammar was contextual, and that water had at least three words and two of those words had strong abstract concepts. His mind was stuttering over the intricacies. Nevertheless, he would be able to write asking for help in Ugarit once someone came back, which he was sure would be soon.

Azariah was learning the grammar quickly. It reminded him of his home dialect of Kahi. His community had farming in their blood. It was part of their souls, and their love for the land made practical speech too flat. The words of a sentence would swirl around the main word or concept. This Ugarit didn't swirl around farming but around their survival and a new mysticism. Azariah had crash-landed at one of their most sacred lakes and cliffs.

The Idmarites had thoughts on the Gate being bombed two hundred years ago and being cut off from the empire. Azariah had heard plenty of oral histories from other planets, but Idmari's poetry exposed him to emotions, dire need, and complete upheaval in terms that a diplomatic setting didn't.

During Azariah's second lonely night, he woke up to frightening loud sounds, like a ship rumbling too close. He tumbled out of his sleeping bag and reached for the tent door. He stepped out onto the white flowers with his bare feet and looked up at the sky. No ships, just the hazy clouds that hid the stars, and the glow from the two trailing moons. But the rumbling noise was louder. The animal part of his brain was panicking, the rest was gathering information. The glow of the moons was enough to light up the landscape.

The noise was an earthquake. Azariah couldn't feel it yet, but he could see it beyond the fence. The earthquake was rippling the ground in sound-shaped waves. One of the earth waves crested like an ocean wave, ripping the earth, leaving an ugly, jutting scar that was visible among the white flowers. The earthquake wave was still visibly coming, and even side-to-side motion was visible. Azariah couldn't feel the ground shake yet. He needed to get to the emergency bag. The anti-gravity tech could support his weight for a short time, but it was too far.

The earthquake wave disappeared when it hit the tuning-fork fence. The deep rumbling that continued to shake the surrounding ground was not touching Azariah, his tent, or the cliff. He watched in fascination as the earthquake jutted against the fence, creating cracks in the ground that pushed soil several feet up the fences, like ocean waves crashing but not receding.

His animal-instinct side calmed down. He looked around, and it was the same for the entire area within the fences; the lake water rippled funny. The white flowers were perfectly fine and still except for the breeze. Now that Azariah knew what to look for, he could see all sorts of ripples and scars in the landscape of varying ages.

"Well, I think this is an excellent demonstration," he mumbled to himself. The fences were special technology that absorbed the kinetic energy of the earthquake. He was fully isolated, with boiling water on one side, earthquakes on the other, and a lava ocean beyond the cliffs. He hoped good company and safety would come soon.

Chapter 41: Azariah, Idmari

Weeks passed.

No one came. Loneliness was enough to make his brain melt. Azariah hiked and climbed cliffs, which revealed only more rippling landscape. Earthquakes were constant enough that he didn't feel comfortable leaving the fenced area for long. The library called them planet quakes. The temperature of the lake was unpredictable enough that he didn't risk a dive to the ship. He boiled tubers in the lake, even though it was terribly unsafe, but there was no fuel to cook them otherwise. He could monitor the *Zayets* communications from the shore, but the dampening field was strong enough to make it pointless.

Azariah felt trapped in a 2D photograph—stuck to one spot in space. Time had no meaning.

One day, he was in the library with projections of Daniel and his mom in chairs to keep him company. He allowed this just one hour a day or he really would go crazy.

"Beep beep," said the proximity alert device.

Azariah was so surprised he fell over.

Soon, an air-cycle approached. His one and only friend on the planet sprang off his cycle, his bright blue eyes still the only visible part of his face. The air-cycle towed an entire cord of wood, which was both exciting and concerning. Azariah didn't want to stay here, but having fuel would improve his circumstances a little.

Azariah still couldn't understand the Idmarite's yelling now, but he was prepared for that. Azariah got out his disc that had a pre-written message on it in Ugarit and showed it to the Idmarite. After reading the first sentence, it was clear that his friend understood the message, and he continued reading. The message was simple, asking for help for *Klipspringer* and the other things the captain had asked for. Hopefully it would be enough that the Idmarite wouldn't leave him here. At the end of the message was a request for the Idmarite to read the message aloud so Azariah could learn to speak. The Idmarite looked at Azariah strangely, got a book from the monastery library, and showed Azariah the back corner of a book. He flipped a hidden switch and the inside of the cover turned on, and with a couple of taps, the Idmarite turned on an audiobook. Azariah was embarrassed that he hadn't found that on his own. But surely he wouldn't be staying so it didn't matter. While Azariah puzzled over the book, the Idmarite shoved the disc with the written message at Azariah, gesturing that he wanted to write. Azariah showed him how the disc worked, hoping for confirmation that the planet would help *Klipspringer* or that the Idmarite would take him away from the sacred lake and monastery. They handed the projected note back and forth as they wrote.

Idmarite: *Why did you land here?*

Azariah: *I crashed! What's your name?*

Idmarite: *Our station disarmed you and aimed you to land in the sea near our largest sea settlement. You disregarded that.*

Azariah: *Not on purpose! I'm sorry! I really, really wish I'd crashed into the sea now! I'm happy to come with you!*

Idmarite: *No. Now that you're here, you will stay here. For ordeal or judgment.*

Azariah: *What does that mean?*

Instead of answering, the Idmarite said some words and took Azariah's disc and put it in his own pocket. Azariah, his heart pounding, wondered about forcefully taking it back, but that wouldn't get him very far. Instead, he watched as the Idmarite dumped the wood and left.

Once Azariah was alone again—the most alone he'd ever been—the disc had so much stored that it was like an extension of his soul—he plopped on a bed of white flowers, laid down, and looked at the hazy sky while tears fell from his eyes. His only spot of hope was that the Idmarites were keeping the ship alive if they were keeping him alive.

Months passed.

Time consumed Azariah and also meant nothing. Time existed like a monster just behind his back, extracting another piece of his soul, grounding him to powder. No one else visited; the cheerfulness was extracted. He learned how to pronounce Ugarit using the audiobook function on all the books and figured out that the Idmarite had said *I need to take your tool. I don't have anything to write with.*

All his tedious reading revealed what *Ordeal or Judgment* meant. Most of the population lived out in the solar system; they came to this planet when they needed to meet with their leader. If two parties couldn't decide on an issue, she would put them through an Ordeal to discover the truth on behalf of the local god named ID. If the parties agreed on the facts, it was her place to carry out the punishment or restitution, or Judgment.

Azariah was pretty sure he was stuck in an Ordeal; if anyone had taken their measure of him, they would know this flat isolation would wring the truth out. This was being done to him.

These expansion worlds were toys to King Nebuchadnezzar. The worlds were tools to get Daniel what he wanted. Azariah had allowed that to guide him too much. These worlds were everything to the residents. Hananiah and Mishael had both told him more than once that he was creating messes for them to clean up. Azariah hadn't cared much about how he was contributing to the destabilization. He thought his little warnings were appropriate, but he had spent little time understanding each planet's perspective. Even now, he had become reflective only because of this Ordeal.

Chapter 42: Azariah, Idmari

"Beep beep," said the proximity alert device, waking Azariah in his tent.

Azariah groaned and rubbed his eyes. He dozed for a few minutes and then reached for his alarm—he had set it to scan more than a hundred kilometers down the valley and up to the top atmosphere, and it hadn't caught any lifeforms except for the one visit.

The proximity alert was for someone at the edge of the lake! He should have been warned a long time ago, even if they were coming by air or underwater. Unless....

Azariah got dressed and stepped into the eerie moonlight. The moons were in waxing gibbous phase, the sixth time he'd seen that.

A steam fog had gathered over the lake. At the edge sat someone with a delicacy he generally attributed to women. She smoked from a pipe and didn't look his way as he approached. The smoke smelled like juniper. She was small and older by at least fifteen Gospel years and wore a gray shawl with a geometric pattern. Her aura was like the priestess on Lughamstone whose hand he had kissed and caused his first interplanetary solecism.

"I am the Oracle Buhlalu. I live in the cliffs and lead my people. You may sit."

Azariah sat crossed legged nearby, plenty of space, and looked out over the lake with her. The Oracle handed him the pipe. He had, in fact, sat close enough that he was well within her arm's reach. Mishael would scold him again for not understanding personal space. Azariah accepted the pipe and inhaled only a little, held the smoke in his lungs for a moment and then breathed out through his nose. He felt a little tickle, but that was it for the immediate effects. He handed the pipe back. To his surprise and relief, she handed him his disc. He held it tightly in his hand and moved the conversation forward with hope.

"I am Envoy Azariah Ramzi. Did you want to talk now? Or am I interrupting?" Buhlalu—he had read interesting writings by other Oracles but nothing by her.

"I knew I would set off your alarm. It's fine if you're here. It's nice to have someone to share my midnight pipe with."

"About the *Klipspringer*—I'm sure you've heard."

"Yes. A few of my ships will meet with them soon. Once we're close enough, we can decrease the effect of the defense field so your ship is more functional. There will hopefully be no incidents."

"Thank you. I have the same hopes. Do you have more information?"

"What would you like to know?" They had a typical desultory initial conversation. Azariah was sleepy and had forgotten to grab gifts. There was nothing to be charming about. He wanted to ask what her intentions were but that wasn't their way.

"That's enough," the Oracle finally said. "I'll take you to my observation station."

"Excellent! Thank you for this honor." Azariah still wanted to get her a gift, but all the oranges were gone, and the tea was terrible.

The Oracle took him to a staircase in the obsidian and basalt cliff. It was dark and warm and took forever to climb. Before they exited, she provided a heat shielding uniform with a protective helmet. She opened a door once they were ready. They were about halfway up the cliff.

The other side was the ocean of lava.

Close to the shore, thousands of feet below, the lava was roiling. Under the influence of the moons, the lava ocean had tides and giant cresting waves. The lava on the surface was continually hardening and breaking apart. The tide influenced movements were sticky but continually moving. The neon yellow of the lava shone between the hardened parts, yellow waves flowing over the shore and then fading away. As far out as Azariah could see, the surface of the ocean was black with bright yellow cracks. It was hot and terrifying and beautiful, much worse than his glimpses during the crash landing.

They watched for a moment and then the Oracle walked to a building. Azariah didn't see why the staircase couldn't have opened right into the building, and then he saw cracks in the basalt indicating shear movement—the staircase and building probably had been aligned at some point. Looking around, he saw giant accordion fans on the very top of the cliff, spaced out and going in both directions along the cliff. Azariah pointed and asked about them.

"Those are a heat shield," she said, her voice coming through a speaker in his helmet as they entered the building. "They keep the worst of this God-forsaken heat away from the sacred lake. Don't take off your helmet yet." She had been flipping switches and turning dials, all of it the old empire technology. "I haven't been to this station for a while and things need to cool down."

Azariah walked around the room. He rubbed his thumb on a ceramic counter. There was a port for a manual connection. The old empire tech sent to colonies was built to last. Colonies might be cut off from resupply, though being cut off due to terrorism hadn't been expected. This working surface was at least two hundred years old but had been maintained nicely. He moved on. The back wall was smooth obsidian. The building was one large room. Three walls were mostly windows with views over the lava ocean. The sight of the yellow lava was impressive as the sun rose. The building was set for observation with no other visible function, not to live here or spend any length of time. There was no sign of visitors.

After a few more minutes, the Oracle took off her heat suit and Azariah copied, hanging it up near the door. She led him to an area with seats made of heavy-duty molded material. They could watch the landscape, fascinating and hellish, and talk.

"Did you read about the sacred hives?" The Oracle asked.

"Yes." Over a hundred years ago there was a planet quake disaster with very few survivors. A main source of food was insects. Sheds of insects broke apart in the disaster and gas clouds killed them. The larvae were left. People ate all the larvae, and they ate almost all the pollinators as well. A woman grabbed the last two hives and ran for safety.

"This cliff observation post is where she hid. She protected the hives until she died, possibly lived off honey and the white manna flowers for decades. No one knew to look for her and when she was discovered she had been dead for five years. Now she is honored as a saint. We don't even know her name." She had left behind writings that Azariah had studied in detail along with stories of how the local god named ID enjoyed participating in the Oracles' judgments. Along with this local god, the Oracles received visits from an archangel named Michael; the scientific community had turned to mysticism.

The Oracle pointed out a side window nearby. There were two hives and a shrine to the first Oracle. "Those are ceremonial, and yes, these particular bees can survive the heat. There are plenty of hives now on the plain."

Azariah so desperately wanted to talk to another human being, but he was out of practice and his diplomatic instincts said to be quiet.

"She is the first Oracle because of the crazy writings. She writes about ID, who visits me. I mean, yes, I call them crazy writings while writing crazy things myself. I shouldn't consider them crazy, but I believe I have always been skeptical right up until now." She frowned at Azariah. "I'm angry at ID, though he doesn't care. All he did was encourage the first Oracle to stay alive to take care of the bees. That's the only thing she did. That's all ID did at the time; he never revealed himself to anyone else during that time. Millions died without any noticeable interference. Now ID helps Oracles with ordeals and judgments, but how is anything he says to me now important?" She looked at Azariah; her question wasn't rhetorical.

Azariah bowed his head. "I've read everything in the library and respect it."

"Would you like to hear my latest vision? I haven't shared it with anyone. Usually once I share it, I don't have it anymore, and I had decided shortly before you arrived that it was time. Then your ship crashed in that lake, and it seemed like a sign, not that ID ever tells me things like that, so I've been walking from the other side of the world and just as I'm here my people are about to reach your ship."

"I would be very honored if you would share such a thing," Azariah said, bowing again.

She stood with a large set of windows at her back. The fiery background was how Daniel described the Ancient Court. "I saw in my vision by night, and behold, the four winds of heaven were stirring up the Great Sea. Four great beasts came up from the sea, each different from the other. The first was like a lion and had eagle wings. I watched till its wings were plucked off and it was lifted up from the earth and made to stand on two feet like a man, and a man's heart was given to it. Suddenly another beast, a second, like a bear. It was raised up on one side and had three ribs in its mouth between its teeth. And they said thus to it: 'Arise, devour much flesh!' After this I looked, and there was another, like a leopard, which had on its back four wings of a bird. The beast also had four heads, and dominion was given to it. What is your answer to that?"

Azariah had little time to compose himself. It was disconcerting to hear Daniel's vision from the perspective of someone else. But if God gave visions to one person, then She could certainly give the same vision to other people as well. Daniel's visions were in the *Klipspringer* database, but this would be an odd trick to play.

"My answer," Azariah said. "Is this: that there is a fourth beast that is terrifying and has ten horns." He could recite Daniel's vision entirely but decided not to.

The Oracle's shocked reaction was immediate. She walked away from Azariah who got to his feet as well.

"No, stay there. Give me some distance."

Azariah watched some scary lava geysers explode and the lava tides roll in.

"I want Idmari to stay cut off from the rest of the galaxy. But what is it you want?" The Oracle asked, turning around.

Azariah looked at the Oracle, expecting there to be more.

"I'm ready to just cut to the heart of it," the Oracle said, "Whatever is going on, on the grander scheme of things, the galaxy wide scheme, I need to know what you want."

That struck him dumb. A few months ago—before he was stuck with himself alone for so long—he would have asked for what Daniel wanted: safety for as many of their people as possible. Now that seemed incredibly wrong.

"If you aren't ready to join the rest of the galaxy, then you shouldn't. In order to make that happen, it would be best for your people for all of us to go home," Azariah said firmly. "I can keep people from trying to come here again. If we stay here, I think more might try to come."

"Still, I must know what you want?"

"I have restitution to perform. I want to perform it. I need to do a better job of keeping safe the worlds caught up in the empire's expansion. And I want to get back to Daniel."

"Well, let's get you home."

"Is it as easy as that?" Azariah had cut to the heart of the matter too —keep the king away.

"I personally have the location of one hidden Gate, just beyond our moons. The location is knowledge that has been passed from Oracle to Oracle. This Gate leads to Tamu Massif, which is a nearby solar system. The two of us were closely connected and we're lucky the Gate between the two of us wasn't destroyed two hundred years ago when our Gates to the greater galaxy were. I am willing to allow all your crew through the Gate on the *Klipspringer* and then I will destroy the Gate on our end. I think you should be able to use the Gate at Tamu Massif to help you get home, but I don't care. Tamu Massif is dead as of our last known contact roughly two hundred years ago. The survivors came here, settled on the other side of the planet, and unfortunately were wiped out about one hundred seventy years ago. We will escort you to the Gate, including me, as I have to be present."

Chapter 43: Azariah

The next day was like a dream. Like every other place Azariah had left, he had only his disc and the clothes on his back.

Now that the Oracle had decided, many people popped out of the woodwork to communicate with him, though since he was leaving the planet in isolation, there was hardly a point.

Azariah left Idmari with the Oracle. There was a ceremony that included a fleet of small ships promenading around her flagship. After a few days of travel through the solar system, they met with the *Klipspringer*. The Idmarite military ships surrounded it. *Klipspringer* was leaving on Idmarite terms. Once the Idmarite ships gathered around *Klipspringer*, they turned back to face the planet and escorted *Klipspringer* to the Gate.

The crew was excited and on edge when Azariah returned. The captain and crew had plenty of questions. Due to all the deaths, ship duties had bounced around and now Wamiri was at the right hand of the captain and also in a rolling chair due to all the stress. She especially had a lot of questions, natural curiosity and also her quality assurance instincts kicking in. *Klipspringer* wouldn't be given time to check on the Gate that was more than two hundred years old with unknown maintenance, but Azariah passed on what information he could.

After the captain's initial excitement, she and Azariah had a serious discussion on the Oracle's intent and honesty. Azariah hid the mystical and prophetic parts.

"She feels like she understands us well enough, and she wants us out of here," Azariah said over a cup of tea with the ship shuddering under him. Everyone else was used to it.

"She doesn't want us to come back? Are you sure? She didn't say."

"She clearly said to me that they want to stay in isolation for possibly hundreds of more years. But she knows we'll do whatever we want. She understands the empire."

"Do you think she's leading us into a trap?"

"No," Azariah said positively. "There are much easier ways to kill us, and if this was dangerous, she wouldn't have left her planet. And if the Tamu Massif Gate is in good enough condition for us to enter the solar system, I'm sure we can use it to get home."

"What are her motivations?" The captain asked, holding onto a plate during an especially bad ship shudder.

"Above all, it's the right thing to do—we are stranded away from home, and she has the power to send us home. Connecting to the Chaldean empire would be a conflict the Idamites don't want. Yes, there are dangers to sending us back, but there are dangers to keeping us and it's wrong to kill us."

"It fits with their collective cultural trauma."

The ride to the Gate was terrible. The ship hadn't used its propulsion engines at full strength and wasn't taking the beating very well. Plus, once they returned to Babylon, *Klipspringer* was expected to make a planet side landing and needed to prep heat plates. There was a lot to do. Azariah didn't sleep much.

Despite the need for rest, Azariah also had a very strong need to spend time with his friends, especially the Jump team. With months of isolation under his belt, interacting with people was something he desperately needed, but it was also something that made him cranky. Everyone was kind and understanding; he had been out of contact for so long that they had considered him as one of the dead. When he asked to have dinner together, he wanted only something small and quiet, but it turned into a big celebration, initially for just for him but then growing as a farewell party for everyone since the *gerru* would be over soon, if the report that Tamu Massif was abandoned was true.

Azariah first had a great time fluttering around between people, but felt overwhelmed soon, so he sat in a corner of the mess hall a little out of the way. The cooks made sure he always had tea with goat's milk in a covered cup in case gravity went out. People found him if they wanted to.

First was the captain, who had been such a good advocate for himself and the crew.

"Tell me, Captain, most people on your crew were forced into their positions. Was that the same for you? What did you do to get stuck here? I'm sure you're connected enough to have been reassigned."

"I volunteered. I saw the captain who had been selected and knew the ship wouldn't get past the first Jump. It seemed like a suicide mission, but it was my duty."

Azariah gave her a tight hug.

"Listen, Azariah, I know you're going to be under a microscope when we get home. Please allow me to help. Even if other people pull away, I won't be one of them. From what you've said, you don't know where you are going to stay when we get home. I definitely have room for you on my property in the Kaspum Mountains."

"Thank you. I'll call you Maria now." Azariah gave her another tight hug and felt his eyes burning. He didn't know what would be waiting for him on Babylon.

Second was Bounthavy.

"Darling Azariah, thank you again for everything," she said, sitting close and giving him a side hug. "Now that we're almost home, I wanted to tell you something. Did you know that there were assassination attempts against you? They originated from the Etemenanki palace and accused you of treason! Anyway, I pulled a few strings and cleared your name. So just stay clear of the palace and you won't have to worry about it."

Azariah was speechless for a moment and just kissed the top of her head as a thank you. "I didn't know you had those kinds of strings to pull."

"Considering all the support you've given me, it was the least I could do."

"I am still in your debt."

After Bounthavy, his surviving friends from Engineering came by and that was a much quieter visit as they grieved for losing so many friends. Park came by, which put him on edge that Beck might drop in too, and that's when he finally left. He had to give Beck a baby. He had refused to think about it, refused to participate, but he knew that he would have to face up to it once he was at home. He would rather face one of Bounthavy's assassins, especially if they were like Sal.

In a matter of days, they were at a distant moon. The entourage stayed together, which made maneuvering a little difficult, but they found what they were looking for: the Gate, surrounded by an abandoned space station and lots of old, falling apart ships and detritus. The Idamites had pulled anything useful through the Gate before closing it.

The Gate turned on, opened, and they were hustled through. *Klipspringer* entered the solar system and by the time the engines had swung them around to face the Gate, it was off. Now it was time to turn it back on, reprogram it, and go home.

After a few days of reprogramming and preparing for Babylon, Azariah was frantic and impatient and exhausted.

The Gate finally opened. He was lightheaded.

Azariah thumbed through his letters and correspondence. Daniel had written a lot, but nothing marked urgent. No other emergencies.

Azariah wrote Daniel a few jumbled lines and then passed out.

PART THREE

CONSEQUENCES

Chapter 44: Daniel

In order to get the Ctesiphon Federation to give up their independence, Daniel ran a campaign in a democratic election. People liked him and believed in him, so he won.

One reason the asteroid citizens liked him was because of his star surfing skills, so at their request, Daniel was out with them again during the active cycle. His Martigny asteroid tattoo impressed some citizens, but he could fake a tattoo in a way that surfing skills couldn't be. Everyone went out the airlock; being among the stars again was heady; Daniel's memories from the Goethe system didn't do the reality justice.

I am leading these people. They chose me. It's okay to enjoy this.

One gravity line had shut down traffic, so a crowd of people was just hanging out. When Daniel joined them the first time months ago, he had been rusty. Now he could join the more talented star surfers. They enjoyed tricks like surfing a 360 spiral around the gravity line or zooming away from gravity as much as possible and still make it back.

"Issiakkum Ravi," Sigazibi said, her voice coming through a speaker in Daniel's helmet. She had stayed on the asteroid.

Daniel stopped, hovering away from the gravity line. Her tone in just those two words was urgent, as were her next words.

"Check your disc."

Daniel had slapped it to the front of his space suit. Now that he looked at it, he could see he had letters from Aza! He hadn't heard the special chime since he was in space. The bundle of letters from Aza was large, the last one flagged and marked as written a half hour ago.

My dearest Daniel, Long story, we just opened a Gate at the twelfth planet, we're coming home for good now! Straight hop through the Gates and then I get to see you in a couple hours! Maybe? We are not sure how fast we can go.

I checked for flagged messages and didn't see any. I hope you can be at the palace.

The predetermined arrival plan was for a grand entrance attended by the king, the only time the *Klipspringer* would enter a planetary atmosphere. The ship would land at the palace for the crew to disembark, and then the ship would be converted into a museum. However, they were all supposed to have more time to prepare. There was supposed to be an end to the eleventh cycle and then Azariah could spend the last cycle deciding what he wanted. But having him home even sooner was perfect. Daniel's heart was singing.

Daniel turned around, gave a signal to his bodyguards that he was leaving. Sigazibi cleared her throat. Instead of heading for the exit, Daniel swerved to say goodbye to the Ctesiphon delegation that he had been surfing with and gave his apologies for leaving early because of an urgent personal matter. When he returned to the asteroid, he repeated his goodbyes to specific politicians Sigazibi pointed out.

Bar-Rabkib and Ben-Hadad were both alike and different. The Ctesiphon population had been stable and insular for thousands of years. The lack of being close to the sun had lightened their skin, and anyone even a shade darker was an outsider. They both had that worldview, but cohesion on racial lines had created opportunities for exploitation, and they were from different classes. Bar-Rabkib had a slight frame and a soft voice. Ben-Hadad physically dominated them and also was louder, more talkative, and just more. The old political structure, which was a series of corporate fiefdoms, had appointed Ben-Hadad. The former power players insisted on their interests being represented in the new government, and they meant for Ben-Hadad to overwhelm any other representation. They were making Daniel as angry as he ever got at anyone. The Ctesiphon Federation provided layers of problems to fix, and this was only one part of his administrative responsibility in Babylonia.

"I have to leave on an urgent personal matter. All these contracts will be invalid in two days. It will be your job to get replacement contracts with the Babylonia solar system as signatory instead of the Ctesiphon Federation."

"Daniel, we've got this," Ben-Hadad, laughed and shook the shoulder of Bar-Rabkib.

"You will refer to me as Issiakkum," Daniel said coldly. "I have to sign off on any work you do. All contracts must be at arm's length."

They glared.

Daniel turned to Bar-Rabkib. "The Ctesiphon Federation chose this union. The Federation elected you to bring them forward."

"I know! I know! I'm eager to do my home asteroids proud." Perhaps Bar-Rabkib was eager, but also they looked overwhelmed.

"The tax agreements are still valid. For the entire empire's existence, Ctesiphon's illegal activity has given you funds to pay tax, and you will no longer have those funds. We've discussed alternatives, like harvesting the gas giant or properly educating your constituents. Choose for yourselves or I'll be choosing for you. I will enforce my wishes if you fall back into old habits; I hope you can understand this without me specifying threats." Daniel didn't want to threaten military action, especially when the king's special forces were excited about the idea.

Daniel's words and accompanying stare were enough for Bar-Rabkib, who paled further and Ben-Hadad, who turned red. By this point, Daniel had reached his ship and was standing just inside.

"I'll see you at the ceremony." Before they could say anything, he shut the door.

Sigazibi and his protection officers were ready to go as he settled into his seat. The rest of his staff were staying behind. They would take a different ship with the Ctesiphon delegation to the ceremony on Babylon in a couple of days. He was supposed to be with them. Instead, he was in his new two percent ship. It would take a day to get to Babylon, and he was worried he wouldn't be there for Aza. Daniel sent a couple of messages. Azariah wasn't available to write back immediately.

Next, Daniel did his best to reschedule the ceremony that would create a united Babylonia solar system with him at the head. He couldn't stand wasting a day right when Aza was back. But Daniel wasn't allowed to reschedule. Birbirru, Oshpenaz, Mishael, and Sigazibi all yelled at him. What was the point of becoming issiakkum-samsi if he couldn't spend time with Azariah to the extent he wanted? But not even Hananiah was the slightest bit swayed.

Hananiah and Piama, his wife from the Kaliopi estate of Gospel, were happy to chat and were ecstatic. Their permanent home was in the South Pole. Hananiah was gone a lot because of his *gerru* duties. This last cycle had been so long that they were free to do whatever they wanted and spent time at the North Pole because of the Ctesiphon Federation union festivities. Tomorrow evening was a party at Daniel's penthouse, which he wanted to cancel, but Birbirru, Oshpenaz,

Mishael, and Sigazibi wouldn't let him. Daniel then called Samwel, his housekeeper, and so on. The time passed faster than he expected, especially once he started reading Azariah's letters.

"Oshpenaz, do I look okay?" Daniel was going to see Azariah for the first time in over three years, except for the short video call, and he hadn't had time to prepare. He didn't feel ready. He had come straight to the docking bay from his ship; he was barely beating the *Klipspringer.*

Daniel and Oshpenaz were in the second story of the king's reception lobby. On the other side of the glass wall were hundreds of people, friends, and family, gathering in the docking bay where the *Klipspringer* crew would disembark. Daniel was not with them. The king had never completely let him go. Daniel was still a part of the king's entourage for events like this. And with all the changes Daniel was making, he was an excellent target for assassination and his bodyguards appreciated it when he didn't mingle in uncontrolled crowds.

Oshpenaz rolled his eyes at Daniel's question. "If you don't look okay, what hope is there for the rest of us?"

"You know what I mean." Daniel held himself for inspection, tucking a curl of hair behind his ear. He was wearing cream-colored linen pants with expensive sandals and an open cream-colored robe that went to the floor with gold embroidery and showed off his arms. It was fancier than his usual clothes because of the ceremonies with the Ctesiphon Federation, and all he had with him.

"Smile. You look like you dropped important work and flew over here," Oshpenaz said drily, "but nothing is dirty, and nothing is stuck in your teeth. Oh look, Chancellor Ospelt is here. Hm." He continued scanning the crowds and murmuring to Daniel or his friend on his other side about who was in the crowd. Many powerful families had sent their black sheep and problem children away on the *gerru,* expecting them to die. This dynamic made the crowd edgy with excitement to welcome the crew home.

"How is our Azariah?" Oshpenaz asked. "I've skimmed over his reports and the letters to me, but I'm sure he lets you know how he really is."

"Idmari was a strange planet. He had a hard time writing about it," Daniel whispered, trying to not lie.

Oshpenaz chuckled, mistaking the discretion for disinterest. "As long as the envoy is okay, you don't care. I wonder if he's read any mail. He might not even know you are issiakkum of Babylon."

"Oshpenaz!" Daniel gasped and laid a hand on his arm. "So much more has happened since his last Gate opened. He might not know anything!" Daniel's innate patience broke. He tried to video chat again and sent Azariah more messages. Nothing Daniel had sent him had been marked as read, though Azariah had sent a message a few hours ago that he was awake and fine.

"Ah, here we go," Oshpenaz said, drawing Daniel's attention up.

Instead of the ship being a blip on a map, they could now see *Klipspringer* burn through the atmosphere. Soon enough, the ship landed like a metal ball. The crowd below gathered as close as they could to the ship on the landing platform outside the docking bay.

"Oh my, look at that. And that." Oshpenaz pointed to where there were enormous boulders embedded into the frame of the ship, barely missing the landing struts. In other areas, large patches of metal covered the original hull.

"Azariah said he was fine," Daniel said automatically. He re-read his two messages. "Wait, he didn't. But I asked Gabriel."

Now the ramp was descending, and Daniel's heart was in his throat.

Azariah was one of the first, coming with the captain. He looked incredible. He was serious, no smile, he looked over people with an unemotional weighing glance. Daniel wanted to run to him, but clenched his fists and tapped his foot instead, staring. Azariah carried himself like royalty and was wearing a deep teal shawl with plum colored embroidery, looking older than twenty-three. He was paler and taller and thinner. Daniel's heart felt like it was going to burst.

Then he smiled, and it was a perfect Azariah smile. It made Daniel smile, even though he wasn't even looking in Daniel's direction. He had found their friends and was hugging everyone: Samwel and Fatuma, Mishael, Hananiah, Piama, and their kids. It was perfect. Watching the tableau was the second best thing to do.

Azariah asked Mishael a question, who pointed at Daniel's set of windows, and they headed to the door on the first level. That was Daniel's signal.

The next few minutes were a blur. Afterwards, Daniel could remember only little snatches. Azariah's shawl under his hands when they greeted each other with a tight hug. Daniel's guards bumped into them as people pressed in. Mishael and Hananiah close by.

Soon enough, they were at another palace landing platform for private high-status vehicles. Once they were free of the tight crowds, Daniel could breathe deeper and enjoy having Azariah so close by.

"Aza, this is your flyer, an Omary model," Mishael led and pointed it out. "A gift from Daniel. The first of many, I'm sure."

Daniel was pleased with himself that he didn't wait until the twelfth cycle started before thinking about all the things Azariah would need once he got back.

Azariah let Daniel put an arm around his waist and guide him around. Now his brow furrowed, thinking.

"I'm the Babylonia issiakkum now," Daniel said as a reply to the question on his face, leaving off whether he was the -mati or -samsi for now. Daniel was one today and would be a different one by the end of tomorrow.

"This is overwhelming," Azariah smiled as they approached the flyer, and reached out a tentative hand to touch it.

Mishael helped unlock it. Daniel had bought it and stored it at his penthouse, but otherwise had nothing to do with it. Mishael, Hananiah, and Piama had taken it for test runs while he was off-planet at the Ctesiphon Federation election.

All four climbed in—and it was like four or five years ago, their last camping trip right before they were thrown in prison. Daniel smiled at the guys in the backseat. They were their usual spots. Daniel reached over to Azariah and placed a hand on his shoulder.

Azariah leaned back in his seat and held Daniel's hand over his heart while looking at the dashboard. He kissed the back of the hand and dropped it so he'd have both hands free to poke at the screen.

Daniel felt his hand tingle where Azariah had kissed it. His entire arm tingled like he had bumped his elbow, and that was when Daniel knew for sure what Azariah meant to him. Daniel didn't know or much care what his own sexuality was, but he knew that having Azariah physically close to him was everything, was giving body to his own soul, and that he would be happy to give Azariah whatever he needed or wanted. A few years ago, Azariah would touch him on the arm and then pull away like he got burned. He had felt this. He wanted the entirety of love, without reservation, and Daniel's internal reservations were gone now. He was frustrated with himself for pushing Azariah so hard three years ago; Daniel had offered Azariah everything at that point, and how could he offer it again in a different spirit and have Azariah believe?

"Let's get home," Daniel said. "My bodyguards here have to stay in the heat until this takes off."

"I can't drive this," Azariah said, running his hands on the dashboard. "I don't even know where we're going, and I crashed the last ship I piloted."

"My turn!" Mishael announced, itching to take over. "Move out of the way."

Instead of getting out of the flying car, Azariah sat in Daniel's lap to switch places—again, something they used to do all the time. Daniel barely had time to put a hand on Azariah's waist before Mishael settled in front and Azariah was now in the back.

"I can talk in here, right?" Azariah asked, glancing at Hananiah.

"Yes," Mishael answered.

Daniel turned and reached back to put a hand on Azariah's knee.

"I couldn't put this in any letters, but there's an Oracle at Idmari who has the same visions as Daniel. It's because of that connection that she let us go when I asked. I didn't ask for anything else." Azariah had a new seriousness in his manner.

"You protected Idmari," Hananiah sighed in relief. "You finally get that."

"I do." He looked at Daniel.

"I get it too. Finally," Daniel promised.

"None of us ever wanted you to go," Mishael complained. "And you've screwed up big time. You have no idea."

"Mishael! That is enough!" Daniel said, using his issiakkum voice, which silenced everyone for a moment. Mishael maneuvered the flyer onto the penthouse platform.

Azariah put his hand on Daniel's, and it was such a thrill. He spoke to the other two. "I have a couple of friends who might be stuck on the ship, if someone can look after them."

"We can go," Hananiah said, indicating himself and Mishael.

"Yeah," Mishael agreed. "We'll get out of your hair, especially if I can borrow this."

Azariah nodded once he realized no one else was giving permission.

"Thanks guys," Daniel said and popped out of his side of the Omary.

Daniel hustled Azariah inside out of the heat. As soon as they were inside, Daniel embraced him, clutching a fistful of shawl, thinking of the last time when Azariah was leaving, and he didn't want to let go. Azariah tucked his chin over Daniel's shoulder and breathed deep.

After a long time, after Daniel holding tight and saying, "I love you," and "I'm so happy," and Azariah said nothing, just nodding and holding tight, Daniel leaned back. Azariah let go.

"Don't let go, I just want to see you," Daniel said.

Azariah sighed and put his hands on Daniel's waist. He has his eyes closed. Daniel ran his fingers down the side of Azariah's face and cupped his jaw with one hand. He had shaved. He was paler than Daniel had ever seen him, making his olive tone look translucent. He'd lost weight, and it brought out the sharp planes of his face. His hair was tied back, and Daniel took the tie out. It was so smooth and clean. Azariah opened his eyes and Daniel was breathless. His eyes were like Daniel remembered, like they'd been in his lucid dream, a brown that was so bright they were like liquid cinnamon, contrasting with the teal of his shawl.

Azariah's eyes held a question. "I have changed. I can feel it even more now, right here with you."

The sound of his voice—the same—made Daniel shiver and pause, smoothing Azariah's shawl down his chest, fingering the embroidery. "When I saw you come out of the ship and greet our friends, you were different and, Aza, it was love at first sight. You would have caught my attention anywhere. It thrilled me that my best friend who I'd been writing to and who had been writing every single little thought to me was also this beautiful, elegant man."

Azariah's face softened as Daniel spoke, and he pulled close. "Can you say it again?"

"I love you. I'm in love with you, it is a full *eros* and everything love. I want to get married and raise a family with you. I told you on your birthday that I wanted a family with you and then in the next breath said no. Of course you had to leave. I'm so sorry. You always had my back, you always let me in, you have for years so naturally. I've changed everything, Azariah, and I can't imagine a future without you as my partner in everything."

Azariah smiled more and more as Daniel spoke. "I love you too."

They kissed. Just like when he kissed Daniel's hand, Daniel felt a crackling energy start at his lips and go through his body, like the nerves connected to his heart and mind. Daniel felt overwhelmed in seconds, never having felt this before, but he couldn't let go.

Azariah broke their kiss. "I want to kiss you more. But remember, before I left, how you would visit me and all you would do is take naps? I think I understand that feeling now."

"You're safe now. You can rest," Daniel agreed and caressed Azariah's face, wiping away a tear. "Let me show you your new suite, Aza. Your home is here."

Chapter 45: Azariah

Azariah woke up in the dark. He thought he was on Idmari, but the air and gravity were wrong. He called for lights; they lit up a strange room. He was alone. The windows were closed, so he stumbled out of bed and hit the light shield—the Babylonian style button was his first major clue. But even that couldn't prepare him for the view: a vivid panorama of Babylon city, down the Turquoise River canyon. Daniel. This was Azariah's suite inside Daniel's home, his issiakkum penthouse. Azariah shook his head. This wasn't the homecoming or Daniel he had expected, and maybe that was a good thing.

Azariah's disc was notifying him about important messages. He retrieved it and sat in a comfy chair near the windows. Daniel and Mishael both had messages in his feed. Azariah wanted Daniel's more. He opened it and it was incredibly long. Mishael had marked his message as urgent, so before Azariah got lost in Daniel's, he checked out Mishael's. His first line was *Don't do what Daniel is asking, here's what's happening.* So Azariah read his message and then went back to Daniel's and took his time. After that, and after a shower and eating— all his favorites were in his kitchen—he peeked out his door to the entrance hall, which was a ballroom today. The entire floor was crowded with people. It was overwhelming, which was not a sensation he was used to. Daniel should be in the crowd, but Azariah didn't see him.

A petite woman was standing right at his door. When she saw Azariah, she pushed him back inside, talking into a device, "No, he's not dressed, just like you thought. He's back inside." Obviously an aide from Mishael. Azariah thought about his messages over the years. Who were his aides?

"Tasroses? Welcome, make yourself at home."

She glared at him.

Azariah gave her a big smile. Before they could say anything else, Mishael burst into the room and dismissed Tasroses, who disappeared out the door.

"Fantastic! We're off to a great start," he said, flicking at Azariah's casual cotton robe.

"I wanted to make sure there really was a party before I got dressed up in that outfit. And hey, you're certainly looking good. I do better braids, though."

Mishael, in a burgundy suit, helped Azariah with the fancy black silk kimono that Daniel had picked out. He said it would complement Daniel's forest green outfit. He also looked like he was going to cry.

"You've changed so much, Azariah. You still sound like the same Azariah in your letters, but this is very unexpected," he said, frowning to keep the tears from falling and handing Azariah a hairbrush.

"Surprise, I made it back," he said lightly. "Give me an update on Daniel. He said he wasn't doing anything important enough to stay away, but he didn't have a choice."

Mishael laughed quite a bit at that and said, "The procession ended about an hour ago. Everyone—King Nebuchadnezzar, Daniel, and the Ctesiphon Federation—paraded this morning to the North Pole where they signed papers, asked for Marduk's and God's blessings, and then paraded back to the palace in front of at least a million people. Now people are throwing big parties, celebrating the union of the Ctesiphon Federation with the Babylonia solar system and Daniel's ascension from issiakkum-mati to issiakkum-samsi, anointed by the king. Daniel's party is one of the most exclusive. So no, nothing important."

"Yesterday Daniel said he wished for me to be with him as his partner but that it wasn't advised, which he didn't understand." They had talked a lot yesterday before Azariah finally slept. While their talking had been on an emotional note that matched how Daniel kissed Azariah, he couldn't reconcile it with the Daniel he had last been with three years ago.

"I'm sure *you* will understand within a few minutes of meeting all of his own new court vipers," Mishael answered, interrupting Azariah's thoughts.

Azariah immediately felt protective and ready to jump into the party. The kind of jump he was used to—right into a mess. But his lengthy isolation had changed him enough that this party felt like a challenge instead of a fun adventure.

Mishael and Azariah left his suite and entered the entrance hall.

Azariah had walked through this entrance hall when he arrived yesterday but hadn't been able to absorb the full extent of Daniel's penthouse. Mishael and Azariah now stood in a ballroom-sized room. One side of the room had the entrance from the landing platform and the far opposite end of the room had the entrance for people who had to use the elevator.

"Is this really all Daniel's?" Azariah asked.

"Yes," Mishael answered. "This is the issiakkum's penthouse. It's two full stories and more that cover the whole of the top of this skyscraper. The views down the valley are fantastic. The prior issiakkum designed it. There's a partial third story for the master suite but Daniel won't use it. Yet."

"How did he even become the solar system governor? Last night I fell asleep before I could ask half the questions I needed to."

"You know Daniel. He decided it was what he ought to do, so he asked the king for it, and now it's his."

They stood off to the side while Mishael pointed out the different swirls of cliques and power centers and old friends, similar to all Azariah's diplomatic parties but in a nicer setting, with a three-story-high ceiling, curvy stairs, onion shaped pillars, Zharqua desert colors, the smell of sage, and a variety of people crammed into the space that had seemed vast when he had arrived yesterday. Before Mishael could go into too much detail, party attendees saw him and wanted to talk with him, and also meet whoever he deemed important enough to talk to. And then Azariah was interesting for himself as the recently returned envoy. Through all of this, Azariah looked for Daniel. Mishael said he would be in the thickest crush of people on the other side of the room. Azariah kept calm. This was a new diplomatic role and, as Daniel's best friend, it wasn't his place to elbow his way to Daniel's side.

"Daniel has met all these people, right?" Azariah asked Mishael.

"Yes. They all have enough of a connection to be invited, at least."

"So I need to meet every single person."

Mishael rolled his eyes.

"If I were to meet every single person over the course of two hours, I should spend about thirty seconds with every group of three people."

Mishael rolled his eyes again. They had been whispering to each other between people approaching, and now Mishael was done. He dumped Azariah onto Wahap, who he was delighted to see, and gave him a big hug. Wahap was indeed ingratiating himself into various circles, as much as he could spend time away from New Godaniya.

"My dear Aza," Wahap said in Oghuric, "I am leaving this solar system tonight. I know I have only a minuscule chance of convincing you to come with me, but you are invited."

"Thank you, my dear friend," Azariah smiled. "I've heard the king is up to something. I need to bear up under it, though it would probably be safer to go." Azariah spoke with him for as long as he could. They introduced each other to different people, but Wahap had to leave too soon.

And on it went. Not too many people made an impression. Azariah couldn't remember anyone's names, but there were a few stand outs.

Beck's parents were ever so glum that she'd made it back, relieved she wasn't there at the party, a bit pleased to tell Azariah they were expecting a grandchild from him, and ever so slightly impressed, though they might have been faking it. They were both in royal court dress, bare to the waist and with Egyptian schentis that had embroidered golden planets.

Moving from one possible set of in-laws to the next, Azariah soon found Daniel's mother and youngest sister and gave them a full two minutes. Out of all the people in the room, Daniel's mother intimidated Azariah the most. She wore a loose, neutral-colored, dour outfit, exactly what you'd expect a mother-of-a-spiritual-icon to wear, and which hid her actual position—a growing power player who owned planets and resources in at least three systems now, ruling at least three billion people. Azariah asked after her other daughters, both of whom were now married. When Azariah congratulated her, she grimaced and said that her new children-in-law were going to be trouble. Azariah made it clear that he hoped to be her son-in-law. She did not say no, which he considered a victory. He hugged Salamasina, who was dressed in a magenta jumpsuit, and he slipped her a last gift, an ear cuff with fire crystals from Idmari embedded in it, a gift from the Oracle, and warned her it was significantly more valuable than any other gift. She got a wild look in her eye; her mother plucked it out of her hands and glared at Azariah, who bowed apologetically over the mother's hand and moved on.

Azariah gave Birbirru a tight hug when he bumped into her. She still had purple hair and wore a long pleated gown that made her look like an Aegyptus queen. "Tell me seriously, how is Daniel doing from your perspective?"

"Azariah, he is wreaking havoc on the empire." She grabbed his arms and shook them gently. "The king says he disagrees, but he isn't stopping Daniel, so everyone thinks the two of them have some secret plan. The power centers of the empire are going to change within the next few years unless they reverse course immediately. The Federation unity seems like a small thing on one hand, but it's going to increase Daniel's power exponentially. So for now—all these people? These are the people who don't wish Daniel dead but instead are deathly afraid or curious of what whim or careful plan might bring them down or lead to new fortune. And his family and friends and whoever loves him are here too, whatever. I've traveled enough to know that -samsi holds so much more weight than -mati, and there's never been a Babylonia issiakkum-samsi. Most people think he's naïve and over his head, but I know him well enough to see through that, and I'm freaking out a little. Ugh, but anyway, how are you? I'm shocked you're still alive."

"Fantastic. You are now one of my best friends and we should have tea a couple of times a month to catch up like this. If I survive the next few weeks, of course." Azariah kissed her cheek and moved on.

After an hour or so, the crush around Daniel lessened, and Azariah started to get glimpses of him through the crowd. Mishael had said their outfits complemented each other. Azariah's was flowing while Daniel's was structured with a forest green floor length vest, pants, gold sandals, and wore his hair in a tight braid. This vest had a high neck, gold embroidery, and two opal buttons near the top, which let the vest flow back and expose his mid-drift. He looked like a demi-god; that's what Azariah had thought when he saw Daniel yesterday, and it was even more true today. Daniel wore his biggest emerald ring, a new signet ring, and on his ring finger, a gift Azariah had sent from the tropical region of Qatna,of beautiful sculptural rings carved from white shells and laid like a lattice between two knuckles. Daniel was reserved as he spoke to people, none of the gentleness from yesterday. When people bent to kiss his signet ring, he had a look of being stiff and severe. Azariah remembered this Daniel and felt better knowing that this Daniel was still there and not just the happy Daniel.

He saw Azariah, finally, and smiled.

The lady next to him gasped, "Is he smiling at me? I've never seen him smile. Oh! He's coming this way."

Daniel approached, bowed to the lady, and asked to speak to Azariah, and then immediately ignored her to smile again. Azariah gave the lady a more polite goodbye and then gripped his arm. It felt like the closest to a hug he could get in such a crowd with so many people watching. This was an important first impression, and different from greeting each other in the docking bay crowd. Daniel was ruling over and working with these people, and Azariah wanted to support him in whatever way he could. Looking at Daniel's soft, happy expression, Azariah knew the gravitas of the moment went over his head. So he let his own concerns about image and diplomacy drop away and took a deep breath. Azariah bowed over his hand formally and kissed the Qatna ring.

Azariah stood up and raised his head. Daniel didn't drop his hand. This was like when Daniel was about to enter the high royal court for the first time, and he'd been scared, but had kept Azariah close by. They had been two lonely young men away from home and now, years later, there was still a small echo of that feeling.

"Congratulations."

"Thank you."

"You can't ever just leave asteroids alone, can you?"

"I have to take care of all of them." Daniel smiled again, a big smile that crinkled the skin around his kohl-lined eyes.

"Thank you for interrupting your trade negotiations yesterday to meet me."

"There are plenty of capable people on my staff who were probably happy to get me out of the way."

"But no one else can star surf. I was thinking of why you would bother with trade agreements in the first place, but a half hour ago I said hi to Te'oma and I wondered if—"

"No, I would never work—"

"—So you do still hate—"

"—hate him with the utmost hatred. I count him my enemy." Daniel's smile lit up his face.

Azariah laughed at him, relieved to connect with him. They could still talk to each other, even if the dynamic was changing.

"No, don't laugh, I'm serious." Daniel was laughing too and everyone nearby was watching. "He's been nosing around for Ctesiphon mining contracts, and I can't decide if maybe I should tolerate the enemy I know or try to find someone better in this God-forsaken spiral arm."

"You, of all people, should know God is here." He was amazing. Azariah was so happy for him.

Mishael appeared out of nowhere and whispered something in Daniel's ear. Daniel immediately dropped Azariah's hand, put his hands behind his back, and was reserved again.

Azariah bowed and said he had some more people to meet.

Daniel nodded, and Mishael pushed Azariah to turn him away.

"I'm annoyed with you already," Mishael hissed, dragging Azariah away from Daniel. "Daniel isn't expendable, not to the king, not to God, or even Gabriel, but the rest of us aren't like that, and you are drawing too much attention to yourself and, therefore, me when you're like *that* in public. You are clearly Daniel's weak point; people can't hurt him directly, but they can indirectly by targeting you."

"I can handle it." Azariah brushed him off and continued working the room. Once he had met the people on the floor, he knew there was still another set of important introductions. Daniel also needed help in a domestic way. Azariah followed the working staff and found a staging room near the largest kitchen. It was a relief to leave the ballroom; in the past, he could have stayed out there all night.

Azariah was in the middle of convincing the house manager, Inthavong, to share her first name when Daniel slipped in, ordered her to always listen to Azariah, and then ushered Azariah out a side door into a hallway.

"So we're not going back to the party? It's okay to speak in Kahi now, right? You have no idea how much I've missed Kahi."

"Kahi is perfect. The only important part of today besides the obvious was making sure that Ben-Hadad and Bar-Rabkib signed off on the collective property agreements which will make my infrastructure changes easier to implement. I can now hand over the whole stupid project to an administrator. I need to make an appearance at the king's party, but I've got a couple hours."

"To spend with me?" As soon as the words were out of his mouth, Azariah realized how hopeful and vulnerable he sounded.

"Of course." Daniel smiled and squeezed his hand.

"Did you need my opinion on the trade agreements?" Azariah asked lightly, trying to pull back from the vulnerability. "I can—"

"Aza. You're the only person I want to spend time with. I finally have you here in person and I want to be close to you." He gave Azariah a heated look, who blushed and felt tongue-tied. "Come on. This way."

Daniel took him down the wide, bright hallway with only a couple of people strolling around, looking like the quiet kind of people who needed a break from the crush of the ballroom. Daniel touched his elbow and led Azariah to a chapel. Azariah smiled. Of course Daniel would have one and of course he would show it off at the first chance.

"As the issiakkum I have to set an example. There are public visiting hours. Um, but this is just on the way to where I want to take you." He put an arm around Azariah's waist and led him down a hall between the stained-glass chapel windows and pillars with heat shields. Past the heat shields was a huge terrace. "That's my midnight vineyard. It's the only time it's cool enough to visit. I like looking at it though. Here we go." He tapped through a door. It opened to a nicely shaped and styled room, terracotta and white, but Azariah couldn't tell what it was until Daniel walked to a nearby closet. He opened up a safe in the closet and took off his rings, then closed the safe. He started unbuttoning his vest.

"Oh! This is your home! Your personal rooms in the penthouse." Azariah said brightly.

Daniel smiled. "Yes. Where did you think we were going?"

"A swimming pool, maybe? A tour? I really don't know where anything is."

"I'll show you around tomorrow, including the penthouse swimming pools."

Azariah was about to ask what they were doing for the rest of this day when Daniel took off his long vest and Azariah went a little speechless. Daniel hung the long vest up in the closet and was about to grab a cotton robe when Azariah stopped him. "You look gorgeous. You've really filled out."

"Thanks. This outfit is going to a museum, so I'm just getting away from it for a bit." He wasn't really catching onto Azariah drooling over him, though he was giving little looks. "I need to undo this braid. It's too tight."

"Let me guess. You still want it up, but in a different way. I'll take it down if I don't like it."

He smiled again and reached up to do his hair. After watching for a minute, Azariah couldn't help but run a finger over his arm. Daniel stepped closer, so Azariah ran his fingers down his torso. Daniel liked it. He leaned into it as he finished his hair. But he was also tense, so Azariah dropped his hands and hugged him instead. It was a different intimacy where he wasn't putting Daniel on display. He could feel Daniel relax.

"This is nice. I'm feeling much better," Daniel sighed.

"Even though you're wearing pants? Have you changed that much on me?"

"No, I still hate them. If I took them off now, I would eventually have to put them back on for the king's party. Way too much of a hassle."

"Noted. Daniel still hates pants so much that they aren't coming off."

"No one teases me like you." He squeezed Azariah a bit tighter.

"Is it selfish of me to not want anyone else to tease you?"

"I'll allow it."

They had hugged like this before. It felt like he was finally home.

"Ah, there we go. You're finally relaxing." Daniel rubbed his back. After a minute, he felt warmer. "Aza, am I still your *sudatim* home?"

"Yes. Of course. You're my only home. You remember me saying that?"

For an answer, he kissed his cheek. And then they were really kissing. It still felt like a dream, like Azariah would wake up to his black and white life on Idmari. But Daniel was lush and potent and solid.

Daniel kissed the corner of his eye and hugged him. "I love you so much."

"I'm starting to believe you."

"I know. Idmari has put you in a weird state and everything here is different. But now that today is over, I can give you whatever you need. I wish I could have spent today with you."

"Don't worry about it. I slept until the party started. I haven't read any of your letters, though it sounds like you've read mine."

"Some of yours. But you had to wake up alone. I didn't want that to happen." He kissed his cheek and wiped away tears Azariah hadn't even noticed.

Azariah kissed him on the lips again, to feel that delicate contact, to feel him lean in—a little kiss, a little shift in balance—and he saw the whole rest of his life reoriented. It was like seeing in color. Without thinking about it, his kissing changed, and Daniel backed off.

"Aza— Azariah, we're going to end up on the floor right here, and my place is really nice. Let's find a couch or something."

Azariah laughed with relief. "There's more than this one beautiful room?"

They went through an entryway arm-in-arm, which triggered the lights. His beautiful suite was full of art and plants. And two people—

"What are you doing here?!" Daniel half-yelled.

Sigazibi shrugged her shoulders and gestured at the woman, who stepped forward.

"I am Hasdrubal," the woman announced to the room in general. Azariah had seen her only from a distance years ago. She was dressed in high court formality, shaved head, face tattoo with an intricate design, schenti with embroidered gold planets, and sandals with laces up to her knees. Pretty fancy.

Hasdrubal's eyes swept over the room and landed on Azariah. She gave him a short bow.

Azariah gave Daniel a kiss on the cheek, let go of him, and returned the bow.

"Envoy Azariah Ramzi, the king requests your presence immediately."

"Oh no," Daniel said. "You're going to die."

Chapter 46: Azariah

"I didn't mean that," Daniel said quickly. "It's not anything bad. I mean, I don't know what it's about. There's no reason for anyone to be upset." Despite these words, he was clearly upset, gripping Azariah's hand and putting himself between Azariah and the king's representative.

Azariah signed into his hand. *What's going on?*

Daniel held his hand tight again, indicating he needed to stop signing. His eyes were darting around, and he was breathing fast. Did he want to escape? That didn't seem like a good idea. Like he could read Azariah's mind, he shook his head no. He turned, put his hands on Azariah's shoulders, and said in a whisper, "Say as little as you can."

Azariah searched Daniel's eyes for anything else. All he saw was worry. He felt more concern for Daniel than for himself at that moment. Daniel relaxed enough to let him go and stand at his side instead of between Azariah and the others.

"What do I need to do? Change my clothing?" Azariah asked Hasdrubal. The obi of his kimono was coming undone, so even if he didn't change, he needed to freshen up. He finally felt a bloom of emotion: annoyance. *Daniel should be unwrapping me like a gift.* He thought to himself and gave Daniel an unhappy frown. *If he wanted to.*

Hasdrubal walked Azariah to Daniel's changing room and pulled out a high royal court outfit. Once he changed, she braided his hair. It was weird.

"Wait, don't leave yet. Come with me." Daniel took Azariah to the closet near the terrace door. He opened the safe and put his spiritual advisor signet ring on one of his fingers and then his new -samsi signet ring on another finger and then took the white shell ring off his hand

and put that on Azariah's finger, too. He kissed all the rings and then kissed him quickly before giving him back to Hasdrubal.

Hasdrubal led Azariah up to the palace and through the maze of hallways, up to the high court and then off to the side, the smaller private chamber without the large terrible crowd.

"Wait, Hasdrubal. I'm going to see the actual king, right? Not a representative? What's the proper genuflection? It's been three years."

Hasdrubal was kind enough to walk him through the steps and words one time. She was emotionless, but in a human way.

As she opened the molded marble and gold entry door, Azariah braced himself for a small terrible crowd, but there were only five people: Dabu'us, Oshpenaz, Erioch, Hasdrubal, and King Nebuchadnezzar. The chamber was in black-and-white marble with intricately patterned tapestries and rugs. Oshpenaz and the astrologist were in a seating area with dark furniture; it looked fancy enough for the king to gather with people, but King Nebuchadnezzar was on a small throne in another part of the room with Erioch, where Azariah could stand before him. The king was in full form; despite having no real audience, he wore his high royal court clothing with a large open robe that took up a lot of space. His hair was elaborate, and his beard was a magnificent version of Hasdrubal's face tattoo. The king did, in fact, in his full regalia, look like the emperor of a growing galactic empire. Hasdrubal led Azariah to kneel before the king and then removed herself to sit with Oshpenaz.

Azariah knelt, staring at the king's feet, and said the required words of respect and allegiance. The almost total lack of an audience scared him more than anything so far.

"You may arise." The king held out his hand for Azariah to bow over.

Azariah looked at Erioch real quick. Was he supposed to grab the king's hand or just hover over it? Erioch indicated Azariah should hold it. He did firmly, like when he venerated Daniel.

The king was wearing a ring, two inches long, a large gem the color of fire, half carved with an eagle and half cut with facets, each facet shining a different shade of flame, twinkling reds and oranges and whites.

"Thank you, Your Majesty, for wearing my gift." Azariah let go of his hand and stepped back. Azariah had brought back a satchel of gifts, with certificates and receipts, all for the king and had survived the last

Jump. This was at a hint from Daniel. That particular ring was worth a year of Azariah's stipend. The satchel was supposed to still be in the ship, but Azariah had been anticipated before he could present them formally to the Treasury, where he thought they would get lost. King Nebuchadnezzar wasn't known for thoughtful, appreciative gestures. Was this some political display that went over Azariah's head?

"I have watched your career for the last three years with great interest. I have not at any point regretted making you an official palace envoy."

Is this a compliment? An obvious sarcastic lie? Either way, Azariah bowed deeply.

"Now, as to why I brought you here, on such an auspicious day, on such a day that ought to be full of celebration only and yet there is a serious enough matter to pull me away and deal with a mere envoy. I am certain that you have information on how to return to Idmari, and you must give me that information now. I read your official report. I am sure you took scans of the Idmari Gate as you passed through. You as good as told the— the— that one person who reported an interesting conversation, a security officer. Why isn't your information in your report? If you're not sure you have good information, that's perfectly fine. I forgive you for not including it. I am a benevolent king, but now it's time to give me what you have, and we'll work on it. We can even work together if you were hoping to trade the information for favors. Well, speak now, don't keep me waiting."

"Your Majesty, my deepest apologies, but I don't have any further information beyond what is in the report. I'm happy to discuss what I have in further detail, but I don't have the kind of information you are asking for. I hardly know how to convince you." Azariah bowed deeply and humbly. He was lying, of course. He had memorized the information and then deleted all traces.

"Hand over your disc."

Azariah did promptly. This might be why the king was wearing that ring—to indicate that everything else Azariah owned had been searched. Erioch started his examination. The king took the time to wax on eloquently.

"I want all twelve planets; I am so close to realizing that goal; only you stand in the way of my gratification. I am your powerful emperor. You are a captive. I have raised you up from destitution. I have blessed you with an Etemenanki palace education and my trust to carry out my will as if it were your own. And you repay me with lies? You've been home for less than two full days and you've stuck your nose into a half dozen doors. You've met with your comrades, you own one of those rare Omary ships that otherwise only royalty has, and you've moved in with the Babylonian issiakkum-samsi. Hasdrubal said you were kissing when he should have been at my party. You're a bad influence."

"Your Majesty, thank you for your blessings. My life has improved and flourished under your reign. My projects over the last six years have been dedicated to you and to the Chaldean empire. My God has blessed you as king; our Prophet Jeremiah has called you a servant of our God."

"How dare you. Even if your God has blessed me, you are too weak to have any real loyalty. Your Paradise solar system is weak. I can see why your God has abandoned most of you. You must all bow to me now."

Azariah stayed silent. The king didn't offer any further information but let Azariah sweat under his glare for a couple of minutes. Erioch handed the disc back, keeping his face blank. Azariah realized—great moment to realize this—that Erioch was armed, a very nice *aliktum* gun. He didn't carry a gun three years ago.

When the tension had risen quite a bit, the king spoke again. "Here is why I'm angry and suspicious. Any of these reasons would be enough to kill you. I have done worse for less. One, you won't give me the Idmari information. Two, you ignored my request to provide Brigette Beck with a baby; I should have received a report that she got pregnant at some point during the tenth cycle, but there is nothing. Three, you were programming an AI Jump. This is the first set of reasons, but there's even more. My General Hammu-Rapi studied Daniel and in his study of Daniel, he studied you and now I have three more reasons to kill you. One, you are color blind and you are wearing contraband contacts right now. Two, you say you were a farmer on Gospel, but you were in fact part of the militia. Three, you used your position at the foundry to pass messages to Gospel. I congratulate you on finding a weak spot in our surveillance, but you will suffer the consequences."

It was hard to hear his history laid out so bluntly. It was harder still to hear Daniel being dragged into this mess. Azariah had used all his training and willpower to not interrupt the king during his speech. He imagined a planet on top of his throat, crushing his ability to speak.

"Yes. You indeed have nothing to say and there is only one

counterargument that could hold any weight: Daniel. I do think his influence is why you have not been as effective as you could be."

Azariah's heart started to race; a credible threat against Daniel was the only thing that could break him. (Apologies to everyone else.)

"That's right. Daniel is a sore point for all of us. Daniel is safe. I could order Erioch here to kill Daniel, and he wouldn't do it. Honestly, I should have Erioch killed for that, but it's his only flaw. I will kill Daniel directly if needed. Erioch wouldn't stop me personally. But I'm not going to. And yet I will put the health of my empire before him. God will continue to give him visions which he will continue to pass to me. I have no other use for him. If I kill you, he can be sad. Whatever, I don't care."

Both Erioch and Azariah saw this for the lie it was and glanced at each other before remembering one might have to kill the other soon. The first time they met, Erioch had assured Azariah he would make his death painless. Azariah felt a terrible welling of laughter and swallowed it.

"So, envoy, there you go. You should be dead at least six times over and yet I have spared you so far for Daniel's sake. But now that you're back, you must live your life for me. What do you say to that?"

What do I say! "Your Majesty, I would be pleased to prove my loyalty to you. Please let me know what you require."

"No, no, absolutely not. I will not give you hoops to jump through. Your loyalty must be lodged deep within your heart, and it's from that natural upwelling that you inherently know how to prove your loyalty. So what will you do?"

Azariah couldn't disagree with the king. He didn't want to bring Daniel into his mess. His silence lasted for two seconds, but apparently that was too much.

"I will decide for you. You will prove yourself to me or die. Leave now."

Press Release from King Nebuchadnezzar

Press release from King Nebuchadnezzar of the Chaldean Empire:

You haven't heard from me for a while and probably think I've been up to something dastardly. Have I been? No! Of course not! I am blessed by God, Daniel's God, who is powerful and favors me above all others. I have not been involved in destruction or violence. I have been working with artists, engineers, and the greatest minds of the empire to create something beautiful and special and that speaks directly to the power that God has granted me specifically and that can be shared with all. No one but myself and Daniel have truly seen our vision and it must be made real. It must be shared with you, my beloved subjects. It is demanded and imperative that such a dream that brought awe to myself and Daniel will also bring awe to the rest of the empire, that those who doubt will indeed either be convinced of my worthiness or suffer the consequences. It is only a small ceremony, typical of emperors.

This will be made available to everyone soon, after the first special ceremony. This is my glorious project, the shining beacon of who I am, the call to all in the Empire that they may know who I am, that they may know what I am capable of, that all, my own people and all others, now know what is possible, that it's possible because of me, and that it's done for me.

I am the king of kings. The God of heaven has given me dominion and power and might and glory; in my hands has God placed all humankind, the solar systems, and the nebulae. Wherever there is life, God has made me the ruler over them all. All else is inferior.

Chapter 47: Azariah

A few days after his little chat with his new best friend the king, they were all gathered in Daniel's suite. Mishael, Hananiah, and Azariah were called by the king to some special off-world party starting tomorrow. Today felt like the eve of a big battle.

Daniel and Azariah were making bread—stress baking—in Daniel's kitchen while waiting for the other two. Azariah was re-learning Daniel, who was still the same in essentials but there were all sorts of small new things, like baking as a hobby, or wearing white and blue batik printed yukatas, or wearing his hair in a high fluffy bun. Azariah could see the back of his neck for the first time ever. He couldn't keep his eyes off Daniel.

"Are you happy with your life?" Azariah asked. "Do you ever wish you could go back? You were a priest for ten years, right?"

"It feels like I've stopped fighting destiny," Daniel replied. "I take better care of myself. I'm helping more people than I ever have. That sounds like a question you ask yourself. You're still settling in, and I want you to build a life you're happy with." Daniel kneaded the bread. "Be honest, do you still see yourself as a farmer? Do you still want to go back to your Zharqua wheat fields?"

"No, I don't. I did finally, at some point, grow out of that. If anything, I'm a potato farmer from Idmari," Azariah said, leaning against the counter with his shoulder pressed into Daniel's.

"So, what would make you happy? Besides never seeing a potato again."

"What about a vacation? Just the two of us." Azariah couldn't see past whatever tomorrow might bring, but he could play along for Daniel.

"Have we been to the beach?" Daniel gave him an intense look, searching his eyes, a response that seemed out of proportion. "I had this lucid dream."

"Like the beach at the Wara Ti'amtum Sea?" Azariah asked. "I was thinking off-planet."

"Not the sea. I meant an ocean beach." Daniel rolled his hand to indicate big waves.

"Ah, you mean the big kind with moon influenced tides that create a lot of turbulence that is soothing to watch, unless it's lava. No, we haven't. What's this about a lucid dream?"

"You've always known—you, always, always you— that I've never been a Paradisian prophet, since the first time I blessed you. You were trying to tell me that in real life over and over and then it came back in a dream." Daniel shook his head slowly, folding the dough.

"Yes, I did tell you that literally several times over the course of several years!"

"I guess I didn't want to hear. I couldn't hear. That's a problem our people have. I understand better why you had to leave. The way I feel about you now— if you were treating me the way I treated you, of course I wouldn't be able to stick around. Of course. And I'm so glad you didn't go to Paradise because you probably would have ended up in the Revelation battle and died. So now I've got you back. We fit together, support each other, even more and better than I thought, and I'm not going to lose you to the king tomorrow!"

God doesn't save everyone. Loving each other is not enough to save people from death, or worse. Azariah thought about saying that aloud but decided to let Daniel keep his bravado. He changed the subject. There was so much to talk about before the king's party-slash-newest assassination attempt. "Tell me more about this fetus you have incubating in your medical suite. You got to go to Gospel to get the egg from my sister. What did you think of my family?"

To Azariah, this felt like pretending still, but it really was happening to Daniel—whatever happened tomorrow, Daniel would have a daughter who was Azariah's biological niece. Azariah knew—had always known—that Daniel would be comfortable with them intertwining their lives to this extent, but tomorrow would end things before they could begin together.

Soon enough, Mishael and Hananiah arrived.

"Hey Azariah," Mishael said after greetings, "Wamiri, your friend from *Klipspringer* wanted me to give you her contact information. I forgot and she ended up contacting me."

"What did she say?" Azariah asked. "Last I heard, she was leaving from *Klipspringer* straight to some special project."

"Well, let's call her now and see if she has an update, and she can tell you."

"Let's see." Azariah brought up a display and sent a communications request, voice and video.

"Surprise! I'm actually answering," Wamiri waved with a smile. "No time for chitchat. I've been doing something that I can't talk about. It's about the party you're going to tomorrow. I think it's hilarious, but you're going to hate it. No, seriously, if you come, you'll die, either a spiritual or physical death. If I were you, I would run back to my precious Wahap. Anyway, I've got to go!"

"That's unsettling," Azariah mumbled as Wamiri ended the connection, thinking about calling a few other people, but Mishael waved for attention.

"That's right, Azariah. Can you see now what a mess you've made of things?"

"I know the king is after me and you are caught in the crosshairs, but honestly, my mistakes have nothing to do with what the king is threatening me about. I wanted to help Paradise and, like Erioch said, that was the silly thing that let me blow off steam. But restitution will put me in much more direct opposition to the king and his goals. Hiding Idmari is an example of that."

"Which is why I want you to just back off," Daniel said.

"No," Mishael said, waving Daniel away, "Let me hear you say it, Azariah. Confess your sins. I want to know that you understand."

"I joined the *gerru* with the intent to help Paradise and I didn't care who I might hurt along the way." Azariah sighed. "I purposely stirred up shit at Lughamstone because they weren't useful to me and it would occupy the empire, take up more of the empire's resources. Lughamstone needs a mediator to calm the civil war down, someone to help restructure their economy, not the current violent dictatorship. I should help do that.

"Sumer. I looked to them as a place for our people to heal, when actually the king wiped the natives out and I should have seen that possibility. There's barely anything I can do but look for and protect pockets of survivors, even if they are cannibals. I should try.

"New Godaniya. I lost interest once the bomb hit because I couldn't ask for help once their conflict revved up again. I still need to ask Wahap for forgiveness. He asked me very directly for specific help, the kind of help I should have been giving all along, but I wanted to just get to the next planet to check it out. Oh and yes, Mishael, I shouldn't have allowed any politically incendiary holidays.

"This expansion project of the king is inevitable, but the way he's carrying it out is unforgivable. And for us, we need to survive, but what else? I mean, the only Paradisians in true chattel slavery are people from Revelation of John who wouldn't leave the planet even after warnings from angels. No one deserves slavery, but who am I to rescue them? Is God bringing me to the king like this to destroy me so that I won't interfere with Her punishment? Not that I really believe God would actively bring anyone into slavery, but unlike a lot of people, we were warned about specific consequences. So it's my own fault for being on the king's radar and I've got to fix things even if I stay on his radar. Sorry, Daniel." And that was only if Azariah got through the king's party alive. Mishael raised an eyebrow at Azariah, who shrugged his shoulders. These were his conclusions after having nothing else to think about for months on Idmari.

"Thank you," Mishael said. "That's a pretty good summary. But you forgot how you've dragged all of us into your mistakes. We're suffering too. Except for Daniel, and I think the fact that he's not invited is very telling."

"The king wants loyalty and recognition that he's the best king. Just give him whatever he wants," Daniel said, waving his hand to dismiss any disagreement. But he couldn't shut his friends up like he could other people.

"I'm not giving up Idmari," Azariah said.

"You should. It's worth your life," Daniel insisted.

"No, we just went over that. Stop being so stubborn."

"At this point, it's way more than just Idmari," Mishael said. "He's going to expect something from us that he knows Daniel wouldn't do."

"And I won't be there, so just do it."

"Really, Daniel?" Hananiah asked. "You're fine with us doing absolutely anything?"

"Daniel," Mishael said before he could answer Hananiah's question, "from the very beginning the king has been trying to tear us up, tear out who we really are. It's why he brought us to this planet in the first place. The three of us don't have the power you do to stay intact."

"My mom and sister have had this argument," Daniel answered. "Physical death or spiritual death. And I know there's a third way."

"You found it for yourself, but we haven't been given the same options. God doesn't need us the way he needs you," Azariah said, taking Mishael's side over Daniel's for the first time in his life.

"Daniel," Mishael said, continuing to agree with Azariah, "if we make a choice that saves our physical lives, it's more than spiritual death for just us. We're all in public enough positions that our choices will affect other people. We have been true to our God, our home, way of life, and all the little- and medium-sized choices we've made over the years. Why did we do that if in the end we give the king what he wants?"

"We don't know what he wants," Daniel said.

"He wants us dead," Azariah answered, immediately recalling at least one assassination attempt. "He wants to make an example of us. He's going to give us an impossible choice."

"That's very melodramatic—" Daniel broke off, probably realizing that the king would definitely do something *melodramatic*.

"I'm not ready to live the whole rest of my life according to his terms," Azariah repeated, hating that their arguments were now going in a circle.

Hananiah broke through. "I've talked with Piama about this, and that's where we landed. This isn't a one-time loyalty test. The king is pushing us in a direction we'll have to follow for the rest of our lives. I'm not willing to do that." And if Hananiah, with a wife and kids, wasn't willing to make the decision to stay alive, how could Daniel ask Azariah.

"Well, Mishael, what about you?" Daniel asked. "You don't have a family who would be under the king's thumb. You don't have anything to protect like Azariah thinks he does. You've gone along with the flow well enough, though you've always protected us."

"Yes," Mishael answered Daniel, "if you look closely, I've always talked as if I agree, as if I'm willing to do as I'm told, but if you look at my actual actions, I've always chosen the right thing to do. The king is forcing all of us to have children, that's one thing Azariah is dying over —but not me. I'm not married, I don't have children, and the king isn't mad at me about it. I know how to play that game. I've used my resources, especially through the Atabek embassy, to help our home. How else do you think a Gospel ruler—Patroness Shelomith—got to Babylon? So far, I've been able to stay unnoticed, underground, and legal. And sure, I'll still say what I need to say. But if tomorrow is more than that, then no, I'm probably not going to come back. I'm too much in the habit of making the right choice."

* * *

After their friends left, Daniel grabbed Azariah and kissed him fiercely. He returned the kisses equally but stopped him after just a few and tucked a curl behind Daniel's ear.

"What about we hang out in your conservatory?" Azariah asked. It had a miniature waterfall and pond with two glass walls and a glass ceiling. The stars and moon were beautiful tonight. Plus, it was safe to talk in there.

"What's wrong with my bedroom?" Daniel asked, pulling Azariah to the stairs.

"Well, it's a little like a monk's cell."

"You mean virginal," Daniel corrected bluntly.

"I really can't kiss you in your sanctum sanctorum."

"You're very difficult," Daniel said, kissing him and changing the direction he was pulling him. "I wish you would promise me to do whatever it takes to come back."

"I can promise you this. If I do come back, I won't ever leave you again," Azariah said, tracing the niobium chain Daniel still wore under his yukata.

Daniel hugged him tight for an answer, clinging in a way Azariah remembered from three years ago but was now more yielding and intimate.

A couple of hours later, they were laid out on a pile of random cushions with his yukata on top of them like a blanket. Daniel was on his back and Azariah had his head on Daniel's chest, tracing his muscles with a finger while he played with Azariah's hair. Daniel had a new tattoo on his forearm that balanced out the Martigny tattoo—a band of small flowers with Kahi letters for Azariah woven in. They had kissed and exhausted all emotional talk, and now Azariah had a piece of business Daniel would hate on multiple levels.

"My *sudatim* Daniel, remember like five years ago how we all learned memorization tricks? Do you remember how to use them?"

"I guess. It's not really my favorite thing. I prefer just referencing whatever I need, not storing it in my brain. Sometimes it feels like my visions push everything out."

"I have something I need you to memorize. You can't write it down."

"What is it?" he asked in a guarded tone after a long pause.

"Even though we're not looking for a safe haven any more, Idmari is special and connected to Gospel and maybe to you specifically. So we need a safe way to get back there if we ever want to." Azariah paused for a moment, but Daniel didn't say anything, just stopped playing with his hair. "I have the information to force a connection to the Idmari Gate. I don't want to be the only person with that knowledge."

"I don't want to do this. Maybe we're not supposed to go back. Maybe it's supposed to be hundreds of years from now. Didn't the Oracle say she would destroy her Gate?"

"I know, I know. But it's important to me. And I don't believe her. Can you do it as a favor for me? I probably would have asked you anyway, just so I wasn't the only person. It's not just about tomorrow."

"You have to kiss me first," his voice was rough.

Azariah obliged. He hadn't had a sexual connection with a man in a long time and while they weren't having sex yet, he had missed this state of being, to feel like his energy and self and enjoyment were doubled, reflected, and shared. Daniel still didn't know the depths of that physical intimacy. If Azariah hadn't left three years ago but taken Daniel's consort deal, Daniel would have allowed himself to feel pleasure, but Azariah had wanted so much more than that—and had it now. Daniel's visions didn't define his reality so much, weren't so important in their moments together, and this didn't end Daniel's world. Instead of staying single, he was creating something with Azariah, and he found that it didn't disrupt his connection to God. It was only different, like serving God by being an administrator instead of an advisor. Azariah hoped that he would come back to Daniel.

Chapter 48: Nebuchadnezzar

The glorious day showcasing my power arrived. I was at my palace ship port with my perfect outfit, my perfect hair and face, which was all the style, which was mimicked by everyone. Once I was on board with my especially curated list of guests, both leaders and dissenters, all powerful in their own way, we would travel to my gold moon in orbit around a nearby planet called Samash.

Yes, a Gold Moon. A perfect sphere of gold, no layers of anything else, completely man-made, nothing that the works of the universe could create. My genius alone has brought this wonder from idea to fruition. No one has even dared to dream such a thing, but now all will wish to visit and bow to my superiority.

"Your Majesty," Hasdrubal announced, "The shuttle is available whenever you desire."

Oshpenaz walked with me to the shuttle, which was made of gold, the insides as well; when I sat, I sunk a fingernail into the armrest to check, and then yelled at someone for missing such a flaw. They moved me and buffed the mark out, and I told them to leave—and everyone knew what that meant.

We flew out. I was absorbed by what I saw out the window. Oshpenaz and whoever is next to him spoke my praises quietly. They were annoying. I had the quartet seated behind me start to play. I wanted the perfect atmosphere for my grand entrance to the gold moon. The other people in the shuttle, my subjects, somewhere behind me (they could see me, but I didn't deign to notice them), weren't as important as I was but they were important enough. I glanced around. Everyone had intense concentration on my glorious work, appearing out the observatory window. My subjects were in holy, spiritual meditation on my own works, people who were grand in their own right, and they were now mine in many ways. Their reverence was natural, and they must carry it forward forever, and to their own people, and into their own works, so that I was everywhere. I did notice a few who did not mimic my own style; not that it's required. I signaled to Oshpenaz that they needed to be at the back so that they wouldn't offend me further. It was for their own good.

The shuttle landed on my gold moon. I was delighted. I won't even pretend to scowl, as if there was something that could be improved— this was perfection, and the perfection reflected back onto me. No fingernails pressed into the surfaces now; I made sure everyone had short fingernails and left all possessions behind. This was meant to be a holy pilgrimage.

Now to use mere small words to describe the greatest wonder of the galaxy. As we walked off the shuttle, the gold of the ground rippled out in all directions, to all the horizons. There was nothing natural, nothing of nature. Each mark and detail was wholly manmade to great beauty.

This time of day, the atmosphere glowed. *The world is charged with the glory of the king.*

In one direction were gardens and orchards; every fruit was gold, every petal was gold, all carefully sculpted to the smallest detail. There were little robot bees made of gold.

In another direction was an ocean of gold, with waves sculpted mid-splash, as tall as a man.

In order to view this area—the whole moon was like this—I built a forum with seating in arcs and tiers.

At the front of this forum was an image of gold, my own likeness, four hundred feet tall. The head, chest, arms, belly, thighs, legs, and feet were pure gold.

Next to the forum was a gold smithery atelier where a blast furnace was still going full throttle, with a molten gold metal lake that turned into a river of gold that flowed around my idol and into the gold ocean. The blast furnace continued to work, to ensure the molten gold wouldn't solidify.

I settled into a place of prominence in the forum, which was like a theatre or sanctuary, with my entourage around me and the rest of the shuttle's passengers filing into the seats. Some were wandering off to examine the works of art but were being shepherded into the seats for the real reason they were here.

The audience consisted of *muma"eru* commanders, *sakinu* prefects, *pihatutu* governors, *mustalum* advisers, *ganzabaru* treasurers, *dayyantu* judges, *ababdum* magistrates and many other empire officials of the strongest Chaldean planets and of the newest Chaldean planets from the *gerru.*

Then Hasdrubal walked to a central place in front of my idol and loudly proclaimed, "Nations and peoples of every solar system, this is what you are commanded to do: As soon as you hear the sound of the horn, flute, zither, lyre, harp, pipe and all kinds of music, you must fall down and worship the image of gold that King Nebuchadnezzar has set up. Whoever does not fall down and worship will immediately be thrown into a blazing furnace."

As soon as the music played, all the nations and peoples of every solar system fell down and worshiped the image of gold that I, King Nebuchadnezzar, had set up. I gazed over all my people. A sense of pride and satisfaction welled up from deep inside. I could cry at this display of loyalty.

Yet—back in the shadows—there were people who had not fallen down, who were still on their feet.

I signaled for the music to stop. I ordered my guards to grab the three men who hadn't prostrated themselves.

I watched as the guards brought down the heretics. They were my favorite heretics—beautiful specimens. A very pleasing symmetry and personalities and gracefulness in all their movements. They would either bow to me and I would win that way, or they would burn and I would win in a much more fun way.

I mused on whether I wanted them to die today. If they died today, I would want it to be as dramatic and memorable as possible, a caricature of violence and terror that would be easy to remember. For instance, if they cried out in tortured pain as they burned alive, that would be very pleasing. I had a concern that flinging them into the gold moon's furnace might not be the right way; they might die too quickly or perhaps might have enough strength to be quiet. But Erioch said that the trial run had gone fine. I'd trust that. I kept my eyes locked on the three men.

Chapter 49: Azariah

They were going to die. Azariah was sure of it. The king, while seemingly calm, did not take his eyes off them like a hawk. His guards were on their way to them, he was sure. They were in the way back so it would take a minute.

Mishael grabbed his hand and Hananiah's hand on his other side.

"Dear Lord, our Father in heaven, and also Dear Christ, our brother in the Holy Spirit," he whispered, "You, who have blessed our brother Daniel, please save us from imminent death. We have followed your word, so we might be worth protecting. And if you let Daniel's lover die, you probably won't be able to give him any more visions, so please keep us alive. Amen."

Azariah wanted to laugh. But he didn't because he was about to die. He wanted to kick Mishael in the shins. God let so many people die all the time.

"So you're saying we still shouldn't worship that idol?" Hananiah asked. "It's our loyalty test, and Daniel said to just play along."

"He wouldn't have played along with this test. That's why he's not here. The king knows Daniel wouldn't bow and the king doesn't want him dead."

"Hananiah," Azariah said, leaning past Mishael, "if you want to bow, that's fine."

"No. If I bow, he'll have his foot on my neck for the rest of my life."

Azariah nodded once. That thought strengthened his own resolve.

Mishael had just a few more seconds to brush Azariah's hair off his shoulders and smooth out Hananiah's robe as the guards came up the stairs to escort them. He took the lead, and Azariah was in the rear. He never thought he would die a martyr, but this was certainly a memorable way to go, not that martyrdom had ever been a priority.

They would do a good job representing Gospel. Azariah saw Hananiah try to reach Babylon again on his disc. No signal. His poor wife and kids. All Azariah's self-involved pity flooded out.

The guards marched them down the stairs in a showy pattern. Azariah knew most of the people they walked past and had talked with them on the trip here. He passed a delegation from Lughamstone that included Leander and Priestess Wilhelmina. He passed a much smaller delegation from New Godaniya that did not include Wahap, but he did see the Vice President and Lieutenant Zikirulla Moydun, who had bowed and gave Azariah a sad look as he walked by.

There was no delegation from Sumer because they had been wiped out. Azariah felt a great pain of loss to think of that genocide and his part in it. There was no delegation from Idmari because he had saved it, and maybe the sacrifice he was making right now would atone for his other willful mistakes.

They were brought to stand before the king, with the ridiculous gold idol rising behind him, with their backs to the crowd.

Hasdrubal addressed the three young men on behalf of the king. "Is it true, Hananiah, Mishael, and Azariah, that you continue to serve God as you choose and will not worship the image of gold I have set up? This entire moon is a sign of the power that God has given King Nebuchadnezzar. You do not decide how the King, servant of God as reported by your own prophets, should be respected, and he is worthy of worship. Now when you hear the sound of music, if you are ready to fall down and worship this glorious image of our worthy King Nebuchadnezzar, very good. But if you do not worship it, you will be thrown immediately into the blazing furnace. Then what god will be able to rescue you from my hand?"

Mishael stepped forward to reply, addressing himself to the king instead of Hasdrubal, "King Nebuchadnezzar, we do not need to defend ourselves before you in this matter. If we are thrown into the blazing furnace, the God we serve is able to deliver us from it, and he will deliver us from Your Majesty's hand. But even if he does not, we want you to know, Your Majesty, that we will serve the creator God in our own way and not worship the image of gold you have set up."

Up until that point, the king had been expressionless, allowing Hasdrubal to do the hard work. The king had even had a benign, benevolent expression, as if this was a misunderstanding, and that the revelation of his power and the weight of his threat would be enough. But now he allowed his rage and fury to show, his face getting red.

"Slaves," he hissed. "Foolish, seditious, arrogant slaves, undermining my empire! Do you think your families will escape?" Only those closest to him could hear.

Azariah felt Hananiah flinch next to him, but that was it. His own family was still on Gospel, just about as safe as any Paradisian could be.

Mishael bowed deeply to the king, but no prostration, and to the king, not to his idol, and stepped back next to Hananiah.

This enraged the king further. "That furnace must be heated to seven times hotter! I want to feel its strength from here!" He aimed this command at someone nearby who ran off with the message. "Erioch, get all your strongest soldiers and tie them up!"

Erioch bowed and indicated what seemed like a small army to surround the three young men. While they were being tied up—they weren't resisting—Hasdrubal had the music play again and led the entire audience through another round of veneration to the gold idol.

The furnace was about a hundred paces away, and by the end of a half hour, Azariah could feel an intense heat on his face, dry and prickly. The people at the front of the audience could feel the heat too; while the king hadn't succeeded in pressuring the three young men, the threat alone was terrorizing the rest of the audience; just the idea that the king would execute like this was effective, even if Azariah and his friends weren't making a scene like the king might hope.

At the king's order, two men picked Azariah up, one at his shoulders and one carrying his feet. It was a bit embarrassing. He would have preferred to walk, but the humiliation was the point. The heat became more intense. Droplets of molten gold were landing around them. One drop landed on the clothing of the guard carrying his feet. He put the feet down to swat at the smoldering fabric. Someone behind them yelled at him to keep going. Azariah watched as Mishael and Hananiah were thrown into the furnace, huge, hot flames engulfing them immediately, and licking at the soldiers, all falling back on fire, rolling around to put out the flames and in pain. The guards carrying Azariah saw their comrades and paused for a moment. Then moved forward. The flames licked at Azariah now, molten gold boiling over the edge of the furnace. They threw Azariah in and he felt himself splash into the molten gold. Azariah watched as his two soldiers screamed as they backed off, one tripping over a pool of glowing gold.

Azariah was not in pain; his nerves must have burned immediately, but he was still conscious and felt himself flow down the river of molten gold, tied up too tight to have any control.

Suddenly, he felt strong hands and arms catch him in his armpits and drag him to a shallow landing. Azariah opened his mouth, but molten gold flowed in, which, again, didn't hurt but was an odd sensation in his mouth. Azariah wondered if his tongue had disappeared, but it didn't seem like it. He felt the waves in the air signifying heat, but he didn't feel anything beyond a typical summer's intensity. He looked for his friends—an angel stood with them. She had cut the bonds of Mishael and Hananiah, who were now standing up. The angel came over to Azariah and loosened the knots in the bonds at his hands just by touching them and touched the bonds around his ankles. As the bonds dropped off him, they sizzled in the flames and disappeared.

He was sitting chest deep in bright molten gold. He lifted a hand up out of the gold and shook off clumps; his hand was fine. He had no burns. He was not in pain. The gold in his mouth felt funny, and he spat it out into his hand, where it cooled quickly into a clump.

Azariah shook off the ropes and stood, the molten gold sloughing off his clothes, walking a few steps through the gold to his friends. Now that he was standing, the gold was a bit below his knees; the angel had brought them to some shallow area on the same shore as the idol and was still within sight of the blast furnace. The river bank next to them was solid gold and steep enough that they would have trouble climbing out.

They watched the guards who had carried them to the furnace. All six had collapsed within reach of the flames; molten gold boiling over the edge of the furnace bubbled around them. They were either unconscious or dead. Azariah looked out past them. The king and crowds were yelling. Erioch and his soldiers were trying to get closer to their fallen comrades.

Mishael touched Azariah's arm. "We should stay in here." He nodded to the angel.

"We're alive," Hananiah said. "Am I crying? I feel like I should be." He rubbed his face. "I feel like I could go swimming in this."

Azariah held Hananiah's face in his hands. "We are alive! You'll see Piama and the kids soon, I'm sure. I can't tell if you're crying either. Our bodies have been transformed."

"When Paul said our bodies would be transformed, I don't think this is what he meant," Mishael said, standing next to the angel. Azariah turned to face them, the molten gold still sloughing off when he moved.

"I am Gabriel," the angel said. She looked at each of them.

Azariah knelt before the angel, like he did Daniel.

"You are not afraid. You do not kneel out of fear. Please arise," Gabriel said. "I am a messenger from God." She was the embodiment of flames. She didn't breathe. Flames licked around her like armor.

"Why are you saving us?" Mishael asked.

"Daniel asked me to save you from corporeal danger. He is a good man," Gabriel answered. "You are good enough, children of God and heirs with Christ."

"I remember. You and the vision of the woman told him a bunch of things that are still confusing, but Daniel only wished to know more about the end of our exile," Azariah said.

"Yes, he did ask," Gabriel said. "You bear the seed of the Daughter of God. All solar systems will know She is the Daughter of God just as they know Jesus is the Son of God and man."

"We get it," Mishael snapped. "Our exile is nothing compared to the glorious future that all our prophets tell us about."

"In one year, one year, and a half year, She will come," Gabriel announced.

"That's similar to other prophecies," Azariah said.

"This is ridiculous," Mishael snapped again, kicking at the molten gold.

"Wait," Hananiah said, "Gabriel, you're giving us the specific year that the Daughter of God is going to be born, aren't you?"

"Yes. I'm sure Daniel understands."

"No, he didn't," Mishael said. "But we'll let him know if we see him again."

"So you've saved us," Hananiah said, bowing a little. "What do you want us to do?"

"That's obvious," Mishael interrupted the messenger of God, the audacity. He was going to get them killed. "We have been given the prophecy of God's Daughter. We will keep that prophecy safe once we get back home. It's a seed to tend to carefully."

"Wait, no, that's not obvious at all," Azariah said. "We are supposed to scatter the seed of knowledge so that all solar systems and sectors know."

"Information can be too easily corrupted," Mishael objected. "We're the literal seed, the bloodline and culture. This is such an old argument. I can't believe we're having it here. I can't believe we think this is a life-or-death issue… well, okay, I can believe that."

"Gabriel, I feel like I understand now why you give Daniel the prophecies, but what would you have us do?" Hananiah asked again.

"As God has said, be good men and prosper."

They waited to see if there was anything else. There wasn't.

"Ah, here comes the king," Hananiah pointed out.

The overheated furnace had blown up such huge flames that they had been hidden from view. Now the furnace was cooling down and the audience could see the three young men.

They bowed politely. The king was still quite a way off.

"Who's in there with you?" Hasdrubal called to them.

Azariah looked at Gabriel. She did not look like she intended to answer the king, or like she had heard anything.

"An angel!" Hananiah obliged.

"Servants of the most high God, you may come out now!"

The friends looked at Gabriel. They weren't going to do anything she didn't want them to do. She touched the steep river bank of gold and steps formed, like they had been carved out in a moment.

They stepped out, but Gabriel didn't follow. Once they were away from the molten gold, she disappeared. The *muma"eru* commanders, *sakinu* prefects, *pihatutu* governors, *mustalum* advisers, *ganzabaru* treasurers, *dayyantu* judges, *ababdum* magistrates and many other empire officials crowded around them. They saw that the fire had not harmed the young men's bodies, nor was a hair on their heads singed; their robes were not scorched, and there was no smell of fire on them.

Then King Nebuchadnezzar said, "Praise be to the God of Hananiah, Mishael, and Azariah, who has sent his angel and rescued his servants! They trusted in him and defied the king's command and were willing to give up their lives rather than serve or worship any god except their own God. Therefore, I decree that the people of any planet or language who say anything against the God of Hananiah, Mishael, and Azariah be cut into pieces and their houses be turned into piles of rubble, for no other god can save in this way."

Epilogue: Daniel

The day after Azariah came back safely, Daniel demanded an audience with the king, and was granted his request.

"I've given them new titles and roles. They're safe. What more could you want?" The king grumbled. Azariah and Hananiah were appointed as special administrators on a council overseeing the planets from the *gerru* expansion. Mishael had opted to work with Zharqua Patroness Shelomith and Prophet Ezekiel to consolidate Paradisian exiles and slaves to only a few systems, which the king was allowing for now.

"I will marry Envoy Azariah Ramzi, and I must have your blessing," Daniel said with a deep bow. Azariah would have to become an empire citizen; the king had not offered citizenship as one of his new blessings.

"When you entered the palace grounds, we dropped a file into your feed. Check it out." The king shared a smirk with Hasdrubal, which Daniel instinctively glared at.

When Daniel opened the file, it projected as an ornate desk in front of him. On top of the desk lay an enormous book that was at least five hundred paper pages with a deep red leather cover. The book was too big for him to pick up. Daniel opened it to the title page. The title was *Daniel and Azariah's wedding*. Daniel flipped through the pages. Tons of information such as a twenty-thousand-person guest list, which included Azariah's biological parents and family. Half a luxury vacation planet reserved for the wedding and celebrations. A date scheduled. Invites and reservations would go out starting tomorrow. It must have taken a month of time for a whole team to do this. Daniel slammed the book closed and turned off the projection.

"Why?" Daniel asked in a strangled voice.

"I knew your creator God would save your friends. I totally knew that. So I prepared a different way to control Azariah," the king said smugly. "Besides, your sister married the Queen of Sheba, and your wedding has to be bigger and better than theirs."

You finished the book! Wow, thank you for reading it! No matter what you thought, I am incredibly excited that you got to this point.

Please, please, please leave an honest review.

Authors can only sell books if they get reviews.

And if I don't sell books, I can't afford cat food.

If you don't leave a review, then Diamond, my tortoiseshell cat, won't get fed, and she is wasting away. Please, think of Diamond.

P.S.

What do you think of a sapphic sequel with Daniel's sister Magdalene and the Queen of Sheba, and also Daniel's sister Hippolyte falling in love with someone?

Or another novel in the same universe with Mishael falling in love with Prophet Ezekiel (it has Daniel's and Azariah's wedding)?

Or possibly a short story with Hananiah and Piama?

Stay tuned!